# the DEN OF SHADOWS
# quartet

Amelia Atwater-Rhodes

# *the* DEN OF SHADOWS
# *quartet*

DELACORTE PRESS

*In the Forests of the Night* copyright © 1999 by Amelia Atwater-Rhodes
*Demon in My View* copyright © 2000 by Amelia Atwater-Rhodes
*Shattered Mirror* copyright © 2001 by Amelia Atwater-Rhodes
*Midnight Predator* copyright © 2002 by Amelia Atwater-Rhodes
Title page illustrations © 2009 by Yuan Lee

Visit us on the Web! www.randomhouse.com/teens
Educators and librarians, for a variety of teaching tools,
visit us at www.randomhouse.com/teachers

*Library of Congress Cataloging-in-Publication Data is available upon request.*

ISBN: 978-0-385-73894-1 (tr. pbk.)
ISBN: 978-0-375-89676-7 (e-book)

Printed in the United States of·America
10  9  8  7  6  5  4  3  2  1
First Edition

# CONTENTS

*the* DEN OF
SHADOWS
*quartet*

# IN THE FORESTS
# OF THE NIGHT

In the Forests of the Night *is dedicated to everyone who contributed to the story, especially:*

*Julie Nann for her excellent teaching skills. Carolyn Barnes for talking to my agent about me. All the members of the Candle Light circle for their slightly insane inspiration. Sarita Spillert for her encouragement. Dan Hogan for enduring a telephone conversation at four in the morning. Laura Bombrun for her house, which coincidentally is exactly the same as Risika's. Also, I need to mention my family: my heroic father, William; my brilliant and inspiring sister, Rachel; my beautiful and slightly telepathic mother, Susan; and my overly insightful cousin, Nathan. I love you all.*

# The Tiger

Tiger! Tiger! Burning bright
In the forests of the night,
What immortal hand or eye
Could frame thy fearful symmetry?

In what distant deeps or skies
Burnt the fire of thine eyes?
On what wings dare he aspire?
What the hand dare seize the fire?

And what shoulder, and what art,
Could twist the sinews of thy heart?
And when thy heart began to beat,
What dread hand? and what dread feet?

What the hammer? what the chain?
In what furnace was thy brain?
What the anvil? what dread grasp?
Dare its deadly terrors clasp?

When the stars threw down their spears,
And watered heaven with their tears,
Did He smile His work to see?
Did He who made the Lamb, make thee?

Tiger! Tiger! Burning bright
In the forests of the night,
What immortal hand or eye,
Dare frame thy fearful symmetry?

William Blake

# PROLOGUE
## NOW

A CAGE OF STEEL.

It is a cruel thing to do, to cage such a beautiful, passionate animal as if it was only a dumb beast, but humans do so all too often. They even cage themselves, though their bars are made of society, not of steel.

The Bengal tiger is gold with black stripes through its fur, and it is the largest of the felines. The sign reads *"Panthera tigris tigris"*; it is simply a fancy name for *tiger*. I call this one Tora—she is my favorite animal in this zoo.

Tora walks toward me as I approach her cage. The minds of animals are different from the minds of humans, but I have spent much time with Tora, and we know each other very well. Though the thoughts of animals can rarely be translated into human thought, I understand her, and she understands me.

Such a beautiful animal should not be caged.

# CHAPTER 1
# NOW

I RELINQUISH MY HUMAN FORM for that of a hawk as I leave the zoo, which has been closed for hours. The security guard fell asleep rather suddenly, as many do upon meeting my eyes, so there is no one to witness my departure.

I could bring myself to my home instantly with my mind, but I enjoy the sensation of flying. Of all the animals, the birds are perhaps the most free, as they are able to move through the air and there is so little that can stop their flight.

I land only once, to feed, and then arrive back at my house in Massachusetts close to sunrise.

As I return to human form, I catch a glimpse of my hazy reflection in my bedroom mirror. My hair is long and is the color of old gold. My eyes, like those of all my kind, became black when I died. My skin is icy pale, and in the reflection it looks like mist. Today I wear black jeans and a black T-shirt. I do not always wear black, but that was the color of my mood today.

I do not care for the new, quickly built towns humans are so fond of scraping up out of plaster and paint, so I live in Concord, Massachusetts, a town with history. Concord has an aura—one that says "This land is ours, and we will fight to keep it that way." The people who live here keep Concord as it was long ago, though cars have replaced the horse-drawn carriages.

I live alone in one of Concord's original houses. Over the years I have made myself the long-lost daughter of several wealthy, elderly couples. That is how I "inherited" the home I live in.

Though I have no living relations that I know of, it is not difficult to influence the thoughts—and paperwork— of the human world. When mortals do begin to question me too closely, I can easily move to another location. However, I make no human friends no matter how long I stay in an area, so my existence and disappearance are rarely noticed.

My home is near the center of Concord; the view from the front windows is the Unitarian church, and the view from the back windows is a graveyard. Neither bothers me at all. Of course there are ghosts, but they do no harm besides the occasional startle or chill. They are usually too faint to be seen in daylight.

My home has no coffin in it; I sleep in a bed, thank you. I do have blackout curtains, but only because I usually find myself sleeping during the day. I do not burn in sunlight, but bright noonday sun does hurt my eyes.

The vampire myths are so confused that it is easy to see they were created by mortals. Some myths are true: my reflection is faint, and older ones in my line have no reflection at all. As for the other myths, there is little truth and many lies.

I do dislike the smell of garlic, but if your sense of smell was twenty times stronger than that of the average bloodhound, would you not dislike it as well? Holy water and crosses do not bother me—indeed, I have been to Christian services since I died, though I no longer look for solace in religion. I wear a silver ring set with a garnet stone, and the silver does not burn me. If someone hammered a stake through my heart I suppose I would die, but I do not play with humans, stakes, or mallets.

Since I am speaking about my kind, I might as well say something about myself. I was born to the name of Rachel Weatere in the year 1684, more than three hundred years ago.

The one who changed me named me Risika, and Risika I became, though I never asked what it meant. I continue to call myself Risika, even though I was transformed into what I am against my will.

My mind wanders back the road to my past, looking for a time when Rachel was still alive and Risika was not yet born.

# CHAPTER 2
# 1701

THERE WAS ASH on my pale skin from helping to put out the fire. As my sister, Lynette, had been preparing the evening meal, flames had leapt from the hearth like arms reaching out to grab her. My twin brother, Alexander, had been standing across the room from the hearth. He was convinced this accident was his fault.

"Am I damned?" he asked, staring past me at the now cold hearth.

How did he want me to answer? I was only seventeen, a girl still, and certainly not a cleric. I knew nothing of damnation and salvation that my twin brother did not know as well. Yet Alexander was looking at me, his golden eyes heavy with worry and shame, as if I should know everything.

"You should ask these things of a preacher, not me," I answered.

"Tell a preacher what I see? Tell him that I can look into people's minds, and that I can . . ."

He trailed off, but we both knew what the rest of the

sentence was. For months Alexander had been trying to hide his powers, which were just as undesired as the fire had been. Shaking with fear, he had told me everything. He could sometimes hear the thoughts of those around him, though he tried to block them out. If he concentrated on an object, he would make it move. And, he had added, if he stared into a fire, he could make it rise or fall. Despite his efforts to control these powers, they were sometimes stronger than he was.

Lynette had been cooking supper. Now she was at the doctor's with our papa, being treated for burns.

"It is witchcraft," Alexander whispered, as if afraid to say the words any more loudly. "How can I tell a clergyman that?"

Once again I could not answer him. Alexander believed far more than I in the peril of the soul. Though we both said our prayers and went to church without fail, where I was skeptical, he was faithful. In truth, I was more afraid of the cold, commanding preachers than of the fires of Hell they threatened us with. If I had the powers my brother was discovering, I would fear the church even more.

"Maybe that is what happened to our mother," Alexander said quietly. "Maybe I hurt her."

"Alexander!" I gasped, horrified that my brother could think such a thing. "How can you blame yourself for Mother's death? We were babies!"

"If I could lose control and hurt Lynette when I am seventeen, how much easier would it have been for me to lose control as a child?"

I did not remember my mother, though Papa sometimes spoke about her; she had died only a few days after

Alexander and I were born. Her hair had been even fairer than my brother's and mine, but our eyes were exactly the same color as hers had been. An exotic honey gold, our eyes were dangerous in their uniqueness. Had my family not been so well accepted in the community, our eyes might have singled us out for accusations of witchcraft.

"You are not even certain *Lynette's* injuries are your fault," I told Alexander. Lynette was my papa's third child, born to his second wife; her mother had died only a year before of smallpox. "She was leaning too close to the fire, or maybe there was oil on the wood somehow. Even if you did cause it, it was not your fault."

"Witchcraft, Rachel," Alexander said softly. "How large a crime is that? I hurt someone, and I will not even go to the church to confess."

"It was not your fault!" Why did he insist on blaming himself for something he could not have prevented?

I saw my brother as a saint—he could hardly stand to watch Papa slaughter chickens for supper. I knew, even more surely than he did, that he could never intentionally hurt someone. "You never asked for these powers, Alexander," I told him quietly. "You never signed the Devil's book. You are trying to be forgiven for doing nothing wrong."

Papa returned home with Lynette late that evening. Her arms had been bandaged, but the doctor had said there would be no permanent damage. Alexander's guilt was still so strong—he made sure she rested, not using her hands, even though he had to do most of her work. As he and I cooked supper, he would occasionally catch my gaze, the question in his eyes pleading: *Am I damned?*

# CHAPTER 3
# NOW

WHY AM I THINKING these things?

I find myself staring at the rose on my bed, so like one I was given nearly three hundred years ago. The aura around it is like a fingerprint: I can feel the strength and recognize the one who left it. I know him very well.

I have lived in this world for three hundred years, and yet I have broken one of its most basic rules. When I stopped last night to hunt after visiting Tora, I strayed into the territory of another.

My prey was clearly lost. Though not native to New York City, she had thought she knew where she was going.

The city at night is like a jungle. In the red glow of the unsleeping city the streets and alleys change and twist like shadows, just like all the human—and not so human—predators that inhabit it.

As the sun set, my prey had found herself alone in a

dark area of town. The streetlights were broken, and there were more shadows than light. She was afraid. Lost. Alone. Weak. Easy prey.

She turned onto another street, searching for something familiar. This street was darker than the one before, but not in a way a human would recognize. It was one of the many streets in America that belong to my kind. These streets look almost normal, less dangerous, though perhaps a bit more deserted. Illusions can be so comforting. My prey was walking into a Venus flytrap. If I did not, someone was going to kill her as soon as she entered one of the bars or set foot in a café, which had probably never served anything she would wish to drink.

She seemed to relax slightly when she saw the Café Sangra. None of the windows was broken, no one was collapsed against the building, and the place was open. She started toward the café, and I followed silently.

I sensed another human presence to my left and reached out with my mind to determine whether it was a threat. Walls went up in an instant. But they were weak, and I could tear through them if I tried. The human in question would feel it, though that did not matter to me.

"This isn't your land," he told me. Though I could sense a bit of a vampiric aura around him, he was definitely human. He was blood bonded to a vampire and probably even working for one, but not one of my kind. He was not a threat, so I did not even bother looking into his mind.

"This isn't your land," he told me again. I knew he could read my aura, but I was strong enough to dampen it, so to him I must have felt young. Even so, he was very foolish or he was working for someone very strong—possibly both. Since there are no more than five or six vampires on Earth who are stronger than I, I had little to fear.

"Get out," he ordered me.

"No," I replied, continuing toward the Café Sangra.

I heard him draw a gun, but he had no chance to aim before I was there. I twisted the gun sharply to the side, and he dropped it so that his wrist would not break. My prey's eyes went wide as she saw this, and she ran away blindly, darting around the corner. Stupid human.

I stopped veiling my aura, and my attacker's eyes went wide as he felt its full strength.

"Is that all you were armed with?" I scoffed. "You work for my kind—you must have more than one gun."

He went to draw a knife, but I grabbed it first and threw it into the street hard enough to slam an inch of steel into the ground.

"Who—Who are you?" he stammered, afraid.

"Who do you think I am, child?"

I tend to avoid most of my kind, and destroy those who insist on approaching. Because of this, few recognize me. "Whose are you?" I snapped when he did not immediately respond. I received only a blank stare in return.

I reached into his mind and tore out the information I wanted. Those of my line are the strongest of the vampires when it comes to using our minds, and never have I found a reason to avoid exercising that power. When I found what I sought, I threw the human away from me.

I swore as I realized who this human belonged to.

Aubrey . . . He is one of the few vampires stronger than I. He is also the only one who would care about my presence in his land.

I had been in this part of New York City before but had never encountered Aubrey or any of his servants here. Yet, according to this human, the place belonged to my enemy.

My attacker smiled mockingly. Perhaps he thought I was afraid of his master. Indeed, I fear Aubrey more than anything else on this Earth, but not enough to spare this boy. Aubrey would learn about my being on his territory one way or another, and this child was bothering me.

"Ryan," I crooned, finding his name as I read his mind. He relaxed slightly. I smiled, flashing fangs, and he paled to a chalky white. "You made me lose my prey."

Before he had a chance to run, I stepped toward him, placing a hand on the back of his neck. As I did so I caught his eye, whispering a single word to his mind: *Sleep.* He went limp, and did not fight as my fangs pierced his throat. I could taste a trace of Aubrey's blood in the otherwise mortal elixir that ran through Ryan's veins, and that taste made me shiver.

I did not bother disguising the kill. If Aubrey wished to claim that street, he could deal with the body and the human authorities. Either way, Aubrey would feel my aura and know I had been there; very few would dare to kill one of Aubrey's servants on his own territory.

Though I feared Aubrey and dreaded what would

happen should I confront him again, I refused to show that fear. That was the first time our paths had crossed in nearly three hundred years; I would not show that I still feared him.

Aubrey . . . Hatred flickers through me at the thought of him.

The long-stemmed rose lies on the scarlet comforter over my bed, its petals soft, perfectly formed, and black.

I pick up the rose, cutting my hand on a thorn, which is as sharp as a serpent's tooth. I look at the blood for a moment as the wound heals, reminded of a time long ago; then absently I lick it away. My mind returns again to the time when I was still Rachel Weatere—a time when I was given another black rose.

Then I did not lick the blood away.

# CHAPTER 4
# 1701

"RACHEL," LYNETTE SAID to me. "You have a caller. Papa is waiting with him." Her tone reminded me of a pouting child.

Nearly a month had gone by since Lynette had been burned. My sister was unaware of Alexander's tortured mind; she knew nothing of the powers that he was so afraid of, and believed the fire to be an accident.

Alexander had not spoken to me again about the things he saw, though I recognized the moments when the visions surfaced in his mind. I alone noticed when his face went dark and his focus changed, as if he was listening to voices only he could hear.

When I reached the door, I saw what had made Lynette unhappy. The caller was a dark-haired, black-eyed young man whom I knew only vaguely. Lynette was fourteen, and she resented the attention the boys in town paid to me, though she would never have said so aloud.

Alexander was looking at the visitor with a dark

gaze. I remembered his confession to me about the things he saw, and how he could hear the thoughts in minds around him. I was afraid to know what he was seeing and hearing now.

Turning away from my brother, I looked at our visitor. He wore black breeches and a crimson shirt. The color was too bold for the time; the dyes for such brilliant hues were expensive. The whole outfit had probably cost more than my entire wardrobe.

"Please come in," my papa was saying. "I'm Peter Weatere, Rachel's father, and this is my son, Alexander. This is my other daughter, Lynette," he added as we joined them. "And of course you know Rachel."

Papa assumed that, since our visitor had asked for me, he knew me. But I had seen him before only in passing, and the one time I had spoken with him, I had not been told his name.

"Aubrey Karew," the young man introduced himself, shaking my father's hand. I heard the faintest trace of an accent, though I could not place it. I had not been given much exposure to different languages.

I looked up, and Aubrey's eyes seemed to catch me. They sent shivers down my spine. Something kept me from looking away, as if I was a bird caught in the eyes of a snake.

"How may I help you, Mr. Karew?" my father was asking. I tried to keep my eyes down, as was proper, but could not. Aubrey's eyes were hypnotizing, and I could not force my gaze away from them.

Then this strange young man handed me a rose, which I took without thinking. I should not have been taking gifts from young men my father had barely met, but the way this man's eyes caught me had startled me, and I took the rose before I even realized what it was.

"Mr. Karew," my father said, frowning, "this is rather improper—"

"You're right," Aubrey said.

Papa stood dumbstruck. I looked at the rose, which I was still holding. It was beautiful—such long-stemmed roses did not grow in the northern colonies. For a moment I thought it was deep red, but soon I realized it was black. One of the thorns caught the skin of my hand, drawing blood, and I transferred the rose to my other hand, hoping no one had noticed.

I looked back up at Aubrey, whose eyes had fallen to the cut on my hand, and another shiver went down my back. He turned abruptly and left. He was gone before anyone could say a word.

My father turned to me, his face stern, but my brother intervened.

"It is too late to discuss our visitor rationally. We need to sleep before the bell rings for church tomorrow." I knew my brother well, and I recognized his tone: he did wish to discuss Aubrey, but not with my father. Papa nodded; he respected my brother.

Alexander had been the only one in my family who noticed my cut. After my father left, he took me out to the well to wash it, his expression worried.

"What is wrong, Alexander?" I asked him, still holding the rose, though I hardly noticed that I was doing so. "You look as if our guest had a serpent's tongue."

"Perhaps he did," Alexander said, his voice hushed and dark. "A black-eyed boy we have never seen comes to our door and offers you a black rose. You take his gift and cannot seem to put it down, even after it has drawn blood from you."

"What are you saying?" I whispered, shocked.

"I may not have signed the Devil's book, but that does not mean there are not creatures out there who belong to him."

"Alexander!" I whispered, shocked by the implication. He had all but accused this Aubrey Karew of being one of the Devil's creatures.

I looked at the rose, which was still in my hand, and then put it deliberately on the ground, trying to convince my brother—and perhaps myself—that such an action was possible.

Even so, my gaze remained on its black petals, and I realized how Alexander had felt when I told him to speak to a cleric after Lynette's accident. What would be said should I explain to a preacher about the black rose I had accepted? After all, I had heard that people signed the Devil's book with their blood, and my blood had been drawn.

Alexander walked back into the house silently, and I watched him leave, not knowing what to say. I could not deny that the rose was beautiful in a way—perfectly shaped, just opened. The color, though, was the color of darkness, death, and all the evil things I had been told of: black hearts, black art, black—

Black eyes. Hypnotic black eyes.

I did not like to believe that I might have accepted a gift from one of the Devil's creatures. I convinced myself that I had not.

Perhaps if I had believed—

Perhaps nothing. What could I have done?

❊ ❊ ❊

The next day would be my last day in that world — my last day to speak to my papa, my sister, or my brother, and my last day to draw a breath and know that without it I would die. It would be my last day to thank the sun for giving light to my days.

I would argue with Alexander and avoid my papa. And, like all humanity, never once would I thank the sun or the air for its existence. Light, air, and my brother's love — I took them all for granted, and someone took them all away.

My last day of humanity . . . Rachel Weatere would die the next night.

# CHAPTER 5
# NOW

I PULL MY THOUGHTS from the past, not wanting to dwell on that night, and my gaze again returns to the black rose. I wonder briefly where it was grown. It is so similar to the one Aubrey gave me three hundred years ago.

I hesitate to pick up the white florist's card that has been lying beneath the rose, but finally snatch it from the bed.

*Stay in your place, Risika.*

The rose is a warning. Aubrey did not like having his servant killed on his own land, and he is reminding me of my past.

I hunt in New York again this night, careful not to stray onto Aubrey's land but refusing to give up my favorite hunting grounds out of fear.

I stop in his part of New York for only a moment. I have burnt the card and leave the ashes in a plastic bag on the front step of the Café Sangra. I take orders from no one.

Some vampires, like some humans, know nothing other than submission. They do not wish to rise in power. But those vampires are rare. Few vampires will allow themselves to show fear of another, for as soon as you are proved weaker you become the hunted. The hunter hates being hunted, chased, or wounded. If it did not, it would not be an aggressive hunter, and those who cannot be aggressive are hunted down while they shiver and hide because the night is dark.

Forever is too long to live in fear.

Even so, I do not go to see Tora this night. I do not wish to draw Aubrey's attention to her until he has forgotten this small challenge. Although I resent being kept away from her, I would rather stay away than have her die so that my pride may be appeased. For Tora, I allow myself to fear Aubrey.

After I hunt, I change to hawk form and return to Concord, my mind still troubled. I fall into bed for the day, but I do not dream—I simply remember.

# CHAPTER 6
## 1701

ALEXANDER AVOIDED ME the day after Mr. Karew visited. We attended morning services as a family, but the rest of the day, Alexander mostly stayed in his room. During the short time he was out he looked dazed, as if he was seeing something I could not see or hearing voices I could not hear. Perhaps he was. I still do not know, and I never will.

When he approached me that evening, the dazed look was gone, replaced by determination.

"Rachel?"

"Yes?"

"I need to speak to you," Alexander told me. "I do not know how to explain to you so that you do not think . . ." He paused, and I waited for him to continue.

"There are creatures in this world besides humans," Alexander went on, his voice gaining strength and determination. "But they are not what the witch hunters say they are. The witches . . ." Again Alexander paused, and I waited for him to decide how to say what he needed to say. "I do not know if Satan exists—I have never seen him, personally—but I do know that there are creatures out there that would damn you if they could, simply for spite."

This was nothing I had not heard before at church. But my brother said it differently than the preacher ever did. I would say it sounded as if Alexander had more faith, but that wasn't quite it. It sounded as if, in his mind, he had proof.

"Alexander, what has happened?" I whispered. His words seemed a warning, but it was not a warning I understood.

Alexander sighed deeply. "I made a mistake, Rachel." Then he would say no more about it.

I went to bed that night feeling uneasy. I was afraid to know what Alexander's words meant, but even more afraid because I did not know.

Around eleven I heard footsteps moving past my door, as if someone was trying without success to move quietly. I rose silently, so as not to wake Lynette, with whom I shared the room, and tiptoed to the door.

I left my room and entered the kitchen, where I caught a glimpse of Alexander leaving by the back door. I began to follow him, wondering why he was sneaking out of the house at such a late hour.

I well knew the abstract look that I had glimpsed on his face: he had seen something in his mind. Whatever vision had driven him from sleep had scared him, and it pained me that he had walked straight past my door, not even hesitating, not willing to confide in me.

Alexander had slipped through the back door, but I hesitated beside the doorway, hearing voices behind the house. Alexander was speaking with Aubrey and a woman I did not know. Her accent was different from Aubrey's, but again it was not familiar to me. I did not know then that she had been raised to speak a language long dead.

The woman Alexander was speaking with had black hair that fell to her shoulders and formed a dark halo around her deathly pale skin and black eyes. She wore a black silk dress and silver jewelry that nearly covered her left hand. On her right wrist she wore a silver snake bracelet with rubies for eyes.

The black dress, the jewelry, and most of all the red-eyed serpent, brought one word to my mind: *witch*.

"Why should I?" she was asking Alexander.

"Just stay away," he ordered. He sounded so calm, but I knew him well. I caught the shiver in his voice — the sound of anger and fear.

"Temptation," the woman said, pushing Alexander. He fell against the wall, and I could hear the impact as his back hit the wood. But she had hardly touched him! "Child, you would regret ordering me away from your sister," the woman added coldly.

"Do not hurt her, Ather." It was the first time I had heard her name, and shivers ran down my spine upon hearing my brother speak it. My golden-colored brother did not belong in the dark world she had risen from.

"I mean it," Alexander said, stepping forward from the wall. "I am the one who attacked you — leave Rachel be. If you need to fight someone to heal your pride, fight me, not my sister."

When I heard this, my heart jumped. Alexander was

my brother. I had been born with him and raised with him. I knew him, and I knew he would not harm another human being.

"You and that witch should not have interrupted my hunt," said Ather.

"You should be grateful 'that witch' helped me stop you. If you had killed Lynette—"

"Which sister matters more to you, Alexander—your twin, or Lynette? You drew blood; you should have remembered Rachel before you did."

"I will not let you change her," Alexander growled.

"Why, Alexander," Ather said, advancing on him again. "What gave you the idea I wanted to change her?" She smiled; I saw her teeth as the moonlight fell on them. Then she laughed. "Just because she accepted my gift?" Ather took another step toward Alexander, and he stepped back. She laughed again. "Coward."

"You are a monster," Alexander answered. "I will not allow you to make Rachel one too."

"Aubrey," Ather said. Nothing more. Aubrey had been standing quietly in the shadows. He laughed and moved behind Alexander, but my brother did not react. He seemed unafraid to have Aubrey at his back.

"Rachel, do come join us," Ather called to me. I froze; I had not realized she had seen me. Ather nodded to Aubrey, who took a step in my direction, as if he might escort me into the yard. I did not step back from him but became angry instead.

"Get away from me," I spat. I had always been outspoken for my time, and Aubrey blinked in surprise. He stepped to the side and allowed me to walk past him toward Ather.

Alexander had said he had made a mistake. Now he was trying to protect me from the two who had come to avenge that mistake. I stalked past Aubrey to where Ather was standing.

"Who are you?" I demanded. "What are you doing here?"

"Rachel," she purred in greeting, ignoring my questions. She showed fangs when she smiled, and I was reminded of the serpent on her bracelet.

"Rachel, do not get angry," Alexander warned me.

"Too late." I spat the words into Ather's face. "Why were you threatening him?"

"Do not demand answers from me, *child*," Ather snapped.

"Do not call me child. Leave my property, now, and leave my brother alone."

Ather laughed. "Does this creature truly mean so much to you?" she asked me.

"Yes." I did not hesitate to answer. Alexander was my twin brother. He was part of my family, and I loved him. He had been cursed with a mixture of too much faith and damnable powers. He did not deserve the taunting he was receiving.

"That's unfortunate," Ather said dryly, and then, "Aubrey, will you deal with that distraction?" I started to turn toward Aubrey, who had drawn a knife from his belt, and barely saw him grab my brother before Ather took my head in both her powerful hands and forced me to look into her eyes. "Now he means nothing."

I heard Aubrey laugh, and then stop. I thought I heard a whisper, but it was so soft, so quick, that it could have been the wind. Aubrey reentered my line of vision, sheathing his blade. Then he disappeared, and I was left watching the place where he had stood. I stared after him, in shock perhaps. I heard nothing anymore, felt nothing.

Then what had just happened seemed to hit me, and I tried to turn to my brother, who was so silent—too silent. . . .

Ather grabbed my arm.

"Leave him there, Rachel," she told me.

But Alexander was hurt, maybe dying. I had no doubt Aubrey had drawn the knife to kill him. How could she tell me to leave him? He needed help.

"I said, *leave him,*" Ather whispered, once again turning me toward her. I stepped back, meeting her black eyes.

Cold shock was beginning to fill my mind, blocking the way of terror and pain. My brother could not be dead—not this suddenly.

"Do you know what I am, Rachel?" Ather asked me, and the question jolted me from my silent world. *This* was reality—not Alexander's death, not black roses. I could deal with this moment, so long as I did not think of the one before.

"You appear to be a creature from legend," I said carefully, worried about the consequences my words might have.

"You are right." Ather smiled again, and I wanted to slap that smile from her face. I remembered Alexander's words—*I am the one who attacked you*—and my surprise at hearing them. I could not believe my brother would ever harm anyone. The idea that such violence was in *me* was shocking . . . yet also strangely exciting.

Ather continued before I could say anything.

"I want to make you one of my kind."

"*No,*" I told her. "Leave. Now. I do not want to be what you are."

"Did I say you had a choice?"

I pushed her away with all my strength, but she barely stumbled. She grabbed my shoulders. Long-nailed fingers twining in my hair, she tilted my head back and then leaned forward so that her lips touched my throat. The wicked fangs I had glimpsed before pierced my skin.

I fought; I fought for the immortal soul the preachers had taught me to believe in. I do not know whether I ever believed in it—I had never seen God, and He had never spoken to me—but I fought for it anyway, and I fought for Alexander.

Nothing I did mattered.

The feeling of having your blood drawn out is both seductive and soothing, like a caress and a gentle voice that is in your mind, whispering *Relax.* It makes you want to stop struggling and cooperate. I would not cooperate. But if you struggle, it hurts.

Ather's right hand pinned both of mine together behind me, and her left hand held me by the hair. Her teeth were in the vein that ran down my throat, but the pain hit me in the chest. It felt as if liquid fire was being forced through my veins instead of blood. My heart beat faster, from fear and pain and lack of blood. Eventually I lost consciousness.

A minute or an hour later, I woke for a moment in a dark place. There was no light and no sound, only pain and the thick, warm liquid that was being forced past my lips.

I swallowed again and again before my head cleared. The liquid was bittersweet, and as I drank I had an impression of power and . . . not life or death, but time. And strength and eternity . . .

Finally I realized what I had been drinking. I pushed away the wrist that someone was holding to my lips, but I was weak, and it was so tempting.

*"Temptation."* The voice was in my ears and my head, and I recognized it as Ather's.

Once again I pushed away the wrist, though my body screamed at me for doing so. Ather was insistent, but so was I. I somehow managed to turn my head away, despite the pain that shot through me with each beat of my heart. I could hear my own pulse in my ears, and it quickened until I could hardly breathe past it, but still I pushed away the blood. I believed, for that second, in my immortal soul, and would not abandon it—not willingly.

Suddenly Ather was gone. I was alone.

I could feel the blood in my veins, entering my body, soul, and mind. I could not get my breath; my head pounded and my heart raced. Then they both slowed.

I heard my own heart stop.

I felt my breath still.

My vision faded, and the blackness filled my mind.

# CHAPTER 7
# NOW

NEVER BEFORE AND NEVER AFTER have I felt the soul-tearing, mind-breaking pain I experienced that night. I have looked into the minds of willing fledglings; never have I seen my own pain reflected. My line's strength comes at a price, and the price is that pain. It has changed us all. One cannot be conscious throughout one's own death and not be changed.

Perhaps that was the worst part. Or perhaps the worst part of my story is yet to come.

The visions of my past linger in the present. Alexander's face floats in my mind, and I cannot seem to make it disappear. My two lives have nothing in common, and yet as I stand in this house I feel as if I have somehow been transported back to the past, before my brother was killed.

Seeking a diversion, I bring myself to New York City. I do not shift into hawk form. I simply bring myself away with the ability that only my kind has—the ability to change to pure energy, pure ether, for the instant it takes to travel in that form to another place. It takes me only a thought, and I arrive in less than a second.

I automatically shield my aura as I appear in the alley, not wishing to announce my presence to the world. Then I walk through the scarred wooden door that leads to Ambrosia, one of the city's many vampire clubs. This place was once owned by another of Ather's fledglings, a vampire named Kala. But Kala was killed by a vampire hunter. Yes, they do exist; witches and even humans often hunt our kind. I do not know who owns this place now that they have killed Kala.

The club is small and looks like any café—or it would if it had windows and more light than the single candle in the corner gives. Of course, I can see by the dim light, but a human would be close to blind in Ambrosia.

At the counter is another of my kind. I do not know him. He has his head down on the counter, and the skin I can see is almost gray. As I walk through the door he does not even look in my direction, though he does raise his head long enough to empty the glass that stands on the counter near him, and to lick the blood from his lips as a shiver wracks his body.

"Who did this to you?" I ask him, curious. There is no disease on Earth my kind can catch, and almost no poison that affects us, so I wonder why he looks ill.

"Some damn Triste," the stranger growls. "He was in the Café Sangra. I didn't even realize he wasn't human."

I wonder how Aubrey would react if he learned a Triste witch had been in the Café Sangra.

The Triste witches appear almost identical to humans.

If one can read auras, their auras feel the same. Their hearts beat, and they breathe. They need to eat, just as humans do. Their blood tastes just like a human's.

However, they are not human in the least. Like vampires, Triste witches are immortal. They do not age, and their blood is poison to our kind. This child who chanced to feed off one is lucky he did not take much, or else he would already be dead.

"Since when does Aubrey allow Tristes in his territory?" I ask. The two kinds—vampires and witches—are usually enemies. The word *Triste* can almost be used as a synonym for *vampire hunter.*

"He doesn't. I was feeding," he answers, cringing a bit. "And then found myself on the floor with my arm broken. Aubrey tossed me away from the witch like some kind of a doll. They got into an argument, and the witch was thrown out. But this witch, he gave me this on the way out," he says, holding up a folded slip of paper. "Said to give it to some fledgling of Ather's."

He adds, "Ather doesn't have any fledglings called Rachel, does she?"

*"What?"* I gasp. I am the only one of Ather's fledglings who has ever been called by that name, and only Ather and Aubrey know it.

"He said, 'Give this to Rachel—Ather's fledgling.' "

I no longer wish to take the paper from his hand. I do not wish to know what it says. Rachel was human, weak, prey. Only Aubrey would call me by that name. Except for Ather, he alone knows all the memories it stirs, and he is the only one who would try to hurt me with it.

*I am not Rachel, and I can never be Rachel again,* I think. *Rachel is dead.*

I leave Ambrosia without another word, my head reeling with anger. I have seen Aubrey only twice since my death, and both times were long ago. Until recently, I have avoided him like bad blood.

When I return to my home at dawn, I find one of Aubrey's servants in my yard. This is my town, and I do not tolerate other vampires, or their servants, in my territory. This applies to Aubrey above all else, because he would take what is mine if I allowed it.

I change to human form less than a foot from the interloper and push him against the wall of the house.

"What do you want?" I demand.

"Aubrey sent—"

I have no patience and reach into his mind, finding the information I want. Aubrey sent him to warn me away again. If Aubrey had come himself we would have fought, and while I know he does not fear challenging me, I cannot see us fighting again without one of us dying.

"Tell him I hunt where I wish," I say to the human. "And I will kill any other servants of his who approach me." It is dangerous to send such messages to another vampire. What I have said is very close to a challenge—one I hope to avoid—but so be it. If I must, I will play thin ice with Aubrey tonight. I do not care that if the ice breaks it will be I who falls through.

I leave the human on the doorstep and return to my room.

# CHAPTER 8
# 1701

I FELT MYSELF DIE. I remember hoping I would wake again, that somehow I would live, but then I realized what that would mean.

I was dead.

I threw myself into the shadows of death and became lost.

Senses and memories came slowly when I first awakened.

I remembered a death, and I remembered that it had been I who had died, but I did not remember who that "I" was.

Trying to open my eyes, I saw only blackness. I thought I was blind, and that terrified me. Was this death, then? Floating forever in blackness, not even remembering who you had been?

As that thought brushed my mind I realized I was not floating. No—I could feel a wooden floor beneath me, and I was leaning against a wall that was cold and smooth like glass. I groped blindly around myself but felt nothing else. Behind me was the glass wall, and in front of me was only blackness.

I forced myself to my feet. Though all my muscles were stiff, after a moment I was able to stand.

I felt for my pulse and could not find it. I tried to shout and realized I did not have air in my lungs to do so. No heartbeat. No breath. I became afraid once again. I was dead, wasn't I? If not, what was I?

Humans breathe when alive, even when they are asleep or unaware of their breathing. Since waking, I had not taken a breath, and I had not noticed until now.

I finally tried to draw a deep breath, but sharp pain shot through my lungs. It knocked me to my knees, then slowly began to fade. Finally it subsided, and I tried to speak, wondering if I would be able to hear myself. Are not the dead both deaf and mute?

I took another tentative breath, and the pain did not strike as hard this time, so I used the breath to ask the darkness, "Can anyone hear me?" I received no reply, and I did not wish to ask again.

I tried to ignore my fear, working the stiffness from my joints and forcing myself to take another breath. The pain was almost gone, but my ribs still felt sore, as if the muscles around them had not been used for a long time. I felt no need to exhale, and I did not become dizzy when I did not do so. Letting out the unnecessary breath, I marveled when my body did not tell me to take another.

I had my senses of touch and hearing. I could speak. I could taste, and the taste in my mouth was sweet and vaguely familiar. I licked my lips and found that it was there as well. A memory tried to surface in my mind, one of pain and fear. I did not want it, so I pushed it away.

I tried to determine whether I could smell anything in the darkness. A honeylike scent wafted in the still, cool air. Beeswax? A candle, perhaps? I could also smell the light, dry scent of wood and an even fainter scent like frost—glass. It did not occur to me that I should not be able to smell *glass*. No human could.

Beneath these scents was something I did not recognize—not really like a smell at all, but like something between a taste and a fragrance that you catch for a moment on the breeze. Or perhaps it was the breeze itself, a gentle movement in the air. I focused on this sensation, and though it did not become clearer, its presence was strong.

Later I learned that this feeling was aura. The aura of death—my death—and of a vampire: Ather, my dark, immortal mother, who gave me this life against my will and who killed my mortal self.

I tried to walk, searching for a way out of the black room I was in, and found it surprisingly easy. The stiffness was gone from my body, and I moved smoothly, more as if I was floating than walking. The wood beneath my bare feet was smooth and cool.

I followed the wall until I reached a place that was not glass—a wooden door. I opened it slowly and blinked at the light that poured in. Turning my face away, I caught sight of the room I had just left. All four walls were mirrored, and my reflection flew back at me hundreds of times. Amazement filled me. Whoever owned this house must be rich, to have so much glass in one room. And yet there were no windows at all: nothing to let in the light and air.

I walked back into the room, entranced by my own reflection, hardly recognizing myself. I approached the mirrored surface and stretched a tentative hand out to the stranger reflected there. Her hair was still my golden hair, and her body had nearly my body's shape, but her form was more graceful, and when she walked she seemed to glide effortlessly. Her eyes were black as midnight, her skin as pale as death.

"Look hard, Risika," a voice behind me said. "Remember it well, for soon it will fade."

I spun toward the voice. Everything about the speaker was black, from her hair and eyes to her clothing, everything but her unnaturally fair skin. My first thought was *witch*. It came from some vague recollection of my past life, though I did not know what that life had held.

My next thought was *Ather*. I remembered her—I remembered the dark halo her hair formed around her pale skin, and I remembered her icy laugh.

A scene flashed through my mind. Once again I remembered my death, but now I remembered before that—Aubrey, sheathing the knife that had just taken a life. Whose life? I did not know and was not sure I wanted to.

"Why have you brought me here?" I demanded. "What have you done to me?"

"Come, now," Ather told me. "Surely you can figure it out. Look at my reflection—look well. Then tell me what I have done to you."

I obeyed her command and turned back to the

mirror. I could barely see her reflection. In the glass her form was so faint that her black hair appeared as little more than pale smoke.

"Now look at your own reflection," she told me.

I did. Once again I looked at the figure in the mirror, wondering if she could truly be me. I had a picture of myself in my mind, and it was not the same as the one I was seeing; though very close, perhaps, it was still very wrong.

"Who am I?" I asked, turning back to her. I truly did not know.

"You do not remember your life?"

"No." Ather smiled as I responded. A cold smile—if a snake could smile, it would smile as she did.

"I thought so," she answered. "Your memory will, sadly, return later, but for now . . ." She trailed off with a shrug, as if it did not matter.

"Who am I?" I demanded. "Answer me." I was angry, but her nonchalance was not the only reason. My mind had been spinning since I awoke. The sensation had been faint at first, but now the edges of my vision were beginning to go red.

"Why?" she responded. "Who you were no longer matters. You are Risika, of Silver's bloodline."

"And who is Risika?" I pressed, trying to ignore the painful shiver that wracked my body. "What is she?"

"She is—*you* are—a vampire," Ather told me. The information took a moment to reach my mind. I knew words like *witch* and *Devil*. This one was foreign. From somewhere, some memory I could not quite see, I heard someone say, *"There are creatures out there that would damn you if they could, simply for spite."*

Surely Ather was one of those creatures the speaker had been talking about. And Aubrey—I remembered him as well. Once again I saw him sheathing his knife, but still I could not remember why he had taken it out.

"You have made me into—" I broke off.

"Do you know I can read your mind like a book?" Ather said, laughing. "You are young now, still partially human. You will quickly learn to shield your thoughts, perhaps even from me. You are strong, even now. He warned me you would be. Was he afraid you would be too strong for me to control?"

I did not say anything, hardly understanding what Ather said. My head was spinning as if I had hit it on something, and I was having difficulty focusing on anything.

Ather paused, looking at me, and then smiled. When she did, I could see pale fangs, and I repressed another shiver. "Come, child," she told me. "You need to hunt before your body destroys itself."

*Hunt.* The word sent dread through me. It reminded me of wolves and cougars, animals who stalked their prey in the forest. Blood soaking into the ground. So much blood . . .

Now I wanted that blood. I could see the scarlet death in my mind. Surely the blood was warm and sweet and—

What was happening to me? These thoughts were not mine, were they?

"Come, Risika," Ather snapped. "The pain will worsen until you either feed or go mad from it."

"No." I said the word solidly, without reluctance, despite the way I felt. I was burning, and there was dust in my veins. I thought of blood and craved it the way I craved water on a long, hot day. I knew what Ather meant when she said *hunt*, but I would not kill to ease my own pain. I was not an animal. I was a human being. . . .

At least, I hoped I was human. What had Ather done to me?

"Risika," she told me, "if you do not feed, the blood I have given you will kill you." She was not pleading with me; she was stating facts. "It will take days before you are truly dead, but by sunset tomorrow you will be too weak to hunt for yourself, and I refuse to spoon-feed you. Hunt or die, it is your choice."

I hesitated, trying to remember. There was a reason that I should not hunt. Someone I knew would have re-sisted, someone I loved but could not remember . . . I could not remember. The only reason I could remember now was the one I had been taught all my life by the preachers—because killing was a sin.

But dying by my own choice was a sin as well.

Perhaps I was already damned.

"Foolish child," Ather said. "Look at yourself in that mirror and tell me that your own church would not condemn you for what you are. Would you refuse the life I have given you to try to save the soul which your god has damned?"

"I will not sell my soul to save my life," I said, though in my mind I was not so sure. My church was cold and strict, but I feared the nothingness of a soulless death just as much as I feared the flames of the spoken Hell. And perhaps she was right. Perhaps it was already too late.

"No," I said again, trying to convince myself more than her. "I will not."

"Brave words," Ather told me. "What if I told you it did not matter?" She was whispering now, as if that would drive her words into my mind. It was working. "You signed the Devil's book as your blood fell onto my gift to you."

In my mind the scene played itself out again. A black rose, the thorns sharp like the fangs of a viper. A drop of blood falling on the black flower as those fang-like thorns cut the hand that held them. Black eyes, much like Ather's black eyes but somehow infinitely colder, watching like a snake as the blood fell. Watching like a viper, like the thorns of the rose, as if he had bitten me . . .

My mind was filled with dark images and darker thoughts of snakes and hunting beasts and red blood falling on black petals. My heart was filled with pain and anger and hatred and the black blood that had damned me.

# CHAPTER 9
# NOW

I PULL MYSELF from my memories. I curse the fool I was to think I could save my damned soul with silly protests.

Aubrey's servant has run from my home, and I sense him leaving my town. He fears for his life, with good reason. Had he stayed I would have killed him. He knows I would, and he knows I can smell his fear.

I may have been changed against my will, but I do not fight what I am anymore. There is no greater freedom than feeling the night air against your face as you run through the forest, no greater joy than the hunt. The taste of your prey's fear, the sound of its heart beating strong and fast, the smells of the night.

I stand in this small town, so near to the dead and almost as near to the faithful in the church across the street, feeling the fear of the human running from my home. For that is what I am—a hunter. I learned long ago that I could not deny that fact.

Every instinct tells me to hunt this running, frightened

creature. I am a vampire, after all. But I am not an animal, and I was once a human. That is what makes my kind dangerous: a hunter's instincts and a human's mind. Humanity's cruel way of toying with the world, laced with the savage, unthinking hunt of the wild animal.

But I do have control, and I will let this human live to tell his news to Aubrey, whom he fears even more than he fears me. He is the bearer of bad news, and Aubrey does not like bad news.

I refuse to allow Aubrey to rule me, but only because it is the way of my kind. I fear Aubrey as much as this human does, perhaps more, for I know exactly what Aubrey is and what he is capable of.

I am restless. Despite the rising sun, I am in the mood to do something.

After making a quick check to make sure there is no blood on me from the previous night's hunt, I leave my house. I walk, partly because I am not leaving Concord and thus not going far, but mostly because I have a craving to move.

Occasionally I visit cafés like Ambrosia, which cater to my kind. But more often I become a shadow of the human world. Human lives, which seem so complex to those who are living them, seem simple from the perspective of three hundred years.

The coffee shop has just opened when I slip through the door.

The girl who works there is human, of course. Her name is Alexis, and she has worked there for most of the summer.

"Morning, Elizabeth," she greets me, and I smile in return. I often visit this place in the morning. Of course, I did not give Alexis my real name. I do not allow myself to grow close to humans. They have a tendency to notice that I never age.

I buy coffee, not because I want the caffeine or even like the taste, but because people will stare at someone who is sitting in a coffee shop without anything to drink.

A few minutes later the prework traffic begins. For about half an hour the shop bustles, and I sit in the corner silently and watch people.

Though I have worked to distance myself from human society, I enjoy watching humans as they go about their business.

The principal of the nearby school hurries in, already late for work, dressed in a somber suit that makes her look even more tired than she is. A minute later a middle-aged man opens the door, stopping in during his morning jog. Two women, sipping their coffee at one of the small tables, get into a quiet argument over an article one read in the newspaper. A teenage girl meets her boyfriend and then is horrified as her father walks into the coffee shop.

I smile silently, watching the various dramas, which will probably be forgotten by evening.

Business slows as the customers depart, many complaining about their destination.

Humans are often this way. They go about their lives, constantly working, complaining of boredom one minute and overwork the next. They pause only to observe the niceties of society, greeting each other with "Good morning" while their minds are somewhere else completely.

Sometimes I wonder what my life would be like if I had been born into this modern time. Sin and evil no longer seem as important as they did three hundred years ago. Would I have been as horrified at what I have become, I wonder, if I had not been raised in the church, with the ever-present threat of damnation?

The two women in the corner who have been arguing about politics now stand and depart together, laughing. I watch them with an ounce of jealousy, knowing their worries are far away and that despite everything they know, they are still innocent.

Innocence . . . I remember when the last of my innocence died.

# CHAPTER 10
# 1701

ATHER LED ME from her house, and I saw no choice but to follow. The moonlight cleared my mind slightly, but my vision was still red around the edges, and my head was pounding.

I did not have specific memories of who I had been, but I knew what a town was, and what a house was. And everything I saw around me was somehow not *right*.

Ather's home was at the fringe of a wood, set far back from the road. After a moment I realized what was bothering me about it: the house was painted black with white shutters, as was the one next door. I had an impression of inversion, like the black Masses I had been told of at which Devil-spawns spoke the Lord's Prayer backward. It was the same, and so very wrong.

"Where are we?" I finally asked.

"This place does not exist," Ather answered. I frowned, not understanding. She sighed, impatient with my ignorance. "This town is called Mayhem. It is as solid as the town you grew up in, but our kind owns it, and no one outside even knows it exists. Stop thinking about things you need not worry about, Risika. You need to feed."

*You need to feed.* I shut my eyes for a moment, trying to blink away the burning sensation. I shook my head, but the pain refused to dull. Would I need to kill to sate it? I did not want to kill, but I did not want to die, but I did not want to kill. . . . What happened to the damned when they died?

"No," I said again, though this time it meant nothing in my ears and nothing in my mind. Thinking was impossible. I only knew I did not want to kill, but all I could think about was blood . . . red blood on black petals, and thorns and fangs like a viper's. . . .

The pain was intense, pushing my reason away from me, and my thoughts were no longer coherent. Ather sounded so sure, so calm.

"Come, child," she said soothingly. "You can feed on one of the witches waiting for death, if that would appease your conscience. They are already doomed to death and worse."

A shiver wracked my body, and the pain in my eyes and head grew. My hands were numb.

I am not sure whether I nodded. I believe I may have.

The next instant I found myself in a cold, dark cell with two of the accused witches. I did not consciously know how I arrived there, but part of me knew that Ather had used her mind to move us both. She appeared beside me a moment later.

I heard a beating that filled the room, and it took me

a moment to realize that it was the heartbeats of the two women who were in the cell with us. One of them had screamed when she saw us, and the other had crossed herself. The smell of fear was sharp, and though I had never smelled it before, I recognized the scent the way a wolf does.

The accused witches tried to move away from us, one reciting the Lord's Prayer, the other still screaming. But the cell was too small for them to go far. I hardly heard the prayer.

I was aware only of their heartbeats and the pulses in their wrists and throats. I heard nothing else, saw nothing else. My vision was red-hazed, and my head was spinning.

*Feed freely.* I recognized Ather's voice in my mind. She smiled at me, and I caught a flash of fang. Absently I brushed my tongue over my own canines and realized that they were the same—too sharp, too long, they did not belong in a human mouth. I could feel the tips, vicious as a snake's, pressing into my lower lip.

I saw Ather walk toward the still screaming woman, who quieted and went limp, as if she had fallen asleep. Ather pulled back the woman's head, exposing the pulse in her neck. Ather's razor-sharp fangs neatly broke the woman's skin, and the scent of blood entered the room.

I lost all ideas of sin and murder then.

I lost all that had once made me Rachel.

I turned to the other woman, whose prayer had become a babble.

I fed.

❈   ❈   ❈

I tasted her life as it flowed into me. Ather's blood had been cool and filled with the essence of immortality. This human's blood was thick and hot, boiling with pure life and energy. It wet my parched mouth and brought down my fever, and I drank it like a healing ambrosia.

Flashes of thought came to me, too fast for me to realize at first that they were not my own. After a moment I gained more control and discovered they were from my victim. I saw a laughing human child. It called to its mother to show her a flower. I saw a dinner cooking in a hearth. I saw a wedding. I saw morning services. My mind focused on this last image.

I could see this woman's mind clearly, and she was innocent of any form of witchcraft. This thought, more than any other, caused a complete change in me. This woman had been sent here to die as a witch, and she was innocent of the crime. Why had her own people accused her? How many more of the accused were innocent?

I tried to draw away quickly, but I moved as if under water. It was so tempting to drink for just a moment more, and a moment more than that, and just a moment more . . .

"And lead us not into temptation." I had spoken those words without faith so many times. If true belief had backed my prayer, would the words have been rewarded? Or would I still have been in that cell, feasting on the blood of an innocent woman?

All I knew at that time was that I did not want to kill, and yet I could not draw away. Even as I heard her heart stop and felt the flow of blood slowing, even as

she died, it was hard to stop feeding. My vision returned as her vision faded, and I looked at the innocent
woman, now pale as chalk and empty of blood.

Beside me Ather licked her lips and dropped her
prey to the stained, dirty floor of the cell. She looked as
satisfied as a kitten with a bowl of cream. I was horrified, but not simply because of the killing. I had been
unable to draw away as an innocent woman died, even
though I could have saved her life.

"It is easy to kill, Risika," Ather told me. "And it gets
easier the more you do it."

"No," I answered. How many times had I said that
word in the past day? What meaning did it have anymore? I was not as sure as I wanted to be.

"You will learn," she told me, taking the woman from
my arms and dropping her to the ground with the other
innocent. "You are a predator now, and survival is the
only rule of a predator's world."

"I will not be a killer."

"You will," she said, walking behind me. I turned to
keep her in my view. She sounded so sure, and I felt so
unsure. "You are above the humans now, Risika, above
even most of our kind. Will you let them rule you because that is how the humans taught you?"

I did not answer, because I could not do so without
agreeing with her.

"The law of the jungle says 'Be strong or be domi-
nated.' The law of our world says 'Be strong or be
killed.'"

"It is not my world!" I shouted. I did not want to belong to this fierce world of hunters who fed on the
blood of innocents.

"Yes, it is, Risika," Ather insisted.

"I won't let it be."

"You have no choice, child."

"You're evil. I won't kill because you tell me to—"

"Then kill because it is your right." She snapped each word off, impatient with my refusal. "You are no longer human, Risika. Humans are your prey. You have never felt sorrow for the chickens you killed so that they could grace your plate. The animals you raised so that they could be killed. The creatures you put in pens so that you could own them. Why should you feel differently toward your meal now?"

She put it in a way I could not disagree with. "But you can't just kill humans. It's—"

"Evil?" Ather finished for me. "The world is evil, Risika. Wolves hunt the stragglers in a group of deer. Vultures devour the fallen. Hyenas destroy the weak. Humans kill that which they fear. Survive and be strong, or die, cornered by your prey, trembling because the night is dark."

# CHAPTER 11
## NOW

I LEAVE THE COFFEE SHOP and return to my home before the sun rises too high for comfort.

I go to bed, fall into a deep sleep, and awaken that evening in a foul mood.

I allow myself to hide in fear. Even as I say I will not let Aubrey rule my life, I let him keep me from the one thing in this world that can still bring me joy: Tora, my tiger. My beautiful, pure-minded tiger, who was once free and is now caged.

Aubrey has stolen so much from me. I have sworn to avenge the lives he has taken, but every time I have been too much a coward to challenge him.

My mood is as dark as Aubrey's eyes, black without end, and I want to fight back. So I deliberately hunt in Aubrey's land—the dying heart of New York City, where the streets are darkened with shadows cast by the invisible world.

I see another of my kind, a young fledgling, in one of

the alleys. She senses my strength and cowers, blinking away like a candle flame in the night.

She is weak and not a threat to Aubrey's claim on this dark corner of the city, so he tolerates her presence. Perhaps he shows off occasionally, simply to keep her afraid. But he knows she will never challenge him. I am Aubrey's own blood sister, created by the same dark mother. If he tolerates me I could be as much a threat to his position as a mongoose in a cobra's nest — not because I am stronger, which I am not, but because it will appear to others of our kind that he fears me, and his pride is too strong to allow that.

I hunt and leave my prey dying in the street. Perhaps it is foolish to bait Aubrey this way, but I have lived too long beneath his shadow and refuse to cower any longer. Aubrey himself does not challenge me as I feed, and my suspicions rise. Where is he, I wonder, that he does not know I am here? Or is it simply that he does not care? Is he that sure of his claim?

I return to my home in a dark mood, but as I enter my room my thoughts turn to ice.

I can sense the aura of one of my kind, one of my kin, and I recognize it very well. Aubrey. Aubrey with black hair and black eyes, Aubrey who saw the blood falling from my hand and smiled, Aubrey who laughed when he killed my brother.

Aubrey is the only vampire I know who prefers using a knife to using his mind, teeth, or hands. I touch the scar I bear on my left shoulder, the scar given to me only a few days after I died, created by the same blade that took my brother's life. The scar that I swore, on the day it was dealt, to avenge, along with my brother's death.

# CHAPTER 12
# 1701

AFTER THE DAY when I lost my mortal soul, I never went back to my old home. I understood I no longer belonged there. I hated to think what my papa was going through, but I hated even more the idea of his learning what I had become. I wanted him to believe me dead, because it was better for him to think I had simply disappeared than for him to know he had lost his daughter to a demon.

I fed on one of the true monsters—one of the many "witch hunters" who interrogated and jailed the accused, seeking guilt where there was none.

How humans can do such things to their fellows is beyond me. They torture, maim and kill their own kind, saying it is God's will.

I no longer try to understand the ways of humanity. Of course, maybe I'm being hypocritical. My kind is often just as cruel to our own. We are simply more direct. We need no one else to blame our violence on. If I kill Aubrey, I will do so because I hate him, not because he is evil, or because he kills, or for any other moral reason. I will do so because I wish to do so, or I will not do so because I do not wish to.

Or I will not do so because he kills me first, which is the end I expect.

Soon after I was transformed, I brought myself up to the Appalachian Mountains for a time. I had been told about them, yet had never seen them. It was incredible to be in the mountains at night. I was a young woman, alone in the wilderness. Had I been still human, such a thing would never have been allowed. I lay in a treetop, listening to the forest and thinking about nothing at all.

"Ather has been looking for you," someone said to me, and I jumped down to the ground. My prey lay beneath the tree. I had taken him to this place with my mind before I fed, to avoid interruptions.

I walked toward the voice. It was Aubrey.

"Tell Ather I do not want to see her," I said to him.

Aubrey was dressed differently than when I had last seen him, and could no longer be mistaken for a normal human. He had a green viper painted on his left hand, and was wearing a fine gold chain around his neck with a gold cross suspended from it. The cross was strung on the chain upside down.

He held his knife in his left hand. The silver was clean, sharp, and so very deadly, just like his pearl white viper fangs, which were, for the moment, hidden.

"Tell Ather yourself—I'm not your messenger boy," he hissed at me.

"No, you just take Ather's orders, like a good little lapdog."

"No one orders me, child."

"Except Ather," I countered. "She snaps and you jump. Or search, or kill."

"Not always . . . I just didn't like your brother," Aubrey answered, laughing. Aubrey smiles only when he is in the mood to destroy. I wanted to knock every tooth out of that smile and leave him dying in the dirt.

"You laugh?" I ask. "You murdered my brother, and you laugh about it?"

He laughed again in response. "Who was that carrion on the ground behind you, Risika?" he taunted. "Did you even bother to ask? Who loved him? To whom was he a brother? You stepped over his body without a care. *Over the body*—no respect, Risika. You would leave his body here without a prayer for the scavengers to eat. Who is the monster now, Risika?"

His words stung, and I instantly tried to defend my actions. "He—"

"He deserved it?" Aubrey finished for me. "Are you a god now, Risika, deciding who is to live and who is to die? The world has teeth and claws, Risika; you are either the predator or the prey. No one deserves to die any more than they deserve to live. The weak die, the strong survive. There is nothing else. Your brother was one of the weak. It is his own fault if he is dead."

I hit him. I had been a young lady, not taught to fight, but in that minute I was simple fury. I hit him hard enough to snap his head to the side and send him stumbling. He righted himself, the last of the humor gone from his face.

"Careful, Risika." His voice was icy, a voice to send

shivers through the bravest heart, but I was too angry to notice.

"Do not speak of my brother that way." My voice shook with rage, and my hands clenched and un-clenched. "Ever."

"Or what?" he asked quietly. His voice had gone darker, colder, and he was standing as still as stone. I could feel his rage cover me like a blanket. I knew in that instant that if anyone had ever threatened Aubrey, they were no longer alive to tell of it.

There was a first time for everything.

"I will put that blade through your heart, and you will never speak again," I answered.

He threw the knife down so that it landed an inch from my feet, its blade embedded in the ground.

"Try it."

I knelt slowly and cautiously to get the knife, not moving my eyes from Aubrey, who was watching with an icy stillness. I did not know what he would do, but I knew he would not simply let me kill him. Yet he stood there, silent, still, and faintly mocking in his expression, and did nothing.

"Well, Risika?" he prompted. "You said you would— now do it. You hold the knife. I stand defenseless. Kill me."

If I had killed him then . . . If I had been able to mur-der him then . . .

"You can't," he finally said, when I did not move. "You can't kill me while I am defenseless because you still think like a human. Well, know this, Risika—that isn't how the world works."

He grabbed my wrist with one hand and my throat with the other. The knife was useless.

"Ather talks about you as if you are so strong. You're just as weak as your brother is."

I had never learned any fighting skills. I had never practiced violence. But in nature survival is the name of the game, and the body touches its long-dead roots. You adapt, because if you cannot, you're as good as dead. I adapted.

I wrenched my wrist from Aubrey's grip while using my free hand to push away the hand that held me. The knife fell, forgotten. My wrist was broken, but there was little pain—the vampire's tolerance for pain is high, and the injury was healing quickly.

I felt a spinning, burning sensation and failed to see Aubrey's next attack. He pounced, knocking me back over the tree roots and onto the ground. I kicked his kneecap with all my strength, breaking it. He hissed in pain and anger, falling to the ground. I started to push myself up, but pain lanced through my arms and back.

A fight between two vampires may look physical, but when they are as strong as my line is, most damage is done with the mind. A strong vampire can strike out with its mind and kill a human without even touching it. It is harder to kill another vampire, but the fighters can still distract and disable each other. I was young and did not know how to fight that way. I was on the ground and couldn't push myself up because of the pain.

Aubrey was there in a moment. He placed one hand

on my throat, pinning me to the ground on my back. Even wounded he was far stronger than I.

He had retrieved the knife and held it against my throat.

"Remember this, Risika — I have no love for you. I think you are weak, and I don't care about your morals. If you challenge me again, you will lose."

I spat in his face. He drew the knife across my left shoulder, from the center of my throat, in the gap between the two collarbones, to the center of my upper left arm. I gasped. It burned like fire and hurt more than anything I had ever felt.

Most human blades will not scar our kind, but Aubrey's blade was not a human blade. Magic, for lack of a better word, was embedded deep in the silver. I learned later that Aubrey had taken his blade from a vampire hunter during his third year as a vampire. Its original owner had been raised as a vampire hunter, but even so he had lost to Aubrey.

Aubrey disappeared as I lay on the ground, riding out the pain. If the blade had been human silver, the wound would have healed in moments; instead it took some time for my body even to get control of the pain.

Once it had subsided from blinding to simply unbearable, I sat up slowly, gingerly tracing the wound. The bleeding had already stopped, but the wound did not close fully until after I had fed again. And it left a scar. My skin was already so pale that the scar showed only as a faint pearl-colored mark, but I knew where it was, and I could see it easily.

Somehow, though I knew not how, and someday, though I knew not when, I would avenge that scar and all that it stood for: Alexander's death, the death of my faith in humankind, and the death of Rachel, innocent Rachel, a human filled with illusion.

My kind can live forever. I would have a long time, and many opportunities, to keep that vow.

# CHAPTER 13
## NOW

I WAS FOOLISH to attack him then, and am equally foolish to bait him now, but I have no other choice. I refuse to roll over and let Aubrey be king without ever challenging him.

I can sense his aura in the room but cannot see him, and he has not spoken.

*Where are you, Aubrey?* I ask him with my mind. *Why do you hide from me?*

I hear his laughing, taunting voice in my head; it is a voice I have come to hate with all my mind, all my strength, and all my soul. He says only four words, not even a sentence.

One line of a poem.

*Tiger! Tiger! Burning bright . . .*

I scream the wordless cry of the eagle, the hunting cry of the diving hawk, the angered cry of a caged beast, and I hear Aubrey laugh in my mind. I know where he was as I hunted on his land.

Even as he laughs I change my shape to a golden

hawk that flies from that room in her animal rage and lands inside the tiger's cage at the zoo. The sign, *"Panthera tigris tigris,"* has fallen, and its wooden post is snapped in two like a twig. The metal bars of the tiger's cage are bent. The guard is lying on the ground, pale and motionless.

I do not care about the guard or the sign, only about Tora, the one creature I have loved since Alexander's death. Tora, who is lying on her side, her paws bound, with a knife in her heart. She was born free, and deserved to live so. Instead she lived in a cage and was killed, bound and helpless. This more than anything makes me feel as if the knife was planted in my own heart instead of hers.

I shift back into my usual form and pull the knife from her, screaming another wordless cry of rage and grief. Tearing the ropes from her paws, I weep at each golden hair that has fallen from her and at each black hair that has forever lost its shine. I weep—weep as I did not when I lost my brother and my life. I weep until my thoughts run dark and my tears run dry.

Love is the strongest emotion any creature can feel except for hate, but hate can't hurt you. Love, and trust, and friendship, and all the other emotions humans value so much, are the only emotions that can bring pain. Only love can break a heart into so many pieces.

The greatest pain I have ever felt rode on the back of love. I loved Alexander, and every injury he received seemed reflected onto me. His death tore my heart out and bled it dry, and now Aubrey has used my love for Tora to push the blade in deeper.

This is why, I have learned, the strongest of the vampires keep all these emotions at arm's length: because they are weaknesses, and if you have weaknesses you can be taken down with all the other prey.

Close to dawn I lift my head, my long golden hair blending with Tora's tiger fur. I do not think, but add the black stripes to my own tiger-gold hair.

"Look, my beautiful," I whisper. "I have stolen your stripes. I will wear them so that your beauty will not be forgotten. My tiger, my Tora, my beautiful—I will not allow this crime to go unpunished." My eyes are dry but sparkle with anger and determination. "I will be sure he is truly dead before he takes another life I love."

I am focused inward, on Tora, and hear no one approach me. However, I feel a brush of air against my hair, the aura of some visitor. My head snaps up, but I see no one. Whoever was there is gone, leaving nothing save a slip of paper next to my hand.

I pick up the paper, my eyes caught on the name that is scrawled across the top in black ink: *Rachel*. I cannot read the words below, which have run together where water has fallen onto the ink. *Not water*, I think, realizing how strongly the aura is mixed in with them—*tears*.

I stare at the name for a moment, then crush the note in my hand, a fine tremor of rage going through me at this creature who dares to taunt me so. I do not recognize the aura on the paper; I do not know who sent it.

"Rachel is dead," I say aloud. "I am not Rachel—she died three hundred years ago."

The tearstains on the paper—whose are they? What human learned of Rachel and was so pained by her story that he sent me this? Or is this note a sick joke of Aubrey's, another way to scar my heart?

"I don't want your games!" I shout. If the one who left this reminder is still near, let him confront me.

No one answers.

# CHAPTER 14
# NOW

MY PAST AND MY PRESENT have combined to taunt me. Shaking with grief and anger, I return to Ambrosia. I glance around the room, checking for Aubrey. I do not see him.

I come to this place seeking a diversion. The ghost of Rachel cannot follow me here.

I see my image reflected in a crystal glass someone has left on a counter. My reflection is a misty apparition, but I can see Tora's markings in my hair and I laugh. This is something Aubrey will never take from me.

In this moment I feel like exactly what I am: a wild child of the darkness. A dangerous shadow in a mood to make trouble.

I look around the room again. Smiling, I toss my tiger-striped hair back from my face and perch on the counter. The girl behind it, a younger fledgling, opens her mouth as if to tell me to get down but then thinks better of it.

"What do you see, Tiger?" someone asks me, and I turn toward him. "You look around this room as if you saw it differently from all of us. What do you see?"

I recognize him, and I know he recognizes me. He is Ather's blood brother, Jager. People say he treats all life as a game that must be played—a cruel and deadly game in which whoever is winning makes the rules.

Jager appears eighteen, with dark skin and deep brown hair. His eyes are emerald green, and they reflect the dim light like a cat's. I know it is the same illusion as my hair. All vampires have black eyes, and Jager had dark eyes even when he was alive—he was born nearly five thousand years ago, in Egypt, and watched the great pyramids rise.

"I see someone who does not show his true eyes," I observe. "What do you see?"

"I see that my warnings to Ather and Aubrey were justified," he answers.

"Was it you who warned Ather I would be strong?"

"It was I who warned her that you would be stronger than she."

He sits on the counter beside me, and the girl behind it gives up, moving to a table on the other side of the room.

"Ather is weak," I comment. "It is one of her flaws. She changes those who will be stronger than her, because it makes others think she has more power than she does."

"She isn't the only one you are stronger than, Risika," he answers. "Aubrey isn't often challenged, because people know he is powerful, and they are afraid of him. He has you afraid of him, although he is not much stronger than you are, if at all."

"Oh, really?" I ask, not believing him. "Then we must be speaking of different Aubreys, because I lost the last time I fought the Aubrey I know."

"You could hide that scar with a thought. You have the power to do that," Jager says, changing the subject.

"I could," I answer. "But I don't."

"You wear it like a warning—a sign that you will avenge it."

"I will avenge more than this scar, Jager."

"When?" he presses. "Will you wait for him to start the music? Or will you start it yourself?"

"I prefer to kill in silence."

Jager gazes at me and smiles. "Happy hunting, Risika." A moment later he is gone.

I lie back on the counter, thinking on his words, and then I too am gone. We are phantoms of the night, coming and going from the darkened city like shadows in candlelight.

I return to my home in a light, detached mood, not bothering with the complexities of revenge. I look out the front window, watching the few who are also returning to bed as the sun rises.

One of Concord's other shadows enters his house—a witch, but only by heritage, as he is not trained. He is not a threat to me.

I also see Jessica, Concord's young writer, looking out her own window. Jessica writes about vampires, and her books are true, though no one understands how she knows what she does. I wonder if I should tell her my story—perhaps she could write it for me. Perhaps it is my story she now writes.

I go upstairs and fall into bed and a vampiric sleep.

My dreams are my memories of the past. I dream of my years of innocence, while I was still fighting what I was.

# CHAPTER 15
# 1704

I DID NOT RETURN to my home for three years, and when I finally did, no one saw me.

It was nearly midnight when I stopped in Concord, which was intentional. I did not wish to run into any humans.

I did not want to be recognized, of course, but more than that I was not sure I could control myself. The last time I had fed had been two nights previous, on a thief who had the ill luck to attack me as I wandered the darkened streets. The thirst beat at me viciously.

Though I consoled myself by saying I only killed those who deserved it, Aubrey's words always echoed in my mind: *Are you a god now, Risika, deciding who is to live and who is to die?* Thieves and murderers sustained me, but only just. I fed only as often as I needed to in order to survive, and the hunger was always near.

\* \* \*

I stood outside the house I had once lived in, perched on the edge of the well, watching the house like a ghost, able to see and hear but unable to do anything else.

Would he recognize me, even if he saw me? The three years had changed me. My fair skin was frosty white, and my golden hair was tangled, not having seen a comb in a while. I wore men's clothing, having lost my patience with long dresses as I explored the forests, mountains, and rivers of the country.

Of course I could have walked up to the door and asked my father if he knew who I was, but I would not. He would only be hurt more when I had to leave again. I would not let him know what I had become.

Lynette was asleep in her room, but my father was awake, and crying. He looked out the window, and though I knew he was looking in my direction, he did not see me. I had learned how to shield my existence from mortal eyes.

The tears on his face sent daggers into my heart. I had a powerful vision of Aubrey and Ather lying dead, with me standing above them. Would anyone weep if they were killed? I did not think so, but I would never have the chance to know. Aubrey had proved beyond any doubt that I would not be the one to give him death.

A woman drifted downstairs behind my father. Her dark hair was tied back, and even from this distance I could see that her eyes were chocolate brown. Her skin was not as fair as my mother's had been. When she put a hand on my father's shoulder, I could see that she did not have the graceful artist's hands my father had often described my mother as having.

"Peter, it's late. You need to sleep."

My father turned to her and gave a weak smile, and for an instant I felt an irrational urge to go inside and *shake* this woman. I had seen my father's thoughts, and I knew without a doubt that this stranger was his wife. Her name was Katherine. Had he married her trying to replace us? Did she even know about Alexander and me? Did she care?

These people were no longer my family, that I knew. But I could not help hating this woman for trying to take my place.

"Jealous?" someone said over my shoulder, and I swung around toward Aubrey, knowing that my eyes were narrowed with hatred. "If she bothers you that much, kill her."

"I am sure you would appreciate that," I hissed.

He laughed. "You have too many morals."

"And you have none," I snapped back, trying to keep myself from hitting him. I refused to leave while he was here, his attention on my father and this innocent woman.

Innocent woman . . . strange, how my opinion changed so quickly. As soon as Aubrey suggested I kill her, I felt the need to protect her.

"I have some morals, I suppose," he argued, though his voice was light. He had taken no offense at the accusation. "But none that interfere with the way I survive. Look at yourself, Risika—you can hardly preach the benefits of morality."

Though I did not hate myself for killing to survive, I feared that I would one day become as indifferent to murder as Aubrey was.

"If you came here to convince me to abandon my morals, you are wasting your time," I snapped.

"You are hardly my only motive for being here," he answered lazily.

My father and his wife had decided to get some air and were now sitting on the back porch, quietly discussing how the farm was doing, Lynette's suitors, and everything else except for the reason my father had been crying.

As if he could sense my gaze on him, my father turned toward me, but this time his eyes went wide, as if he could see me despite my efforts.

Standing, he took a step in my direction before his wife put a hand on his arm. "There's no one there, Peter," she insisted, and my father sighed.

"I could have sworn I saw her. . . ." He shook his head, taking a raspy breath.

"You could have sworn you saw her a few days ago, but she was not there. You thought you saw your son the week before that, but he was not there. They never are, Peter, and they never will be. Let them go."

My father turned about and went inside the house. Katherine closed her eyes for a moment and whispered a prayer.

Why did she not help him herself? Was she so blind that she could not see how much her words had hurt him?

Aubrey laughed beside me. "You *are* jealous."

I spun toward him again, losing my temper. "Could you go somewhere else?"

"I could," he said. "But this is more fun."

"Damn you."

He shrugged, then looked past me to my father's wife, who had just stood and moved toward the house.

She hesitated, then turned slowly, sensing eyes on her back.

"Leave her alone, Aubrey," I commanded.

"Why?"

Katherine looked up as if she had heard a sound, and then walked toward us, though I could tell that she did not really see Aubrey or me.

I clenched my fists, knowing that he was baiting me and knowing equally well that if he had set his mind on killing this woman, there was no way I could stop him.

Katherine gasped as Aubrey stopped hiding himself from her. She froze, eyes wide.

"Fine, Aubrey—you have made your point," I snapped, stepping between him and his prey. "Now leave."

"And what point would that be?" he inquired. "I do not share your reservations, Risika. I hunt when I wish, as I always have."

"Hunt somewhere else," I said. His eyes narrowed.

"Who . . . Wh-What do you want?" Katherine stammered, backing away from us. She was breathing quickly, and her heart was beating fast from fear.

Aubrey disappeared from where he stood and reappeared behind her. Katharine stumbled into him and let out a gasp.

Aubrey whispered into her ear and she relaxed. Then he reached up and gently pulled her head back, exposing her throat. . . .

# CHAPTER 16
# NOW

I SNAP AWAKE, instantly alert.

There is someone in the house, in the room.

I rise from my bed. "Why do you hide, Aubrey?" I ask the shadows. "Do you finally fear me? Are you afraid that if you challenge me again you will lose?" I know this is not Aubrey's fear, but I am in the mood to taunt, just as I know he is.

There is one taunt that almost guarantees a vampire's response: accusing him of being afraid.

"I will never fear you, Risika," Aubrey answers as his form coalesces from the shadows of the room.

"You should," I respond. Vampiric powers strengthen with strong emotions—hate, rage, love—and Aubrey brings all those emotions to the surface of my mind.

Despite my hatred, if I fight him I will lose. This is a lesson I learned well years ago. Aubrey is older, stronger, and much crueler.

For now, though, he lounges against the wall, throwing his knife into the air and catching it. Throwing, catching. Up, down. The faint light glints on the silver blade, and I have a sudden picture in my mind of Aubrey missing the knife, and of it slicing across his wrist.

He has modernized his style since the 1700s: he wears black jeans tucked into black boots, a tight red shirt that shows off the muscles of his chest, and a metal-studded dog collar. The green viper has been replaced by the world serpent from Norse mythology, which played a part in the destruction of the world. On his upper arm is the Greek Echidna, mother of all monsters, and on his right wrist is the Norse monster Fenris, the giant wolf who swallowed the sun.

I wonder what Aubrey will do when he becomes bored with these designs. Maybe cut them off with an ordinary knife. His flesh would heal in a matter of seconds. Maybe I could volunteer to help. . . . No one would mind if I "accidentally" cut his heart out in the process.

"Why are you here, Aubrey?" I finally ask, not willing to wait for him to speak.

"I just came to offer my condolences for the death of your poor, fragile kitten."

My body freezes with rage. Aubrey knows how to hurt me, and how to make me lose my temper. He has done so before.

I start to move toward him—to hit him, to make him hurt as much as I do.

"Careful, Risika," he says. Just two words, but I stop. "Remember what happened last time you challenged me."

"I remember," I growl. My voice is heavy with pain and rage. I do remember—I remember very well.

"You still wear the scar, Risika. I can see it even from here."

"I have not forgotten, Aubrey," I answer him. He wears the same face he had then: cold, aloof, slightly amused, slightly mocking. He knows what Tora meant to me, and I know that he has visited me to try to bait me into attacking him again.

I wonder what kind of life made Aubrey the way he is. A psychologist would love analyzing him. Aubrey knows exactly what to say and do to make those around him weep, laugh, beg, hate, love, fear, or anything else he wishes. I have seen brave men run in fear, humans wage wars, and vampire hunters turn on their own, all because of Aubrey.

He is far stronger than Ather, physically, mentally, and emotionally. As I have said, Ather's largest flaw is that she changes people who are strong—people who will be stronger than she is. She does this because, though others of our kind might challenge her alone, they assume that her fledglings would avenge the attack.

I may never understand why Ather decided that Rachel was a human who demanded her attention, but I do not hate my blood mother. She was the one who tore me from my human life, but she was also the one who forced me to look upon the darkness of humanity. Had it not been for her, I would have lived and died as prey and nothing else.

Though I would not lift a finger to defend my blood mother, I do not go out of my way to attack her.

Aubrey, on the other hand . . . Three hundred long years ago I knew that Aubrey was stronger than I, and indeed, I fought him and lost. I fear what will happen if we fight again. He eggs me on every time we meet, knowing well that I fear him. I hate him all the more because of that fear, and he knows this as well.

He is still waiting for my response to his taunt.

"Considering you killed Tora, your condolences aren't worth much," I tell him.

He raises his eyebrows questioningly.

"Don't look like that. I could feel your aura there, and even now I can smell her blood on you."

Aubrey just laughs.

"Get out of my house, Aubrey," I growl. I have no wish to fight him. I only want him to be gone.

"You don't seem in the mood for company," he comments. "I'll stop by again later, Risika."

I hear the implied threat but have no chance to reply before he disappears. He has accomplished what he came here to accomplish and has no reason to stay.

I remember my dream the night before, and my mind returns to it, my anger at Aubrey forcing me to remember the rest.

He did not kill Katherine. He only killed the remainder of what might have been my soul.

# CHAPTER 17
# 1704

I REFUSED TO WATCH HIM kill her.

Ignoring the consequences, I jumped at Aubrey, tearing him away from Katherine. The woman stumbled, falling to the ground, still hypnotized. Aubrey spun around and grabbed my arm, throwing me to the ground too. I did not immediately try to stand. I did not want to fight him again, because I knew that if I lost, he would kill me.

"You never learn, do you?" he snapped. "Stand up, Risika."

I stood slowly, watching him warily, but he only pulled Katherine to her feet.

She had caught her hand in a raspberry bush when she fell, and I had to turn my head away from her, my already faltering self-control weakened further by the scent of blood.

Once again Aubrey pulled her head back, and this time my gaze caught on her throat, riveted by the

blood that was flowing just beneath the surface. I hesitated an instant, during which Aubrey leaned forward.
He showed no reluctance as his fangs pierced her
throat.

"Let her go, Aubrey," I somehow managed to growl,
fighting the bloodlust that was trying to convince me to
feed.

He looked up, and his black gaze met mine for
a moment; he licked blood from his lips, and a
wicked smile spread across his face. "You really want
me to?"

"*Yes,*" I snapped back.

"Here."

He pushed the woman into my arms, then disappeared.

I stumbled, shocked, but when I recovered I found
myself holding the unconscious woman gently.

Her bleeding hand was resting on my arm, and I
could feel her pulse beating against my skin. A thin line
of blood ran down her throat, and before I even realized what I was doing, I had licked it away.

I felt every pulse of her heart as if it was my own,
and each beat was like fire being forced through my
veins. I turned my head away, trying to capture some
measure of control, but that simple move brought on a
spell of dizziness.

I had not fed in days.

The thirst was so strong, and her blood seemed the
sweetest I had ever taken. I let it roll across my tongue,
savoring the taste, knowing I should not but unable to
stop myself.

I heard a hoarse cry, and my head snapped up. I saw my father. There was no recognition in his gaze.

I dropped Katherine, forcing myself to let her go. I had not yet taken enough to harm her; she would survive.

I disappeared into the night.

# CHAPTER 18
# NOW

AFTER THAT NIGHT I fed well, never again allowing myself to reach the point where I could lose control. Aubrey had accomplished his goal, as always.

My anger at Aubrey turns into anger at myself. Then as now, he managed to use my emotions against me.

*Why do you let him make you so upset?* I ask myself. *You know he does it intentionally. Why does it continue to bother you?*

"Coward," I say to myself. "That's all you really are—a coward. You've worn that scar for three hundred years, and you've done nothing. You can't even keep your temper long enough to *think*!"

I realize that despite everything I have said, I have still been clinging to some part of my humanity.

For three hundred years I have avoided him, refusing to fight. When I was human, I was controlled by my father and my church. Now Aubrey controls me, and I do not fight because I am afraid of the consequences.

I might die, but that has never been my real fear. I fear that if I start the fight, it will be proof that I am the monster I have tried for so long to pretend I am not.

Who am I pretending for? Alexander used to be my faith. He clung to his morals even when he thought he might be damned, and I have tried to do the same. Why? Alexander is dead, and no one else cares.

*So why bother? Why pretend?* I ask myself. *You have not been human for nearly three hundred years; stop acting as if you are.*

*What else do you have to lose?*

I change out of my black tank top into a gold one that hugs my body and shows a bare line of flesh just above my black jeans. My moods change like shadows in a candle flame, and I am in a playful mood now. I sketch the rune of gambling in the air, remembering it from somewhere in my long past: Perthro, shaped like a glass on its side, for people who are willing to bet everything, win or lose.

I am in a far more destructive, reckless mood than ever. I remember the stories I have been told about Jager—how he flirted shamelessly with the virgin followers of Hestia in the Greek era, danced in a fairy ring at midnight under the full moon, and spiced up a ceremony performed by a few modern-day Wiccans by making the elements called actually appear. I am in that kind of mood. I have nothing left to lose, and I want to change something. Destroy something.

I spin the mirror so that it faces away from me. I know what I will see if I look into its reflective illusion.

✢   ✢   ✢

I bring myself to a small town in upstate New York that is hidden deep in the woods, beyond the sight of the human world, called New Mayhem. *New* Mayhem — the Mayhem Ather showed me three hundred years ago was nearly leveled by a fire a few years after I was first there.

I have been to New Mayhem several times, but I am the only one in my line who does not sleep within its boundaries. Aubrey has his home inside the walls of New Mayhem, and so I have always made mine elsewhere.

Even with the new hotel suites that house the mortals, the new bars, the new gyms, and the paved streets, New Mayhem is still an invisible town. The bartenders never ask for ID, the hotel doesn't keep records of who comes and goes, and the nightclub is as strange as an ice-skating rink in Hell. No one ever comes, no one is ever there, no one ever leaves — at least, there would be no way to prove it should anyone ever look for receipts, or credit card numbers, or any written record of those who were there.

The heart of New Mayhem is a large building on which is painted a jungle mural. Around the doorway pulses a glowing red light from inside the club. This is where I go, barely even reading the name on the door: *Las Noches*.

The red strobe lamp is the only light inside Las Noches, giving the room a spinning, blood-washed effect. Mist covers the floor. The walls are all glass, mostly mirror, but in places there are eyes painted beneath the glass. The tables are polished black wood and look like satanic mushrooms growing from the mist.

Pounding music, bass heavy enough that it makes our bodies vibrate in time with the beat, slams down from a speaker somewhere in the shadowed ceiling.

At the counter, which is also black wood, is a black-haired girl called Rabe, one of New Mayhem's few inhabitants who are completely human. This early in the night Las Noches has a mixed crowd—more human than vampire, actually—but Rabe works here even when the crowd is completely vampire.

I turn away from Rabe and scan the room for the one person I seek. I find him sitting at a table with a human girl, though they do not appear to be talking. I walk purposefully to the back of the room, and ignoring the human, sit on the table. Chairs? Not for me, thank you.

Aubrey's eyes widen, no doubt wondering when I became so bold. I do not look at the human girl, though I know she has not left the table. She is sitting very still, but I can hear her breath and her heartbeat.

"Risika, why are you sitting on the table?" Aubrey finally asks me.

"Why not?"

"There are chairs," he points out. The girl behind me is slowly standing, inching away as if I might reach out and grab her if she catches my attention. I almost laugh. I am already smiling—the slow, lazy, mischievous smile of a cat.

"It seems your date is leaving, Aubrey," I comment, and the girl freezes. "Is she more afraid of me than she is of you?"

"Go away, Christina," Aubrey says to the frightened girl, who darts off.

"You have no class, Aubrey."

He frowns momentarily at my words but then decides to ignore them. "I forgot to comment on your new style of hair, Risika," he says. "It reminds me of that dumb beast in the zoo."

"I noticed that you tied her up before you killed her. Was one tiger too much for you to handle?"

We play this deadly game well, each of us striking at the other without blows—and it is indeed a deadly game. Who will lose their temper first? Who will strike the first physical blow?

"Risika, no one creature is too much for me to handle," Aubrey laughs.

"Oh, brave Aubrey," I say. "Save us from the defenseless animals!"

He shoves my shoulder, taking me by surprise and pushing me off the table. Then he stands. So far he has not drawn a weapon.

I sit on the floor, in the mist, and laugh. "You fool," I say. "You complete fool."

# CHAPTER 19
# NOW

SEVERAL OF THE HUMANS have gathered around us, wondering what is going on. This is not a smart thing to do when two vampires fight. However, humans are curious to the point of stupidity, and they do not think about possible casualties if the fight gets out of hand.

I stand from the mist, my laughter gone from the air but still in both our minds.

"You're like a child, Aubrey," I say. "The neighborhood bully, I suppose. You can terrorize humans and children, but what would happen if someone fought you who knew what they were doing?"

"Get out, Risika. I don't want to fight you again. We've done this before." His voice is cold, meant to frighten, but I do not heed it.

"We've done this before, have we? Where is your fancy blade then, Aubrey? You offered it to me and asked me to kill you if I could. I think I deserve a second chance."

"Why do you feel compelled to challenge me again, Risika? You still wear the scar I gave you last time. Are you so determined to bear another?"

"I wear this scar as a sign that I will one day repay it. 'Do unto others as you would have them do unto you,' Aubrey. I will avenge this scar and every scar you have put into my heart."

"Really? How, Risika?" he asks me, leaning against the table casually. "I am far older than you—"

"Does it matter, Aubrey?" I respond, slowly circling him. He does not turn to keep me in sight until I am completely behind him, but he does turn. He does not like having me at his back.

"Perhaps not, but I am meaner, Risika, and I am deadlier. A viper, hidden in the grass."

A viper—how apt. Does he know how often I have compared him to that exact creature?

"A garden snake, Aubrey, hiding in the grass. I am not weak anymore, but I think you are." I lean forward, my hands on the table between us.

I am lying, of course. I know he is stronger than I, but I am not about to admit that to him.

"That remains to be seen, does it not?" he answers, turning away from me as if he doesn't care where I am.

Another deadly game. We circle each other. *I am not afraid to have you behind me—I do not fear you that much,* we say to each other. Yet we watch our backs, because we are both vipers, willing to kill and simply waiting for a chance.

"Shall we find out?" I suggest coolly. I am not bothering to hide my aura, and I can feel it stretch out, strike Aubrey's aura, and crackle around it. I search his aura, looking for weaknesses, as I know he searches mine.

"Why are you so eager to lose, Risika?"

He *is* afraid of me, I realize. He is playing for time—trying to make me lose my nerve. Why? Because he is afraid he might lose? It does not seem possible that Aubrey thinks I could win.

I walk around the table toward him until I am close enough that he turns, not trusting me.

"Why are you stalling, Aubrey?" My power snaps out and hits his like a whip. He staggers a bit—I am strong, and I am reckless, and I really do *not* like him.

His own power lashes out, and I feel a burning in my veins. My vision mists over for a moment, a moment in which Aubrey draws his knife.

"You always need your blade, don't you, Aubrey? Because without it you'd lose, wouldn't you?" I circle behind him, and he turns to keep me in sight. Like the game of insults, this is one I can win: Follow me, watch me, but do not let me get behind you, because you know I hate you and will kill you if given a chance. It is only in the actual fight that I fear I might lose.

"Come now, Aubrey—just like old times. You threw your blade down then and dared me to pick it up; are you too afraid to do so now?"

I lash my power around his wrist. His muscles spasm, but he holds on to the knife.

" 'Yea, though I walk through the valley of the shadow of death, I will fear no evil.' I have nothing to fear, Aubrey—what about you?"

His power flares out with his anger, and I hear wood

crack. One of the tables splits down the middle, and a human jumps out of the way barely in time.

"Impressive," I say scornfully, and lash out with my own power. The mirrored walls fracture into spiderweb patterns with no single inch left whole. Hairline cracks run through every surface, but not one piece falls out. Aubrey backs up a step, away from me.

"Coward," I say. "Do you back away from me?" I take a step forward, ever aware of the knife in his hand, and he steps back again, almost running into one of the humans, who jumps away quickly.

Aubrey glances behind him and notices the crowd for the first time. It is mostly human, but there are some of our kind. I see Jager lounging against the wall and Fala, Jager's fledgling, sitting cross-legged on a table.

"Are you all talk, Aubrey? Are you too afraid to fight?" I circle to the left as he moves to get behind me, so that I end up behind him. Once again he has to turn to keep me in his sight.

"Why would I be afraid?" he asks, his tone mocking. "It would not hurt me to destroy you, Risika."

"I'm sure it wouldn't, Aubrey, but we will never have a chance to test the theory," I answer.

"Test it again, you mean," he says. "We have tested it once before."

I ignore his words and reach out, my aura striking his in its center and latching on. The average human sees nothing, and the vampires see only a shimmering space between us, but Aubrey feels it, and I feel it.

He stumbles again, bringing his shields up and throwing my power back at me. I hold on with my mind, though I fall into a table, and feel his power crackling around my own.

Humans have one thing to use in a fight: their bodies. Among my kind, opponents fight with their bodies, but also with their minds. I can feel Aubrey's power beating against my shields, trying to get into my mind, trying to latch on to my own power. I push him away from my mind, trying to get into his, all the while circling, moving closer, dodging the knife, circling away.

My eyes mist over for a moment, and my veins burn as Aubrey lashes out again. I stumble, and he strikes out with his blade. I narrowly dodge, falling back, barely catching myself before I fall to the floor. Aubrey is there in a moment, but I am not.

His power, which has attached itself to my aura, keeps me from using my mind to move. But I push him back long enough to change to hawk form and fly away. Fighting his mind and holding hawk form is nearly impossible, and I return to human form. Aubrey's mind is stronger than my own, but for the first time I realize that the difference is small. Were he as strong as I thought, he could have stopped me from changing at all.

I came here expecting to lose but refusing to run. For the first time I realize I might be able to win.

Aubrey's power wavers for a moment as my fear drops, and I strike out again with all my strength. Aubrey falls back a few feet, and I advance and strike again. He disappears for a moment, and suddenly the knife is at my throat.

I know that if I use the small strength I have left to move, I will not be able to hold up the walls keeping him out of my mind.

# CHAPTER 20
# NOW

I FREEZE, feeling the faintest burning where the blade presses against the skin of my throat. With that blade, it will be fatal if my throat is slit.

"I told you long ago that you cannot win against me, Risika." Aubrey thinks he has won, and he is not paying as much attention to his shields. I do not feel him pushing as strongly against my mind. Why fight when you think you have won? "I do not kill my own unless forced to, Risika, and you are not enough of a threat to force me. So go."

He moves the knife away for a moment, and I hit his wrist, breaking it. The knife falls to the ground, and I shove him into the fractured mirrors that make up the walls.

I laugh.

I pick up the knife before he can recover, striking him with my mind, keeping his shields down. I lock on to his mind with my own, forcing him down.

"Aubrey, I've learned. In fact, you taught me this

little trick. You think that once you turn your back I will stay away, afraid. Well, know this, Aubrey," I say, feeding his words back to him. "That isn't how the world works."

Now he begins to fight again. He was taken by surprise for a moment, but he grows desperate. He lashes out along the line of power I am using to strike him, and as I stumble for a moment, losing my hold, his walls return.

We both now know that this fight is serious. But he is weak, and I can feel that he is afraid. He has forgotten his knife, which I now hold; his every instinct is focused on survival.

I throw his strike back at him, forcing him away from my mind. He stumbles slightly but then throws all his power at me. I fall into the table Fala sits upon and instantly feel her power strike out against me. For just a moment I lose focus, dropping the knife, and Aubrey pins me to the ground.

He has retrieved his knife.

This scene is familiar. I remember three hundred years ago, lying upon the forest ground, Aubrey pinning me, knife in hand. The memory brings a thread of terror, and I react instinctively. I do what I was not able to do then.

I throw Aubrey off me—not far, just a foot or so. But in the moment when he is off balance I shift into another form I know inside and out, one with the strength to fight.

The Bengal tiger is the largest feline on earth. Aubrey does not know the mind of a tiger, the pure animal instinct, and cannot find a hold. I slash at him, scoring his chest. The wounds heal in moments, but I have pushed him down again.

Aubrey tries to roll away, but I pin him to the ground. I am physically stronger than Aubrey, and though he is stronger when using his mind to fight, my mind is powerful enough to hold him off when I am in this form.

I look into his eyes, in which I can see a flicker of fear beneath a sheet of resignation. He almost looks as if he was expecting this moment.

I prepare for a killing strike. But he does not want to die.

"You've proved yourself, Risika," he tells me. "Years ago I gave you a choice between giving up and fighting to the death. Do I get no such chance?"

I hesitate. *Aubrey, I know how this game works,* I answer with my mind, as I cannot speak the human tongue when I am in this form. *If I let you go now, what is to stop you from stabbing me in the back as soon as I turn away?*

*This doesn't need to be to the death, Risika,* Aubrey insists. I can sense his desperation.

*You gave me a choice because I was weak, Aubrey. I am stronger than you — we have proved that here — but I swore long ago that I would avenge all you have taken from me. And you took so much; the price is so high.*

He moves his head back, exposing his throat, and I pause, waiting for him to explain. *I paid a high price long ago for this life. I do not want it to end yet,* he tells me with his mind. *I offer you my blood in return for the blood I have spilled.*

He is serious. The fool really would do anything to survive. My taking his blood would make me far stronger and open his mind to me completely. There would be no way for him to shield his mind from me, and no way for him to harm me with his mind, which would make it nearly impossible for him to hurt me. Physically he would have the same strength, but he could make no move that I could not read from his mind ahead of time.

I pause for only a moment, then return to human form and lean forward. My teeth pierce skin, and the blood flows. Vampire blood is far stronger than human blood.

His blood tastes like white wine, only thicker and far more potent, and I feel giddy when I pull away again, wiping blood from my lips. The wound on his throat heals instantly, but I know the wound to his pride will last as long as I do.

I pick Aubrey's knife up off the ground and contemplate it for a moment. He is defenseless, and if I struck him in the heart he could not raise a hand to protect himself. I trace the scar from my throat to my shoulder, remembering, and then, like lightning, I draw the knife along Aubrey's collarbone in an identical wound.

"Remember this day, Aubrey. The wound you dealt long ago has returned to you. I'll be satisfied with your blood, though it doesn't begin to replace the lives of Alexander and Tora. Now get out."

I let go of his mind, yet I can still feel it completely. It is an eerie sensation. I stand easily, his blood racing through my veins, replacing the power I lost in the fight and far more.

Aubrey pulls himself up into a sitting position, using a nearby table. His skin is flour white, and his eyes are almost empty as he raises his hand to the wound on his shoulder. No one has ever wounded him and lived to tell of it.

He slowly stands to leave, and the humans move away as he walks through them. Those that remain know what we are, and they know what such blood loss has done to his hunger and how hard it is for him to maintain his control as he leaves the room.

I turn my back on him, unafraid, and return my gaze to Fala, who is still sitting serenely on the table. She does not seem to remember almost causing my death.

I lash out with my power, and she jumps up gracelessly as the wooden table catches fire. Fala disappears, not wanting to fight.

# CHAPTER 21
# NOW

I WALK TOWARD JAGER, and humans bump into each other to get out of my way. I laugh as they hurry from the room.

"Come to see the show?" I ask him.

"I told you you were stronger than Aubrey," he says. "The coward. I didn't expect him to offer so much just to live. You are probably one of the strongest of us now—maybe as strong as I. It would be interesting to find out."

"Another time, Jager," I answer. The adrenaline and energy from the fight are still in me, and part of me wants to fight something stronger. But the rational part of my mind tells me I am far too giddy to fight anyone seriously.

"Of course, Risika," he agrees. Jager fights simply for the challenge, not for a prize, and he does not fight anyone who he does not think has a fair chance unless it is necessary. At the moment I am drunk on Aubrey's blood, and I would lose. "Your eyes are still golden from shifting to a tiger," he tells me.

"I like them this way." I laugh, looking into the shattered mirror. My once misty reflection is now completely gone, but I can see myself in my mind's eye. My hair is still tiger striped, and my eyes are as golden as my silk tank top—the color they were when I was alive, before vampirism darkened them to black. I run my tongue along my teeth, licking off the last traces of Aubrey's blood.

Jager disappears, and I realize that almost everyone has left. Tossing a black strand of hair off my face, I feel for the first time a familiar aura in the back of the room. I remember it from a letter I received recently, a letter with a tearstain on the page.

"So my stalker would visit me in person," I say to his back. In this light the blond hair looks almost exactly as my own once did. I reach out with my mind, and even though I cannot read him I realize what he is. I remember the Triste witch who had been in the Café Sangra, who had given a note for Rachel to his vampiric victim.

I did not think much about it at the moment, but now I wish I had. I swear, suddenly realizing the truth I should have realized long ago.

"I was hoping I could convince you not to follow those creatures . . . but I guess it's too late, isn't it?"

I remember wondering why I never heard him fall.

"Rachel—" he starts to say.

"Alexander, don't talk to me." He has waited three hundred years to tell me he is alive? I damned myself years ago. I had—or thought I had—nothing left to lose, then. All the years I was alone. All the pain he could have spared me . . .

What pain has he known? I never went back to my father, because I did not want him to see what I had become. Had I known my twin was alive, and immortal like me, would I have chosen to spend the years with him? Would he choose to spend them with me, knowing I'm a monster?

He turns around, and for a moment I look into golden eyes that are mirror reflections of my own. But then he looks past me, at the area where Aubrey and I fought. I see Alexander's gaze linger on the blood that pooled on the ground when I cut open Aubrey's shoulder.

"Why?" he finally asks, his voice soft. "There had to be some other way to deal with this."

I look into Alexander's eyes again and see the judgment there. It does not matter that I am his sister. He *does* think I am a monster.

I laugh, and Alexander flinches, because it is a bitter sound. "Would you rather I just let Aubrey get away with it?" I say. "I thought he killed you, you know. Did you want me to just *forget* that? Or did you think I could turn the other cheek and ignore murder?" Alexander looks away for a moment, pain filling his features as he hears my scornful use of words from the Bible, which he always held so dear when we were children.

"I thought you would hate me for what I had done," he says.

"And just what have you done?"

He pauses, shaking his head, and then reluctantly

meets my gaze. "After Lynette was burnt, I would have done anything to protect her. I prayed that I would learn how to control my power, and . . ." He takes a deep breath, steadying himself. "A woman heard me praying. A Triste. She taught me more than I ever wanted to know about the vampires and every other monster on this Earth. I listened because she also taught me how to use my gifts."

*From a curse to a gift,* I think. *Does he still consider himself damned?*

"A few nights before Ather . . . changed you . . . I caught her trying to feed off Lynette. I stopped her, but . . ."

I can guess the rest of the story. Ather is too proud to let anyone take away her prey without seeking revenge. She changed me to hurt Alexander, because my faithful brother would be torn apart by his sister's damnation.

Alexander pulls his gaze from mine, and this time it falls to Aubrey's blood on my hands. "Rachel, how could you do that? I never thought I'd see you with blood on you, willing to kill another. You walk with them as if you are one of them."

I could argue—after all, I did not kill Aubrey—but I do not.

I loved Alexander long ago, and I suppose I still do. But things have changed in three hundred years. At least, I have changed. Alexander does not understand.

He tried to protect me once. He tried to keep me away from the darkness and death, because he did not want Ather to change me into what I now am. He tried, but he did not succeed, and there is no way to undo the damage that has been done since. I have been a monster too long, and as much as I care about him, I cannot change my nature now.

My golden brother still does not belong in this dark world. His sister is dead, long dead, and I cannot bring her back to protect him from all the pain I know seeing me has given him.

The only way I can protect him now is to make sure he never understands how easy killing can become.

"Alexander, listen closely. Rachel is dead," I say, forcing my voice to be cold so that he will not argue. I speak quietly, driving my words to his brain. "I am one of them."

I consider the words as I say them. It is true—I *am* one of them. But no one—not Aubrey, not Ather, not my father or brother—controls me now.

I could have killed Aubrey. I could have used my strength to be like him. But I remember my humanity.

I am one of them.

But I am also Rachel.

I am Risika.

# DEMON
# IN MY VIEW

*Dedicated to Jessica Guenther, who is a pillar of strength in rough times, an inspiration, and one of Aubrey's greatest admirers.*

*Thanks also to everyone who has helped me:*

*Sarah Lancaster, Sara Keleher, Andrea Brodeur, and Carolyn Barnes for their support and friendship, my sister Rachel for hours of work looking through poetry, Rick Ballard and Steve Wengrovitz for their help editing, and Natasha Rorrer and Nathan Plummer for listening patiently to all my complaints and offering their suggestions. To anyone I missed, thank you. I never could have done this without you.*

# Alone

From childhood's hour I have not been
As others were — I have not seen
As others saw — I could not bring
My passions from a common spring —
From the same source I have not taken
My sorrow — I could not awaken
My heart to joy at the same tone —
And all I lov'd — *I* lov'd alone —
*Then* — in my childhood — in the dawn
Of a most stormy life — was drawn
From ev'ry depth of good and ill
The mystery which binds me still —
From the torrent, or the fountain —
From the red cliff of the mountain —
From the sun that round me roll'd
In its autumn tint of gold —
From the lighting of the sky
As it pass'd me flying by —
From the thunder, and the storm —
And the cloud that took the form
(When the rest of Heaven was blue)
Of a demon in my view —

Edgar Allan Poe

# PROLOGUE

THE NIGHT IS FULL OF MYSTERY. Even when the moon is brightest, secrets hide everywhere. Then the sun rises and its rays cast so many shadows that the day creates more illusion than all the veiled truth of the night.

I have lived in this illusion for much of my life, but I have never belonged to it. Before my birth, I existed for too long in the realm between nothingness and life, and even now, the night still whispers to me. A strong cord binds me to the dark side of the world, and shields me from the light.

# CHAPTER 1

THE BLACK OBLIVION OF SLEEP was shattered by the caterwauling of some singer on Jessica's clock radio. She groaned and viciously beat the alarm clock into silence, then groped blindly for the light switch. The somber red glow of her Lava lamp provided just enough light to read the time.

Seven o'clock. The red numbers glowed sadistically, and Jessica swore. Only two hours of sleep again. How she managed to remain in the conscious world at all was a mystery, but she dragged herself into the shower, where the cold water finished what the alarm clock had started.

*Only one hundred and eighty days of school left,* Jessica thought as she prepared for the first day of her senior year of high school. There was barely enough time to get dressed before she had to pull her backpack onto her shoulders and dart down the street to catch the bus. Breakfast? A fleeting dream.

*Ah, Ramsa High School. What a perfect little niche of Hell,* she thought as the bus pulled up to the school. *In one year, you will be out of here forever.* That fact was the only thing that had convinced Jessica to get out of bed that morning: if she passed senior year, she would never need to succumb to the grasp of Ramsa High again.

She had lived in the town of Ramsa since she was twelve, and had long before realized that the other students would never accept her. Few were openly hostile, but no one could be described as warm and fuzzy, either.

As she neared the building, Jessica was acutely aware of how many students walked in groups of friends. She had known these people for five years, but that didn't seem to matter as they moved past her without a word. She even saw two girls notice her, whisper to each other, then quickly retreat as if Jessica was somehow dangerous.

One senior, a boy Jessica had known since her very first day at Ramsa Junior High, crossed himself when he saw her. She was tempted to start chanting satanically in the hopes of scaring him. He had long before decided that she must be a witch, and she had no idea why. Occasionally, out of spite or simply boredom, she encouraged his belief.

The thought was amusing in a way. The only witches she knew lived solely in the confines of the novels she'd been writing for the past few years. One of her witches could walk right in front of this idiot and he would never recognize her as what she was; Jessica's witches tended to be rather human in their manner and appearance.

More humorous, though, was the fact that her old enemy was holding the book *Tiger, Tiger* by Ash Night.

Jessica wondered how he would react if he knew that she would soon be receiving royalties from his purchase.

Jessica had been struck by the idea for *Tiger, Tiger* several years before, when she and Anne had been visiting one of Anne's old college friends in Concord, Massachusetts. She had spent nearly the entire weekend vacation locked in her room, and those hours of work had finally paid off.

In homeroom, Jessica sat in the back, alone as always. She waited in silent contemplation for attendance to be taken. The teacher was a young woman whom Jessica had not seen before; her name was written on the board and had received a few snickers from the students. Kate Katherine, high-school teacher, must have had sick parents. On the other hand, her name was probably easier for people to remember than Jessica Ashley Allodola.

"Jessica Allodola?" Mrs. Katherine said as if cued by Jessica's thoughts.

"Here," Jessica answered absently. The teacher checked off the name in her book and went on to the next person on the list.

The words of Jessica's adoptive mother, Anne, echoed through her mind.

*"Tomorrow is the first day of a new year, Jessie. Could you at least try not to get sent to the office? Just this once?"*

*"Don't call me Jessie,"* she had answered.

*"Just try, Jessica,"* Anne had pleaded. *"For me?"*

*"You aren't my mother. Don't tell me what to do."*

*"I'm the closest thing to a mother you have!"* Anne had snarled, losing her patience.

*The remark had stung, and Jessica had stalked to her room, mumbling, "My real mother was smart enough to get rid of me early."*

Snapping back to the present, she wondered bitterly if Anne considered it bad luck that Jessica was the child she had ended up adopting. Jessica wrenched herself from these thoughts as a pretty girl with chestnut hair tentatively entered the room.

"I'm sorry I'm late," the girl said. "I'm new to the school, and I got a bit lost." She introduced herself as Caryn Rashida. Mrs. Katherine nodded as she found Caryn's name on her list.

Caryn looked around for an empty seat; one was conveniently located next to Jessica. But when she saw Jessica she hesitated, as if she might go sit somewhere else. Jessica wasn't surprised. The residents of Ramsa all seemed to shy away from her almost unconsciously.

However, Caryn made up her mind and walked resolutely across the room. Extending a hand, she spoke. "Hi. I'm Caryn Rashida." She stumbled a bit over her own last name. "Why are you sitting all alone here?"

" 'Cause I want to," Jessica answered coolly, leveling her emerald-green eyes at Caryn's pale blue ones. Caryn held the gaze for a moment longer than most people could, but then looked away.

With disgust, Jessica had noted the girl's unease and her decision to make an effort despite it. Jessica had no wish to be taken under Caryn's wing like a homeless child. Dislike she understood; pity she could not stand.

"Wouldn't you rather have some company?" Caryn asked, her tone more subdued but no less friendly.

Ignoring Caryn's attempts at conversation, Jessica pulled out a pencil and started to draw.

"Well, then . . . I guess I'll leave you alone," Caryn said, voice muted. She moved to another table. Jessica continued drawing, ignoring Caryn and the teacher, who was droning on about locker assignments.

Mrs. Katherine asked Caryn to help distribute the locks, and when Caryn had finished, she lingered a moment at Jessica's table. Jessica wondered grimly at the girl's persistence.

"I've never been able to figure these out," Caryn muttered as she fiddled with her lock. She spun the combination a dozen times without success. "Maybe it's broken . . . You want to give it a try?"

Jessica plucked the lock from Caryn's hands and had it open in a second. "Hope you don't need to use the locker too much this year."

"How do these things work?" Caryn laughed at herself cheerfully.

"Figure it out yourself," Jessica answered as she shut the lock and tossed it back to Caryn.

"What did I do to you?" Caryn asked, finally deflated, and Jessica wouldn't have been surprised to see her eyes start to tear. "Why do you have to be so nasty to me?"

"It's who I am," Jessica snapped, closing her notebook and putting it away. "Learn to live with it."

She turned her back to Caryn as Mrs. Katherine led the class to their lockers. The girl didn't try to talk to Jessica again for the rest of the day. No one else did either; besides the arrival of Caryn, nothing had changed.

# CHAPTER 2

"HOW WAS YOUR FIRST DAY of school?" Caryn's mother asked as soon as the girl entered the kitchen.

Caryn's mother, Hasana Rashida, was a slightly plump, attractive woman with hair of a rich brown, cropped in a serious yet flattering style. She was obviously tired from her day at the bookstore, of which she was the new manager, so Caryn decided not to bother her with details of the icy putdowns she had received that morning.

"It wasn't awful," she answered instead as she fished a spoon from the silverware drawer and went to serve herself some ice cream.

The thought of Jessica made her uneasy. There was something in Jessica's aura that she hadn't been able to identify—something darker than normal. At first, it had almost kept Caryn from approaching. After only one day, she could see that it also kept other students away.

Of course, that was logical. Caryn wouldn't have

been in this town if Jessica had been a normal high-school student.

Caryn had tried despite her unease to get to know Jessica, more because the girl had seemed so alone than because Caryn had been asked to do so.

Prompted by these thoughts, she asked, "Where's Dominique?"

Hasana sighed. "She left to deal with some trouble involving her daughters, but she should be back soon."

Dominique Vida was one of the few people who could give Caryn the chills just by entering the room. She was the leader of the oldest living line of witches, and her power was impressive. She was the one who had tracked down Jessica's address and maneuvered Caryn and Hasana into this town, finding a house for them and employment for Hasana in less than two weeks.

Either despite this power or because of it, the woman was emotionally cold as ice in almost any situation. She needed to be: Dominique Vida was a vampire hunter. She could not allow emotion to cause hesitation in a fight.

If anyone else had asked Caryn to move into this town, where she could barely breathe for the aura of vampires, she would have refused. But Dominique was the leader of all four lines of witches, including the Smoke line — Caryn's own.

Dominique could order Caryn to go into the vampires' lairs alone, and Caryn would do so or risk losing her title as a witch. As antisocial as Jessica seemed to be, at least watching the writer didn't seem dangerous.

Following the same train of thought as her daughter, Hasana asked, "Did you meet Jessica?"

"Yes. She hated me on sight," Caryn answered gloomily. "And considering how she's treated, I'm not surprised."

Caryn had been shocked at the way Jessica's classmates seemed to view her—as if she was a poisonous spider. One of them, an athletic senior who'd been flirting with Caryn only a few minutes before, had called Jessica a witch. Hurt by his words, Caryn had needed to swallow an argument; Jessica was further from being a witch than the boy who had made the accusation.

Caryn glanced down at her bowl, her appetite gone. Her ice cream was melting.

# CHAPTER 3

ANNE CONFRONTED JESSICA as soon as she walked in the front door. "You're late."

"Sorry," Jessica answered sardonically. "They love me so much, they asked me to stay a bit longer."

"Jessica . . . on the first day of school?" Anne's voice was heavy with disappointment.

"Learn the art of sarcasm," Jessica suggested. "I needed to walk off some energy, so I swung by the woods on my way home."

"Thank god." Anne smiled and started to fill out the forms that the school had mailed home. An awkward moment went by in silence.

"Anything interesting happen at school?" Anne asked eventually, though Jessica could tell that her mind was not on the question.

"Nope," Jessica answered absently as she searched through her bag for a letter one of her teachers had given out for parents. She handed it to Anne.

After scanning the letter, Anne asked, "How are your teachers?"

"Fine."

"That's nice."

As usual, their conversation was more of a mandatory social gesture than a method of communication. Anne and Jessica had learned long before that they had nothing in common and had little chance of ever engaging in a truly two-sided talk about anything. Occasionally one actually paid attention to what the other was saying, but such circumstances usually led to arguments.

Another moment of silence ensued.

"I'm going to my room," Jessica announced finally. Leaving her backpack on the couch, she went upstairs and into the dimly lit cavern she had created for herself.

The windows were covered by heavy black curtains, and the shades were down. A small beam of light squeezed underneath the curtains, but that was all.

The bed, which was little more than a mattress on wheels, had been pushed into a corner. The sheets and comforter were black, as were all but one of the pillows. The exception was deep violet and made of fake suede. Anne had bought the pillow for Jessica several years ago, when she had still been attempting to influence the girl's tastes. Besides the pillow and Jessica's magenta Lava lamp, there was little else in the room that wasn't black.

A laptop computer and printer stood out brightly against their dark surroundings. They sat atop a black wooden desk, which they shared with a strewn assortment of floppy disks. The computer was one of the few things Jessica cherished. Here, in the shadowed niche she had created for herself, she churned out the novels that had been her escape from the world since she moved to Ramsa.

The twenty-nine manuscripts that she had written in the past five years, the brown envelopes that held her contracts for two of them, and a few copies of the published book *Tiger, Tiger* were the only other nonblack objects in the room.

It had been only two years earlier that she had first begun the search for a publisher; she could hardly believe how quickly things had gone since. Her first book, *Tiger, Tiger,* had been released about a week before, under the pen name Ash Night. The second one, *Dark Flame,* was presently sitting on her editor's desk awaiting the woman's comments.

Jessica flopped down onto her bed and looked up at the ceiling. Sometimes ideas for her books would strike as she lay like this, staring into oblivion, but usually they came from her dreams.

Even while she was writing, it was as if she was in a dream—one which her waking mind did not understand. She never quite knew what was happening in any of the numerous novels that she was working on at any given time. But she had learned not to read the manuscripts until they were finished. The only time she had broken that pattern, the flow of words had abruptly stopped. That had been the only story she disliked. The scenes written after she had read it seemed forced and unnatural. Trying to think them up had been a chore.

She didn't realize that she had drifted into sleep until she was awakened by Anne's knock on her door.

"Jessica?"

"What?" she asked tiredly.

"It's dinnertime," Anne announced. "Are you going to come down?"

Jessica closed her eyes for a moment more and then got up and turned on her computer.

"I'm not hungry," she called to Anne. "Go ahead and eat without me."

"Jessica—"

"I'll eat later, Anne," she snapped. Normally she would have at least joined Anne for dinner, just to maintain the illusion of a familial relationship. But when she was in the mood to write, that pull was stronger than her desire to get along with her adopted mother.

# CHAPTER 4

WITHIN FIVE MINUTES Jessica was writing quickly, lost in the bubble of her imagination. The entire night passed as she typed. It was sunrise when the flow of words halted.

Exhausted, Jessica turned off the computer, stood to stretch, and fell into bed and a sleep filled with nightmares.

*Jazlyn collapsed to her knees, unable to stand any longer. Her head pounded as her body fought the strange blood that was trying to overtake her system.*

*She knew this sensation. She had felt it once before, on the day she had died, years ago. It had not hurt so much then. It had not hurt to die.*

*It had not hurt to die . . .*

*Why did it hurt so much to live again?*

*Her vision went black as her heart beat for the first time in more than thirty years. She drew a slow, painful breath.*

*The heart in her chest labored, unaccustomed to its task. Her*

*lungs burned with the constant intake of oxygen, which seemed*
*to sear her throat. All the muscles of her torso cramped each*
*time she inhaled.*

*Finally she fell into blissful unconsciousness.*

Jessica woke, gasping for breath.

That same dream had frequented her sleep for years,
but she had yet to become used to it. The pain was always so vivid.

She turned on the Lava lamp and let the glow of magenta light calm her. The clock read 6:13 A.M. Though it
was less than an hour after she had fallen asleep, she
was no longer tired. As always, that dream had forced
fatigue far away.

After showering and dressing quickly, she paused to
study herself in front of the full-length mirror in the
bathroom. Jessica well knew she had a body and face
to die for. At five feet, five inches tall, she was slender
but not bony and had well-toned muscles despite the
fact that she rarely worked out. Her skin was naturally
fair and had been kept that way by her aversion to sunlight. Unlike those of many girls her age, Jessica's com-
plexion was flawless and always had been. Her long
jet-black hair tumbled around a face with high cheek-
bones, full lips, and expressive green eyes.

Yet despite her attractive appearance, Jessica had
never so much as had a date. Occasionally that fact
bothered her, though she usually had plainer insults to
deal with than oblique dismissals from the boys in her
grade.

Annoyed, she finally turned away from her reflection. Again she'd been unable to find the flaw that made

people hesitate when they saw her on the street or in the hall.

Downstairs in the kitchen, Anne was finishing a batch of pancakes.

"Morning, Jessica," Anne said as she slid two of the pancakes onto a plate. "Sit."

Jessica sat. She was in no hurry this morning, and the pancakes smelled delicious. She realized that she had eaten very little the day before.

"Smells good," she offered.

Anne smiled. "Thank you. I do try."

By the time she left for school, Jessica was in a good mood. She even had the heart to smile at Mrs. Katherine when she saw her in front of the building, and the teacher returned her gesture with a nod. Then Caryn walked by, and Jessica's cheer vanished.

# CHAPTER 5

As she entered the building, Jessica came upon a group of girls who had gathered near the main office.

"Nice body," she heard one of them whisper, referring to someone in the office.

"Who is he?" another girl asked.

"No idea," the first one answered. "But you've got to admit he's cute."

"Cute?" a third girl repeated. "He is totally *hot*."

Jessica couldn't see the subject of this profound conversation. *Probably some handsome blond substitute who will turn out to be the most hated teacher in the school,* she thought pessimistically.

"Who are you looking at?" she asked the three gawking girls.

The quietest, a senior named Kathy, looked over her shoulder, recognized Jessica, grabbed her friends' arms, and pulled the girls away.

Jessica scowled as she watched them go. At least most people were *subtle* about moving away from her.

She quickly forgot the girls' behavior, however, when she glanced into the office and saw the object of their admiration.

His face could have been modeled after the portrait on a Roman coin. Hair the color of raven feathers contrasted with his fair skin, and when he turned a bit she saw that a few strands had fallen across his eyes, shading them. He was dressed entirely in black, except for a gold chain around his neck. The pendant on the chain looked like a cross, but Jessica couldn't be sure from where she was standing.

A shock of recognition struck her. *Aubrey.*

Aubrey was, without a doubt, her favorite character from the books she had written. He had been the villain in *Tiger, Tiger* and the main character in *Dark Flame.* Gorgeous, powerful, and somewhat mysterious, he was every teenage girl's fantasy . . . or at least, he was hers. Considering her present status in the world of teenagers, she couldn't pretend to speak for the rest of the female population.

Of course, Aubrey was a vampire.

*Get a grip, Jessica. You write fiction,* she reminded herself. *Aubrey doesn't exist.* She would hardly have minded if her vampire hero *had* existed, but such a thing was impossible. Vampires were not real.

Yet the resemblance between this new boy and Aubrey was uncanny, and the sense of familiarity lingered despite her efforts to shake it. She forced herself to turn away and walk to her homeroom before the boy could notice her watching him.

She sat in the back of the room once again, and this time no one came to talk to her. Caryn looked over once from the group she seemed to have been accepted into, but Jessica sent a fierce gaze her way and Caryn cringed, visibly shaken.

A few moments after attendance had been taken, the boy from the office walked in. He handed a form to Mrs. Katherine but didn't bother to explain why he was late.

"Alex Remington?" Mrs. Katherine asked, reading the form.

He nodded, barely paying attention to the teacher as he sought out an empty seat.

Alex paused when he saw Caryn, who was watching him with wide eyes. Unlike most of the other females in the room, Caryn looked terrified.

When the bell rang, Jessica watched with curiosity as Caryn pulled on her backpack and slipped quickly through the crowd and out of the room. She was clearly being careful to stay as far from Alex Remington as she could.

Before Alex had even reached the door, a girl named Shannon caught up with him. Jessica could recognize Shannon's methods of flirtation a mile away and shook her head in disgust. Shannon already had a boyfriend, but that had never stopped her when there was a drop-dead-gorgeous male in her line of vision.

Jessica was about to leave when Alex glanced up for a moment, meeting her gaze over Shannon's shoulder. His eyes were jet-black and shadowed by dark lashes. Jessica smiled wryly in response to the amusement she saw in those eyes—no doubt a reaction to Shannon's not-so-subtle advances.

Then something Shannon said caught his attention and he looked away from Jessica, returning his gaze to his more assertive admirer.

A bit reluctantly, Jessica headed down the hall, leaving Alex at the mercy of Shannon the Conquerer.

# CHAPTER 6

JESSICA WANDERED into the courtyard at lunch-time, having no desire to sit alone at a table in the cafe-teria so that she could be assaulted by the stench of the day's mystery meat.

Her thoughts traveled for a moment to Alex; she re-membered how he had caught her eye. Then she men-tally chided herself for focusing on a guy who probably had already forgotten she existed. And even if he hadn't, he would never be desperate enough to risk his social standing by associating with the leper of Ramsa High.

She pulled an unlined notebook and a mechanical pencil from her backpack and proceeded to sketch, sim-ply for something to do with her hands, as she dis-creetly watched the people around her.

Shannon was standing with a few of her friends, but instead of talking to them, she was staring intensely across the courtyard at Alex. Alex, leaning casually against a tree, was smirking slightly as another boy berated him. Jessica recognized the guy as Shannon's boyfriend, and she judged by his posture and tone of voice that he had heard about Shannon's conversation with Alex that morning.

Finally Alex seemed to lose his patience. He locked eyes with the other boy, who, though a few inches taller than Alex and much broader, took a step back. The boy said something Jessica couldn't hear and left quickly.

Jessica shook her head, not surprised. Something about Alex made it evident he wasn't someone to mess with.

As Jessica had watched the confrontation, she had continued to draw. Now she looked down at the pencil sketch and felt a chill run through her.

Even though her model had been nearby, the likeness was remarkable. But the thing that struck her the most was the pendant, which she hadn't yet been able to look at closely but had somehow drawn in careful detail.

The cross was upside down and carefully molded with a viper twined around it. It was the same design as the one that Aubrey wore, and it startled Jessica to see that she had drawn it into her portrait of Alex.

"Mind if I join you?" someone asked.

Not just someone. *Alex.* Jessica recognized his voice and whipped her notebook shut. His tone was confident, unmarred by adolescent awkwardness. Hearing his silk-smooth voice made her shiver, because she was once again assaulted by a wave of familiarity.

*Snap out of it,* Jessica ordered herself. Over her mental argument, she heard her voice calmly reply to Alex, "Go ahead."

Suspicious of his motives, she couldn't immediately come up with anything more to say. The last time any guy had tried to talk to her, he had done so only on a dare. With that painful memory in mind, she kept her expression cool, waiting for Alex Remington to explain himself.

As he sat down near her, she studied his appearance. The pendant was exactly as she had drawn it — exactly like Aubrey's.

"Do you always keep to yourself out here?" he asked.

"Do you always go out of your way to talk to people who look like they want to be alone?" she answered, instinctively defensive. She bit her tongue after speaking the words. If Alex actually wanted to get to know her, she was an idiot to try to chase him off.

He just looked amused. "Would you prefer to be alone, or are you avoiding someone in particular?" As he asked this, he glanced over at the windows of the cafeteria. Jessica followed his gaze and noticed Caryn sitting inside with a group of other seniors.

"If I was trying to avoid anyone, it would be Caryn," she answered truthfully. "She seems convinced that my inner child needs a friend."

A mixture of empathy and annoyance crossed Alex's features. Jessica felt confident that the annoyance was reserved for Caryn.

"It's her nature to try to draw people out of the dark," he said.

"You two know each other?"

"Unfortunately," he answered. The scorn in his voice was palpable.

He silently watched Caryn for a moment, until she looked up as if she could feel his gaze. When she saw Jessica and Alex sitting together, she stood, gathered her belongings, and hurried away.

"She sure doesn't try to draw *you* out of the dark," Jessica commented.

"They've tried, and they've failed miserably," was his reply.

# CHAPTER 7

CARYN HAD RETREATED to the school library after seeing Jessica with the creature who was calling himself Alex. She had a study hall there soon, anyway; other students were already spilling out of the cafeteria and going to their classes.

She had been staring out the window for about five minutes when she suddenly saw Alex and Jessica walk past. It seemed there was no escape from them.

"Are you stalking me?" she heard Jessica say to Alex in a light, maybe even flirtatious, tone. Caryn frowned at how easily Jessica seemed to trust him. Alex was the last creature on Earth that any human should trust.

"Why would I do that?" Alex asked with pretend innocence.

*Why indeed?* Caryn thought. *Maybe because you're a manipulative leech?* If only Jessica knew what she was talking to.

"Anyway, I'm not quite so obvious when I'm stalking

someone," Alex was saying to Jessica, amusement in his voice.

Caryn shook her head. *Of course you are,* she thought. *If they don't know you're there, they aren't afraid.*

Suddenly she heard his mocking voice clearly in her mind. *I suppose you would know from experience?*

She threw up her mental shields, even though she knew they were little better than glass against his kind. *Get out of my head,* she thought angrily. Alex laughed in return.

Meanwhile, he and Jessica had continued to speak. It was obvious that Jessica had no knowledge of the silent conversation that had been going on. Her tone was jovial and unguarded, as if she was speaking to a friend.

*Friends with the leeches but not with the humans,* Caryn thought bitterly.

She couldn't exactly blame Jessica, though. Even knowing the truth about Alex, Caryn herself could barely sense his bubble of mental control. Without conscious effort he kept humans in thrall, so that they were comfortable around him despite their instinct to avoid his kind.

Only twice during the day had Caryn seen him let down his guard: with Shannon that morning and with the boy who had insulted him at lunch. Shannon had quickly stopped her flirtation and slunk away but had managed to laugh about her sudden unease when describing the situation to Caryn later.

Caryn forced herself to start her homework rather than think about Alex and Jessica any longer. She had no fighting skills with which to defend Jessica physically. And the girl had made it clear that she wanted no part of Caryn's friendship, so she certainly wouldn't be willing to heed her warning.

Caryn was not going to get in Alex's way—especially here, surrounded by so many defenseless humans. Arguing with a vampire in the middle of a crowd would only get people killed.

# CHAPTER 8

AFTER SCHOOL Jessica took the bus to the center of town. She walked to the bookstore, hoping to find *Tiger, Tiger* on the shelves. The book was supposed to have come out more than a week before, but this was the first chance Jessica had had to look for it. The advance copies she had at home didn't hold quite the same allure as the sight of her work in a bookstore display.

Jessica sighed when she saw Caryn browsing the shelves, but she wasn't about to let the annoying teen chase her away.

"Oh . . . hi, Jessica," Caryn said, sounding surprised. "You looking for anything?"

"A book. What else would I be in a bookstore for?" Jessica answered crossly.

It took her only a second to spot *Tiger, Tiger* on the shelf next to Caryn, and she reached past the girl to grab a copy. As the book was written under Jessica's pseudonym, Ash Night, Caryn wouldn't be able to connect Jessica with it. Even so, Caryn's eyes widened when she saw the book.

"I've read that one," she said in a voice that sounded falsely casual.

"So have I," Jessica answered, turning away from Caryn and toward the counter.

"I wonder what the author is like," Caryn commented. "Where do you suppose her ideas come from?"

Jessica ignored Caryn effortlessly until she added, "What if it was all real? If Ash Night's vampires actually existed? If Ather and Risika and Aubrey—"

Jessica spun on Caryn as she spoke that last name. "Vampires don't exist," she snapped. "Get over it." After having had this conversation with herself all day long, she was glad to finally have an excuse to say the words aloud.

"But—"

"Caryn, I've been subtle, rude, and even offensive," Jessica interrupted. "Now it's time for direct." She met Caryn's delicate blue eyes with a glacier-cold glare. "I don't care if you think vampires exist. I don't want to talk about it, just like I don't want to chat about combination locks or anything else. I don't want to talk to you at all. Do you understand?"

With a bit of a sigh, Caryn nodded, deflated.

That had been rather satisfying. Next Jessica just had to convince herself that Alex Remington wasn't the Antichrist, and she could return to the regularly scheduled tedium of her daily life.

"Cold," she heard behind her. "Very cold. I approve completely."

Jessica turned and saw Alex leaning against a shelf. His gaze as he watched Caryn hurry away reminded Jessica of a wolf watching a rabbit run to cover.

"Maybe I'm paranoid, but I could swear you've been following me." The words were out of Jessica's mouth before she had a chance to consider them. Hearing her own tone, she almost choked. If she caught herself flirting, she was likely to become ill.

"On and off," he answered vaguely, and didn't add anything more. He turned to wander down the aisle, glancing from shelf to shelf as if looking for something. After a few yards he looked over his left shoulder to see if she was still behind him, and it occurred to her that *she* was following *him*. Embarrassed, she stopped doing so.

"Anything good in here?" he asked, returning to the shelf where Jessica had found *Tiger, Tiger*.

"What's your definition of good?" she asked, making a point not to move toward him.

He pulled a book from the shelf: *Renegade*, by Elizabeth Charcoal. Showing it to Jessica, he said, "You'll love it. Trust me."

"You've read this?" Jessica had seen a magazine article about the author, though she hadn't had a chance to read the book. Elizabeth Charcoal claimed that she was a vampire, and that *Renegade* was actually her autobiography.

"I know the author," Alex answered matter-of-factly. "She gave me an autographed copy of the manuscript. Right after she tried to slit my throat, but why sweat the details?"

"Oh, really?" Jessica said skeptically. He was either teasing her or trying to impress her.

He shrugged. "We got into an argument."

"Does this happen to you often?"

"Fairly frequently," he answered, his tone nonchalant. "Elizabeth and I don't like each other very much, but her book is . . . interesting. It's the kind of thing you'd like."

"How do *you* know what I like to read?"

"I can tell," he answered cryptically, and then he turned to the checkout. He paused so that she could catch up and walk beside him, not behind.

The woman at the counter looked at Alex with contempt and whispered something under her breath.

"Hasana, what a surprise." Alex greeted her coolly. He smiled malevolently. The woman glared at him, but he ignored it.

"You two know each other?" Jessica asked foolishly, seeing the angry sparks fly between them.

"Hasana is Caryn's mother," Alex offered, as if that explained everything. Jessica remembered Caryn's reaction that morning when she had first seen Alex, and wondered what had happened between him and this family.

"Watch out for this guy," Hasana warned, nodding toward Alex. "He probably knows more about you than your taste in books."

"And how could that be?" Jessica asked dryly.

"I can read your mind, and learn your secret fears and darkest desires," Alex answered.

Jessica paused, examining his expression. She had

written those exact words, Aubrey's words, in *Dark Flame*, the novel that was presently waiting on her editor's desk. She couldn't remember whether she had used them in *Tiger, Tiger*.

"Do you always talk like that?" she asked, unnerved.

He looked at her challengingly as he said, "Don't you know?"

She just shook her head, alarmed but unwilling to show it.

As Alex paid for his book, Jessica realized that she was still holding *Tiger, Tiger*. She placed it on the counter, not intending to buy it; she had plenty of copies at home.

Alex's gaze drifted to the cover, and his expression leapt immediately from amusement to anger. He spun away and, without another word, stalked out of the store. Jessica was left staring after him, too shocked to react.

"If I were you, I'd just avoid him," Hasana advised.

"Why? Is he going to hurt me?" Jessica's sarcasm was sharpened by her confusion regarding Alex.

"Unless you keep away from him, he most likely will," Hasana answered seriously. "He has a temper."

Jessica was out of sharp remarks. To hide her discomfort, she picked up the copy of *Tiger, Tiger* and said, "I guess I'll put this away before it makes anyone else freak out."

"If you want it, just keep it," Hasana answered softly. "You *are* the author."

Jessica froze, dumbfounded.

"I'm sorry," Hasana said quickly. "I just—"

"How did you know?" Jessica interrupted, annoyed

to learn that this woman had connected her to Ash Night. She had used a pen name to *avoid* recognition.

"I've read it, and I . . . recognized you as the author," Hasana fumbled. "You just have a look about you . . ."

"What *look*?"

"Never mind," Hasana said, shaking her head. "Take the book and the advice, and ignore me."

She turned away, suddenly very busy with some papers, and Jessica left in a daze.

# CHAPTER 9

AUBREY HAD LEFT THE STORE to avoid hurting someone — probably the witch.

Though he had a house on the fringe of town, he preferred to spend his time in the heart of New Mayhem, in his room behind the nightclub known as Las Noches. There he paced angrily, wondering what to do about the human called Jessica.

She didn't know that everything she wrote was true. She thought vampires were just another myth. She thought her characters were just figments of her own imagination. She had no idea what Alex was.

That wasn't quite true. He knew that Jessica had recognized him the instant she saw him. Only her human rationality had kept her from believing that Alex Remington was actually Aubrey.

Aubrey had heard of the author Ash Night through a young vampire who worked as an editor at Night's publishing company. The vampire had even given Aubrey a copy of the *Dark Flame* manuscript. The news of this book had quickly spread through the vampiric community, as it had when Elizabeth Charcoal had published her autobiography.

The difference was that Ash Night was not writing about herself, but about things she had no right to know. *Dark Flame* was Aubrey's own history, which no one but he knew in total. Yet Ash Night had written his past correctly, down to the last detail.

Aubrey didn't mind the thought of *Dark Flame*'s being published. In his history he had almost always been stronger than those around him. However, the others who were mentioned in the manuscript came across as often weak, and in the vampiric world, there was no worse threat to one's position than an apparent weakness. *Dark Flame* had earned its author some dangerous enemies.

The vampire from the publishing company had not worked with Ash Night directly, and she must not have known about the author's first book. Seeing *Tiger, Tiger* in the store today had taken Aubrey completely by surprise. The cover made it strikingly clear whom the book was about. Despite the artist's ignorance of his subject, Aubrey had instantly recognized the portrayal of Risika. He had lived this book as well — or unlived it, as the case might be. He knew what would be printed on its pages.

Aubrey lightly touched the scar that stretched across his left shoulder, which Risika had given to him a few years ago. For the first time in nearly three thousand years he had lost a fight, and he had lost it badly. Risika could have killed him in the end. Instead, she had taken his blood and let him live. The action had opened his mind to her completely; she could now read him as easily as he could read most humans.

The sight of the book was like the thrust of a knife into his still-bleeding pride.

Aubrey had been the first of his kind to search out the author, and most of the other vampires were satisfied by the knowledge that he was dealing with the problem.

Though Jessica had requested that her true name and address remain private, Aubrey had easily pulled the information from the mind of her editor. Her town, Ramsa, New York, was only a stone's throw away from his home in New Mayhem, one of the strongest vampiric cities in the United States. Aubrey had drifted into Ramsa to see how much of a threat this Ash Night was.

What had he expected? Anything but what he found: a seventeen-year-old human who had no apparent connection to the vampire world. She did, however, have a darkness in her aura that was almost vampiric. This close to New Mayhem, Jessica's aura was strengthened by the vampires in the area. Humans reacted to it instinctively and drew away from her, as they had from Aubrey until he had started influencing their minds.

He had tried to influence Jessica. He should have been able to reach into her mind and tell her to stop writing. With any other human the task would have been easy, but with Jessica he had been blocked completely. That fact alone had fascinated him enough to refrain from killing her the first time he'd been given the chance.

Indeed, there were many things about Jessica that interested him despite his usual distaste for humans.

Foremost was her unnerving lack of reaction when he had caught her eye earlier. Most humans would have become disoriented, momentarily trapped in his gaze, but Jessica had been unaffected.

Aubrey closed his eyes for a moment, taking a breath to calm himself. He stopped pacing and once again wore the dispassionate mask that he had developed over his many years of life.

But the craving for movement would not die as cleanly as he had hoped, so he left his room and walked down the short hallway to Las Noches.

The nightclub's atmosphere was intense. Red strobe lights flashed through the room, disorienting everyone but those who had spent as much time inside the place as Aubrey had. Bass-heavy music pounded from speakers hidden somewhere in the shadowed ceiling, and mirrors covered the four walls. Risika had shattered every inch of these mirrors during her fight with Aubrey, so the numerous reflections were now distorted.

Until Jessica saw Las Noches, walked inside, and tried to keep her mind from spinning, she would never be able to accurately imagine the psychedelic bar and nightclub that was the dark heart of New Mayhem.

Of course, Jessica didn't believe that New Mayhem even existed.

Now, in the hour before sunset, the crowd was the usual mix of humans and vampires. The mortals were comforted by the sunlight that still bathed the world outside; most of the vampires in the room would not hunt until after dark. The bartender on duty was an ebony-eyed girl named Kaei. With her pale skin and the curtain of ink-black hair that fell down her back, Kaei had looked like the traditional vampire even when she'd been human. She had been born in Mayhem and had been responsible for its nearly complete destruction three hundred years earlier. She had offered Aubrey her blood more than once, and in return he had probably saved her life a dozen times.

"Moira was looking for you," Kaei told Aubrey as he approached. "She mentioned something about helping you 'dice the writer into bite-sized pieces.' " Moira had complained many times recently that Ash Night had made her seem weak. The author had not needed to try very hard. Though Moira was strong in comparison to most others of their kind, she was one of the weakest of their line. She had been changed more than five hundred years before Aubrey but had never gained his strength.

Most of their line had been strong as humans; that was how they attracted the attention of the vampires who would ultimately change them. Fala had met and fallen in love with Moira, then changed the human woman to save her life.

Despite Moira's weakness, she and her blood sister Fala were feared because of their reputation for being fond of causing pain. Moira had been born before the Aztecs, and shortly after she'd been changed, she had pulled the heart out of one of their priests with her bare hands.

"Fala asked for you too," Kaei continued, her expression grim. "She was talking about turning the author into ash—making her 'fit her name better.' " Unlike Moira, who preferred weaponry, Fala was fond of fire.

Aubrey sighed, having no desire to deal with either of the two vampires. "Maybe they could draw straws," he answered wearily.

"Do what you will," Kaei answered, knowing that what she said rarely mattered. She walked away without another word.

Aubrey pulled one of the unlabeled bottles from under the bar. Though not exactly sure what it was, he knew it wouldn't harm him. He could down a liter of cyanide and not notice any effect. Some of these bottles held wine, others liquor, and others blood that was always cold. How the bar was kept stocked was a mystery, as there was rarely a bartender working and the drinks were all free.

# CHAPTER 10

AUBREY WAS STILL AT THE BAR when he heard a familiar voice behind him.

"Welcome back," Jager said in his usual cool tone. Jager was the second oldest in their line and one of the few vampires who might rival Aubrey for pure strength. However, he was rarely interested in fighting.

"Did you meet Night?" Jager asked when Aubrey did not instantly volunteer the information.

"I did," Aubrey answered, not elaborating.

"Did you kill him?" It was an offhand question. Killing was the logical way to deal with a human who could be a threat to their kind. Whether or not she knew it, Jessica possessed truths that were dangerous to the vampire world—and she had chosen to share them.

"Her," Aubrey corrected. "No, I didn't kill her."

He didn't know quite why he hadn't killed Jessica. It would not have been difficult, and the death would not have created much of a stir, after a few whispered words into the minds of Anne Allodola and Ash Night's business associates.

"I hope Risika isn't a bad loser when it comes to bets," Jager commented. "She assumed you'd kill the author."

"She would," Aubrey answered dryly. *What would Jessica think,* he wondered, *if she knew there were bets being made about her potential death?*

"May I ask why you *didn't* kill her?" Jager said, not disguising his curiosity.

Aubrey wondered about the answer himself. The phrase "she's beautiful" came to mind, and of course it was true. Jessica seemed almost to embody the graceful perfection of a vampire. But Aubrey had never before hesitated to kill someone because she was attractive.

More than her physical appearance, Jessica had a rare aura of strength about her. Aubrey remembered Ash Night's describing him as having the same kind of aura while he had been human, but he had seen it in very few others. Risika had been one of the exceptions; that strength had drawn Aubrey to her before she had ever caught Ather's eye. Now Jessica was another.

"Is the question too difficult?" Jager asked, his tone patronizing.

Aubrey resorted to the simplest answer. "I wasn't in the mood."

Jager accepted the explanation, and the two vampires sat awhile in companionable silence.

Suddenly the fiery Fala appeared in front of them.

"I see you've returned from your little game in the sunlight," she purred at Aubrey. Her voice was like poisoned chocolate, deceptively smooth and sweet. As she brushed by Jager, she gave him a quick kiss on the cheek.

Fala was Jager's first fledgling. Born in Egypt, she had naturally dark skin that had paled little in the almost five thousand years she'd been a vampire. Her black hair was pulled back from her face by bloodred combs, but that was the only bit of color in her otherwise black outfit.

"I suppose you've met Night," Fala spat, as if the name was not one to be mentioned in polite society. "Is she quite dead, I hope? Even better, is she writhing in pain somewhere?"

"She's alive," Aubrey answered, not in the mood to exchange sadistic banter with Fala.

"Mind if I kill her for you?" Fala asked casually as she walked behind the bar and poured herself a drink from Aubrey's bottle. "This is good," she commented, holding the bottle up to the red light, which did not help to illuminate its contents. "Anyone know what it is?"

She emptied the rest of the liquid into her glass, then threw the unlabeled bottle over her shoulder. The bottle shattered, and several people at the tables turned at the sound. One human stood up and brushed glass off her jeans, but she didn't seem upset. Breaking glass was hardly an unusual occurrence at Las Noches.

Fala sighed luxuriously as she turned back to Aubrey and Jager. "I love the sound of breaking glass. Now, about Ash—"

"No, you can't kill her for me," Aubrey interrupted.

"You're going to stop me?" she asked, her voice going lower, slightly menacing.

"I have more of a quarrel with her than you do," he

answered coldly, not bothering to explain the statement.

"Unless she has drawn blood, Aubrey, you have *nothing*," Fala snapped back, stalking closer to him.

Fala was referring to one of the few standing rules of their kind: blood claim. Humans, unless they lived in New Mayhem, were free prey of any vampire. However, if a human drew the blood of a vampire, that human could only be hunted by the vampire who had been harmed. Had Jessica attacked Aubrey and somehow made him bleed, Fala would have been unable to hurt Jessica without Aubrey's permission.

"She hasn't, and she never will," he answered.

"You wouldn't admit to being wounded by a human even if you had been," Fala scoffed. She finished her drink and threw the glass over her shoulder. "But I suppose you wouldn't be in such a good mood if you'd lost *another* fight."

She said nothing more. Aubrey struck her with his mind, and she fell backward into the bar, hissing in anger. Several heads turned toward them, and a few humans chose that time to exit Las Noches; it was dangerous to be in the same room with two fighting vampires.

Jager was still nearby, and he was watching the argument with narrowed eyes.

"Would you care to repeat that?" Aubrey asked Fala, his voice cold as ice as he casually threw another bolt of power at her, causing her to double over in pain. He hadn't even broken a sweat.

"Aubrey." Jager spoke only his name, a calm but clear warning.

Aubrey answered by drawing back his power instead of hitting Fala again. Jager would not start a fight over what had happened thus far; Fala wouldn't appreciate the help. But even so, Aubrey knew that Jager was too fond of Fala to look the other way if she was truly threatened.

"Damn you, Aubrey," Fala cursed. She scowled but was wise enough not to insult him again.

"Already been done," he answered calmly.

"Damn you again!" she shouted, delivering a glare that would have stilled serpents in their dens.

"Too late," he quipped. "And after five thousand years, I'd think you could come up with something better than that."

Fala growled but didn't attempt to attack him. Though she was far older than he was, he had always been stronger, and he was a better fighter. If she fought back, she would lose.

"Fine," she snarled. "But if you don't kill the human, or otherwise dispose of her, I *will*. Is that perfectly understandable to you, Aubrey?"

"Yes."

In the next moment they were both gone, Aubrey retreating to his room. The nightclub's heavy music reverberated through the building, but he was used to it. He fell into bed and a sleep of complete oblivion. Like most of his kind, he did not dream.

# CHAPTER 11

WHEN AUBREY WOKE he brought himself to the edge of Red Rock, the forest that surrounded New Mayhem and fringed Ramsa. The ability to instantly move from one place to another was a power he used often, as he had for more than two thousand years.

The full moon was about a week away still, but Aubrey could easily sense a few untrained witches and some werewolves lurking in the busy forest. There were also several vampires nearby, all of Mira's bloodline.

Ramsa was supposedly Mira's territory, but that barely worried Aubrey. Mira, though ancient, was one of the weakest of their kind, and her fledglings were little stronger than most humans. Few in Mira's bloodline had lived through Fala's extermination of them a few hundred years before, and now they were hardly even considered part of the vampiric community. Most of them were so sensitive toward their prey that they only fed on animals and willing humans.

There was a party going on at a house on the edge of

the woods. Shannon had unwittingly invited Aubrey to it, before he had frightened her. The house was filled with people, and the faint scent of alcohol floated from it to where Aubrey stood watching, many yards away. He easily reached out with his mind and sifted through the thoughts of those inside.

The minds he touched were hardly entertaining—either hazy from drinking, silly from joking, or angry from gossiping. He found Shannon quickly. She had drunk some beer and her defenses were down; little effort was necessary to convince her to come outside alone.

Shannon wandered absently into the woods, and jumped in surprise when she came upon Aubrey.

"Um . . . Hi, Alex."

She greeted him tentatively, glancing back at the house in obvious confusion as to how she had arrived here. Before she could decide to leave, he reached into her mind and her nervousness faded.

"Shannon, right?" he asked, taking a step toward her.

"Yeah," she answered with a coy smile. "Why are you hiding here in the—"

*Sleep.* Aubrey sent the command to her mind as soon as he was close enough to catch her as she fell.

She collapsed, unconscious in an instant, and he caught her without effort. He could have caught someone ten times her weight with no difficulty. Though he could control any human physically, he didn't relish the possibility that the girl would scream and attract inconvenient attention. It was easier to have her asleep as he fed. He had done this many times before.

He tilted Shannon's head back to expose the artery, which was covered by nothing more than a thin layer of skin. His canines, which looked normal enough most of the time, extended to razor-sharp points. These fangs pierced the skin of her throat quickly and precisely, and within moments he was lost in the sensation of the rich human blood that ran over his tongue and quenched his thirst.

# CHAPTER 12

CARYN HAD SENSED Aubrey's presence even before she saw Shannon leave the party with a dazed look on her face. She had felt the pressure of his mind on Shannon's.

Caryn had no idea what she would do once she encountered Aubrey, but she felt compelled to follow Shannon anyway. A group of boys had bunched together at the door, and Caryn was delayed for a few minutes as she tried to slip through the throng. Once she was finally outside, it took her only a short moment to find the vampire and his prey. She could easily sense Aubrey's aura, which was like a shadow flickering just outside the normal spectrum of vision. She could feel his power slither across her skin.

This ability was her line's gift—or curse, as some would say. Though her family, the Smoke line, had always been healers, most witches were vampire hunters. Caryn had a witch's blood, which was sweeter and stronger than a human's, and a witch's knowledge, which made her dangerous to the vampires. But she did not have the ability to fight. She had always known herself to be easy prey, and had tried out of self-protection to avoid their kind, unless doing so meant risking an innocent person's life.

Throughout her childhood, Caryn had been taught to respect life, and to protect it whatever the cost. She knew Aubrey too well to look the other way while he cast his lure.

"Aubrey!" she called as soon as she had found him.

The vampire was standing several yards into the woods, holding Shannon, who was motionless. Aubrey had an arm around her waist to keep her from falling, and his other hand cradled the back of her neck. His lips were at her throat. Shannon was pale but still breathing.

"Aubrey!" Caryn shouted again when he didn't respond.

Aubrey glanced up and glared at her as he continued to feed. *What do you want?* he growled.

Caryn jumped at the intrusion into her mind but somehow managed to find her voice. "Let her go, Aubrey."

"Is that a threat?" Scorn laced his voice as he dropped Shannon. He mockingly licked a trace of blood from his lips.

Caryn hurried to Shannon's side. She was unconscious but would live.

"How many people have you murdered like this?" Caryn demanded, her voice wavering.

"I don't think you really want to know," Aubrey answered coolly.

"Don't you have any conscience at all?"

"Not that I know of," he said with nonchalance. "Now, much as I love your company, I really do prefer to dine alone."

He was enjoying this, Caryn realized. He could easily have avoided the argument by disappearing and finding prey elsewhere, but instead he was playing with her.

"You'll kill her," Caryn protested.

"So?" Aubrey responded, sounding amused, as he took a step toward her. Caryn flinched but did not move away from Shannon. If he was determined to kill tonight, she had no hope of preventing it, but her conscience would not allow her to leave. "Are you planning to stop me?" he mocked. "If you were one of your cousins, I might at least *pretend* to be worried . . . though probably not. As it is, I know you'd never fight me even if you had the strength."

He was speaking the truth. No one in her line had harmed another creature since Evelyn Smoke, the first of the Smoke line, had stopped hunting vampires.

"Please, Aubrey," Caryn entreated, beginning to despair.

"Caryn, go away. You're beginning to bore me."

"Let her go," Caryn persisted, though her tone was hardly commanding. She was sickened by his game, and worse, she worried what would happen when he reached the end of his patience.

"That would accomplish very little," Aubrey pointed out. "I would just have to draw someone else from the house. Would you like to say that this girl's life is more important than, oh, her boyfriend's? Or—"

"You're having a great time, aren't you?" Caryn finally

shouted, standing and stalking toward him as her anger gave her courage.

Waiting for her to continue, Aubrey lounged casually against an oak tree. Had she been from any other line — Vida, or Arun, or even Light — she would have killed him then. But the last of the Light line had died nearly three hundred years earlier, and the Vidas and Aruns had other vampires to deal with that night. So Caryn Smoke did the only thing that her training would allow her to do in this situation.

She took a deep, calming breath and stretched out her left arm with the palm up, exposing the pale tracery of veins at her wrist.

"Here," she said softly, her fear almost hidden. "My blood is stronger than human blood." Her voice quaked for a moment, but she forced herself to continue. "You wouldn't need to kill me."

Aubrey's gaze flickered to the pulse point on her wrist, but that was the only sign that he cared for the offer at all. "And what is to stop me from draining you dry?"

"Your word that you won't."

She saw the amusement in his gaze. Had the situation been reversed, she would have understood the humor. Taking his word for her safety was like a vampire's accepting the word of any other witch. Most witches lied and broke promises almost by habit when it came to Aubrey's kind. Vampires weren't considered people, so even the proud Vida line had no hesitation about deceiving them. In general, only the Smoke line considered honesty important when dealing with Aubrey's kind.

A vampire's word was said to be broken as easily as a

wineglass, and Caryn had no doubt that Aubrey's was just as fragile. In reality, the only thing that might keep her alive was Aubrey's awareness that killing a Smoke witch brought down instant retaliation from all the vampire hunters in the other lines.

Caryn's heartbeat quickened with fright, but she used all the discipline she'd been taught to keep her resolution from wavering.

Aubrey took the wrist she offered and used it to draw her toward him. He put a hand on her forehead and gently tilted her head back. Her heart rate tripled in an instant, but she balled her hands into fists to keep from trying to pull away.

*Don't worry,* she heard him say in her mind. *It won't hurt.*

She felt a sharp stinging when his teeth pierced her skin, but it faded almost immediately. The combined anesthesia of vampiric saliva and his whispering voice in her head dulled the pain completely. Caryn's legs gave out under the pressure of Aubrey's mind, and she felt him put an arm around her back to hold her up.

*You taste good,* he said absently.

*I don't know whether to take that as a compliment or a threat,* she mused. Her fear had disappeared, and her thoughts were becoming incoherent as she lost blood and his mind tightened its grip on her own.

Caryn tried to focus. She had been taught so much discipline . . . why couldn't she *think*?

She had been prepared for pain, but there was none. She felt extremely relaxed, as if she was floating . . . She was dreaming . . . wasn't she? Did it matter?

She imagined herself resting on a beach in the warm sun, or maybe meditating atop a mountain beneath the full moon. She was relaxed, peaceful, calm, happy to forget . . .

Forget what?

Caryn tried to focus, but it was nearly impossible. Aubrey's mind pulled at hers, numbing and soothing it. With intense effort, she drew herself out of her trance. There was far too much danger to forget what was happening.

His mind still held hers, and it was increasingly difficult not to let herself fall back into the seductive void. But if she gave in, would she ever surface again? He would probably kill her.

*Would you rather it hurt?*

Caryn had the vague idea that Aubrey was taunting her, but she could do nothing about it.

Eventually, after what seemed to be hours, Aubrey reluctantly pulled away. Caryn collapsed, suddenly aware again of her own body.

She was dizzy and weak, and her pulse was hurried as her heart attempted to circulate her thinned blood. Through foggy vision, she saw Aubrey hesitate, as if debating whether he really wanted to let her go.

Then he disappeared.

She put her head down for a moment, trying to clear her mind, then carefully crossed the clearing to make sure Shannon was all right. Hopefully, when the girl woke she would just assume she had drunk too much. She would never know how close she'd come to dying.

With this thought, Caryn put a hand over her own heart, feeling the rapid beating. Unlike Shannon, she was completely aware of how close Death had brushed by her tonight.

# CHAPTER 13

JESSICA HAD BEEN WRITING all evening, but by the time midnight came the inspiration had died. She was restless and knew she wouldn't be able to fall asleep anytime soon. The best way she could think to burn some energy was to go for a walk.

The round moon lit her path through Red Rock Forest, and she soon found herself at her favorite spot: a large oak tree about a quarter of a mile in. She pulled herself onto one of its large branches and relaxed. Something about the night always calmed her.

Finally, under a broad canopy of leaves, she drifted into sleep.

*Jazlyn's heart labored hard, unused to its task. Her lungs burned with the constant effort of breathing. But finally she fell into blissful unconsciousness.*

*Instead of the death-sleep that she had grown accustomed to, she dreamed of the world she was now trying to escape. She dreamed that she was running through a city street at midnight, chasing her frightened prey. She dreamed that she was flying far above the nighttime desert in the form of an eagle. She dreamed that she was walking in a graveyard, toward the grave of her once-husband.*

*Jazlyn woke gasping for breath. It took her several moments to realize where she was, which was something that hadn't happened to her in a long time. Her very survival had frequently depended on her ability to wake instantly.*

*During those confused moments, a vague memory flashed in her mind of meeting a witch who called herself Monica, a witch who had offered to give her back her hard-lost humanity.*

*But why had the witch—*

"Do you usually sleep outside in trees?"

Startled awake, Jessica sat up too quickly and almost fell from her perch. Alex was the one who had spoken. He was sitting, completely at home, on another branch.

"Couldn't you rustle some leaves next time?" she grumped, though she felt herself beginning to smile at her odd but welcome visitor. "I nearly fell out of the tree. How'd you get up here without my hearing you?"

"I flew."

Jessica just shook her head.

"Well, if you don't like it, I'll get down." Alex jumped from the branch and landed gracefully, like a cat. Jessica followed more slowly, having no desire to break an ankle by showing off. They walked aimlessly through the darkened woods as they spoke.

"Don't you live somewhere? Or do you just follow me around all day?" Before, she had asked him a similar question as a joke, but this time she truly wanted an answer. It seemed a bit too much of a coincidence that he was out here tonight.

"I *live* nowhere," Alex answered, his voice serious despite the hint of teasing she could see in his eyes, "and it isn't day."

Jessica shook her head again as she realized there was no way to get a straight answer from him.

As she contemplated this fact, she noticed a design on his right wrist, which was only visible because his sleeve had slipped up when he had leapt from the tree.

"What's that?" she asked, pointing to the tattoo.

Alex rolled up his sleeve to reveal the entire design: a black wolf with golden eyes and white fangs stalked across his wrist. Jessica knew this beast; it was Fenris, the giant wolf who swallowed the sun in Norse mythology. Aubrey had the same design on *his* right wrist.

She took a deep breath to keep herself from speaking until her thoughts were under control.

This could not possibly be a coincidence.

Over the past day, she had struggled to come up with an explanation—besides the impossible one that Alex *was* Aubrey—that would account for all the similarities between the two of them. Now a stunningly obvious scenario at last occurred to her: Alex was a fan of Ash Night. Aubrey was described down to the last detail in *Tiger, Tiger*. What would stop someone, if he was so inclined, from getting black contact lenses, a matching pendant, and replicas of Aubrey's tattoos?

But before Jessica could comment on Alex's tattoo, he asked her, "What are you doing out here so late at night?"

"I couldn't sleep," she answered, still unnerved. "You?"

"Maybe I *am* stalking you," he teased.

"Well, then I'm flattered," she joked back, though the light words masked more serious thoughts. If her theory about his fascination with Aubrey the vampire proved true, how far might he take this role-playing game of his?

She began walking in the general direction of her house, and he walked with her. Their conversation fell into silence.

"You're quiet suddenly," Jessica observed. They were within sight of her house, and she had stopped walking to look at him. "What are you thinking about?"

Alex sighed. "Nothing you would care to know."

"Why don't you tell me, and let me be the judge of that?" she pressed.

"Blood and death and people who know too much," he answered, his voice more tired than threatening. "Go inside, Ash Night. I'll speak to you another time."

He walked away silently, not giving Jessica a chance to respond. By the time her mind had processed his words, he was out of sight.

Her anger rose again for an instant, in reaction to the fact that yet another person had somehow discovered who Ash Night was.

However, the anger was quashed by a prospect that was intriguing, yet frightening. If he was Aubrey, and vampires did exist, and he and his kind knew who she was . . . her life could end up being a great deal shorter than she had intended.

# CHAPTER 14

"HOW CUTE," Fala spat, approaching Aubrey as he entered Las Noches. "How disgustingly cute."

"Excuse me?"

Fala laughed, a biting sound that told anyone within hearing to beware. "Do you honestly think I haven't been keeping my eye on the author, after all the trouble she's been causing? And you've been out there practically *flirting* with her!"

For a moment Aubrey hesitated, fighting an urge to check on Jessica and make sure Fala hadn't harmed her after he had left.

"Leave Jessica alone," he commanded, his voice hard. It wasn't wise to show any attachment to a human, but he refused to let Fala harm the girl.

"What is it about this human?" Fala sneered. "Aubrey the almighty, the hunter, the warrior, who feels nothing but contempt for anything mortal . . . If I didn't know better, I'd say you were attracted to her."

He laughed in answer to her taunt, which she had

obviously hoped would bother him more. "You've made up my reason, Fala. What's *your* interest in her? Fala, the child who has been abused and hunted by almost every immortal creature on Earth, the coward who wants power without risk, the fake goddess . . ." He paused and watched the rage flicker through her eyes in response to his references to her humiliating past — the past Ash Night knew all too well. "If I didn't know better, I'd say you were jealous."

Aubrey knew this last accusation was ridiculous. Fala hated him far too much to be jealous of his attraction to anyone, much less a human. But the expression on her face as he said those last words was priceless.

"You vain, arrogant, human-loving *idiot,*" Fala snarled. Then she disappeared before he had a chance to retaliate.

Aubrey ignored her words and chuckled as he wandered over to the bar. He wasn't worried about Jessica for the moment. Had Fala actually killed her, she would have made it clear that she had done so. She would have insisted on sharing every bloody detail with him.

# CHAPTER 15

CARYN RASHIDA WAITED inside the front door as Anne Allodola went to wake her daughter. Caryn ran over possible scenarios in her mind for the hundredth time.

"She'll be down in just a moment," Ms. Allodola said as she returned.

Caryn nodded nervously. She had made up her mind, and this time she would not let Jessica's frosty putdowns turn her away. Of course, waking her up might not have been a good idea, but how was she to know that Jessica would still be sleeping? It was almost noon.

When Jessica finally came downstairs, Caryn could instantly tell that she was in for a challenge. Jessica's aura hummed with annoyance and anger, as well as some confusion. As soon as she saw Caryn, the emotions found an outlet.

"What the hell do *you* want?" Jessica snapped.

Caryn flinched slightly. "I need to talk to you, Jessica."

"About what?"

"Alex."

Jessica's eyes narrowed as soon as Caryn said the name, and she stopped trying to herd Caryn out the door.

"What about Alex?" Jessica asked carefully. When Caryn looked toward the kitchen, where Anne was not-so-subtly eavesdropping, Jessica sighed. "Come upstairs. We can talk in my room."

Caryn hesitated at the doorway to Jessica's room, which was threateningly dark. There was no light besides the glow that came from a red Lava lamp on the shelf. Jessica removed the lamp's bottle so that the light shone pure white, but that only served to illuminate the room's gloomy monochrome.

"This is your room?" Caryn asked before she could think not to. She noticed one lonely hint of color: a violet pillow on the corner of the bed, half lost beneath the black comforter. She wondered how Jessica would react if she told her that violet was the color of humanity.

Caryn had a sudden, irrational desire to rescue the pillow from the blackness. That much she could do easily. Unlike Jessica, the pillow would not fight her.

"Say what you came to say, Caryn," Jessica growled.

Caryn went over the million different scripts she had prepared to tell Jessica the truth, then discarded them all. She walked to the shelf and sifted through the rough manuscripts until she found Jessica's copy of *Dark Flame.*

"I've heard about this," she said. Most of the world—excluding the humans—had heard of Ash Night's *Dark Flame.*

Jessica frowned, and Caryn could tell she was trying to make sense of the comment. Before she could formulate an answer, Caryn continued.

"How did you . . . get the idea for that book? And *Tiger, Tiger*?" she asked.

Jessica laughed, appearing shocked by the ordinariness of the question. "You came here to ask me how I get my *ideas*?"

Caryn took a deep breath to steady herself. "Not entirely." Her next words came out in a rush. "I wanted to ask if you knew they were true."

Jessica's expression was suddenly drained of its amusement.

"Get out, Caryn," she ordered coldly.

Caryn took a step back from Jessica's sudden vehemence. *Denial,* she reasoned. Jessica knew the truth but refused to accept it. It made perfect sense that she would fight back against anyone who attempted to convince her of what she was desperately trying to ignore.

Caryn inhaled deeply when she realized that she'd been holding her breath for the past few seconds.

"What do you know about Alex?" Caryn pressed. Jessica was exceptionally strong. When forced to see the truth, she would be able to accept it. If only Caryn knew how to convince her!

"I said, get out of my room," Jessica repeated.

"Will you think about what I said?" Beyond that simple request, Caryn was out of ideas. "Please?"

"If you'll leave." The answer was little more than a growl.

Caryn reached into her pocket and pulled out the

letter she had written earlier, after several drafts. She held it out to Jessica, who snatched it from her hand.

"Happy now?" Jessica snapped.

Jessica's rampaging emotions were starting to make Caryn dizzy, so she nodded meekly and hurried out of the room. As she paused in the hallway, wishing she could think of some way to reason with Jessica, she heard the lock turn in the door. A few moments later loud music began to spill into the hall.

# CHAPTER 16

JESSICA SPRAWLED across her bed with mindless noise blaring in her ears and tried to reason things out.

Caryn was playing with her. She knew the Rashidas and Alex had some relationship; they hated each other too much to be perfect strangers. For all she knew, Alex and Caryn used to date. Now they had ganged up to play a game of "let's mess with the author's mind."

It was cleverly done, she admitted reluctantly. Alex's portrayal of Aubrey was perfect. She wondered who Caryn was trying to be. If it was a game, it was well practiced and planned between them.

*There is no if,* she scolded herself. *Vampires do not exist!*

Jessica had no love of mind games, especially ones played by childish idiots like Caryn. She wondered if Caryn realized just how little sense of humor Jessica had when it came to her books.

Frustrated, she opened the letter that Caryn had handed her and scanned it quickly.

Then she read it again, more slowly, and then a third time.

*Jessica —*

*I realize how confused you must be now. I don't know how to explain to you that everything you are thinking right now is true. I can't imagine how you got involved in this world; all I know is that what you write puts you in danger.*

*With your permission, I will try to help you, but I can't do anything unless you ask me to. I'm not a fighter, but I know others who are. If you will let me, I will ask them for help.*

*Stay away from Aubrey, away from all of them. Stop writing your books about them. Maybe then they will not see the need to destroy you. You well know how dangerous they are. Please, be careful.*

*Blessed be,*
*Caryn Smoke*
*Daughter of Macht*

*I am signing with my true name now. I don't wish to lie to you as all the others would.*

"What is going on here?" Jessica asked the black walls. They said nothing — they rarely did, though when she was dead tired they sometimes made an exception.

Everyone who had read Ash Night's first book knew who Aubrey was — what he looked like, where he was from, how he spoke, and how he thought. The two books that had gone through her editor's office revealed the dark corners of Aubrey's past and his present, and had reached into the wider vampiric world to show its customs and politics.

Never once had these books mentioned the Smoke line of witches or their immortal mother, Macht, whom Caryn had so casually referenced in her letter.

Without conscious thought, Jessica picked up one of the manuscripts that had been sitting on her shelf for months now. Though she hadn't read the novel since she had written it, she remembered the characters inside. The story was set years earlier; the witches mentioned in it would be Caryn's distant ancestors. Jessica knew, through the eyes of her vampiric characters, all about the Smoke line. But *only* she should have known, because the manuscript had been read by no one else. The fine layer of dust on the binder was proof that no one had picked it up recently. There was no way Caryn could ever have read it.

The girl's words echoed in Jessica's mind: *What if it was all real? If Ash Night's vampires actually existed?*

And more recently: *I wanted to ask if you knew they were true.*

Though Jessica hadn't delved too far into the world of the Smoke witches, simply because they were of little interest to her vampires, she knew their basic beliefs. If a Smoke witch was aware that someone was in danger, it was that witch's duty to protect him or her.

If it was true, Jessica was certainly in danger.

If they were all real . . .

If Aubrey existed, and Jessica had met him, then why was she still alive? He had no scruples about killing, and she had shown the world every weak moment of his past. Yet when she mentally replayed her conversations with him, there was no sense of threat. He seemed more to be flirting with her than hunting her.

She needed to know if it was true. She knew these characters better than she knew even Anne. They had been her thoughts and life for years. If there was the slightest chance that they were real, she needed to know.

She needed proof, and to get that, she needed to see for herself.

# CHAPTER 17

IN JESSICA'S NOVELS, New Mayhem was the base of vampiric power in the United States. The town, which was hidden from the human world, was home to the ruling class of vampires—Silver's line, including Aubrey. Their presence had given it a flavor of darkness that Jessica knew she would recognize if she saw it.

She searched through her manuscripts and found various clues to the location of New Mayhem, which was Ramsa's secret neighbor. She had always assumed that she had located New Mayhem near Ramsa out of familiarity, but perhaps instead some trick of the vampiric world had caused *her* to be located *here*.

One of her manuscripts, at this point untitled, caught her eye. The story was that of Kaei, the mostly human bartender at the vampire nightclub Las Noches. Kaei had been born and raised in the original town of Mayhem. She had been responsible for the fire that had nearly leveled the town three hundred years earlier, and in punishment had been blood-bonded to Jager. Kaei was not a vampire, but she would not age as long as Jager was alive.

After that episode, the witches had mostly believed that Mayhem was gone forever. When New Mayhem was built, the mortal Macht witches and the immortal Tristes had not been informed. The vampire hunters had not known about New Mayhem.

Until *Tiger, Tiger* had revealed its existence. Jessica silently contemplated this latest realization as she walked down the darkened road toward the town that might or might not be there.

The walk was longer than she would have liked, but not painfully so. Perhaps three miles went by before Jessica noticed a narrow, unnamed path off to the side of the road. Normally she would not have given the path a second glance after all the nearly identical driveways she had passed, but tonight she saw beside it the sign she had been looking for: a rosebush, which climbed the base of an oak tree.

The last of the blooms was still on the bush, and when she stepped near it, Jessica saw that the flower was black. For more than five hundred years, the vampires had used a black rose as their symbol.

She knelt for a moment, her fingers resting on the silky petals of the rose as she tried to calm her breathing. She no longer needed to see the town to convince herself that everything was true; though her mind might still protest, she believed despite it. Now there was a more compelling reason for her to follow the path. It would lead her home. She had seen New Mayhem through dozens of views but had never even glimpsed it with her own eyes, yet as she walked, she had the strangest sensation that she was finally heading home.

The path went on for what seemed an interminable time. Walking down that path was a test of courage that most people would have failed. The darkness was oppressive, and the forest was unnaturally silent. The isolation pressed against her like a physical weight. Yet, unafraid, she welcomed the night and the loneliness like old friends.

The woods began to thin so gradually that Jessica hardly noticed the change until she saw the first building in New Mayhem. It was Nyeusigrube, which meant "den of shadows." Jessica knew the name well.

She leaned against the side of the building, her legs suddenly weak as the truth slugged her in the gut.

She was all but numb from shock, but not from denial. She believed; she had no choice but to believe.

The black rose had been the symbol of the vampires for more than five hundred years; that alone was daunting. But five hundred years might have been the blink of an eye to some of Ash Night's characters, and for a moment Jessica felt the weight of all the lives she had juggled in her books. Thousands of years' worth of love and hate and pain and pleasure had somehow been compressed into Jessica's subconscious mortal mind.

For a moment she wondered if she should just stay here instead of returning to her human world. She could disappear, as Mayhem had disappeared three hundred years before.

But as tempting as the world of Ash Night might be, Jessica knew that a human in New Mayhem was seen as a lower being. In comparison to the vampires, mortals were weak, foolish children. Jessica's pride would not allow her to be submissive to these characters whose every weakness she had written about.

However, there was no way for her to simply turn back and ignore what she knew. Instead, she had an irrational desire—no, a *need*—to see the creatures of her novels.

In a daze, she made her way to the heart of New Mayhem, not hesitating to push open the door and enter the chaos known as Las Noches.

Jessica couldn't tell if it was the room or her head that was spinning. Her reflection was distorted wildly by the shattered mirrors, and the black wooden furniture seemed to dance in the moving lights.

As she stood just inside the door, she was hit by such a strong sense of recognition that she reeled back a step. She knew almost everyone in the room.

A slender, dark-skinned woman leaned against the bar. She lifted the crystal glass she held and sipped from it a viscous red liquid that Jessica had no desire to identify. She did recognize the vampire, though: it was Fala.

Fala looked up, and her black eyes immediately fell on the human author with distaste.

*Welcome to my world.* Fala's icy voice echoed through Jessica's mind, sending a chill down her spine. *Or is it your world?*

Jessica knew she was being tested, but she only shook her head. *It isn't mine,* she thought in answer, knowing Fala would hear her.

*Damn right.* The ancient vampire lifted her glass as if to propose a toast. *To knowledge, and to pain.*

Understanding the threat, Jessica turned away and left quickly. She had no wish to engage in any kind of confrontation with Fala.

Outside Las Noches she stopped and leaned against the cool wall, waiting for her dizziness to subside. But after a minute or so, she forced herself to move. Though vampires were not allowed to kill humans inside New Mayhem, Jessica doubted that anyone would object to Fala's making an exception in the case of the author Ash Night.

# CHAPTER 18

JESSICA WAS BARELY OUT of New Mayhem, still in the woods that surrounded the single path back to the human world, when she heard the rustle of leaves behind her.

Spinning to face the potential threat, she let out a tight breath as she saw Aubrey.

He had murdered any illusion of the human Alex Remington. The golden pendant had been replaced by a spiked dog collar, and he was wearing a black T-shirt that hugged his form and showed off the many designs on his arms: Fenris on the right wrist, and Echidna, the Greek mother of all monsters, high on his left arm. The Norse world serpent was wrapped around his left wrist, and a new design had recently been added: Cerberus, the three-headed dog who guarded the gates of Hades. The World Serpent was partially covered by a black leather knife sheath, which held the silver knife Aubrey had taken from a vampire hunter a few thousand years earlier.

His hair was slightly tousled, as if he'd been running, and a few strands fell across his face.

Looking at him now, Jessica couldn't imagine how she had ever mistaken him for a human. But illusion was Aubrey's art. And it was simple to fool people who expected nothing else.

For the moment, Aubrey appeared to be exactly what he was: stunning, mischievous, and completely deadly all at once. She could feel the aura of power that hung about him, a tangible sensation like a cool pocket in the still night air. Here, outside the confines of the sunlit world, Aubrey was every inch the dark, seductive vampire of popular myth.

"Leaving so soon?" he asked, glancing for a moment back at New Mayhem.

Jessica's thoughts turned to Fala. "I might have stayed longer, but the threats were a bit discouraging." Her tone was light, despite the truth in her words. She had always preferred sarcasm and jokes to fear and pleading.

"Many are calling for your blood," Aubrey answered seriously, "but there are actually very few of my kind who would dare to kill you."

She could not read the emotion in his face as he spoke those words, but there was something there, just beneath the surface—a meaning she was missing. However, she knew the danger of holding a vampire's gaze, so she didn't try to read the truth in his eyes as she otherwise might have done.

Instead she stepped forward, on the offensive. She was tired of this guessing. "I suppose you're one of the few," she said, but somehow the words didn't ring true.

Aubrey's voice when he answered was soft. "I'm one of the reasons they wouldn't dare."

"And why is that?" she pressed, moving still closer.

He didn't respond, but instead watched her, the look in his eyes disconcertingly intense.

"I don't like being toyed with, Aubrey," Jessica announced, forcing her thoughts back into focus. "If you or anyone else is planning to kill me, then get on with it. I have better things to do than wait for you to act."

Aubrey looked vaguely amused, but at the same time she could tell he was becoming defensive. She knew he wasn't used to hearing any human speak to him boldly. Still, he raised an eyebrow, inviting her to continue.

She answered by slapping him, hard enough that his head snapped to the side and her palm stung.

The act had not been planned. Impatience and anger and confusion had been rising in her system for too long and had simply reached their zenith.

She had wanted him to take her seriously, and now he would. The expression on his face had changed to pure shock. Jessica knew that he would kill most humans for less, but right now she was too stirred up to feel afraid.

# CHAPTER 19

AUBREY'S AGITATION rivaled Jessica's. He had never been more surprised by a human than he was at this moment. Despite the fact that she had just committed a shockingly reckless act, the expression on her face was utterly fearless.

She stepped forward again, aggressive. Her ebony hair tumbled down past her shoulders like a waterfall of midnight.

"Well? What does your kind want with me?" she demanded. "Why am I not dead already?"

"That seems to be a point of dispute," he answered, trying to keep his voice nonchalant.

"You're the only one here. What's stopping you?" she challenged, meeting his gaze without the slightest hesitation.

She stood in front of him, arms across her chest, head held high as if she was looking down at him, black hair shaken back from her face, green eyes strong and defiant. Her entire stance screamed "predator."

A predatory mind-set was something one was or was not born with. Even some vampires still acted like prey. Jessica acted as if she was afraid of nothing.

"Well?" she said, stepping forward again. She was intentionally invading his space, forcing him to react.

"What do you want from me?" Aubrey asked finally. Her mind was a blank to him at the moment. Despite all the years he had spent learning to manipulate every situation, he had no idea what she wanted him to do.

"I know as much about your kind as you do," Jessica said. "Probably more. I've written it all down and allowed other humans to read it. I've even told them about the only fight you've ever really lost in your life. And I'm not going to stop writing, no matter how many times your kind threatens me with death. I'm not afraid of the inevitable." She took one more step forward so that she was all but spitting her words in his face. "What do you want to do about it?"

Jessica looked into his eyes fearlessly. She stood so close that he could feel her breath, but he held his ground, his arms motionless at his sides. They were locked into a challenge that was like a confrontation between two wild cats, each refusing to be the first to look away.

Aubrey was struck by the color of her eyes: a perfect green he had never before seen in any human — somehow impossibly deep. For a moment he experienced the disorientation that he knew his own gaze had so often caused.

His shock was now complete. Jessica had looked into his eyes brazenly, and *he* had been the one caught.

He blinked once, trying to clear his mind, and his thoughts returned to her question.

Over the past few days, he had occasionally wanted to throttle her for her unrealized knowledge and stubborn innocence, and he had once or twice entertained the idea of simply sinking his teeth into that fair and tender throat, which the outfit she wore tonight displayed so well. Most often, though, he had had the urge to do exactly what he wanted to do right now.

"What do I want to do about it?" he mused aloud.

Jessica gasped as he wrapped an arm around her waist and pulled her forward to close the few remaining inches between them. Before she could react, he caught her lips with his own. The kiss was strong but over quickly, and then he willed himself away.

# CHAPTER 20

JESSICA STOOD STUNNED for a few minutes after Aubrey had disappeared; then she flopped back
against a tree and tried to make sense of the world.

She had thought she was facing death tonight. She
had resolved to face it unflinchingly. Instead . . .

The scene replayed in her mind, frame by frame. The
stillness while she had waited for Aubrey to answer her
challenge. The vision of him standing there like a creature formed from the very breath of night.

Finally there had been the brief sensation of his lips
on hers, over before she could respond, but potent
enough to make every thought in her mind lose its co-
hesiveness.

If he had simply killed her, she would have understood. But this . . . this she could not explain.

The night air did nothing to cool her thoughts as she
headed home, finally slipping into the house at nearly
one in the morning.

Sleep eluded her, so she paced in her room for nearly

an hour before turning on the computer with the hope of losing herself in her writing. Sometime shortly before sunrise, exhaustion finally claimed her restless mind. She dreamed.

*For a few moments, Jazlyn didn't know what had happened or who she was. She had vague memories of meeting a witch who called herself Monica Smoke, a witch who offered to give her back her hard-lost humanity.*

*But why had the witch made this offer? Why had Jazlyn accepted? Everything was so faint in her mind. Monica had been afraid to even speak to Jazlyn. Why had she given back the life that Jazlyn had willingly tossed away?*

*Jazlyn's mind drifted back to the night she had died.*

*She had known for years the black-haired, green-eyed creature who called himself Siete, and she had been offered immortality often. She had refused every time. After all, she was twenty-five, she had a husband, and life was perfect.*

*Siete had twice changed humans against their wills, and both times the result had been disastrous, so he accepted Jazlyn's refusals with good grace.*

*Then everything had changed. Carl, the love of her life, her husband for three years, was hit by a drunk driver. He died in a hospital bed while she wept in the waiting room.*

*Her parents had both passed away several years before, and her friends were few and far between. There was no shoulder she could cry on. The only one who was there for her was the immortal Siete.*

*She still said no. Immortality was not what she wanted. Immortality without Carl was meaningless. She wanted only to be left alone and given time to grieve. Even this was denied her—*

A knock on the door woke Jessica.

She lifted her head from the desktop and rubbed her eyes as she heard Anne call her name. According to Jessica's computer, it was now just past ten in the morning.

Sleeping at her desk for five hours had left her with some kinks in her neck. She stood and stretched, then shut down her computer and opened the door to answer Anne.

Anne, wearing her Sunday best, had been about to knock on Jessica's door again.

"Are you running early or is my clock wrong?" Jessica asked, confused as to why Anne was all dressed up for church when she didn't need to leave for another hour.

"I told Hasana Rashida I'd meet up with her for a coffee before the service," Anne explained. "Hasana is your friend Caryn's mother. Have you met her?"

Jessica nodded once and managed not to add anything that might offend Anne.

"Caryn will be with us, if you'd like to come," Anne added hopefully. She offered the invitation every week, though Jessica never accepted.

Part of Jessica's dream gnawed at her: Monica *Smoke*. If anyone would know about Jazlyn, Monica's relatives would.

However, she had no desire to make small talk with Caryn and Hasana, so she declined the offer, deciding instead to speak with one of them outside the church. She took a shower and dressed slowly while Anne gathered her belongings and left the house.

Walking, Jessica reached the church about fifteen minutes before the service was scheduled to start. She waited at the corner of the building as Hasana, Caryn, and Anne approached, laughing. She didn't try to get their attention, and vaguely realized that she reminded herself of one of her characters, stalking prey.

As Hasana and Anne became lost in the crowd near the church doors, Jessica caught Caryn's arm.

"Caryn, I need to talk to you," she said in a hushed tone.

The girl jumped a bit but seemed to relax when she saw who had grabbed her. They slipped out of the group and into a less crowded area of the church-yard.

"About?" Caryn asked.

But before Jessica could answer, Caryn gasped. Her face froze in a look of horror as she pointed toward the side wall of the church.

It took Jessica a few moments to register what Caryn was seeing. The second she did, she bounded across the yard—toward Anne and the vampire who had her in his grasp.

Jessica didn't recognize the vampire, which she supposed was a good sign; if she hadn't written about him, he probably wasn't very strong. She was counting on that fact.

Tearing the vampire away from Anne, she slammed her fist into his jaw before he could even figure out what was happening. Anne stumbled back against the wall, and Caryn and Hasana, from opposite ends of the churchyard, hurried to her side. The rest of the church-goers, clearly under the mind control of the vampire, continued to chat and make their way cheerfully into the building.

Before Jessica had a chance to check on Anne, the vampire turned and hit her hard enough that she found herself on the ground, her head spinning.

The vampire looked nervously from the witches and Anne to the group of people near the doors of the church, and Jessica could all but see his thoughts. If Caryn and Hasana interfered, he wouldn't be able to keep his control over the crowd, and this confrontation would get even messier.

Then he looked at Jessica, staring fiercely at her for one long moment. She tried to stand but couldn't find her balance; he had probably given her a concussion with that little love tap. She braced herself for his next strike. But he was gone.

Why had he left when he could have killed her in an instant? Suddenly last night's conversation popped back into her head.

*There are actually very few of my kind who would dare to kill you.*

*I suppose you're one of the few.*

*I'm one of the reasons they wouldn't dare.*

"Thank you, Aubrey," she said softly.

Caryn moved from Anne's side to Jessica's. Her face was pale, and she said nothing for a moment.

Jessica tried again to stand, and a wave of blackness passed over her vision. Caryn put a hand on her arm to help her up, then gently touched the side of Jessica's head where the vampire had hit her.

Jessica jerked back when she felt the warm wave of energy that flowed out of Caryn.

"Jessica—"

"I'm fine," she snapped, infuriated by her own weakness. She refused to accept help from Caryn.

But as she pulled away, she forced herself to add, "Thank you." The dizziness was gone completely.

As her thoughts focused, Jessica asked, "What about Anne?"

Caryn looked at her mother, who just shook her head.

Jessica's legs went out from under her.

"Jessica, I'm sorry . . ." Hasana was speaking, but Jessica hardly heard the words.

Caryn tried to take her hand, but she shook it off and went to Anne's side.

Anne was pale, but Jessica could tell that it wasn't blood loss that had killed her. The vampire hadn't had the time, so instead he had broken her neck.

She balled her hands into fists, so tightly that her nails drew blood from her palms. Why had he killed her? He had done so intentionally, not just to feed.

As she took the dead woman's hand, Jessica saw a piece of paper tucked into Anne's grip. Pulling it out, she needed to read no more than the first line before she recognized it as a page from the *Dark Flame* manuscript. It was a page on which Fala was described.

Scrawled on the back, in sharp black ink, were four words: *Stay in your place.*

Jessica found herself shaking with anger—at the nameless vampire who had killed Anne, and especially at Fala, who must have put him up to it.

Fala would never have been able to convince one of her kind to go directly against Aubrey, even if for some reason she hadn't wanted to kill Jessica with her own hands. But Anne was free and defenseless prey.

Hasana put a hand on Jessica's shoulder. "Come, Jessica. There are other people to deal with this. You don't need to stay here."

Jessica shrugged out of Hasana's grip, still looking at the only human who had ever bothered to care for her.

# CHAPTER 21

AUBREY PACED IN HIS ROOM, as he'd done shortly after he'd first met Jessica Allodola, trying to reason out his emotions. It was nearly noon, and he was still awake; that alone was enough to make him irritable. Coupled with his confusion about last night's confrontation, he was very much in the mood to pick a fight.

She had stared him down. He couldn't help respecting her for it. Not to mention her all-but-suicidal challenge—

*Not so suicidal,* he reminded himself, interrupting his own thought. *She won, after all.*

Jessica was like a sand viper: beautiful, not apparently formidable, but fearless and deadly poisonous.

"Damn you, Fala," he whispered as the vampire's taunt echoed in his head: *If I didn't know better, I'd say you were attracted to her.* "Why aren't you ever wrong?"

Of course, there was more than the physical attraction Fala had speculated about. The actuality was far more dangerous both to his own position—as was any emotional attachment to a human—and to Jessica if any of his many enemies guessed the truth.

Furious with himself for letting this girl get under his skin, he went into Las Noches, where he was immediately intercepted by Fala herself. Apparently he wasn't the only one who couldn't sleep this morning.

"You didn't kill her," Fala accused as soon as she saw him. "She was strutting around our land as if she owned it, practically begging for death, and *you didn't kill her.*"

"No, I didn't," he answered in a growl.

"Aubrey—"

"What is your obsession with killing this one human?" he snapped.

"She's a threat," Fala answered calmly, obviously pleased by how close he was to losing his control. She looked almost amused, which made him wary. Fala was clever; she was the one most likely to figure out his feelings toward Jessica.

"And how is that?" he argued. "Just because she writes about things that almost every vampire in the world already knows and most mortals disregard as fiction?"

"*Most* is the key word there, Aubrey," Fala chided. "Have you forgotten those not-quite-insignificant mortals called vampire hunters? Kala is *dead*, Aubrey. Your blood sister, Ather's second fledgling. And she was run through by a witch practically on the front steps of Las Noches. That witch wouldn't even have known this place *existed* if it hadn't been for Ash Night."

"Jessica had nothing to do with Dominique Vida's

finding Las Noches," Aubrey argued. "And since when are you afraid of vampire hunters?"

Fala let out a half-curse, half-scream as she began to lose her temper. "What is she going to write next, Aubrey? The only reason she's gotten this far is because *you're* protecting her. Fine, you've established your power. Now why don't you just *kill* her?"

He turned away from her, refusing to answer.

Behind him Fala snickered. "It's true, isn't it? You're attracted to her. I was right all along."

Aubrey reeled back around as her words hit him.

"She's a good-looking young woman, I'll admit," Fala continued. "But that isn't the issue, is it? You've—"

"Fala," he warned, his voice dangerous.

"It isn't that unusual, you know," she continued, sounding even more amused. "It's our line's curse, you could say. *Love.*" She spat the word as if it was some kind of insect.

Finally Aubrey's voice returned. "No truer than in your case. Isn't that *curse,* as you put it, why you're here? Isn't that why Jager changed you in the first place?" Jager and Fala had met while she'd been awaiting death in one of the sandy cells of ancient Egypt. He had changed her the same day. It was still obvious to any idiot how fond they were of each other.

Fala started to retaliate, but he continued. "Not to mention Moira. It seems that the awful, infectious disease has hit you several times." Fala's eyes narrowed at the mention of her beloved Moira.

Then she sighed. "Look what she's done to you, Aubrey," she said, her voice soft, almost sympathetic. "Kill her . . . or change her. If you're really so fond of her, give her your blood. Do whatever you want with her, but *stop* her." She paused, suddenly unnerved. "You know, Silver once gave Jager this same advice — about Kaei."

Aubrey remembered the argument, which had occurred shortly after Kaei had sliced open Silver's arm and shortly before she had set fire to most of Mayhem.

"I hardly think that's relevant," Aubrey answered. "Jessica certainly isn't going to —"

"I think it's very relevant," Fala interrupted. "Jager refused to kill her."

# CHAPTER 22

HASANA HAD INSISTED that Jessica go home with them, instead of staying with the police and the medical units. No matter what her personal feelings toward Jessica, Hasana was still a mother, and Jessica could see the motherly care in everything she did.

Jessica refused at first to go anywhere with the Smoke family, but she gave in when Hasana had Caryn go fetch her belongings—including her computer. At least they understood that she wouldn't go anywhere without a way to write.

Her anger over Anne's death had been replaced by a dismal apathy so overpowering that when she was confronted, the moment she stepped through the Rashidas' door, by Dominique Vida, she didn't even bother to make a biting response.

Dominique, despite her classic beauty, had all the social skills and warmth of an icicle. The air near her hummed with strictly controlled energy. Perhaps the apathy was helpful; otherwise, Jessica might have been tempted to kill Dominique on the spot.

Unlike the Smoke line, Jessica knew Dominique and her kin well. Dominique had murdered so many of the vampires that Jessica had known and cared for that the girl had developed a deep hatred for the witch before she had even met her.

Only when Caryn put a hand on her shoulder did Jessica realize that she was glaring death in Dominique's direction. The vampire hunter was fully returning the glare.

"What is *she* doing here?" Dominique demanded.

Caryn took the initiative to lead Jessica away and into a guest room while Hasana dealt with Dominique's questions.

"You should get some rest," Caryn suggested, trying to pull Jessica out of her inner world of death and pain and hatred.

"Only if there's a way to make sure no one kills me in my sleep," Jessica answered, looking out the door as if Dominique might walk down the hall any moment.

Caryn looked horrified. "She wouldn't . . ." She trailed off. "Why would she want to hurt you?"

Jessica shrugged. That question had an easy answer at least. "Because I can't help hating her," she answered truthfully. "And because she knows I would rather be a vampire than risk being their prey." Jessica thought back to poor Anne, who was just as dead no matter how many vampires Dominique and her kin had killed.

"I'll keep that in mind," answered Dominique, who

had just entered the room, with Hasana behind her. Caryn paled.

"No one is going to hurt anyone in my household," Hasana said firmly. "Jessica, you don't know what you're saying right now —"

"She knows," Dominique interrupted. Turning to Jessica, she said bluntly, "If you'd rather be with them, then go. I won't stop you. But if you choose their side, then I won't protect you, either."

"I don't need your protection," Jessica growled in answer.

"Jessica, please, get some rest," Hasana coaxed. "Dominique, leave the poor girl alone. Her mother was just murdered." She ushered Dominique out of the room. The hunter went willingly; she had said all she needed to say.

Jessica had no desire to sleep, and she told Caryn as much.

"You should try," Caryn answered. "It will help clear your mind."

Instead, Jessica began to pace.

Caryn caught her arm, and only a few seconds later, sleep enveloped her. Later the thought occurred to her that despite Caryn's usual passivity, she was still a strong witch. She had easily induced sleep in Jessica's strained mind.

*Jazlyn said no. Immortality was not what she wanted. She wanted to be left alone and given time to grieve. Even this was denied her.*

*A week after Carl's death, Jazlyn learned that she was pregnant. Looking at her, no one would have been able to tell, but the tests had returned positive.*

*Why would the universe not leave her alone? She was only twenty-five, and she was a widow. How could she raise a child by herself? Carl's child deserved better than what she, who was still in mourning, could provide.*

*A cruel God gave her this life.*

*The next time Siete visited, Jazlyn did not say no. She knew that whatever life she woke up in would not be the life she was leaving.*

*But any decision made out of desperation is later regretted. The world of eternal night and lawlessness was no better than the human world she had fled, yet Jazlyn had no more choices.*

*The years passed and faded, meaningless and empty. Often Jazlyn found herself remembering things like the beach on which Carl had proposed. She remembered being married outdoors and honeymooning in France.*

*Tears came frequently. This was not what she had wanted at all.*

*Just past Valentine's Day 1983, Jazlyn visited Carl's grave for the first time since his funeral. She brushed off the thin layer of snow and read the stone for the first time: "Carl Raisa, 1932–1960. 'I shall smile from Heaven upon those I love. My death is not my end, and in Heaven shall I meet my beloved again.'"*

*But he wouldn't, because she was never going to reach Heaven. Her kind was evil; she had killed so many times to sate the bloodlust that she would never be forgiven.*

*Jazlyn lay weeping in the snowy graveyard that Valentine's night, wondering why the world had chosen her to torment.*

*That was where the witch who called herself Monica Smoke had found her — weeping there for the one she loved. Monica was the first one in more than twenty years who offered her a shoulder to cry on. Then she heard the story and gave Jazlyn the one thing she had thought could never be returned: her life.*

# CHAPTER 23

AS SOON AS SHE WOKE, Jessica sought out her hostesses. Avoiding Dominique Vida, she quickly found Caryn in her room.

"Do you know of anyone in your line called Monica?" she demanded, closing the door behind her.

"Yes," Caryn said after a moment of hesitation. "She was my aunt, my mother's sister."

"Was?"

"She died. Mother never told me how." Caryn frowned. "Why, Jessica. What's wrong?"

Jessica didn't answer, her mind focused on her own questions. "Have you ever heard of someone called Jazlyn Raisa?" Jessica was determined to understand her own birth, even if that was the only part of her life she did understand.

"Jazlyn Raisa . . . No. But maybe my mother would."

Jessica nodded quickly.

"Jessica, what is this about?"

She shook off the question, impatient to find Hasana and hear the truth.

As Jessica entered the kitchen, Hasana looked up from whatever she was cooking. She seemed to sense Jessica's urgency.

"Jessica, do you need something?"

"Jazlyn Raisa," Jessica answered without prelude. "I want to know about her."

Hasana's face betrayed her mistrust. She paused, taking a breath, and then asked, "What do you know about Raisa?"

"She was a vampire, a direct fledging of Siete," Jessica answered. "And your sister offered to give her back her life."

Hasana's eyes narrowed. "I didn't believe it was possible, but Monica insisted she could do it. She died trying, and I heard nothing more about it."

"She succeeded," Jessica filled in.

"Raisa didn't deserve it," Hasana growled. "If you know so much, why are you asking me?"

"Jazlyn was pregnant when Siete changed her," Jessica explained, and she saw shock fill Hasana's expression. "I want to know what would have happened to the child when Jazlyn became human again."

The idea seemed far-fetched. Though Jessica knew plenty about her vampires, she knew nothing about anyone who had ever become human again besides what her dreams had told of Jazlyn. Only a witch would know if a baby carried in a vampiric womb would regain its life with its mother.

"I didn't know there was a child," Hasana whispered.

"Now I understand. Monica wouldn't have risked her life to save a vampire. But a baby . . . Monica must have believed that it would survive."

"What happened to the child?" Jessica shouted. She had to force herself not to grab Hasana by the shoulders and try to shake the information from her.

"I didn't know there was one," Hasana repeated, shaking her head apologetically. Jessica turned away and returned to the room she'd been given, needing to think.

Her mother. The term brought a moment of pain. The woman who had raised her was dead; now she had been replaced by a phantom who had never wanted Jessica. Jazlyn Raisa.

Jessica paced softly in her room, trying to organize her thoughts.

Siete was the first of the vampires. He was ancient, even compared to Fala and Jager and Silver, and his mind was powerful enough that he could easily know everything that Jessica had written. His blood ran through her veins as surely as it had run through her mother's, and her link to him was no doubt as strong as the link he had with his fledglings. The difference was that she was human and had no shields against his mind. So when she slept or simply drifted, she shared his dreams and his thoughts.

The puzzle had come together finally.

Jessica's gaze fell on her computer. Without making a conscious decision to do so, she sat down and booted it up, wanting to hear the comforting hum.

The familiar compulsion struck her. But ignoring

the book she had been working on, she began another, though she had no idea how this one was going to end.

*The night is full of mystery. Even when the moon is brightest, secrets hide everywhere. Then the sun rises and its rays cast so many shadows that the day creates more illusion than all the veiled truth of the night.*

Several hours and many pages passed before the flow of thoughts ceased. Who, she wondered, would finish it if she died?

# CHAPTER 24

NEEDING TO GET AWAY from the magic-choked atmosphere of the house, Jessica slipped out of her room and down the stairs.

"Where are you going, Jessica? I'm just about to serve dinner."

She froze, hearing Hasana's voice, and turned to see Dominique and Hasana standing together in the next room.

"I was planning to go for a walk, perhaps wander in the woods a bit," she answered. "Is there something wrong with that?"

Hasana sighed. "Jessica, do you really think you should be going out there alone?" Jessica could hear a hint of annoyance in her voice.

"Do *you* really think I can stay inside until Dominique has killed all the vampires?" Jessica snapped in return. She knew Hasana was trying to help, but she felt like a wolf caged in the shepherd's barn.

"I could at least deal with a few of them," Dominique

said, watching Jessica as if for a reaction. "After a while, the others will probably decide you aren't worth the trouble."

"After you *murder* another dozen or so of them," Jessica choked out. She had a sudden, vivid image of Aubrey with Dominique's knife in his heart. She would not wish Dominique even upon Fala.

"It isn't murder to kill something that died thousands of years ago," Dominique argued. "Murder is what *they* do every night, when even you know they don't need to kill in order to feed. Murder is what they did yesterday to your mother."

Jessica took an involuntary step toward Dominique and felt the first warning strike from the hunter: a slight burning sensation on the surface of her skin, which flared for a moment and then faded.

Hasana put a hand on Dominique's arm to get her attention. "Dominique, I hardly think that comment was necessary."

Dominique sighed. "If she's going to be staying in this house with you and Caryn, then I need to know whose side she's on," she asserted. "Well, Jessica?"

"If it's a choice between you and them," Jessica spat in answer, "then I would choose the vampires any day. At least they don't preach the morality of their killing."

She spun away, trying to ignore the tension between her shoulders, where she expected any moment to feel the point of Dominique's knife.

# CHAPTER 25

IT WAS NOT YET SUNSET when Jessica arrived, once again, at the doorway to Las Noches.

There were fewer people in the room than the last time, which was probably related to the fact that Fala and Aubrey were fighting near the bar.

They stopped in surprise as Jessica entered and began walking fearlessly toward them.

Fala recovered her wits first and slammed Aubrey back into the bar. The sickening crack of a broken bone reached Jessica's ears even above the music of Las Noches, but she knew he would heal almost instantly.

However, Fala used Aubrey's moment of pain to whisper a threat into his ear. Jessica could only hear the end of it as she approached. *Either deal with it now, or I will.*

Fala left the club without giving Jessica a second glance.

Aubrey stretched, already recovered from Fala's attack. As he turned toward Jessica, she saw him check for the knife at his waist, then shake his head, seeming neither surprised nor concerned to find it gone.

"You're an idiot, you know that?" Aubrey said as Jessica approached. "We both are."

"How do you figure that?" Jessica asked. She ignored the fight that she had just witnessed; she knew she was probably the reason behind it.

Parched from the walk in the sunlight, she considered trying to find something to drink in Las Noches's bar, but worried that she might knock herself out if she chose the wrong thing. While there was nothing in the bar that could kill a vampire, there was plenty that could damage a human.

"You know most of my kind is trying to kill you— particularly the one who just left—and still you come into New Mayhem at sunset," Aubrey answered dryly.

Jessica had to laugh at that. "My mother was killed yesterday beside a church in broad daylight. If any of your kind was really trying to kill me, it wouldn't matter where I was."

She decided that she could probably identify water if she saw it, so she rounded the bar to search.

"Are you trying to poison yourself?" Aubrey inquired, watching her.

"Oh, bite me," she taunted automatically, before the irony of the remark registered.

But Aubrey took her at her word. In a graceful movement, he wrapped a hand around the back of her neck and pulled her toward him.

"A tempting offer." He gently brushed the hollow of her throat with the thumb of his free hand as he spoke.

"You wouldn't."

He leaned down and she felt his lips at her neck. *It would never occur to you to be afraid, would it?* he silently asked.

*If you wanted to kill me, you would have done so long ago.* She projected the thought and knew that he could hear it.

*Are you so sure?*

*No,* she answered. *But if you bite me I'm going to bite back, and do you really want this crowd to see a human do that?* She was well aware that they had an attentive audience by now.

*Is that what* you *want?*

Jessica didn't quite understand Aubrey's question, but he must have sensed her confusion, because he added, *I did something similar to Ather, and we both know how that turned out.* Aubrey had been changed shortly after a fight with Ather. He had slit her throat when she had tried to feed on him. *Even Fala has suggested that I change you.*

*You're right, you* are *an idiot,* she commented in response. *And yes, that is what I want, which means you can't do it.*

Jessica was referring to the fact that Aubrey's line retained its power because every one of them fought. That struggle, as the blood was drained out, was what gave them their strength.

Yes, Jessica was more than willing to become one of their kind. Her hatred of Dominique had finally convinced her. But her readiness meant that she wouldn't fight, and her strength as a vampire would suffer. She would certainly be weaker than Fala. In essence, if

Aubrey changed her now, it would be the same as his allowing Fala to kill her.

Aubrey knew all this as well, of course, so he released her and she stepped back casually, smoothing her shirt as if the confrontation had been normal. He reached past her, into the bar, and pulled out a bottle of water. She accepted it calmly and took a drink.

# CHAPTER 26

WHAT WAS HE TO DO about the human called Jessica? Aubrey had had that thought before, and the answer was no more forthcoming than it had ever been.

Jessica had no idea how close she'd just come to having every drop of blood drained from her body. The feel of her pulse beneath his lips had almost broken even his self-control.

He needed to hunt, but he hesitated to leave her alone. Fala's threat was still fresh in his mind.

The decision was made for him as he heard a faint cry coming from just outside the building. It was a distressed voice he knew well: the voice of Kaei. That girl could get herself into more scrapes in an hour than most humans could accumulate in a year.

Nodding a silent goodbye to Jessica, he quickly made his way to Kaei's side. She could be a nuisance and worse to those who treated her badly, and had caused more than her fair share of trouble, but she was unwaveringly loyal to those she considered her friends.

Fala would probably not attack Jessica in a crowd, and even if she did, Jessica was intelligent enough to fend her off for a minute or two until he returned. Kaei did not have a talent for getting herself out of trouble.

Almost the instant he appeared, he found himself on the defensive. A strike meant for Kaei hit him hard, mostly because he was unprepared. The mental blow had the distinct aura of a witch to it, so he quickly turned his attention to the attacker.

He swore aloud as he recognized Dominique Vida. She had probably followed Jessica here and run into Kaei on the way. Kaei had had more than her share of arguments with witches.

Dominique fell back slightly into a stance of readiness, recognizing that she suddenly had a new, far more powerful foe.

Dominique was one of two vampire hunters who had ever won a fight against anyone in Aubrey's line. The other one he had dealt with accordingly. As for Dominique, no one had managed to get inside her guard sufficiently to plant a knife.

For a moment he was grateful Fala had taken his knife from him during their fight earlier. Dominique could have used it against him; her ancestors' magic had forged it.

Then Jessica returned to his thoughts. As much as he'd like to draw out this confrontation with such a worthy foe, he didn't have time to dally here with Dominique.

Instead, he did the only thing he could to get her out of the place.

He changed shape into the one he favored—a black

wolf—and lunged, taking Dominique to the ground. She didn't expect him to be so reckless, which was the only reason her knife swiped across his stomach instead of plunging into his heart.

He clenched his teeth against the pain as the silver blade sliced his skin open. The wound was shallow, but the magic in the knife made it burn. He would likely have a scar.

Before the witch could recover, he used his mind to bring them both far away from New Mayhem. Then he rolled off her and sprinted, gaining as much distance as he could. Once he was far enough away that she could no longer latch on to his power and follow him, he disappeared, returning to Las Noches with a prayer that Jessica would still be there.

# CHAPTER 27

JESSICA CUT THROUGH THE WOODS on her way back to Caryn and Hasana's house. A small river ran behind New Mayhem; it went through Red Rock Forest and eventually tapered off into Aqua Pond, which was close to the witches' home. She followed that river instead of taking the less direct route along the roads. As she had said to Aubrey, if anything wished to kill her, it would do so just as easily in the woods as on the road or anywhere else. She was too tired to take the long way.

At one point she paused to admire the full moon as it bounced and flickered on the river's surface. In the midst of that peaceful moment, someone grabbed her by the throat from behind.

"So the author would grace me with her presence." The mocking voice was one Jessica recognized instantly: Fala's. Jessica could feel the vampire's cool breath on the back of her neck; it sent a shiver down her spine.

"Leave me alone," Jessica said, her voice calm despite her fear. If Fala had decided to kill her, then she would not be swayed by groveling or cries for mercy. She would probably enjoy hearing them, but they wouldn't motivate her to do any less damage. Talking, at least, might buy time — time in which Fala might simply grow bored, or Aubrey might show up to beat her into a bloody pulp.

"Ha!" Fala exclaimed. "After all the trouble you've caused?"

Jessica had no time to answer; Fala shoved her, nearly sending her into the icy river. She turned back around in time to watch Fala approach.

"You human fool," Fala said, smirking. "You act so sure, so unafraid, so . . . *important*, as if you can't be killed just as easily as any other human. Just like your mother—"

"What do you know about my mother?" Jessica felt her anger rise at the reference, and again she saw Anne in her mind's eye — not killed by Fala's hand, but dead by her order nonetheless.

Fala's smirk widened. "About Raisa, you mean?" she asked sweetly. "About that poor, selfish half-wit Siete had us all practically baby-sitting for? I was there when she gave birth," Fala spat. "I would have killed you on the spot if Siete hadn't told me not to."

Jessica recoiled, the slow-boiling rage that was emanating from Fala, overshadowing even Jessica's surprise. So this was the reason for her hatred. Jessica knew Fala too well not to understand how she reacted to commands.

Once again Fala didn't give her time to respond, but

instead disappeared. Jessica turned to search for her and felt a sharp tug on her hair. Fala was behind her again.

"Ever heard of fighting fair?" Jessica barked, grabbing the hand that was holding her hair, though it was strong as a steel clamp and not about to be forced open.

"Life isn't fair, and neither is death," Fala answered, yanking harder. As she did so, the tight grip forced Jessica's head back, baring her throat. "But I'll make it a bit more sporting. . . ."

Fala drew a knife that had been hidden in her tight clothing and flashed it in front of Jessica's face for a moment before she threw it across the clearing. Jessica couldn't see where it landed, but she heard the thump as it hit a tree. "Maybe I'll even give you a chance to retrieve it if I get bored, Jessie."

"Don't call me Jessie." It was an automatic reaction and was rewarded by another yank, and then a pain, sharp and strong, as Fala's teeth pierced the skin at her throat.

The pain faded quickly, replaced by a floating sensation as five thousand years of vampiric mind pressed against her own. Fala wrapped an arm around Jessica's waist, holding her in place as well as keeping her standing when she finally lost awareness of her body.

Jessica was weightless—sea foam on the back of a wave, or perhaps a feather carried by the breeze.

Then she recognized the trap, and a tendril of fear snaked into her mind. But the pain would begin only if she fought; she could simply stay here, resting—

Before she could let Fala's mind control convince her otherwise, she drove an elbow back into the vampire's gut, at the same time slamming herself back to throw Fala into a tree behind them.

Fala let go with a hiss of rage, and Jessica hurried across the clearing, knowing Fala's injuries would stop her for no more than a few moments. She could feel a trickle of blood sliding down her neck and onto her black shirt, but the wound wasn't likely to be fatal. Fala hadn't had enough time.

*Yet,* she amended as she saw the cold fury in Fala's eyes.

"That's *it,*" Fala hissed. "Do you seek death, Jessica? Or are you just fond of pain?" Each word was filled with venom. "I would have made this so much easier on you, but you chose to do it the hard way."

"I might die, but which one of us will hurt more tomorrow?" Jessica snapped before she could think better of it.

"I will be very sure you feel every drop of life as it leaves your veins," Fala threatened, her voice almost a whisper, "and that your body screams when it starts to starve from oxygen loss, and that you hear the silence when your heart finally stops."

She grabbed Jessica by the throat and threw her almost casually into a tree. As Jessica's right shoulder slammed into the trunk, she gritted her teeth past the pain. The bone probably wasn't broken; Fala would do worse before this was over.

"I guess you know what you're describing," Jessica growled, her anger rising above her common sense. "From your days in that sandy, dirty cell where you were chained like the dog you are."

Fala was almost upon her. Jessica struck Fala's

cheekbone with her closed fist, which fazed the vampire for only a second before she caught Jessica's wrist and tossed her into another tree. Jessica's hands and arms hit the tree first, absorbing some of the blow, but then she felt her head and bad shoulder strike the unyielding wood, and black spots danced in front of her eyes. She suspected this was her second concussion in as many days.

"Damn you, human!" Fala spat. "You aren't going to wake up. Your death will be your death. Do you understand? You are prey, and always will be. Mortal . . . weak . . . *prey.*"

Jessica stood painfully, trying to clear her vision. She had far too much pride to face Fala like the feeble prey-beast the vampire saw her as.

"I know your talents at inflicting pain, Fala," she grumbled. "But even with them, you will never make me your prey."

# CHAPTER 28

RAGE FLICKERED across Fala's face for a few seconds, until a lazy, dangerous smile grew to replace it.

*Wise up, child,* came Fala's voice, suddenly smooth and eerily civil. Jessica felt a moment of panic as she heard the voice in her mind—as she felt the words overlaying her own thoughts. Then the fear faded, and there was only the sound of the cool, unarguable voice.

*I've read your writing,* Fala continued calmly, and Jessica had no choice but to listen. *You know the difference between predator and prey. You were born human, and you will die human—prey and nothing more.*

As Fala stepped forward, Jessica moved to meet her. Fala pulled Jessica's hair back yet again to bare her throat, and Jessica relaxed, allowing the vampire to do so. Fala was simply a higher race, and there was no arguing with the fact. By nature she was a predator.

And Jessica was just her prey. . . .

*Prey?*

That last thought didn't sit well. Instead, it brought

crashing down the house of cards Fala had so easily erected in Jessica's mind.

Jessica shoved the vampire away with both arms, ignoring the screaming pain in her right shoulder as she did so.

"Get the hell out of my mind." She spat the words, a hoarse command, and Fala's expression went still, frozen in anger and disbelief. Jessica had slipped her mind control twice now.

"It seems to me that you were human once, Fala," Jessica continued, ignoring the blood that trickled from several of her wounds, and the black spots that bounced along the edge of her vision. "But I suppose you don't need to be reminded of *your* experiences as prey."

Fala's hand whipped forward and clamped over Jessica's throat, pressing her into a tree and cutting off her oxygen. "Watch your words, human. Unless you want me to squeeze your vertebrae straight through your windpipe."

Jessica couldn't answer as she struggled to breathe. Fala let go, throwing her to the ground hard enough to send splinters of pain through the arm she caught herself with.

"You picked the wrong person to fight, Jessica," Fala told her, pacing near her head. "Because I like pain—your pain—and I *really* like causing it."

"That's called sadism, and I think it's some kind of psychological disorder," Jessica grumbled, rolling onto her front so that she could use her left arm to push herself up.

Fala kicked her in the back of the head while she was

still on her knees. "So are suicidal tendencies," she countered.

Black and red spots fought for domination in Jessica's mind as she felt herself being yanked to her feet by one of her injured arms. The world suddenly lost all focus, and she was dropped back to the ground.

"Pitiful," she heard Fala grunt.

Slowly, excruciatingly, Jessica forced herself to her feet as Fala walked away to lounge on the riverbank. Leaning against a tree for support, Jessica touched the back of her head and found it sticky with her own blood.

As soon as she felt capable of walking, Jessica scanned the clearing for the knife that Fala had thrown earlier. She spotted it partially embedded in a tree trunk nearby and staggered to it. She bit her lip to hold back a yelp of pain as she wrapped her hands around the knife's hilt and yanked it from the wood. Both her arms screamed at the effort.

She recognized the blade as Aubrey's and was surprised that Fala had managed to steal it from him. Though simple, it wasn't a knife one would mistake; the word *Fenris* was inscribed in the handle. Jessica knew the damage it could do to vampiric flesh, with all the poisonous magic burned deep into the silver of the blade by the vampire-slayer witch who had forged it. The knife felt almost alive in her hand, and she could feel its magic slither up her arm. Some of the pain dulled.

Never having handled a knife before as a weapon, she had no hope of fatally wounding Fala, but maybe she could hurt her enough that she would go away.

Jessica planted the knife loosely in the tree, a plan slowly forming in her mind.

"So, I see you're walking again," Fala sighed, appearing in front of her only seconds after Jessica had stepped away from the tree. "I must not have hit you hard enough."

Jessica backed up toward the knife, protecting her right arm. The wounded-bird routine was old but effective. Fala wouldn't consider the knife a threat because it would be impossible for Jessica to remove it one-handed, behind her back.

Fala stepped forward again, and Jessica felt behind her with her left arm as she backed up. Her hand was on the knife, but before she could do anything with it, Fala grabbed her again and dragged her forward.

Jessica's vision spun at the sudden movement, and the next instant she felt the sting as Fala's teeth pierced her throat once more.

This time, Fala made no effort to make it easy on her. The pain began instantly, not dulled by mind control or any hint of tenderness.

Though she had written about it many times, Jessica was not prepared. The pain in her head and her arms was nothing compared to the burning, suffocating sensation that now replaced those earlier annoyances. Despite her efforts not to, she heard her own voice shout out, a useless cry.

A wave of blackness spread across her vision, but she managed to fend it off as she yanked an arm free from Fala's grip.

Fala shifted a bit, and Jessica felt as if her skin had just been flayed from her body; she moaned in agony as her knees gave out under her, but somehow, just barely, she was able to grope for the knife.

She pulled the knife forward in an arc, and though she had no strength and no sight with which to aim, the blade glanced off Fala's side, slicing open the vampire's arm.

To a human, the wound would surely have been fatal. If Fala had been weaker, she too might have died. As it was, Jessica was certain it hurt like Hell.

Fala shrieked in rage and pain and hit Jessica, hard, on the left side of her chest. Jessica heard something snap and was knocked backward into the tree, hitting the wound on her head again.

Fala disappeared, cradling her arm against her chest. That was all Jessica saw before she sank into unconsciousness.

# CHAPTER 29

FALA COULD SHIELD HER MIND too well for Aubrey to locate her, and neither Jager nor Moira would help him.

Only twenty minutes had passed since the tussle with Dominique, but he well knew the damage Fala could have done even that quickly. He had spent the time looking for Fala and berating himself for leaving Jessica alone, and little else. He hadn't even bothered to replace the shirt Dominique's knife had bloodied, but had simply tossed it in the trash somewhere.

Now Aubrey paced in Fala's room, waiting for her to return, all the while envisioning the new forms of pain he could introduce her to if she had killed Jessica.

When Fala finally did enter the room, she looked quite a bit worse for wear. Her arm had been sliced open, and blood was still dripping from the slowly healing wound. She was trembling, though Aubrey couldn't tell whether the cause was pain, chill, or rage.

"Damn both of you to Hell and back!" she growled

when she saw him. "Get out of my room or I'll tear out your heart and feed it to Ahemait myself."

Judging by her mood, she might very well try. Ahemait was the Egyptian devourer of the dead. When Fala brought up the mythology of her human background, she was best avoided.

Instead, Aubrey's anger responded to hers.

He slammed her against the wall, his hand around her throat, and heard the crunch as her windpipe broke. The injury would heal quickly, but he could tell that, despite her high tolerance for it, Fala did not appreciate the pain.

She threw a bolt of her power at him and he stumbled back a step. Dodging quickly, he barely avoided his own knife when she threw it at him. The blade stuck in the wall.

"What did you do to her?" he demanded.

"Only what *you* should have done a week ago!" Fala snapped.

This time it was Fala's turn to stumble as Aubrey lashed out, his anger making the blow even harder. "Where is she?" he said quietly, his voice cold.

Fala laughed. "You honestly expect me to tell you?"

Meeting her gaze, Aubrey paused before answering. He saw her expression change as she recognized the complete, smoldering rage in his eyes. "Yes."

"She's somewhere on the river," Fala spat, wise enough to recognize that fighting him at this moment was a dangerous idea. "I hope the crows have gotten to her by now."

Aubrey disappeared, bringing himself to the edge of New Mayhem, where the river passed by.

Once again he changed himself into a wolf, a creature that could move faster and more surely through the woods. Following the river, he covered a mile in only a few minutes. Finally, less than two miles from New Mayhem, in the thick of the forest, he caught Jessica's scent and brought himself instantly to her side.

Jessica was pasty white, her breathing was wet and shallow, and her heart alternated between racing and threatening to stop.

She was alive, but not for long, and he knew no way to help her. Three thousand years of killing had taught him nothing about undoing this kind of damage.

After a moment of hesitation in which he swallowed his pride, he left Jessica's side and brought himself to the home of Hasana and Caryn Smoke. He could sense Caryn's magic, stronger than her mother's, even outside the house.

Had he not killed all his gods long ago, Aubrey would have prayed that Caryn would be willing to help. Anxiously he brought himself to her side.

# CHAPTER 30

CARYN HAD NEARLY FAINTED from fright when Aubrey first appeared in her room, but his rapid explanation had shoved all personal concerns out of the way, making room for the disciplined healer to come forth. She had been working now for nearly an hour.

She was from the oldest known line of healers on Earth, but even her abilities had limits.

She felt weak from fatigue. Her clothing was soaking wet from when she had accidentally fallen in the river, and her heart was beating twice as fast as normal. Her face was stained with worried tears as she chanted and held her left hand, palm down, over Jessica's heart, channeling much-needed energy into the dying girl. Her other hand was constantly moving—soothing Jessica's brow, holding her hand, or drawing power from the earth.

Jessica's heart had been beating evenly for several minutes, but now it skipped once and Caryn gasped in pain, her chant stopping.

"I can't do this." Fresh tears rolled down her face.

"Should I get Hasana?" Aubrey suggested. "Maybe she—"

"She won't," Caryn interrupted, remembering her mother's anger when Jessica had left the house the day before. "She hates your kind and calls Jessica a traitor to the human race. Monica would have helped; she could have done it. But I just *can't*. I can't save her, and I could kill myself trying."

"Is there anyone else?" Aubrey asked, sounding frantic.

"Vida would kill her," Caryn answered, "and Light's dead." She cast Aubrey a sharp glance, knowing that his kind had murdered Lila, the last in the Light line. "All the others are too weak. Whoever did this broke one of her ribs, and now there's blood in one of her lungs; she's going to start drowning in it soon. Besides that, she's just about drained. It's amazing I can even keep her heart beating at all. Plus, she's got at least a dozen other injuries . . . I don't know of anything in science or magic that can heal her."

Caryn looked beseechingly at Aubrey, hoping he knew something she did not.

He knew nothing she wanted to hear. "I can kill—I can't heal," he sighed.

"I've been channeling my own . . . I don't know what to call it . . . *life* into her, but if I keep doing it we're *both* going to die. No witch short of an Arun could survive this, and they're part vampire . . ."

Caryn trailed off, defeated.

"I could."

She looked at Aubrey blankly for a moment after he spoke those words.

"Unless Fala decided to tear her heart out, her injuries are really rather insignificant to my kind," he clarified.

Finally Caryn understood. She had channeled from other witches in the past. If she could take energy from a vampire and give it to Jessica . . . would that heal her?

It might.

"I could kill you accidentally," she warned him.

"I've lived a long time."

"This is very definitely going to get me disowned," she muttered, hoping her mother would find some way to forgive her. "I need you on my right," she told Aubrey.

After he had shifted position, Caryn placed her right hand just above Jessica's heart, one of the three strongest energy centers. For healing, the heart center was best.

There were no words to accurately describe what she did next. Her own energy centers were open, forming a path from Aubrey to Jessica, and now as she tapped into Aubrey's —

She gasped as the power flowed through her. That was all it could possibly be called. Not life, not *chi* as Hasana called it or simply energy as Monica had taught her, but pure, unrestricted *power.* No wonder his mind was so strong . . .

Caryn forced herself to control the power, which required all her years of practice, and then focused on channeling it into Jessica.

Jessica's own aura was strong, and Caryn wasn't surprised to note vampiric traces in it. She directed

Aubrey's power to the areas of Jessica's injuries, where the girl's aura was weakest.

First she focused on the crack in Jessica's skull. It knitted itself together within seconds, and the blood that had pooled inside was reabsorbed into the veins as they repaired themselves.

The lung came next. The organ collapsed into itself and then regrew—small like a child's at first, but quickly expanding to full size. The rib mended in moments.

The rest of Jessica's body healed just as quickly, simply from the overflow of power. Caryn was grateful, since she was becoming sleepy. How could she be so exhausted with all this power running through her?

She was trying very hard not to think about what this process was going to do to her. She knew only one story that involved channeling the vampiric aura: Midnight Smoke, mother of Ardiente Arun, had drawn the vampiric aura into herself to save a human from becoming one of them. Since then, all Midnight's ancestors had carried a vampiric taint. Ardiente and Midnight had split from the line they had been born in and become the first in the Arun line. Caryn was descended from their relations, who had continued the Smoke line.

Caryn was feeling light-headed. There was nothing more she could do for Jessica; if this wasn't enough, then nothing would have worked. She quickly closed off Aubrey's power centers, then her own, aware that if she passed out before doing so she would probably kill all three of them.

With her eyes closed, she focused on Jessica yet again, trying to ascertain what still needed to be done.

While most of her body had healed, Jessica was still all too human. The newly healed areas needed the support of more blood than she had. Fala had taken too much.

"We should get her to a hospital, or she's still going to die," Caryn said, her voice uneven. "She needs blood."

For a moment Aubrey looked up, and his black eyes held no warmth as they focused on Caryn and then fell to her throat. She could see the effort as he turned his head away.

He was no longer the perfect, drop-dead-gorgeous immortal he had been. He was paler than ever, and his eyes were unfocused. He looked as if he had been drained as surely as Jessica had. Of course, when it came to his kind, power and blood were often all but interchangeable.

Caryn lay down as another wave of fatigue washed over her, and watched silently as Aubrey tried to rouse Jessica.

# CHAPTER 31

JESSICA COULD BARELY BREATHE past the pain in her chest. Every muscle in her body had cramped, and she was shivering with cold.

*Jessica!* She recognized Aubrey's voice in her mind, though she had never heard him sound so distraught.

Slowly she dragged herself into the waking world.

*No, not dead . . . I wouldn't hurt so much if I was dead,* she thought absently. It was difficult to form a coherent sentence.

Aubrey pulled her attention back to him. *Not dead yet,* he said quickly, bluntly. *But you will be soon if we don't do something.* He paused, shaking her a bit to keep her attention from drifting away.

*Careful. I'm not sure that arm is still fully attached,* she answered, her wry humor returning to her.

*I can bring you to a hospital, and they can give you blood. There's probably still time,* he told her. *Or if you want it—I know you said before that you did—I can give you mine.*

If she'd had the breath to do so, she would have laughed.

Did she want to be a vampire? To stay in New Mayhem, in the community that had been her life for years; to be with Aubrey, the only one she'd ever felt completely at ease with; to never be prey again?

Then there was also the bonus of immortality, and the tempting idea of pummeling Fala into a bloody smear on the wall.

*You need to ask?* she finally said, and heard Aubrey sigh with relief.

Of course, she would be the first of his line — *her* line, she amended, realizing she'd soon be a part of it — to have been asked. They had been changed for various reasons — on a whim, out of spite or hatred or love. But not one of them had had a choice in the matter.

Jessica smiled wryly as she realized the favor that Fala had unintentionally given. Jessica had fought for her life when Fala had taken her blood, and now had free choice as Aubrey offered his.

Aubrey drew his knife — the same one he had used to shed Ather's blood years ago, when he had been changed. He slid the blade across his skin at the base of his throat, and he pulled Jessica toward him to drink.

She had known this moment in the lives of each of her vampiric characters; had described it in words and tasted it in dreams. But never had she fully understood it.

As she drank, she closed her eyes and abandoned herself to the sweet taste and the feeling that came with it. The English language had no way to properly express this rolling power that filled her like blue lightning, slipping into every molecule of her body and changing everything it touched.

Jessica tried to cling to the sensation, but a gentle numbness began to ease across her skin and into her mind, like the first tendrils of sleep. She was only vaguely aware of the fact that her heart had slowed and stopped, and only distantly did she realize that she was no longer breathing. The inevitable blackness of death stole over her, and she succumbed to it willingly, trusting that she would wake shortly.

*Jazlyn was in constant pain for the first few days, but even that pain served as a welcome reminder that she was alive.*

*The first thing she did was go to the church, inside which she had not dared set foot since the day she had been changed. The priest blessed her and listened to her confession, which she abridged for the sake of his sanity.*

*She thought she had been given another chance—a chance to leave behind the life of darkness and evil. When the child came—Carl's child, whom she should have had years before— she thought it was a sign that she'd been forgiven.*

*Instead, the child was a reminder of her past. Jessica was flawless, brilliant . . . and shadowed by the night. She looked nothing like Carl or Jazlyn; instead, she had Siete's fair skin, black hair, and emerald eyes.*

*Those eyes could look upon someone and see the darkest parts of their soul.*

*Jessica had spent more than twenty years in Jazlyn's womb, kept alive only by Siete's blood. She was more his child than Jazlyn's.*

*There was no way for Jazlyn to raise the child who brought back her every painful memory. No child deserved to have a mother who could not brush her raven hair, or look into her gemstone eyes, without shuddering.*

*Jazlyn put the child up for adoption, so that she could be given to caring parents who knew only of sunlight and laughter. Jessica deserved that life; she had done nothing wrong.*

*Jazlyn prayed that her child would never be touched by the darkness of her past.*

# CHAPTER 32

JESSICA'S HEART HAD STOPPED. Her face was almost white, and as cool as the fall air surrounding her. She had died only moments before, as Aubrey's blood had entered her system. He left her side reluctantly to check on Caryn.

Caryn's breathing was slow and deep, and she seemed to be fine except for the cataleptic sleep she was in. At the moment Aubrey's hunger was more of a danger to the witch than anything else.

Almost without thinking, he brought both girls and himself to his seldom-used house in New Mayhem, where no one would bother them. The forest had far too many predators in it to leave them alone there, and he didn't know what Caryn would want him to tell her mother.

He put Caryn in the one bedroom with windows, knowing that no witch would want to wake and not be able to see either the stars or the sun. But he left

Jessica in a bedroom with heavy blackout curtains that would block the sun while she slept.

Then, before the mingled scents of Jessica's and Caryn's blood could defeat his usually iron self-control, he went searching for dinner. Having fed well, he returned home to watch over the girls, and finally allowed his mind to turn to other things.

Like how many ways he could fillet Fala, for one. Or how many ways he *would* fillet Fala, for two.

An hour before sunset, Aubrey dragged himself away from Jessica's side. Fala needed to be dealt with before Jessica woke.

He appeared just behind Fala in her room, his knife at her throat and his mind clamped on hers to hold her in place.

"I hope she sliced you open *very* well," he snarled, pressing the edge of the blade into her throat just slightly.

"And I hope she's very, *very* dead," Fala answered in kind, softly so as to not put any more pressure against the blade. Despite her caution, a thin line of blood appeared on her dark Egyptian skin. "If she isn't, I'll correct that error soon."

"I suggest you don't," he said. Considering how the last fight had gone, Jessica might win if Fala chose to pick another.

"She drew blood, Aubrey," Fala answered. "I have claim, and you can't stop me from acting on it."

What he had done for Jessica would have been illegal had Fala conquered her pride earlier and admitted that Jessica had been the one who wounded her.

Instead, she had waited until now to actually call on blood claim, and now was too late.

"The law only applies if she's human," he answered coldly.

Then his attention was drawn away as he sensed a familiar presence just outside the door.

Jessica had washed the blood off her skin, but her pallor showed that she still needed to feed.

"Don't stop her," Jessica said. Aubrey released Fala but didn't move away; Jessica was certainly not strong enough to best Fala in a fight now, before she had even fed. Yet she walked calmly toward Fala, looking at the vampire with scorn. "Wounded by a human . . . what a blow that must have been to your pride."

Fala growled, but she restrained herself from attacking with Aubrey so near.

"I have no desire to fight you," Jessica said simply, almost regally.

Fala's eyes narrowed in response, but she made no immediate comment. Aubrey knew that Fala could tell as well as he could how strong Jessica would be once she had fed.

"However," Jessica continued, just as controlled, "if you ever harm anyone I care about, or come anywhere near me, you will very quickly learn just how many interesting stories about your past I still have to share."

She didn't wait for Fala to react. Instead, she disappeared, presumably to feed.

# CHAPTER 33

JESSICA RETURNED SHORTLY to Aubrey's home in New Mayhem, her fair skin flushed with the blood meal she had taken in a sleazy corner of New York City only minutes before.

Aubrey was lounging on one of the couches in the living room when she entered. He stood and approached her. "Caryn went home, but she left this for you," he said, handing her a letter.

Jessica scanned Caryn's letter—a long, rambling, maudlin farewell. She made a point to hide her own emotions as she silently said her goodbyes to the person who had probably been her last tie to the mortal world.

"And," Aubrey added reluctantly, glancing toward the table, where Jessica's computer now sat, "she had me bring that here."

Jessica smiled wickedly. How harmless the contraption appeared—plain black plastic without a single scratch or mark to show how much tumult it had helped her cause. She wandered to the table and brushed the laptop's case affectionately.

Aubrey had followed her. "Do you really need that?" he asked.

"I can't write without it," she answered, assuming the closest she could manage to an innocent expression before the underlying mischief showed through.

"You live to make trouble, don't you?"

"Life is nothing without a little chaos to make it interesting." She turned to face him and playfully raised her gaze to meet his, challenging. "What do you want to do about it?"

# SHATTERED MIRROR

*Dedicated to Carolyn Barnes, who knows these characters as well as I do, understands all my vague references and odd humor, and can push me on when I've all but given up. Carolyn, I owe you.*

*As always I must mention my family, especially my sister Gretchen. Thank you for believing in me, for listening to my dreams.*

*My love to Indigo of the Round Table. Carolyn, Sydney, Irene, and Valerie, where would I be without you all? You—and Alexandre, and TSB, and Londra, and Hawk, and Ysterath, and even the evil fairy (whom I never liked even if he was a good guy)—are the people who make my life interesting.*

*More thanks go to the members of the Rikai Group for all their encouragement and support while I was editing* Shattered Mirror. *My deepest gratitude goes to Kyle Bladow, who believed in me even when I didn't, and to Darrin Kuykendall, who showed me how to put water on my cereal while I waited for the milk.*

*Last but not least, thanks to my editor, Diana. Without her suggestions and comments, this book would never have become what it is today.*

## The Two Trees

Beloved, gaze in thine own heart.
Gaze no more in the bitter glass
The demons, with their subtle guile.
Lift up before us when they pass,
Or only gaze a little while;
For there a fatal image grows
That the stormy night receives,
Roots half hidden under snows,
Broken boughs and blackened leaves.
For ill things turn to barrenness
In the dim glass the demons hold,
The glass of outer weariness,
Made when God slept in times of old.
There, through the broken branches, go
The ravens of unresting thought;
Flying, crying, to and fro,
Cruel claw and hungry throat,
Or else they stand and sniff the wind,
And shake their ragged wings; alas!
Thy tender eyes grow all unkind:
Gaze no more in the bitter glass.

W. B. Yeats

# CHAPTER 1

SARAH VIDA SHIVERED. The aura of vampires seeping from the house in front of her was nearly overwhelming. She drove around the block once, then stopped her car a couple of yards away from the white Volvo she had been following. Her sapphire Jaguar was flashy, and she hadn't had time to change the plates.

She was lucky she had been planning on crashing a different party, or she would never have been ready for this one. She had come across the white Volvo's owner at a gas station and had tailed her here.

She cut the motor and ran her fingers through her long blond hair, which was windblown by the drive in the convertible. Flashing a killer smile at no one, she checked her appearance in the rearview mirror. The girl in the glass appeared attractive, wild and carefree. The core of stone was not visible in her reflection.

As she stood, Sarah smoothed down her blue tank top and cream jeans and automatically checked to make sure her knives were in place—one in a spine sheath on her back and one tucked into each calf-high boot. Only then did she approach the house.

With blinds and shades pulled, the house appeared empty from the outside, but the illusion was quickly shattered. Before she even had a chance to knock, someone pulled open the door.

*Leech*, Sarah thought, disgusted, as she flashed a smile as practiced as the one she had given her rearview mirror at the vampire who had opened the door.

*Whoa*. Her smile did not waver, even though the vampiric aura in the house hit her like a sledgehammer to her gut. Her skin tingled at the sense of power, the feeling as unpleasant as sandpaper scraping across raw skin.

Unpleasant feeling or no, she began to mingle, looking always for the prey she was risking her neck to find—Nikolas.

Nikolas was one of the most infamous of his kind, a vampire who had hunted blatantly since the 1800s. His first known prey had been a young mother named Elisabeth Vida. Elisabeth had been a witch, a vampire hunter, and incidentally, Sarah's ancestor. Her family had been hunting Nikolas ever since—without success.

Nikolas was clever—he had to be to have eluded hunters from the most powerful family of witches for so long. But he was also vain, and that would be his downfall. Every one of his victims wore his marks, decorations cut into their arms with the blade of his knife. Nikolas allowed some of his victims to live, but he twisted their minds to make them sickeningly loyal to him. Hunters had caught more than one of those warped humans, but they each professed to choose death before they would betray the vampire.

One of them, however, had made a mistake. A flat tire on the way to this bash had left her fuming at a gas station off Route 95, and she had been too preoccupied to cover the scars on her arms. The attendant, a member of the hunters' complex system of informants, had called Sarah; she had followed the girl's white Volvo here.

Taking a breath to focus her senses, Sarah searched the room with all six of them. Human scents mingled with the overpowering aura of vampires. Sarah felt pity and a slight disgust for the living who flitted among the vampires like flies clinging to dead flesh. Though Sarah did see one human boy leaving just after she came in, most of these humans would stay, out of either ignorance or perverted loyalty.

She didn't like being inside this group without backup, but the short drive between the gas station and this house had only allowed for a few cell-phone calls, which had reached only busy signals and answering machines. She couldn't risk making a serious kill, outnumbered as she was, but if she played nice tonight, she had a good chance of wangling an invitation to the next bash this group hosted. She could bring in the big guns then.

The trick was to avoid being killed—or munched on. She was posing as free food, human and helpless, but letting a vampire feed on her was further than she was willing to go. Besides, even the weakest vampire would be able to taste the difference between the bland vintage of human blood and the power in her own witch blood.

It was past ten o'clock at night, and the back of Sarah's neck tingled with apprehension. Any hunter worth her blade generally knew better than to stay at a bash after midnight. Called the Devil's Hour, midnight was when the killing was done.

Yet if Sarah wanted an invitation, she needed to stay and convince these creatures she was one of the idiotic humans who bared their throats willingly. Any hunter, from the most amateur to the most respected, would give his right eye and his life for a chance to take down a group of vampires this strong.

Sarah befriended the girl she had followed, and within fifteen minutes she had charmed her way into receiving one of the slick white cards that stated the time and location of the next bash this group was hosting.

Now all she had to do was follow the two simplest rules any hunter ever learned: Don't get caught, and clean up after yourself.

As the Devil's Hour drew near, Sarah found the weakest of the vampires and made sure she was alone with him when the clock struck.

"I don't think Kaleo meant this room to be open to the public," her companion pointed out, referring to their vampire host. Sarah recognized the name with revulsion. Nikolas was not the only creature in this group the hunters would love to take down.

Hiding her thoughts, she smiled and put a hand on her companion's shoulder, forcing herself to ignore the unpleasant thickness of his aura. "Maybe I just wanted you all to myself," she teased, meeting his black vampiric eyes.

The fiend got the message and leaned closer to her. Sarah ran her fingers through his ash blond hair, and he wrapped a slender hand around the back of her neck, gently urging her forward.

She leaned her head back, knowing where his gaze would travel. He fell for it, as they always did, and as she felt his lips touch her throat, she reacted.

Shoving him back into the wall, she used his moment of confusion to draw the silver knife from the sheath on her back. Before he could recover his wits, she slammed the blade into his chest, then twisted the knife to make sure his heart was completely destroyed. Vampiric power lived in the blood, and any well-trained hunter knew to twist the knife and obliterate the source of that power. Even Sarah, with a silver blade forged by magic thousands of years old, was still careful. The Vida blade would poison any vampire it scratched, but there was no reason to be careless.

The kill was silent and quick; no one outside even knew this monster was down. Sarah absently wiped her clean hand on her jeans, brushing away the tingling aftereffect of touching him, and touched her throat to reassure herself that there were no puncture marks.

She tucked the body into a corner, knowing this house would probably be abandoned for a while after this bash—that was one of the techniques the vampires used to keep hunters from tracking them down. They were rarely stupid enough to sleep in the same house where they killed.

For a moment she paused, pondering the lifeless body, wondering how any person would willingly become a creature who fed on humanity, a monstrous parasite. He would have taken her blood and killed her had she not killed him first.

She shook her head. It was dead, as it should have been when the vampire blood first froze its heart years ago. That was all that mattered.

Checking herself for blood and finding none, she took a moment to relax as she waited for some time to pass.

She sensed another vampire behind her but forced herself to turn slowly, as if a little groggy. She recognized the vampire immediately. Kaleo had pale blond hair and sculpted features, which would have made him attractive had his aura not been enough to make Sarah's stomach churn. In the midst of his blond features, his black eyes seemed infinitely darker. Kaleo was one of the oldest in his line, and more powerful than any creature Sarah had ever faced.

For a moment, Sarah debated going for her blade. Attacking Kaleo by herself with so many of his kind near would probably mean the end of her life. But it might be worth it.

Before Sarah could make a move, though, Kaleo glanced pointedly to the doorway behind which Sarah had hidden her prey. "What excellent taste," he congratulated her. "He was rather a pain."

A prepared vampire was more difficult to fight than an unsuspecting one. Without hesitation, Sarah went for her knife.

# CHAPTER 2

"YOU DROVE HOME LIKE THIS?"

Sarah nodded sharply in answer to the healer's question.

Caryn Smoke shook her head but made no comment.

She was the strongest living member of her line, and had nearly been disowned recently due to her associations with vampires. Sarah had disliked the girl ever since the trial, but Caryn was an effective healer, and Sarah only turned to the best.

Sarah had been raised to ignore pain so it would not incapacitate her in a fight, and tonight those lessons had proved invaluable. Both bones in her right forearm had broken when Kaleo grabbed her wrist and threw her into a wall; her head had hit hard enough that had she been human it would have knocked her out. Instead, she had simply drawn another knife with her left hand.

Fortunately, Kaleo and his guests had all been more interested in the pleasures willingly provided by their human sycophants than in fighting a vampire hunter, and had quickly lost interest in Sarah and allowed her to escape.

Sarah had been lucky. She had survived because the vampires had gotten bored. That—added to the fact that she hadn't seen Nikolas—grated on her.

It was almost five o'clock in the morning by the time Caryn was finished setting the arm. The healer moved on to deal with Sarah's numerous other scrapes, bruises, and minor sprains when Dominique Vida returned from hunting and came to see her injured daughter. As she sized up Sarah's condition, her expression was calm, but marked with distinct disapproval.

"You were careless," Dominique chastised, after she heard the details of Sarah's night. "You went into that group unprepared, and you stayed past midnight."

Sarah lowered her gaze, but did not allow her defiant expression to fall.

Finally Sarah spoke up, her voice sure despite Dominique's reproach. "Nikolas was there." Dominique could complain all she liked about Sarah's carelessness, but if Nikolas was part of that group, then they had a lead to finding him.

"Nikolas?" Dominique's voice was sharp. "You saw him?"

Sarah shook her head. "One of his prey—marked."

"That doesn't help much unless you saw the vampire himself," Dominique pointed out dryly, and Sarah set her jaw to keep from arguing. "And now we have no way of tracking him down." Sarah did not bother turning over the invitation she had received. After having teased and released the hunter they had found in their midst, the vampires would know better than to host the bash she had mistakenly been invited to.

"You're set," Caryn said, her normally quiet voice raised to interrupt the conversation. She patted the cast on Sarah's arm gently. "You'll need a week or so to heal completely, and until then I recommend that you take it easy. Okay?" The last was said with a sharp look to Dominique.

The Vida matriarch nodded. "Thank you for your help, Caryn. Sorry to bother you so late."

Caryn shrugged, her fatigue visible. "No problem. I was in the neighborhood, at a SingleEarth hospital."

Dominique did not react to the remark, and Sarah copied her mother's neutral mask. SingleEarth. The organization was growing by leaps and bounds, with humans, witches, vampires, and shapeshifters joining, all working toward a common cause: unite all the creatures on Earth. Though a noble goal, it was never going to work. Vampires were hunters, evil by nature, and most were incapable of containing their need for bloodshed. Even the vampires at SingleEarth, who survived by feeding on animals or willing donors, admitted that it was painful to live without killing.

"I guess you probably won't be at school tomorrow?" Caryn asked on her way out.

Sarah glanced to her mother, but saw no sympathy. "I'll be there." No matter how hard a night Sarah had had, Dominique was not one to allow her daughter to slack off, not even for a few days so she could start at her new school on Monday. Sarah would start bright and early on Wednesday morning.

Sarah had been expelled from her last school for

fighting on school grounds. In the process of extinguishing a vampire, some school property had been broken, and the administration had not been particularly understanding. Only some quick thinking by Sarah's sister, Adianna, had kept anyone from finding the body.

After the incident, Dominique had decided to move her daughter away from the constant excitement of the city and into a dull Massachusetts suburb named Acton. Caryn and her family lived there.

Dominique returned upstairs to sleep, and Caryn caught Sarah's good arm.

"I should warn you. There are a few vampires in the school." Upon Sarah's look, she added sternly, "They're harmless, and they have every right to be there. If you hurt any of them—"

"If they're harmless, I'll just ignore them. I can't afford to get kicked out of another school, anyway. Okay?" Sarah offered. Caryn nodded.

Sarah's pride, already ground into the dirt, deflated even more when the door opened again and her sister entered the house.

"Hey, little sis," Adianna greeted her. Noticing the cast, she added, "Rough night?"

Adianna Vida, one year Sarah's senior, was almost as perfect as their mother—intelligent and controlled. She had graduated last year, but was taking a semester off before starting college to train harder, and to "look out for" her little sister.

Right then Adianna's blond hair was tousled, and Sarah saw a smear of blood on her dark blue jeans as if she had wiped a knife clean. She had obviously been fighting, and she had just as obviously won.

Adianna patted her sister's shoulder as she passed toward the stairs. "Rest up. The world will survive without you for a week or so."

# CHAPTER 3

SEVEN-THIRTY-FIVE *is a beastly hour to begin school,* Sarah thought, as she opened her locker. The bell rang and she sighed. Hopefully being the new girl would excuse her tardiness. It certainly had no other perks. She thought fleetingly of the hunting companions she had left behind, with whom she had crashed bashes and stalked the darkest corners of the city. By morning, rarely had a blade been left clean.

She forcibly banished such thoughts. She was here now, and it was time to begin this new life.

Her first block was American history, and though she located it easily, the class had already begun when she slipped through the door.

"Sarah Green?" the teacher confirmed as Sarah turned over the folded pink pass from the office. Mr. Smith was a balding, tired-looking man whose crisp suit pants and shirt seemed out of place in the high school. He gestured toward the class. "Take a seat . . . there's one open right next to Robert—"

"Actually, someone's sitting there," one of the boys in the back of the room called. As Sarah's attention turned to Robert, she realized that he looked vaguely familiar, but she couldn't place his face in her memory. He had looked up just long enough to see who had come in the door, and was now writing something in a notebook. The desk next to him appeared empty to Sarah; the chair was vacant.

Mr. Smith looked surprised, but he skimmed the class again.

"There's a seat here," someone else called, and Sarah glanced to see who had spoken.

Black hair, fair skin, *black* eyes. Vampire. She recognized him instantly, but Mr. Smith was already hustling her toward the empty seat.

"Christopher Ravena," the leech said, introducing himself as she slid into her chair. He nodded across the class. "That's my sister, Nissa." The girl he had gestured to waved slightly. Though her hair was a shade lighter, the resemblance between the siblings was marked — including the mild vampiric aura.

"Nice to meet you," she answered politely, though inside she grimaced. *This could be a very long year.*

The aura of the vampire beside her was so faint that her skin wasn't even tingling. He was either very young or very weak, and she could tell that he did not feed on human prey. Probably SingleEarth, harmless as Caryn had said. His sister was almost as weak, and although her aura showed a hint of human blood — probably from one of the plethora of humans at SingleEarth willing to bare their throats — it was obvious she did not kill when she hunted. Neither of them would be able to sense Sarah's aura, so unless they knew her by sight, they would likely assume that she was just another human.

Mr. Smith was talking to her again, and she turned her attention back to him. "Sarah, as you'll see, I like to begin class with a conversation about current events, to keep us involved in the present as well as the history." Raising his voice to address all the students, he asked, "Now, who has something to share?"

The number of hands raised—none—was not overly surprising. Most of the students looked like they were still asleep.

"I know it's early," Mr. Smith said, encouragingly, "but you are allowed to wake up any time now. Who heard the news last night? What happened in our world?"

Finally a few hands tiredly rose, but most of the students had better things to do. The girl sitting in front of Sarah was reading a book that looked like it was probably an English assignment. Nearby, another student was doing Spanish homework. The teacher was either oblivious, or he just didn't care. The news story that was being repeated by a girl in the first row wasn't all that fascinating, anyway.

"Did you just move in?" Christopher asked, his voice quiet to avoid the teacher's attention. He had a slight accent—not quite a drawl, but smooth and unhurried, with a hint of the South.

Sarah nodded, trying to keep a small portion of her attention focused on the dull classroom conversation, while keeping the rest on the two vampires. "My mother got a new job, teaching in the next town." It was a plausible lie, which she had come up with earlier.

Mr. Smith moved back in time to the Civil War, and Sarah took notes furiously for an excuse to avoid Christopher's attempts at conversation. The class was dull, and she already knew most of the information, but if she made a good impression now, Mr. Smith was more likely to cut her some slack later.

Christopher's silence lasted only until the bell. "How'd you hurt your arm?" he asked as Sarah awkwardly shuffled papers into her backpack after class.

"Thrown off a horse," Sarah lied effortlessly. "She's usually a sweet creature, but something spooked her." As she lifted the heavy backpack, she wondered how in the world humans could possibly carry these things around all day. Her witch blood made Sarah stronger than an average human—her five-foot-four, 130-pound body could bench-press 300 pounds—but she wondered how the humans managed.

"Do you need help with that?" Christopher offered, gesturing to the bag. "What class do you have next?"

"Chemistry," she answered. "I can handle it."

"I didn't mean to suggest you couldn't," Christopher responded smoothly. "You just shouldn't have to bother. I've got biology next, anyway, so our classes are near each other."

She examined his expression, but he appeared sincere. For whatever his reasons, he was honestly trying to play the part of a human teenage boy—an unusually polite one, but human nevertheless.

She didn't want to make a scene, so she surrendered

her backpack, and Christopher carried it without effort, which did not surprise her. If she could lift 300 pounds, as a weak vampire he could probably bench-press a ten-wheeler with about as much effort.

"Thanks," she forced out, glad the words sounded sincere.

Though her chemistry class was blessedly human, Christopher's sister was in sculpture with Sarah for the third block of the day.

Sarah's skills with clay were minimal; she had signed up for this class mainly so she could do something low stress without homework. She'd be lucky if she could make a ball. Nissa, on the other hand, had a great deal of talent, which helped Sarah place her in a way that the girl's weak aura had not: Kendra's line.

Kendra was the fourth fledgling of Siete, creator of all the vampires. Though Sarah had never met her, the woman was rumored to be stunning in form and fierce in temper. She was a lover of all the arts, as were almost all of her descendents. Kaleo, with whom Sarah had had her uncomfortable run-in the night before, was Kendra's first fledgling.

All these thoughts passed through Sarah's mind quickly as she watched Nissa craft a young man's figure in the soft clay, humming quietly to herself as she worked. He sat upon a rustic bench, a violin perched on his shoulder. The bow was a fine coil of clay supported by a piece of wire at its neck.

Nissa looked up from her work and noticed Sarah watching.

"That's really impressive," Sarah offered, surprised to find her words completely sincere.

"Thanks." Nissa smiled, looking back at the form. "But I can't get the face quite right." She indicated the shapeless globe where the features should be, surrounded by carefully etched hair.

"Better than mine."

Nissa laughed lightly. "Considering you just started today and you're only working with your left hand, it's not bad."

The vampire carefully wrapped her figure in plastic so it would not dry, and then shifted over to offer suggestions on Sarah's project, which was a sickly-looking clay dog. They worked together for the last ten minutes of class, during which Sarah almost forgot what she was talking to.

"You could put a wire in his tail so it wouldn't fall like that. What kind of dog is it?" Nissa asked.

Sarah shrugged. "I don't really know. My mother doesn't like dogs, so I've never had one."

In fact, Dominique hated dogs. She was very against animals and witches mixing; the Vida line was one of the few that had never used familiars in its magic.

"It could kind of look like a Lab, if you squared off the nose," the girl suggested. Under Nissa's expert assistance the smooth white clay turned into an almost-recognizable animal.

"What do you have next?" Nissa asked as they packed the dog in plastic.

"Lunch, I think."

"Great! You're with Christopher and me." The girl's

exuberance was infectious, but still Sarah hesitated at Nissa's implied invitation. She could be sociable during class, but there were pages of laws in the Vida books detailing how far any relations with vampires could go. While the school cafeteria was not mentioned by name, Sarah was pretty sure it would be considered unnecessary association.

Still, Nissa walked with her through the halls, and even followed Sarah to her locker when she tried to use it as an excuse to drop the vampire.

Inside the locker, on the top shelf, Sarah noticed something she had not put there: a white piece of paper, on which a profile had been drawn carefully in pencil. She immediately recognized the figure as herself; her hair spilled over her shoulders and onto the desk as she wrote.

Nissa just shrugged when she saw the drawing and gave an understanding smile as Sarah read the initials signed in light script in the bottom corner. *CR.* It was from Christopher; he had probably drawn it while sitting right next to her in history class, when Sarah had been trying to ignore him.

# CHAPTER 4

NISSA LED THE WAY to the table where she and
her brother usually sat; Christopher was already there.
Sarah thought again how lucky it was that neither
Christopher nor Nissa was strong enough to read her
aura.

*Lucky* . . . yeah, right. If she had been lucky, they
would have recognized her and avoided her from the
start. As it was, she was going to need to find some way
to break off the friendship they were obviously
attempting to form—preferably without broadcasting
her heritage to two vampires she knew next to nothing
about.

"Sarah, sit down," Christopher called. "How was
sculpture?"

"Much more interesting than Mr. Smith's history lecture," Sarah answered vaguely. She hesitated by the
table's side, but as Nissa tossed her backpack on one of
the chairs, Sarah reluctantly grabbed a seat of her own.

"Hey, Nissa . . ." A human boy approached Nissa,

but hesitated when he saw Sarah. She recognized him as Robert, the boy from her first class. The look he directed at her was anything but friendly. He turned back to Nissa. "I was wondering . . . if you're going to the dance this weekend."

Nissa looked from Robert to Sarah. "I'm going stag."

"Oh, um . . . ." He paused, then said something hurriedly that might have been, "See you there," before he slipped back into the mass of students.

"What was that about?" Nissa asked as soon as the boy was gone. "Did you kill the boy's baby sister or something? Robert usually goes after anything with legs," she joked.

"I never met him before today," Sarah answered honestly, watching his sandy brown hair bob through the crowd.

Christopher shrugged. "Don't worry, you're not missing much," he said lightly. "Robert has been hitting on Nissa ever since he first saw her, and he's a royal pain."

Sarah did not brush off the interaction as lightly as Christopher and Nissa, but she did allow them to change the subject, while her mind stayed focused on the incident.

Sarah was of average human height, and well shaped from a high metabolism and a vigorous exercise routine. Her fair blond hair was long, with enough body that it fell down her back in soft waves, and her sapphire eyes were stunning. To top it off, her aura was powerfully charismatic, and humans were drawn to it. Though she had heard about humans who were naturally anxious around vampires and humanity's other predators, that was obviously not the case with Robert;

and while Sarah had received numerous phone numbers from strange boys, she had *never* met one who instinctively disliked her.

The only possibility she could think of was that
Robert was somehow bonded to the vampires. Sarah
would have sensed a blood bond, but maybe . . . the
thought trailed off with disgust. There were humans
who were addicted to vampires. They didn't need to be
blood bonded to one monster; they gave their blood
willingly to any who would take it. Enough contact
with the leeches, and he could have formed the same
kind of instinctual aversion to witches that most humans had for strong vampires.

"Sarah?" Christopher's voice pulled her back to the
real world. In her mind she played back the conversation she had missed.

"Yeah, sure." Then, "Wait, no. I can't."

They had asked if she was going to go to the dance
the school was hosting on Saturday—the Halloween
dance, which, according to Nissa, was the only school
dance worth going to until the senior prom in the
spring.

"Why not?" Christopher asked, obviously disappointed.

Nissa added, "If you're worried about getting a cos-
tume, I'm sure we could find something for you, and
they sell the tickets at the door."

"No, it's not that. It's just . . . I've got family coming
over that weekend, and my mother would never let me
go out."

"Shame," Christopher sighed, slightly wistful. "Nice
family, or wish-you-could-lose-them family?"

272 AMELIA ATWATER-RHODES

Actually, the "family" included many of the local witches—the rest of the Vida line, some of Caryn Smoke's kin, and a few young men from the Marinitch line. Even human Wiccans celebrated Samhain, and for Sarah's kind, it was one of the few holidays still left that they could celebrate without unnerving the human world. Dominique Vida hosted a circle on October 31 every year, open to every descendant of Macht—the immortal mother of Sarah's kind.

"Some nice, some barely tolerable," Sarah answered, thinking of the Smoke witches in the second group. The peaceful healers had a tendency to preach about peace and unity—an idea that would have been tolerable, had it not included vampires. Luckily, Caryn herself, along with many of the most offensive give-peace-a-chance callers, would celebrate at SingleEarth instead of spending the holiday with hunters.

Yet even as she thought with contempt of Caryn's association with vampires, here she was speaking with two leeches who might or might not belong to the painfully overgrown SingleEarth.

She had to end this. *Some tolerant association is necessary to preserve human safety and forbearance, but friendship and love with such creatures as you hunt is impossible, dangerous, abhorrent, and as such, forbidden.* She could quote the Vida laws back to front, and that line stood out in bold in her memory. Going beyond the bonds of what was necessary to keep her cover in school could at best stain her reputation; other hunters would not trust someone who had befriended the monsters. At worst, Dominique could call her to trial, and that would be a disaster.

"I've got to go," Sarah said abruptly.

The two vampires seemed startled, but they did not try to stop her. "See you later," Christopher said amiably.

"Yeah . . . maybe." She hoped not.

She ducked out of the cafeteria and swung into the girls' bathroom, shuddering as she caught sight of herself in the mirror. What had she thought she was doing? She had dropped her guard around them. Already she thought about the pair with some affection—they were Christopher and Nissa, not two leeches she might one day have to kill.

That was dangerous. Knowing your prey can cause hesitation, and when one is a vampire hunter, hesitation ends in death.

Sarah managed to avoid them for the rest of the day. She had calculus with Christopher, but the only free seat was across the room from him, and for that she was grateful. She needed some time to decide on how she would deal with them before she had another chance to talk to them.

# CHAPTER 5

SARAH SLEPT POORLY that night. With her broken arm, she felt like a caged leopard with too much energy and nothing to use it on. It was nearly three o'clock when she finally drifted into sleep, and even then she was restless, plagued by nightmares.

By the time she got to school, she felt less like a leopard and more like a slug. It was a pity that human drugs were neutralized by her system upon absorption, because she could have used some serious caffeine.

It took her two tries to get the combination to her locker right, and as she tossed in her coat, she managed to knock something down from the top shelf.

The vase shattered upon impact with the dirty school floor, scattering water, glass, and three white roses. The sound of breaking glass drove a shiver up Sarah's spine, bringing back all too vividly her dream from the night before.

Memories of her father's death often haunted her

sleep. Though she had tried to forget that day, to perfect her control the way Dominique and Adianna had, she wasn't strong enough, and she never had been.

At seven years old, she had stumbled across her father's body on the front step of the house. The vampires had caught the hunter and kept him for weeks, bleeding him a little each day. Bloody kisses marked his arms where the leeches had cut into his skin so they could lick the blood away.

Adianna had dealt with the news calmly, as had Dominique. Every hunter knew how dangerous his life was, and was prepared for death. But Sarah had been so young, and when she had stumbled over the cold body of her father, when his blood had coated her hand, she had lost control.

She had hit a window, demolishing it pane by pane until Dominique had dragged her away, horrified not by her husband's death, but by her daughter's reaction.

The death had become a lesson. Dominique had bound Sarah's powers for a week afterward, both as a punishment and to teach her how to deal with pain. She had healed as slowly as a human, from three broken fingers and numerous lacerations on her hand and arm. In the meantime Dominique had her train with the older hunters, fighting until her hand throbbed and every muscle ached. Though binding her magic could not take away the years of training, her reflexes, or even most of her strength, the loss had left her shaken and her abilities meaningless. That weakness had terrified her ever since.

Shuddering from the memory, Sarah dragged herself

back to the present. Ignoring the glass, she carefully picked up the roses and the card that had been tied to the vase with a white ribbon.

The white blooms were beautiful, perfect, with the sweet scent that so many long-stemmed roses lacked. A picture done in professional charcoal accompanied them—a pair of eyes framed with the pale lashes Sarah saw every time she looked into a mirror.

She read the poem at least ten times before she even reached class, and finally resolved to speak to Christopher.

*Blue like sapphire beneath a morning sun,*
*Burning with fire of a crystalline soul.*
*A laughter that never quite reaches inside,*
*Where secrets weather like untouched gold.*

The words were beautiful—and truer than Christopher realized. If he had known even the slightest of Sarah's secrets, he would never have spoken to her in the first place.

She had steeled herself to talk to him by the time she reached her history class, only to have Mr. Smith immediately divide them into groups for a project. Her group included two humans she had not met before, and the mysterious Robert, who was not hiding his hostility any better today.

"What's eating *you*?" one of their other group members demanded after he shot down yet another of their ideas. "If you don't want to help, then just keep your mouth shut. Don't make *your* bad day *mine*."

By the time the class was over Sarah was glad to get

away from Robert—the human had been putting out waves of contempt and distrust strong enough that they were making her stomach churn. She would need to speak to him sometime soon, but not here, not in front of other humans.

She had calmed down slightly by sculpture, where she continued to work on the sickly dog Nissa had named Splotch. Nissa finished her figure. Under her expert hands, the violinist gained clear Roman features, sympathetic eyes, and wicked, sensual lips.

"Someone you know?" Sarah asked. The face was so vivid, so alive, she felt like she should recognize it.

Nissa nodded, pausing in her work. "Yeah." Her voice was soft, sad.

"Who is he?"

"A . . ." She trailed off, as if none of the words she had been thinking of would work. "Someone I used to love. His name is Kaleo."

Sarah's heart skipped as she heard the name. Kaleo had a reputation for ruining lives on a whim, and changing young women into vampires whom he fancied himself in love with.

If Nissa was one of Kaleo's fledglings, Sarah had to pity the girl.

"Anyway, it's over," Nissa stated. "I miss him some-times, but . . . it's over."

"Then why are you sculpting him?" The question was sharper than Sarah meant it to be.

"He is beautiful," the girl said wistfully. Then she jumped as the bell rang for lunch.

They did not speak as they cleaned up their stations, and Nissa stayed behind to talk to the teacher while

Sarah swung by her locker. Inside she found another present from Christopher—a picture of her left hand, which she had been writing with since she had broken her right arm.

Her nails were cut short so they wouldn't hinder her grip on her knife; there was a small scar on the back from the glass window she had punched the day her father had been killed. It looked like a pale teardrop.

On the back of the drawing was another poem.

*Skin like ivory, perfect; A goddess, she must be.*
*Slender fingers, unadorned; beautiful simplicity.*
*A single teardrop; when did it fall?*
*Could this goddess be mortal, after all?*

*If only he knew,* Sarah thought dryly. That scar was left over from the least perfect moment of her life.

Yet somehow Christopher had made the flaw beautiful, no longer a badge of her dishonor, but a mystery for an artist to unravel.

# CHAPTER 6

"CHRISTOPHER . . . are these from you?" she asked at lunch, careful to make her tone light as she placed the two picture-poems on the table. Christopher's eyes fell to them, and he smiled.

"Yes."

He didn't ask if she liked them, and he didn't seem embarrassed.

Sarah was flattered, and somewhat surprised by Christopher's easy confidence. Even so, her natural suspicion surfaced. "Why?"

"Because," he answered seriously, "you make a good subject. Your hair, for one, is like a shimmering waterfall. It's so fair that it catches the light. It makes you seem like you have a halo about you. And your eyes— they're such a pure color, not washed out at all, deep as the ocean. And your expression . . . intense and yet somehow detached, as if you see more of the world than the rest of us."

Flustered, she could think of no way to respond. Did

he just say this stuff from the top of his head? Only her strict Vida control kept her from blushing.

Meanwhile Nissa entered the cafeteria. She started to sit, then glanced from the pictures, to Christopher, to Sarah. "Should I go somewhere else?"

Christopher nodded to a chair, answering easily, "Sit down. We aren't exchanging dark secrets—yet."

Nissa flashed a teasing look to her brother as she took a seat. "As his sister, I feel the need to inform you, Sarah, that Christopher has been talking about you incessantly."

Christopher smiled, unembarrassed. "I suppose I might have been."

"Especially your eyes—he never shuts up about your eyes," Nissa confided, and this time Christopher shrugged.

"They're beautiful," he said casually. "Beauty should be looked at, not ignored. I try to capture it on paper, but that's really impossible with eyes, because they have a life no still portrait can capture."

Sarah's voice was tied up so tightly she thought she might be able to speak again sometime next year. No one had ever talked about her—or to her—with such admiration.

Luckily, Nissa changed the subject. "Christopher is an incredible artist, but he refuses to take classes."

Christopher laughed, shaking his head. "I draw when I see something I need to draw; I can't draw on command. Nissa convinced me to try an art class once, and I failed it."

They talked casually for the rest of lunch. Sarah

found herself relaxing in their company as they told jokes and teased one another good-naturedly. Visions of shattered glass faded from her mind, replaced by light banter. This was easy; these people were kind. What could be evil in their friendship?

"Sarah?" The voice just behind her left shoulder was questioning, a bit sharp.

"Adianna." The muscles in Sarah's neck clenched so tightly she felt like they would tear when she turned her head.

"Can I talk to you?" Adianna's tone was pleasant, so it wouldn't make the vampires suspicious, but the expression that glittered in her eyes was dangerous.

"I'll be right back." Sarah gathered her backpack, leaving the two pictures on the table so as not to draw Adianna's attention to them, and followed the other witch into the hall.

"What was going on there?"

"They're in a few of my classes," Sarah answered, forcing herself to be calm despite the fact that she felt like she was on trial during the Spanish Inquisition. "They're perfectly harmless."

"To humans maybe," Adianna answered instantly. "Not to our kind. What if Mother found out? You honestly think she would see them as 'harmless'?"

"She won't find out," Sarah snapped, softly. "Could we have this conversation outside? If they try, they'll be able to hear us here."

Adianna nodded and remained silent until they reached the hill outside the school. "Sarah . . ." She sighed. "What are you trying to do to yourself? Mother would throw a fit if she knew you were hanging out with their kind. Even I can barely stand the thought of it."

"Dominique doesn't need to know everything I do during my life—"

"Sarah!" Adianna's voice was sharp, but Sarah knew it was more due to surprise and worry than censure. "I don't understand why you would even want to spend your time with them, much less break Vida law to do so. As for what Mother does and doesn't need to know—Dominique is the one who decides what information is her business, and you well know what she would think about your having vampiric friends."

"Are you going to tell her?" Sarah's voice was soft, cool. She couldn't stop Adianna if she insisted on going to Dominique, but she made it very clear by her tone that she would not easily forgive the betrayal.

"Sarah, I understand what you're going through." There was obvious effort behind Adianna's even tone. "I've been there. You aren't one of the humans. You don't have any friends here. You just lost some of your oldest hunting partners by moving here, and faced one of the closest encounters you have ever had with death. It's understandable that you have doubts."

"I have no doubts." Sarah had to take a breath to control herself before she continued. "They don't know what I am—they think I'm human. They aren't a threat." After a pause she decided to speak the truth. "Haven't you ever once wanted someone you could talk to about something besides killing? Someone who has no idea about your power and is simply a friend? It's really nice, Adianna. To have someone treat me like a human girl instead of like a killer is really, *really* nice. What's even better is that I don't have to worry every night whether some screwup of mine just got them killed. I don't have to watch my back every moment—"

"That is exactly why the law says you can't befriend them," Adianna interrupted. "Because you relax your guard. They are *killers*, Sarah. I don't care if they don't kill now, or even if they never touch a human and survive on animal blood. They kill by nature, and eventually that nature will destroy whatever shreds of humanity they may have left. If at that time they are still your 'friends,' it will simply mean you are handy for a snack."

Adianna paused to collect herself, then added more softly, "I don't want to lose you, Sarah. I don't want you getting killed by these two when they turn on you—and note I say when, not if. But worse, I don't want you getting killed for these two. Do you really care so much for them that you will risk getting yourself disowned?"

"Adianna—"

Adianna shook her head, looking tired. "I can't physically stop you from talking to them, but I won't let you get yourself killed for a leech's friendship," she stated clearly. "I won't tell Mother what I've seen so far, but if you three get any closer, I will, while there's still a chance that she'll let you off with a warning." She turned to leave, then added, "And, Sarah? If they ever get you hurt, whether they do it directly or it's because Dominique finds out you have been talking to them, I will kill them myself."

Sarah wanted to respond with anger, but thought better of it. Adianna was letting her off easy, so she just nodded.

"If you care about them like you claim to, leave your new friends alone," Adianna suggested in a rare show of compassion. "Remember them fondly if you care to, but let go of them, or you'll all end up dead."

Adianna glanced back toward the school. "I'm sorry to have to threaten you, Sarah. That wasn't what I came here for."

"I figured."

"I came to tell you that Dominique is flying off this afternoon to train a group of amateur hunters, and I've just received a call to deal with some leeches up in Chicago. We should both be back in time for the holiday." Sarah took in the news without surprise. If it had not been for Adianna's attempts to keep her little sister informed, Sarah would probably never know where her family was. "You'll be fine here?" Though phrased like a question, the last line was a statement. Sarah had spent plenty of time home alone when Adianna and Dominique were off on their various missions.

"Be careful," Sarah told her sister.

Adianna answered seriously, "You too."

They separated, Sarah going back inside the school, and Adianna toward the parking lot.

The bell had rung while Sarah had been speaking with Adianna, so she went immediately to her class, arriving late. Luckily, the teacher was tolerant because she was new to the school; Sarah was in no mood for a detention tonight. She had too much on her mind.

What was she going to do about Christopher and Nissa?

Adianna's worries were legitimate—at least the ones involving Mother and Vida law. If Dominique found out about her budding friendship with two vampires, she would kill them.

Sarah flexed her hand. Old phantom pain reminded her of the other danger. Sarah had had her powers bound once; she could not imagine what it would be like to have them stripped forever.

Sarah almost convinced herself to give up her new friends, for their safety as well as her own. She managed to avoid Christopher's questioning looks in calculus that afternoon, and she said nothing but a casual greeting in response to his hello after class.

Christopher had to stay after to talk to the teacher, and Sarah managed to slip out before he was free. She was home, sitting on her bed, before she found his next gift tucked into her calculus notebook; she had no idea when he had managed to slip it there.

It was another drawing—her, dressed in a pale gown. Above her outstretched left hand, the sun and the moon were suspended; she held the earth in her right hand. A sash was tied about her waist, embroidered with stars. In elegant script, a poem had been written down the page on the figure's left side.

*Fantasy, a shining goddess,*
*She controls the tides.*
*Fantasy, a brilliant goddess.*
*She controls our lives.*

*Fantasy, a golden goddess—*
*In her hands is the light.*
*Fantasy, a silver goddess—*
*In her hands is the night.*

Sarah got up and tucked the card into her desk. Next time she saw Christopher she would tell him the truth—about her family, and about all the laws she was breaking. She would tell him the truth, and he would be able to leave her alone without getting hurt.

# CHAPTER 7

"SARAH, IS SOMETHING WRONG?" Nissa asked the next day during sculpture. "Christopher told me you were avoiding him yesterday afternoon . . . he was sure he had done something to offend you."

Christopher? Offend? She doubted he was capable of such a thing.

Sarah grasped at, and then lost, a handy lie. "Look, I . . . it's nothing really, okay?" Sarah said awkwardly. "I can't really explain."

"That's fine." Nissa's voice was soft, understanding. "If it's none of my business, I'm not going to be a pain. But don't just ditch Christopher—he's a nice guy, and he deserves an explanation if you're not interested."

By the time Sarah saw Christopher at lunch, her resolve to break off the friendship had wavered. He greeted her with a smile and a hello, not asking about her efforts to ignore him the day before.

"Hey, I'm sorry about yesterday—"

"No big deal," Christopher answered easily. "I was kind of worried about you, but . . . well, if you're talking to me again today, it can't have been anything too awful."

"I'm sorry anyway." But his light words and easy confidence made Sarah smile again. "Christopher—"

"Look, we've got to duck out soon to meet with our partners about that history project," Nissa apologized before Sarah could finish her sentence. "Are you sure you aren't going to the Halloween dance this weekend, Sarah? It'll be a lot of fun."

Sarah shook her head. Dominique would throw a fit if she missed the holiday celebrations. "I really can't." She debated asking them to meet up with her after the project, somewhere private where she could tell them and be done with it, but they were already on their way out before she could make up her mind.

Christopher touched Sarah's shoulder as he walked by, a casual gesture that nevertheless made her flinch; physical contact with a vampire made her skin crawl, no matter how weak he was. If he noticed the withdrawal, Christopher did not react to it.

"Catch you later."

"Yeah."

A test kept them from talking in that afternoon's calculus class, but Christopher caught Sarah afterward.

"How'd it go?"

The vampire rolled his eyes skyward. "Math is not my thing." Changing the subject, he said, "I've got to run to a drama club meeting, so I can't talk long now,

but . . . well, since you can't go to the dance, I was wondering if you might want to go for lunch on Saturday."

"I don't know." She *did* know, actually, and the answer was "Absolutely not." Spending time with vampires at school, where she had little else to do, was one
thing; spending time with them otherwise, when she
could be training or hunting, was twisting the laws further than even she could rationalize.

"Give me a call sometime, okay?" He jotted down his
phone number on a piece of scrap paper, and then hurried away to his meeting.

Sarah skimmed the paper after Christopher left, and
tucked it into her pocket.

Nine o'clock that evening found Sarah on the phone,
trying without success to get through to Christopher or
Nissa. Nissa was right—they both deserved more than
to get a simple brush-off. She had decided to call,
arrange a time when they could talk, and tell them
everything.

*Beep . . . beep . . . beep . . .*

The sickly B-flat of the busy signal sliced through
her yet again, as it had every time she had heard it over
the last two hours.

She hung up the phone with a sigh, and pulled out
the local yellow pages to find the Ravenas' address. Her
mind was made up, and she didn't want to risk chicken-
ing out again. She patted the coat's pocket to make sure
her keys were in place, and instinctively checked for
the knife on her back—a hunter never went anywhere
without it—then slipped out to her car.

As she drove, she found herself hoping wildly that Christopher and Nissa would tell her they were part of SingleEarth. If they were, then even Dominique could not forbid Sarah to associate with them—it would be an insult against the witches who ran that organization. Dominique would be furious at her daughter, but she couldn't kill them, or disown Sarah.

*Considering how weak they both are, they're probably part of SingleEarth,* Sarah tried to reassure herself. *Please, let them be in SingleEarth.*

She jumped, swerving, as a squirrel darted in front of her car. *Calm down, Sarah. Focus.*

Try as she might, her strict control was shattered. She had been purely scatterbrained all evening, and was grateful that she wasn't expecting a fight tonight.

As she parked in Christopher and Nissa's driveway, she thought she heard faint music from the house, but it might have been her imagination. Bracing herself, she knocked on the door.

# CHAPTER 8

SOMEONE SARAH DID NOT KNOW opened the door. Black eyes gave him away as a vampire, but his light aura showed him to be almost as weak as Nissa.

"Come on in," the vampire greeted her. Sarah could only nod mutely as she realized what was going on. She had just walked in on a bash.

"Thanks," she answered, dazed. The vampire gave her a strange look, but Sarah paid no heed to him, because her attention had just been drawn to a couple seated on the couch.

A more naïve guest might assume they were making out. One pale hand was wrapped around the back of the boy's neck, and the girl's long hair fell around her face, blocking from view the seam between her lips and the human boy's throat. His eyes were half closed, and one hand twined absently in the vampire's hair, holding her to his throat.

Sarah recognized the dark hair, the slender form, and she wished she did not. Nissa.

Forcing her attention to the rest of the room, her aura brushing over the others, Sarah picked out the vampires easily. This crowd was weak, not killers—and for that she thanked every god and goddess she had ever heard of—but she did not recognize any of them from SingleEarth, either.

That meant there was some danger here for her. Even vampires who did not frequently kill would be nervous in the presence of a Vida, and entering a large group of them, barely armed and weakened by injury, seemed a bad idea.

She was about to leave, but the vampire who had opened the door was talking again. "I haven't seen you around here before," he said. "Who invited you?" Though his tone was not exactly suspicious, she could tell the vampire was uneasy around her. Having someone ask about her was unusual; at most of the bashes she had crashed, the vampires didn't care who a guest was, so long as she could bleed.

"She's with me." Sarah turned, barely checking her instinct to draw her knife, as she sensed someone approach behind her.

The vampire who had been asking sighed. "I should have known." He wandered off.

Christopher ran his hands through his short black hair, nervous. "Sarah . . . I would have invited you, but . . ." She could guess his thoughts. *How do you explain something like this to someone you assume is human?*

"You don't have to explain," Sarah offered in an attempt to save the vampire the unease of beginning the conversation. She could sense Christopher's shock even through his midnight eyes.

"I don't?"

Out of the corner of her eye, Sarah saw Nissa release the human she had been feeding on. He lay back, a bit dazed, but he looked like he would be fine; if there was anything a vampire knew, it was how much blood a human could afford to lose without being harmed.

The girl looked up, and her eyes widened as she saw Sarah standing with Christopher. She wiped her lips clear of blood with the back of her hand.

"I already know what you are." The sentence had been directed at Christopher, though Sarah was busy reading Nissa's features. Seeing blood on her friend's mouth had unnerved her.

"Why don't we go upstairs for a minute?" Christopher suggested, looking from his sister to his unexpected guest. Nissa nodded.

"That sounds good," Sarah answered. Christopher led the way, and Sarah saw Nissa quickly snatch a mint from a table next to the couch before the wall cut her off from view.

A few moments later, the three gathered in Nissa's room, which was not open to guests. Sarah hesitated in the doorway as Nissa and Christopher made themselves comfortable.

The room was surprisingly normal. While Sarah had known better than to expect a coffin, bats, and bricked-over windows, it was still surprising to see the scattering of schoolbooks that littered the desk. A composition book had been tossed casually in a corner amidst a flurry of crumpled paper and pens, and the pastel blue walls were decorated with posters from musicals like *Rent, Les Misérables,* and *West Side Story.*

"Well, then," Nissa breathed, and Sarah caught the scent of mint barely disguising the reek of fresh blood.

Sarah meant to speak instantly, telling them who she was, but Christopher forestalled it, asking hesitantly, "Are you part of SingleEarth? Or . . ."

She barely managed not to laugh at that question. Sarah Vida, a member of SingleEarth? Oh, Dominique would have a heart attack at the very suggestion.

Nevertheless, she was here, talking with two vampires, two *friends* who just happened to be bloodsucking fiends.

She was flattered at least that he thought of SingleEarth before the alternatives. He still thought she was human, and if she was tolerant of his kind, then it stood to reason that she was either part of SingleEarth, or one of those pathetic creatures who chased after the vampires in order to have her blood taken.

"No, I'm not," she said slowly, trying to decide how best to tell the truth. She would rather have been somewhere else, anywhere but in the middle of a house full of vampires she did not know and whose behavior she could not predict. "I didn't know you had a circuit," she stalled.

"It's Nissa's," Christopher answered, nodding to his sister. "She hosts. I just hang out."

The vampire bashes that Sarah frequently crashed followed a pattern. The members of each party circuit alternated hosting, so as to keep the hunters guessing where the next one would be. All that Sarah had attended had been violent, deadly for any humans who attended, but she had heard about ones like this, where the human guests were simply that—guests, not a main course. They donated blood occasionally, but not at risk to their lives.

"Do you go to bashes often?" Nissa asked from her perch on the bed.

"When I can," Sarah answered truthfully, wondering how—and if—she should ease into the topic she had come to discuss. The presence of several unknown vampires downstairs made her a little hesitant to reveal herself.

Christopher flinched, worry in his eyes. "Not all of them are as safe as Nissa's group."

"I know."

"The worst is Kendra's circuit," Nissa warned. "If you stumble on one of theirs, they'll probably kill you without a thought." Softly, she added, "That's the one Kaleo travels in." The name seemed to strike a chord in both vampires, and Sarah remembered Nissa's sculpture of the leech.

*Stop stalling, Sarah,* she ordered herself, even as she commented, "You were telling me about Kaleo in sculpture."

"Kaleo . . . was the one who changed me," Nissa said hesitantly. She glanced at her brother, who just shrugged.

"If you want to tell it, it's your story," he pointed out.

"We grew up in the South, just before the Civil War," Nissa began softly. "Our father worked at a nearby plantation and I took care of the owner's two daughters, while my brothes worked as stable hands for one of the other wealthy families. We weren't rich, but we were happy. My mother died when Christopher and his twin brother were both very young, and I more or less raised them."

With a sigh, she continued, "We were an artistic family. I was the singer, though both of my brothers had talent in that area too. Christopher would write songs and poetry. Even when he said grace at night, his words could bring you to tears.

"That's what damned us—music and art," Nissa went on. "Because it drew Kaleo to me. He was also an artist. If he hadn't learned about my talent, he never would have given me more than a passing glance. As it was, he fell in love with me . . . and I with him." That admission sounded painful. "I was seventeen, a romantic and an optimist, and Kaleo was—*is*—very handsome, and very charming, especially when he has it in his mind to win someone over." Nissa paused in her story.

When she continued, her voice was barely more than a whisper. "For a while our relationship was wonderful, but I learned what he was when I caught him feeding on the woman I worked for." With difficulty, Nissa explained, "He did not have time to hurt her before I interrupted. She woke up later, unharmed, and I stupidly assumed that Kaleo wasn't dangerous, that he would not have hurt her even if I had not interfered."

Her voice wavered as she confessed, "I forgave him, and even came to love him more. Then he offered me immortality, and I said no." Nissa took a deep breath to keep herself composed. A hint of anger entered her voice, overlaid with sorrow.

"I thought for a while that we could continue as before, but Kaleo doesn't take no for an answer.

Eventually he became so insistent that we argued every time we were together, and finally I told him to leave me alone." A moment of silence passed before she continued. "My brothers were twelve and I was barely nineteen when Kaleo killed our father. I could have stopped him, had I been home a minute earlier, but instead I ran in moments after he died. Christopher's twin was there, and he saw everything. Kaleo made it very clear that he would not hesitate to snap my brother's neck if I refused again.

"So I agreed." The words seemed to catch, as Nissa choked back the memory. "I stayed with my brothers for a few years, but my kind does not exist easily in the human world. There was . . . an incident. I changed my brother, and he changed Christopher the next night. And now we're here."

"What happened to your other brother?" Sarah asked. The instant the words were out of her mouth, Christopher's expression made her regret the question.

"He doesn't run with us," Nissa answered quietly. It was clear she didn't want to go into the topic, and Sarah decided not to press.

The silence hung heavy, both vampires obviously contemplating their painful history. Sarah's mind drifted back to her purpose here, but she couldn't tell them now. Not when they had just opened their hearts to her. She couldn't betray a trust like that, even if she hadn't asked for it.

No one seemed to know exactly how to get over the conversation, so Sarah got up and walked around the room a bit. Once again she noticed the school textbooks.

"Why do you go to school?" she asked. "If you're . . .

that old, then why bother?" She did not want to do the math to figure out exactly how old.

"If you spend too much time away from humans, you forget your own humanity," Nissa said, her voice distant. "It gets harder to remember that you used to be one of them, and easier to think of them like . . . cattle," she finished apologetically. "Most of our kind is like that. They don't see anything wrong with killing humans. Christopher and I decided we needed a reminder." Sarah remembered with unease Adianna's comment about the vampire blood slowly destroying the last shreds of humanity, and was glad she was not immediately called on to speak. Nissa continued with what sounded like forced brightness, "It's nice to actually be part of the human world for a bit, though I suppose I could imagine places more glamorous than high school." With a brief glance to some flyer on her desk, she added, "Speaking of, are you sure you won't come to the Halloween dance? It will be a lot of fun."

Sarah started to argue, but instead just shrugged. *What the hell,* she thought, *I can do this one last thing, can't I?* Dominique would be furious, but the dance would be over early enough for her to make the ceremony at midnight. As Nissa had said, sometimes it was nice to just be a part of the human crowd for a while.

She heard herself answer, "Sure. I'll find a way to come."

# CHAPTER 9

SATURDAY NIGHT, Sarah wrote a note to Dominique: *I am going to attend a dance at school, but will be back in plenty of time for the ceremony. Sarah.*

She dressed carefully, added a hint of makeup, and pinned the sleeves of her dress to hide the spring-loaded knife sheath on her left wrist. She could trigger the mechanism with a small burst of power if necessary. Another knife was on her back. She trusted Christopher and Nissa, but no vampire hunter went out unarmed, especially at this time of year. The moon was full, it was the witches' New Year, and her aura flickered around her, strong and bright. She had too many enemies in the vampire world that would be able to recognize it.

Sarah met up with Christopher and Nissa just outside the door to the school.

"Sarah, you look great!" Nissa exclaimed.

Nissa's full skirts billowed around her as she crossed

the floor. She was dressed in an emerald-colored Renaissance-style gown that laced up in back and showed off her perfect figure. Christopher had dressed as a Gypsy, with a colorful vest and a multicolored scarf pulled around his waist.

Sarah was wearing the same dress she would wear for the ceremony later, a light, silvery cotton gown that flowed around her legs when she moved. Around her waist, in place of the silver belt she would wear at midnight, was a sapphire sash that matched her eyes. It was embroidered with silver stars, and had been hidden somewhere in the back of her closet. She had not worn it in a very long time; it had been a gift from her sister, before Adianna had given up such frivolous things like sisterly teasing and birthday presents in order to follow in Dominique's emotionless footsteps.

The constellations on the barely worn sash reminded Sarah of the picture Christopher had drawn. Since she could hardly go around holding planets, she wore sun and moon earrings.

When the three met up outside the gym, Christopher's eyes said that he recognized the outfit.

As they entered the dance together, the brush of another witch's aura caused Sarah to stretch out a tendril of power and try to locate its source, but the crowd of students was so thick she could not.

A slow song started, and Christopher looked to her. "Want to dance?" he asked as he reached for her hand.

She saw an edge of nervousness in Christopher's expression when she hesitated, and before she could think it through she answered, "Sure."

She tensed when Christopher touched her. Stretching out her senses to locate the other witch had made her hypersensitive to his vampiric aura. He looked so human, so fragile, and yet his presence made her every sense shriek in warning.

She distracted herself by focusing on the other witch. The power she sensed was familiar enough that it made her uneasy. She wasn't supposed to be here, but Dominique wouldn't have come to fetch her, would she? If she was at the dance, or if Adianna was here . . .

Everything about the moment was wrong. At this distance, at this time, Christopher's aura ran over her skin like thousands of spider legs scampering across bare flesh.

She stopped dancing at the same time she saw Adianna in the crowd. How distracted she must have been not to have recognized her sister's presence.

"I can't do this," she whispered, stepping back from Christopher, shaking her head violently. If Adianna saw him, after having given her warning . . .

"What? What did I do?" Christopher asked. The hurt in his eyes was so raw she wanted to comfort him.

But "I'm sorry" was all she could say before she turned away. She who had been taught to fight to the end, win or lose, now ran from one of the very creatures she hunted.

Leaning against the wall outside, completely alone, Sarah felt better. A moment later the doors opened again and Adianna came out, her eyes moving sharply around the area as she checked for any possible threats.

"Sarah, Mother is throwing a fit. She asked me to

find you. What are you doing here?" Adianna winced at the obvious answer when the door opened again and Christopher followed them out.

Christopher froze, no doubt sensing danger but not fully understanding it.

"Please, Adia, let me handle this," Sarah asked softly, catching Adianna's wrist before the other hunter could move.

*Sarah*—Adianna said, reaching out with her mind.

Responding the same way, Sarah interrupted, *I'm going to tell him the truth, and then I'll come home. I care about him, and about his sister. I don't want either of them hurt. Just let me say good-bye my own way. And don't tell Dominique.*

Adianna could read Christopher's aura almost as well as Sarah could, and knew the vampire was not a threat physically. She nodded. If Sarah was going to tell him who she was, and end the friendship, then Adianna would let her do it.

Adianna backed away, keeping her gaze on the vampire until she slipped around the corner to the front of the building.

# CHAPTER 10

"WHAT WAS THAT ABOUT?" Christopher asked, bewildered.

"Adianna . . . doesn't like you." It was the most she could think to say. "Come here—away from the door. I need to talk to you, and I don't want someone wandering into our conversation." She led him to the back of the building.

"What did I do?" Christopher asked when she hesitated to explain.

"You"—*are a blood-sucking leech*—"didn't do anything wrong," Sarah answered. She took a breath to brace herself for her next words, because they would hopefully end the closest thing she had ever had to a true friendship. "But I need you to leave me alone." Only seventeen years as Dominique Vida's daughter kept her own pain from her voice. She couldn't continue this double life, and Christopher would be safer knowing nothing. "I want you to stay away from me," she continued, driving the knife home. "Don't talk to me. Don't come near me. Don't even look at me."

"If that's how you feel," he answered, his voice cooler than a moment ago, though she could still hear his hurt in it. She had hidden enough of her own emotions in her life to recognize that he was trying to do the same.

"I'm sorry."

"Don't be—you aren't the first to turn me down, and you probably won't be the last."

"I don't want you getting hurt, Christopher." He shrugged, turning away, as if it didn't matter.

"It's harder to do than one might think," he answered bitterly.

The words gave her a moment of pain. "Christopher, turn around." She couldn't leave him like this, without understanding. She was trying to protect him; she did not want to hurt him.

"I'm leaving. I won't bother you."

*"Christopher, look at me!"*

He turned around, his face completely neutral except for a hint of anger behind his eyes.

"What?" His voice was cold, controlled—very different from the Christopher that Sarah had come to know. She wondered when in his life he had needed to learn how to show nothing of his thoughts, nothing of his feelings.

"It isn't you," she said quietly. She couldn't stand to let him leave without telling him her reasons. "It isn't who you are . . . and it isn't even what you are. Well, in a way it is, but . . ." She sounded like a bumbling idiot, she knew, but the necessary words did not come easily to her. "It's not just what you are. It's what I am."

Christopher started to ask a question, then paused.

"Christopher, I'm a witch. A Daughter of Macht," she elaborated. Unlike the modern Wiccans, her kind was not human, had never been human.

"I don't care if you're Dominique Vida herself," Christopher declared brazenly.

Christopher's words caused a hysterical giggle to catch in Sarah's throat. Her mother was the most famous—or in vampire circles, infamous—vampire hunter born in hundreds of years.

In answer, she drew the knife from her back; the moon glinted off its silver hilt. Christopher swore under his breath, and she smiled wryly. "Christopher, Dominique is my mother."

Now he looked at her with a small amount of skepticism, which was the last thing she expected. Most vampires were far more wary of her kind. "You? But you're . . ."

She sheathed her knife, trying to show that she meant no threat to him. "I'm what?"

"I've met a lot of hunters in my time, Sarah . . ." He raised a hand, gestured vaguely. "You don't seem like the type."

Stepping forward, she put her right hand flat-palmed against his chest and her left over his throat, pushing him back into the wall.

Shock filled Christopher's features, but then he said, "Your knife is still on your back, and if this was a real fight, we both know I could kill you before you could reach it."

She closed her right fist, drawing Christopher's attention to its position above his heart, and then moved her hand to the wall.

With her mind she reached out and triggered the spring on the knife she wore on her wrist, and the blade snapped out, slicing two inches into the wood paneling of the wall.

"Don't underestimate me, Christopher."

"Are you going to kill me, Sarah?" he asked, but there was no fear in his voice—just an edge of anger. He was getting defensive, trying not to let his hurt show. She recognized the act; anger was much less painful to feel than the sorrow.

"I'm not going to kill you. I don't want my *family* to."

"I can take care of myself." So fearless. Most vampires were afraid of her kind, but Christopher did not seem the least bit worried.

"Meaning what? If my mother or sister attacks you, you'll kill her? There is no good situation here, except for you to leave me alone. I'm not right for you."

"Sarah, I don't care who you are," he repeated. "I've taken a knife from one of your line before. I have a scar, but I'm still alive. If someone attacks me, I leave. That's how I've survived for more than fifty years."

She flinched. How had he taken a Vida knife and lived?

That question was shoved from her mind as she processed the comment about "fifty years." According to the story Nissa had told, he was easily three times that old.

She bit back her questions, and focused on the issue at hand.

"Christopher, maybe you don't care, but I have to."

"You're a teenager—it's your job to act out against

your parents. What's the worst they could do to you?" The question was shockingly naïve.

"The worst? Christopher, you don't understand. I am Sarah Tigress Vida, youngest Daughter of Vida. If my mother finds out I have befriended a vampire, she will *disown* me. I'll lose my title, my name, my weapons, and even my magic."

"That could be rough, but you're strong enough to get through it," Christopher said, still not understanding.

"I would be defenseless. I've killed too many of your kind before. I've made a lot of enemies. If I can't fight back, I'm dead. If my line disowned me, it would be the same as them killing me."

"That's why you want me to leave you alone?"

She paused for only a moment. "They'll kill you, too, if they see you with me again. Maybe you're willing to risk that, but I'm not. I would hate myself for doing it, but I need to defend myself, so if you come near me again, I will have to act."

For an instant, some trick of shadow combined with Sarah's guilt made Christopher look not like a friend who had been betrayed, but like an enemy who had been wronged.

"Fine," he answered, and now his voice was like a steel door, closing on some of the best times Sarah had ever had.

# CHAPTER 11

AS SOON AS Christopher was out of sight, Sarah ran from the school grounds, vaulted into the driver's seat of her car, and put the key in the ignition. Her hands were trembling; as soon as she noticed, the movement ceased.

Sarah Tigress Vida was not perfect, but she hadn't lost control since her father had died, and she didn't intend to now.

But she absolutely could not face her family right now. Dominique and Adianna were the last people she wanted to see. Neither did she care to see the other vampire hunters with whom her family would be celebrating the New Year.

At nearly eleven o'clock, she pulled into the brightly lit parking lot of SingleEarth Haven. The mishmash of brilliant auras seeped out of the magically protected building—vampires, shapeshifters, witches, and humans.

She found Caryn near the door. The healer took one look at Sarah and led her to an empty room.

"Why the gloom?" Caryn asked gently, as Sarah collapsed onto the bed.

When Sarah did not answer, Caryn put a hand on her shoulder, friendly despite the fact that they had never been friends. The other witch's aura was like a warm breeze, gentle and soothing as it brushed over Sarah's skin.

"Sarah, what's wrong?"

"Can I just stay here tonight? I can't face my mother right now." Sarah grimaced. "If I don't come home tonight, she's going to want to know where I've been. She'll be upset if I miss the gathering, but it's not against the law for me to be here."

Caryn sat on the bed next to the flustered hunter. "So long as you're here peacefully, you're welcome to stay. But I would have thought you'd want to spend the New Year with your family."

Sarah closed her eyes, trying to clear from her mind Christopher's expression. "There are some things I need to think through before I see them again. And I don't want to fight with Dominique on a holiday."

Caryn patted her hand. "Stay as long as you like. If you're feeling up to it, you should come downstairs, meet some of the others. Even a hunter needs peace in her life sometimes."

"And how would SingleEarth react to a hunter in their midst?" Sarah asked dryly.

"If you walk in there, some vampires will be nervous, but they'll give you a chance." Sarah laughed, but Caryn went on, saying, "It's the effort that matters. Every vampire, every witch, still has a human soul."

Sarah hesitated, but spending the night alone in this

little room, listening to the music from downstairs and staring out the window, was not how anyone would want to spend a holiday.

Caryn led her downstairs, where the SingleEarth party was bustling with activity. Humans mingled with vampires and witches, laughing and joking together as if they were all the same kind.

Sarah rotated her shoulders, trying to work the tension from between her shoulder blades. No matter how light and happy the revelers were, she kept expecting to feel a knife in her back.

"Loosen up, Sarah," Caryn encouraged her. "Introduce yourself to someone, and ask him to dance. Just have fun. SingleEarth is a safe, neutral place—no one's going to bite."

Despite Caryn's urging, Sarah's feeling of being misplaced refused to fade. She did not join the party, but watched from the edge, until at nearly two o'clock in the morning there was some excitement outside. Someone grabbed Caryn's arm, pulling her toward the doorway.

Caryn paused when she saw whatever it was that stood beyond the door, but she quickly gathered herself and stepped outside, with Sarah hurrying after.

The yard was bright, and Sarah recognized the figure that was leading Caryn toward a dark corner. She trailed behind unobtrusively, not wanting to speak with Christopher if she could help it, but not willing to leave Caryn alone with any non-SingleEarth vampire, even one that she knew. Christopher had blood on his arm, and a small streak of it on his cheek as if he had brushed hair out of his face without realizing his hand was bloody.

Christopher had driven to the party, which was odd in itself, since he, like even the weakest of vampires, could have traveled more easily with his mind. He was driving a sleek white Le Sabre that Sarah had never seen before. She understood instantly, though, when he opened the door to the backseat to reveal an injured human.

Sarah relaxed a bit when she realized Christopher was here to help a human friend, but then her suspicions rose. How had the girl been injured in the first place?

Caryn slipped into the car, ignoring the blood, while Christopher knelt beside the open door.

"Apparently she was at a bash, and she got into a fight," he explained quickly. "One of the vampires there asked me to get her help."

"Why didn't he bring her himself?" Caryn asked, her voice faint, as most of her concentration went to examining the human.

"Just help her," was all Christopher said in answer.

A second later, Sarah heard Caryn's breath hiss in with surprise.

Curious, Sarah stepped forward to look into the car.

The girl's naturally smooth, dark skin was marred by bruises and shallow wounds, and Sarah could tell that the unconscious victim's jaw was probably broken. She was bleeding in several places, and her breathing was quick and shallow.

Sarah could only see the girl's right arm, but that was

enough. Faded scars marked her skin—a rose on her right shoulder and a strand of ivy on her wrist. This girl was one of Nikolas's victims. Had Nikolas beaten her, or had some other vampire caused this more recent injury?

*And what was Christopher doing with Nikolas?*

"Sarah, Christopher, give me some room," Caryn ordered. Her voice was soft, but the authority was unmistakable. Sarah could feel the gentle pulse of magic emanating from the healer—a warm, peaceful glow, so different from the painful Vida magic.

Sarah could see tension in Christopher's movements as he slipped past her without a word, and moved further away from the light.

"Who is she?"

Christopher paused. "Her name is Marguerite," he answered cautiously. "They asked me to take her, because no one in that group is allowed within a hundred yards of SingleEarth."

"Why you?"

"Probably because they could find me." His voice was growing cooler. "Blood calls to blood—a lot of the people in my line are in that circuit." The words seemed a challenge, as he flaunted his connection to the killers.

She glanced at the car, where Caryn was still working. "What happened to her?"

Christopher shook his head. "I didn't see it. All I know is that another vampire insulted Nikolas, and Marguerite took a swing at him. She nearly got herself killed before someone dragged the two of them apart."

*So Nikolas wasn't the one who hurt her,* Sarah thought, almost disappointed. If Nikolas had caused this, Sarah could probably have gotten some information from the

girl, but if she had attacked a vampire in defense of
Nikolas, then Marguerite was not likely to tell much of
anything to a hunter.

"You know Nikolas, then?" she asked aloud.

"Don't, Sarah." Christopher's voice was sure, and
made it very clear that he had no intention of telling her
anything.

"Were you at the bash?"

"Do you think I'm the one who hit her?" Christopher
asked, his voice quiet, but taut with anger.

No, she did not think Christopher would ever hurt a
human. But if he was hanging out around Nikolas and
other killers, then she would have to start wondering if
her impressions were correct. "Did you?"

"I didn't hurt her," he said, turning away. "I wasn't at
the bash. I don't follow that circuit." He sounded hurt.

"I had to ask." But that was a lie. She could read his
aura, and more than that, she knew Christopher. He
wasn't a killer.

Sarah had nothing more to say to him. Dominique or
Adianna would have had a knife to his throat immedi-
ately, demanding information on Nikolas and his group.
Had he been speaking to any Daughter of Vida but
Sarah, Christopher would not have lived through the
next five minutes.

The tense silence lasted for several moments, until
Caryn called for Christopher to take the girl home.
Marguerite needed rest, but she would be fine.

Sarah didn't know what bothered her more—that
Christopher had been so frosty, or that she was watching two people who could have given her information
on Nikolas drive away from her.

# CHAPTER 12

CHRISTOPHER WAS NOT IN CLASS on Monday. The seat next to Sarah in history was painfully empty. No new poems showed up in her locker or in her backpack.

In sculpture class, she avoided Nissa. She knew that if she allowed herself to maintain even a casual in-school relationship with the vampires, she would never be able to keep the necessary distance that Vida law demanded.

By lunch she was surprised to realize she already missed them fiercely. She didn't even go into the cafeteria, but brought her sandwich out to the courtyard and ate on the grass, alone.

In calculus, she began to worry about Christopher. Again he wasn't in class. Vampires did not get sick, and it took a lot to even injure them. While it was possible that Christopher had just decided to avoid school — and her — she hoped that wasn't the case. He had been genuinely enjoying playing human; she didn't want to think that she had chased him away from it.

Of course, if he hadn't planned to be absent, then she didn't like to think about why he wasn't here. While human myth often ascribed to vampires the title "immortal," Sarah well knew they could be killed.

Sarah's resolve not to talk to Nissa might have held, had she not run into the girl in the parking lot after school. She was hurrying to meet up with Caryn to have her cast removed when she nearly collided with Nissa.

Jumping back, she asked, "Is Christopher okay?" The words were out of her mouth before she had a chance to think them through.

Nissa hesitated, apparently surprised. "I think so. He . . . was upset after the dance, and went to visit his brother. He came home and crashed a little after sunrise this morning."

"His brother?" Sarah parroted, her stomach plummeting. She leaned back against a nearby car, running her hands through her hair. They had made it clear earlier that Christopher's twin had not decided to follow the same peaceful route as his siblings. "Look, Nissa—"

"Excuse me." The voice was dry, and decidedly unhappy. Sarah turned to see Robert, standing sulkily a few feet back. "That's my car you're leaning against."

Nissa grabbed Sarah's arm and pulled her away from the car. Robert went around to the driver's side and popped the trunk.

"I don't know what to make of Robert," Nissa said

under her breath, softly so the human would not overhear. "Christopher stumbled across him last night at the
bash when he went to help Marguerite."

After that, Sarah stopped paying attention, because
quite suddenly she realized where she had seen Robert
before she had joined this school. Her barely healed
arm was a testament to the night.

"Excuse me, Nissa." No matter what happened, she
was a hunter first. Robert had been at the bash where
Sarah had run into one of Nikolas's victims, as well as
at the bash where Marguerite had been. If he was part
of that circuit, then she had a chance to get back to it.

She turned her back on Nissa and hurried to
Robert's car, where he was just opening the driver-side
door.

"Robert!" She closed the door with one flat palm,
and the human jumped, moving his fingers in just
enough time to avoid having them slammed in the door.

He tried to ignore her, reaching for the door handle,
but he had not accounted for her strength. She wasn't
as strong as a vampire, but she could easily outmuscle a
pureblood human.

"What do you want?" he finally asked.

Sarah glanced back to where Nissa had been, but the
girl had disappeared. With no one to overhear, she answered Robert's question honestly. "I want to know
what you were doing at a bash on Halloween night."

"I was invited," Robert snapped.

"By who?"

"Can't you just read my mind or something?" He
shouldered her aside, and the mixture of his words and

the movement forced her off balance enough that she let him.

He thought she was a vampire. Oh, that was rich. Nearly laughing, she caught the door before he had a chance to get in the car.

"Robert, you have no idea what you're talking about—"

"Leave me *alone.*"

"I'm not a vampire." Her mind was working quickly. He had seen her at the bash, and had made the obvious assumption. What she couldn't figure out was why, if he thought she was a vampire, he had hated her almost on sight. Though there were always plenty of humans who were invited to a bash purely as entrees, most repeat guests attended because they *liked* being fed on. Robert obviously wasn't part of the first group, but his aversion to her proved that he wasn't part of the second, either.

The only other humans who attended bashes were blood bonded, or thought themselves hunters. Sarah would have sensed a blood bond.

"Then what are you?" Robert pressed. "You sure as hell aren't human."

"I'm a witch."

Robert snorted. "And pigs fly."

He had just begun to slide into the seat when she added, "And I'm a vampire hunter."

Finally the human paused, and again she sensed him sizing her up.

Technically, Sarah should have asked Dominique's permission before telling any human she was a witch.

Depending on how Robert handled her revelation, Sarah would either have to wipe his mind to make him forget she had said anything—something that was difficult, but possible—or she might be able to enlist his help.

Robert glanced around the parking lot, where other students were gathering in the postschool flurry of activity. "Get in the car," he finally said. "Tell me what you know."

He pulled out of the parking lot before Sarah could think how to begin. Her silence seemed to make him uneasy, so he spoke instead. "Look. Just because I'm listening to you doesn't necessarily mean I believe you. But maybe if you tell me what you were doing at the bash . . ."

"You must have left early if you don't know the answer to that one," Sarah said, thinking of the disaster that night had turned into.

"About ten," Robert answered, with a nod. "I couldn't find the person I was looking for, so it made sense to ditch."

"Who were you looking for?"

Robert had been driving aimlessly, apparently, but now he stopped at the side of the road. Voice cool and level despite the suspicion, he asked, "Why do you care?"

Sarah could see he wasn't going to give away information for free, and unlike the vampires, she did not have the ability to reach into his mind and find what she needed to know. She had to tell him something. "I want someone dead, and you might be able to help me," she explained.

Robert hesitated for only a fraction of a heartbeat. "You're after Nikolas." When Sarah nodded, he looked at her with absolute skepticism, sizing up her slender figure. "You really think you could get that . . . creature?"

"I'm going to try," she snapped before she could catch herself. His implication had struck a chord, but Robert didn't know what he was talking about; getting mad at him wouldn't help things. She forced herself to control her tone the next time she spoke. "I'm not planning to arm wrestle him, Robert, and I'm not as helpless as you think. I'm not human; I'm stronger than your kind, and I have more power. And I've been trained to kill vampires my entire life. I know what I'm doing."

"Well, good luck," Robert answered sarcastically. "I've killed my share of vampires, but I've still been after this bastard for months."

She had to restrain herself from snickering at his bravado as she noticed Robert hadn't elaborated on the exact number of leeches he had put a knife through. She wasn't surprised. He was only human, after all, and though she hadn't seen him fight, his ignorance of her kind told Sarah that he was probably relatively new at wielding a knife. He was lucky he had not run into Nikolas yet, or his little extracurricular activity would have gotten him killed already.

"How long have you been hunting?" she asked.

"Since Nikolas." His response was short, but clear.

"What did he do to you?"

Robert took a deep breath, his gaze somewhere past Sarah's left shoulder. "Not to me . . . my sister." He spoke slowly, considering his words carefully before they emerged. "Her name was Christine."

"Was?" Sarah would be far from surprised to learn the leech had slaughtered the poor girl.

"We call her Kristin, now. She doesn't respond to her real name." He paused. The silence was so long that Sarah began to wonder if he was finished, but finally he continued, "One of her friends, Heather, brought her to a party . . . I didn't know then, but it was one of Nikolas's bashes. She didn't come home that night, or the next morning. My mother called the police, and they must have checked the hospitals." Again he took a deep breath as if to brace himself, and she could see the vision forming in his eyes. "She had lost a lot of blood. He had carved his name into her arms, then left her nearly dead on some stranger's front lawn."

As he spoke, emotions surged across Robert's aura—fury, frustration, hatred. He forced his lungs to take in a deep breath of air to calm himself, but it did no good. "At first she was just scared and skittish when she got home. She wouldn't let us call her Christine anymore, and she stayed in her room all the time. If you asked her, she would talk about Nikolas, about how . . . handsome and gentle he was." The last words were spat like a curse. "She always described him as black and white, and after a while she made herself that way too. She shudders away from anything colorful, and she screams when she sees anything red."

Sarah didn't like doing it, but she probed his memory wound for useful information. Robert would have to deal with the pain if he wanted to help his sister. "Is that all you know?"

"Only that it gets worse every day. No doctor has been able to help her." He shook his head. "I went to the house where the bash had been a few days after Kristin got home, but it was collapsing in flame. There was this old man watching the fire—he lived next door, and invited me in for iced tea. Said the vampires had been living beside him for years. Usually, he said, he didn't mind unless they put the music on really loud. But when they left Kristin on his lawn, he got fed up and torched the place . . ." Bitterly, Robert added, "He had known all along what they were, and what was going on over there. But he hadn't gotten angry until they trampled his garden when they left Kristin. *That's* when he acted."

Sarah found herself pulling back from the human, who was trembling with rage strong enough to make her head spin. Yet she forced herself to say, "Robert, I need to talk to Kristin."

He gave her a you-have-got-to-be-kidding-me look. "She doesn't talk to anyone, not even me."

Sarah wanted to argue further, but held back. A visit now would be wasted. She needed time to think of a way to approach Kristin so the girl would talk to her.

Robert gave her a ride home, and as they arrived Sarah took a pad of paper from her backpack. Scribbling down her phone number, she ripped out the sheet and handed it to Robert. "Give me a call sometime soon." Hesitantly, she added, "You really should talk to my mother, too. She can train you to fight." Sarah did not know if the human would admit he needed help, but Robert wasn't going to live long if he wasn't trained.

As she slid out of the car, Robert grabbed her arm. "Wait just a sec." He paused, then seemed to make up his mind. "If you really think you have a chance at him, I have something for you."

He tore off the bottom of the paper where she had written her number, and jotted down an address. "I was at a bash here on Halloween. I left when a fight broke out, but I was there long enough to know it's his house. It's about two hours away."

Sarah smiled, glad for the first bit of truly helpful information Robert had been able to supply. Soon she would be facing one of the longest-hunted vampires in the Vida records. Not even Dominique and Adianna would be able to belittle *that* fight.

"Thanks."

"Tell me how it goes?"

With a nod, she closed the car door. She was glad her cast was coming off tonight.

# CHAPTER 13

SARAH SKIPPED SCHOOL the next day. Posing as her mother, she called early and excused herself.

No well-trained hunter was mad enough to stalk a vampire on his own turf at night. While real vampires were not confined to coma-like, coffin-enclosed sleeps whenever the sun was up, they were naturally nocturnal. Christopher and Nissa were prime examples that vampires could function fine in the daylight world, but the stronger a vampire grew, the more irritating sunlight became, and the less natural a diurnal schedule was.

So she was fairly sure that at ten o'clock in the morning, Nikolas would be asleep. At least he would be alone, and not hosting a bash. She wasn't suicidal enough to approach him in a group of his kind, but she believed she could handle one vampire on her own—even the legendary Nikolas.

When she reached the address Robert had given her, she drove past it once, checking for lights and sounds.

It was hard to tell over the vampiric aura that saturated the area, but she thought she sensed humans inside.

The next time around the block, she parked down the street. She stopped the Jaguar at the boundary of two property lines, so if either of the houses' owners saw her, they would each assume she was a guest of the other.

Breaking into a house at ten o'clock in the morning was not generally a good idea, but somehow she doubted she would be welcome if she simply knocked on the door. Swathing herself in magic, she approached through the side yard. If a human glanced in her direction, he would see her movement as the rustle of leaves in a breeze. She wasn't invisible, but humans saw a great deal that they didn't consciously notice. She hoped her magic would keep her safe from detection of the blood bonded humans inside as well, since if any of them saw her, the vampire would shortly follow.

The house was upper middle class, nondescript but for a string of clematis that bloomed a brilliant violet around the mailbox and wraparound porch. Trees grew heavily in this neighborhood, providing plenty of shade in which simple plants grew. Someone had devoted time to gardening.

The image of a long-hunted vampire practicing horticulture was amusing enough to bring a smile to her face, although she doubted he was the gardener.

From the yard, she sized up the house. It was three stories, four if it had a basement. The top floor had a large bay window on the northern side, but white curtains blocked Sarah's view.

After a quick check to make sure all her knives were

in place, Sarah swung onto the porch, her sneakers barely making a sound. A quick burst of laughter alerted her just before two girls came around the corner of the house. Focusing her power, Sarah threw a burst of it at the two, the magical equivalent of a hammer to the head. Both girls collapsed, instantly unconscious. They would wake awhile later, groggy but unharmed.

Taking a deep breath to regain her focus, Sarah stepped past the girls and slipped through the open door they had just exited.

Instantly she felt color-blind. *Black and white,* Robert had said. She was in the right place.

The carpet of the living room was plush black. The walls were white but for abstract designs that had been painted onto them in black. The furniture was a combination of black and white.

Her head nearly spinning at the abrupt change of scenery, Sarah barely avoided knocking a vase of white roses off a black table. Their green leaves were the only bit of color in the room.

She passed through the first floor quickly, easily satisfied that it was empty. On the second floor she passed one door behind which she sensed another human. This one was probably sleeping, but Sarah didn't risk checking. The rest of the house was empty but for the vampire she sensed on the top floor, probably in the room with the bay window.

Climbing another flight of stairs, she sensed him very close by. If he was sleeping, she still had a chance to surprise him. More likely he had already sensed her the same way she could sense him, and was expecting to fight.

She opened the door that she knew must lead to Nikolas's room, but what she found there threw her entirely off balance.

The walls were pure art, covered with pictures drawn in careful black paint, like a sketch enlarged to become a mural.

And she *recognized* the figures. Kaleo and Kendra, and other high-society vampiric killers, each in aloof portraits, graced the walls. Worse, she recognized her friends—Christopher and Nissa.

Still dazed, she spun when she sensed someone behind her.

*Christopher?*

He was dressed entirely in black—black boots, black jeans, and a black T-shirt. His hair was much longer than it had been when she saw him last, and the ebony waves were tied back.

He looked exactly the same except for the hair, but something was very *wrong*.

His expression was dark and angry, as opposed to the open, smiling one she had grown so fond of. But the wrongness didn't reach her brain until he pushed her back into the wall, forcing the breath from her lungs. The vampire's aura washed over her like ice water—too strong, too dark. Christopher did not feed on humans, but this vampire did, and probably had for more than a hundred years.

*So this is the brother,* she found herself thinking. She remembered how Nissa and Christopher had clammed up when she had tried to inquire about Christopher's twin. *Would have been nice to know before stumbling in here.*

Too late—she had hesitated for that vital instant and

now Nikolas had the advantage. He grabbed both her wrists with one of his hands and held them against the wall, careful to avoid the spring-loaded knife she was wearing on her left arm. He stood to her side, carefully out of kicking range.

Sarah was concentrating, preparing to strike him with her mind, when his free hand came from nowhere and hit her.

"Don't try it, Sarah." His voice was similar to Christopher's—a slight southern accent, so like the one she had come to trust.

She pulled her mind away from Nikolas's family—he was a threat, and that was all that mattered.

Yet he wasn't doing anything threatening at the moment. Instead, he was regarding her with curiosity. "Sarah Vida, I presume?" he inquired, voice civil.

"Making sure introductions are out of the way before we fight?" she asked flippantly.

"I'll admit I'm flattered to have such a prestigious hunter track me down," he answered calmly, "but I haven't the faintest idea how to deal with you."

That threw her off guard. So far as she knew, there was only one way vampires "dealt with" hunters who entered their lairs.

"Want to hear my suggestions?" she asked, voice light, the words a cover as she started to raise power again.

He raised one eyebrow. "I don't think we're—" He broke off and hit her again, the blow making her head spin. "I said not to try it."

So he could feel her building power; that much was obvious. She would simply have to wait for a chance when he was distracted, which meant she might need to wait for him to bite her.

"If you're going to kill me, go ahead. If you're waiting for me to scream or beg, your expectations are way off."

"Your control is really that good?" She heard in his voice that he had taken her words as a challenge.

It was a challenge she knew she could win. He could break her neck easily if he wanted to, but if he wanted to hear her scream, he would have to hurt her. Badly. That would take time, and time would give her a chance to escape. "Yes, it is."

Nikolas pulled a knife from his pocket: an ivory-handled jackknife with a rose inlay made of black stone. Opening it, he pressed it against her left wrist, just hard enough for her to feel the sharpness of the blade against her skin.

"If that's supposed to be a threat, it won't work," she informed him as he glanced to her face as if to gauge her expression. "A cut there would bleed out quickly. If you mean to feed on me, you won't waste so much blood."

"And if I just mean to kill you?" he inquired.

"You would have done so already," she answered, her voice calm despite her uncertainty.

"You sure you won't beg?" he asked, offering her one last chance to avoid pain.

"Quite sure."

Still holding her wrists with his right hand, he held the knife in his left hand, and pressed the blade into her shoulder—one sharp cut, about an inch in length.

Her muscle twitched as the knife cut through it, but

Sarah refused to let pain show on her face. She used her training in order to not react, since he was looking for a response. She could take a lot of damage and heal from it. Sooner or later, he would slip up, and then he would be dead.

He pulled the knife upward, this cut at a slight angle to the last one, and then down again, as if making a Z.

Or an N.

The next cut was just beside the last line of the first letter, a half-inch line, and the next was a line parallel to the second letter. She knew what he was writing, and sighed, realizing this could be a long night. Two more short lines followed the most recent, making a K, and then a rough, squared-off circle.

*Nikolas.*

If it scarred, she was going to be really annoyed.

"Is your control really this good, or are you a secret masochist?" Nikolas asked as he cut the tail of the S, a jagged underline.

"Is this a ritual thing, or are you just a sadist?" she returned, impatient. Though he was enjoying his busy-work, he wasn't focused enough for Sarah to act.

"Both," he answered, laughing, as he turned to the other arm. "You can ask me to stop any time now." She understood what he really meant—*You can break down and beg.* "Or must I continue?"

"Hurry up, would you?" She yawned. "I have to get to the drugstore before it closes. We're out of Band-Aids at my house."

Nikolas laughed. "Don't worry about that—you won't need them."

The rose petals were more difficult, and Nikolas did

not say anything as he worked on them. When he moved to the ivy she took a deep breath, preparing herself. The ivy's stem twined around the wrist; in order to cut the full design, Nikolas would need to shift his grip.

Her arms had gone numb from the abuse and from being held above her head so long, which was actually a good thing. The pain was dulling.

"I hope that blade is clean. I would hate for this to get infected." She spoke to break the silence and keep hold of her bravado.

As she had predicted, Nikolas loosened his grip for a split second, and Sarah seized her moment, wrenching her arms down and drawing her knife at the same time. Nikolas only barely managed to avoid the silver blade as she swung it in his direction.

"You're not as quick as some of your kin, Sarah," he informed her, from just outside striking distance.

She laughed slightly. "Quick enough."

"Quicker than Elisabeth?" he inquired, and her eyes narrowed as she remembered the long hours of history. Nikolas was one of very few vampires who had killed a Vida and survived to speak of it.

"How much of a fight did she put up?" Sarah snapped. "Did she at least get a knife in you before she died?"

"Not in me." The words were almost a growl. "Get out of my house, Sarah. I will see you shortly."

He disappeared before she could react.

As she relaxed, the knife fell from her numb fingertips. She picked it up with her left hand, which wasn't much better.

She leaned back against the wall and stretched out

her awareness. While she had been occupied with Nikolas, the humans in the house had fled—even the ones she had knocked out were gone.

Her stomach churned with the unpleasant nausea that comes with blood loss. After bandaging her arms as well as she could with the scant supplies she kept in the car, she picked up her cell phone and dialed Adianna.

# CHAPTER 14

ADIANNA TOOK SARAH to Caryn Smoke's house, to be patched up for the second time in less than a month. Sarah had managed to fend off her sister's questions only with stoic silence so far.

"We're going to have to wash the blood off before I can see the cuts," Caryn explained as she unwrapped the crude bandages Sarah had made with the rough first-aid supplies she kept in her car.

She had cleaned most of the blood from the ivy before she could see enough to tell what the full design was.

"Oh, Goddess . . ." The healer looked up, her pale blue eyes wide with shock and full of question.

"What?" Adianna stepped forward to see what the healer had seen.

"Give me some room," Caryn ordered, her voice steady.

Adianna nodded, and leaned back against the opposite wall.

Caryn turned to the rose. When she got to the other shoulder she cleaned around the wound, revealing more of the damage.

*Nikolas.* Caryn whispered the name, and Sarah saw Adianna's gaze whip toward them as she heard it.

The hunter was on her feet instantly. *"That's* who you were after today?" Sarah nodded once, and saw Adianna's eyes racing over the careful designs. Finally she asked Caryn the question Sarah had been avoiding. "Will those scar?"

Caryn's face was grim as she said, "I'm afraid so. I can heal the deeper damage so there won't be any permanent injury to the muscles, but the wounds are bad enough that I can't do much more."

"My little sister went after Nikolas," Adianna stated with some surprise in her voice. "He got away, didn't he?" Again Sarah had to nod.

"He's had hunters on his tail for more than a hundred years, Adia—he's clever, and he could feel when I tried to build power to fight him. I didn't have a chance."

*Yes, you did,* another part of her mind argued as she remembered her moment of hesitation when she had first seen him. *But he looked like Christopher, so you didn't take it.*

Adianna just shook her head, making her feelings clear: If Sarah had not had a chance to fight, it meant she had screwed up somewhere. Again.

# CHAPTER 15

CARYN BANDAGED SARAH'S ARMS for school the next day. Sarah didn't want to explain the marks. Her story, when anyone asked, was that she had been in a minor car accident.

She was glad that Christopher was not in school again. She had no desire to confront her friend about her enemy. So at her locker that afternoon, she was surprised to see the newest gift. A single white rose and a small white florist's card.

*129 Ash Road, November 4*

She read the words twice, not believing them.

She, youngest Daughter of Vida, had been invited to a bash . . . *intentionally.*

Looking up, she caught sight of Nissa, who was talking with some of her human friends. Closing her locker, Sarah stalked over to Nissa and grabbed the vampire's arm.

"What is this?" she demanded, flashing the card. Nissa's friends all backed up, not sure what to do.

"It's a—"

"I know *what* it is. I want to know why it was in my locker."

"I have no idea," Nissa answered, her brows drawing together in a puzzled frown. "Christopher told me what you said, and I would never . . . can I see it?"

Sarah handed over the card and Nissa went paler, if possible, than her already unnaturally pale color.

"You can't go. Tell me you won't go."

"Why not?"

Nissa looked at the card again. "Where did you get this?"

"It was in my locker. If it's not from you or Christopher, then who would have put it there? And why does it scare you so much?"

Nissa looked back at her human friends, then dragged Sarah away, lowering her voice so the humans would not hear them. "I've been to a bash in that circuit before, but would never go back. Sarah, they'll kill you. If they know who you are—"

"Who are *they*?" Sarah pressed.

"It's . . . it's one of the harshest of the party circuits," Nissa explained. "Tizoc Theron goes to these," she added, naming one of the best-known vampiric assassins in the world. "Kaleo, Jessica Shade, Chalkha, Kamerine, Jega . . . even Kendra herself might be there." Sarah took in the names, trying to match them with the faces she had seen at the last bash she had attended. Nissa continued, "Even *I'm* afraid to go to one of their bashes, and I haven't been human in a long time. These vampires are *not nice*, Sarah. I've known them to brazenly invite vampire hunters just for the fun of it. If they invited you, then they know who you are, and they plan to kill you."

"Is Nikolas part of this group?"

"What?" Nissa asked, very softly.

"Will Nikolas be there?" Sarah demanded again.

"He—" Nissa's eyes flickered to the bandages on Sarah's arms. "My god, Sarah . . . do I want to know what's under there?"

"I think you already do."

"You're going to go, aren't you? To murder my brother." Nissa leaned back heavily, hitting the lockers with a metallic clang. "That group will kill you, Sarah."

"They didn't manage to last time." This was not a conversation she wanted to have. No matter how peaceful, Nissa would surely not appreciate hearing Sarah's plans for her brother. "Don't worry, I'll bring friends."

"*No.*"

"I'm not going to let him get away with this."

"Sarah, I . . . don't bring anyone else in. You'll—" Nissa took a breath to brace herself. "If Nikolas marked you then he's watching you. Anyone you would bring with you, he already knows about—they would be fair game. If you insist on going, go alone."

"Even I'm not fool enough to go into the crowd you're describing alone."

"They won't hurt you," Nissa said quietly.

Sarah laughed.

"Most of the people in that circuit are either afraid of Nikolas, or loyal to him," Nissa argued. "If he marked you it means he's claimed you. No one else will touch you so long as Nikolas is alive."

"Fine—I'll kill him and then leave quickly. How's that?"

"Nikolas alone is dangerous no matter how much training you've had." Nissa continued as her voice took on a pleading tone. "Even the humans there will turn on you as soon as you try to fight him."

"Nissa, I know he's your brother, but do you have any idea how many people he has killed?" Sarah demanded. "If I let him go because I'm scared of him, he's going to keep killing."

"You think I don't know?" Nissa responded, her voice strained. "I'm the one who gave him the vampire blood, Sarah. Every kill he makes *I* feel the guilt for."

# CHAPTER 16

"WHAT?" Of course she had known, but hearing Nissa state it so bluntly was a shock.

"I changed him to save his life. He was in jail, waiting to be hanged for murder." In response to Sarah's horrified expression, Nissa continued, "He was my *brother*, Sarah."

Nissa's words started to come quickly, as if she had waited so long to tell the story to *someone*, and now she simply needed to get it out.

"Nicholas and Christopher were twins, as you know . . . Christopher was actually born first, but Nicholas always acted older. After my father was killed, Nicholas . . . he became more protective. Christopher had barely understood what happened, but Nicholas . . ." She trailed off. The reality of Nikolas did not need to be detailed.

"When they were eighteen their employer's daughter returned from school in Europe. She was rich, and beautiful, and both my brothers adored her, though

Nicholas would never have challenged Christopher for anything.

"She, of course, wasn't interested. We were too poor and too uncultured for her high-society airs. The only reason she even acknowledged my brothers' existences was because it amused her to tease them. She was always trying to pit the twins against one another."

Nissa's gaze was lost on the past, but Sarah caught a glimpse of anger as she described the girl. "Her name was Christine."

Nissa paused a moment and then went on, "It was at a May Day picnic that things changed. Kaleo was well respected in the town and he had found an invitation for us. Nicholas and Christopher looked so handsome, all dressed up. They had taken extra care to look nice for Christine.

"Christopher asked her to dance." Nissa's voice gave away the next part of the story even before she said the words. She took a heavy breath and then continued, "Christine turned him down. Worse, she laughed at him. The things she said to my brother . . . I would have killed her myself, if I had had a chance.

"Nicholas lost it—he was so protective, and he attacked Christine, furious that she had hurt Christopher. He killed her, in plain sight of the entire town, and was sentenced to be hanged."

"He was my brother." Nissa's eyes begged for understanding. "I had already lost my father, and I could not stand to lose Nicholas, too. Not when I could save him.

"I changed Nicholas, but after that . . . The only thing I've ever been grateful to Kaleo for is that the first time he took me hunting, he didn't let me kill. The police were looking for Nikolas, and while I was trying to deal with them, Nikolas woke. It was the middle of the day, far earlier than he should have woken. He ran, and would have died if one of my kind had not taken him in." Nissa shook her head. "Kendra took him hunting, and she taught him to kill.

"He changed Christopher the next night. They both disappeared from my life for months. Kaleo had everyone he knew looking for them, but no one could find them.

"During that time, they made the decision to give up everything that reminded them of their human lives, and that included me. They even changed how they signed their names." She took a breath, her eyes pained. "They never contacted me. I didn't even know they were still alive until I learned a year later that they had killed a witch, Elisabeth Vida. After that . . . well, they seemed to be everywhere at once."

Nissa met Sarah's gaze, her voice hard. "If you kill once, the bloodlust returns twice as strong. It hurts, and after you've been living off death for more than a hundred years . . . it hurts a lot. You have no idea how hard it was for Christopher to give it up, no idea how tempting every human being in this entire school is.

"I have given everything for my brothers, and they have both saved my life more than once when I wasn't strong enough to defend myself from others of my kind. I would probably never forgive myself for harming a friend—and I do consider you a friend, Sarah—but if you hurt my brother, I *will* kill you, or die trying."

Sarah flinched at the passion in Nissa's voice. "I can't let Nikolas live."

"Sarah, please—" Nissa broke off, as if knowing there was nothing she could say. The vampire disappeared, but Sarah would not allow her determination to waver.

She threw out the rose Nikolas had sent with the invitation. Nissa had taken the card, but Sarah remembered the necessary information. The bash would be tonight, at 129 Ash Road. It wasn't the same house she had found before, but considering his age and notoriety, Sarah was not surprised that Nikolas had more than one.

She wouldn't miss this for the world.

If Nissa was telling the truth, then Sarah would only be in danger from Nikolas . . . until she took him down. There was no need to endanger other hunters. If Nikolas knew who her allies were, he would alert the group immediately, and the other hunters would not have even the scant protection that Nikolas's marks gave to Sarah. *How ironic,* Sarah thought grimly. Nikolas's marks would enable her to kill him.

# CHAPTER 17

SARAH FELT A LITTLE GUILT as she lied to Adianna, telling her that she was going to hunt in the relatively safe city.

She wore black jeans and a white tank top, and her jacket hid the bandages, as well as the knife on her left wrist. Her primary knife was on her back, and she had two slim silver daggers in her boots.

Nikolas was playing with her, which meant he would give her a chance to fight. As soon as she had that chance, she would use it. This time there would be no hesitation.

The house appeared dark as Sarah approached it. All the shades were down, but she could hear a haunting melody from inside, a mixture of pain and loneliness. The door opened just as she reached for the knob, and she was again confronted with the peculiar—and powerful—world of Nikolas.

*Black and white.*

The walls were black with a white design running across them, spiraling and plunging, the lines all slightly wrong, drawing the eye to seemingly impossible shapes. The other house she had seen had been crisp in its lack of color; the abstraction in this one made Sarah's vision spin, so she turned to the vampire who had opened the door for her.

Kaleo's red shirt in the black-and-white interior of Nikolas's house was a startling blot of color. Sarah tensed as she remembered her last encounter with him.

"Sarah Vida, nice to see you again," he said, his voice lilting with sarcasm as she met his black gaze without fear. "Nikolas told us to expect you. You can relax, take your jacket off, and make yourself at home. It's only eleven."

"I don't make myself at home in a place like this," she answered, and he just laughed and reached over to close the door behind her.

"Sarah, so good to see you."

She looked toward the voice, but her eyes took a moment to differentiate the figure there from the background.

Nikolas was wearing white slacks and a black silk shirt, and his hair was tied back with a black ribbon. He had not yet fed tonight, and the skin that she could see was almost white, pearl-like. Black and white, colorless, he matched the room perfectly. *Is that what his mind is like?* she wondered. *All sharp contrasts without color or emotion?*

"Welcome to my home, Sarah. Please, come away from the door. May I take your jacket?"

This time it was her turn to laugh. "You can drop the act, Nikolas."

"There is no act, Sarah. Acting, like lying, is an art I have never perfected. Come into my parlor."

"Said the spider to the fly," Sarah finished for him, and he smiled, taking her jacket.

"I never kill until the hour, Sarah."

"Am I really supposed to believe that?" she asked skeptically.

"I never lie."

He hung her jacket in the closet and turned his back to her, leading her deeper into the house. She wanted so much to put a knife into his back immediately, but his next words discouraged her.

"What about you, Sarah? I do not kill until midnight. As it is, I'm not sure that I plan to kill you at all. Do you have any rules for yourself, or should we forget all manners and throw ourselves on the mercy of chaos?"

"You want me to wait until midnight to kill you?" she asked incredulously, and Nikolas turned back to face her.

"If that's what you plan to do tonight, then yes, I would like for you to wait until midnight to *try*. You are a guest here this time—you must abide by our rules."

"Hardly." She leaned back against the wall, crossing her arms. Her right hand rested over the handle of the knife strapped to her left wrist, and she was comforted by the cool feel of silver beneath her fingertips.

"Honor, Sarah," Nikolas sighed. "Does the Vida line no longer teach its children honor? I invited you, and you accepted the invitation. It would be rather unsporting to spoil the game because you are impatient."

"I am never impatient."

"Just like you never shout out," he answered. "And

never cry, even when you make enemies of your friends. Yes, Nissa told me about your conversation," he said before she could ask. "So, will you follow our rules?"

"I can wait until midnight."

"Do I have your word on that?" he asked, his gaze intense.

She did not answer immediately. When a Vida gave her word, she kept it, so Sarah was careful how she phrased her answer. "Unless you threaten me, I will wait until midnight to kill you. You have my word on that."

Nikolas smiled, and for an instant the expression reminded her of Christopher. "Very well, then. Enjoy the bash—you'll probably never make it to another one."

# CHAPTER 18

By ELEVEN-THIRTY, Sarah had been introduced to others, some humans, some vampires. She wondered just how much needed to be done before these killers would drop their social detachment and retaliate, and whether Nikolas even cared that his father's murderer was among the guests.

"Not until midnight." Kaleo's voice slipped through the noise of the room, a hint of laughter in his tone, and Sarah repressed a shiver. She glanced over to see a young woman gazing up at Kaleo with the intensity of love—or terror.

"Midnight is only half an hour away," she argued.

"Is there some hurry, dear?" Kaleo bent his head to kiss his victim's throat; she sighed, leaned her head back, and when he stood again she leaned against a wall, clearly disappointed.

Sarah jumped when she felt hands on her shoulders. "I thought you never reacted," Nikolas said, laughing.

"I'm standing in a slaughterhouse where the cattle

are begging to become hamburgers. I have a right to be jumpy."

"Ah." Nikolas followed Sarah's gaze. "Heather is Kaleo's favorite. She has been frequenting these bashes for longer than I have been alive."

"God," Sarah whispered, sickened. A blood bonded human did not age. This girl could remain alive, Kaleo's personal prey, for thousands of years unless he tired of her and killed her. *Or,* Sarah thought, forming an instant hatred of the vampire, *until I kill him.*

"Welcome to my world, Sarah," Nikolas answered. "Why are you wearing these?" He reached to the bandages on her right arm as she pulled away. "Are you ashamed of what they hide?"

"Ashamed?" she echoed, incredulous. "Should I be *proud* to show the world that you've sliced your name into my skin?"

Nikolas laughed. "Look around you."

The comment was well placed. Sarah had already seen several humans with Nikolas's marks on them. When he entered the room, they greeted him with adoration. While they were discreet in human society, in Nikolas's own lair they wore tank shirts or sleeveless dresses, going out of their way to show off the marks.

"I'd rather burn them off, personally," she growled.

"If you really want to, you can always do that later, though I've heard it's painful," Nikolas commented, apparently serious. "Of course, I don't suppose you would mind a little more pain, would you?"

Before she could react he grabbed her wrist, pulling her toward him sharply enough that she stumbled and needed to catch herself on the arm of a nearby couch.

"I thought you played by the rules," she hissed, snatching her other wrist away when he reached for it.

"I do. I'm simply removing these," Nikolas answered, carefully unwinding the bandage on the wrist he had a hold on.

"Let me go."

He let go of her arms, but continued to undo the bandages until each of his marks was revealed.

The sudden movement had opened one of the cuts on her shoulder, and he bent his head down to the wound. She felt the soft sensation of his lips on her skin and tried to pull away, but Nikolas grabbed her right arm and held her still.

Pressing her left hand to his chest, with the tip of the spring-loaded knife only inches from his heart, she said, "I consider this a threat. Let me go, or I will kill you where you stand."

"You're right," Nikolas said, lifting his head and releasing her. The taste of her blood, stronger and sweeter than any human's, had caused his expression to darken with bloodlust. "It isn't midnight yet, is it?"

# CHAPTER 19

"*Damn*, Sarah."

She spun toward the familiar voice, and nearly swore when she recognized her sister. Kaleo, lounging against one of the walls, watched the confrontation with malicious pleasure—he must have let Adianna in.

"You really have gotten yourself into trouble this time, haven't you, little sister?" Adianna asked, sizing up the situation.

"What are you doing here?" Sarah demanded, frustrated by her sister's appearance. Adianna was going to get herself killed.

"Touchy today, aren't we?" Adianna responded.

"How did you know where I was?"

"I wanted to know what was up with you. I asked this"—she gestured to Nikolas—"thing's brother, Christopher, and he told me you were here."

Sarah cringed inwardly. Adianna didn't *talk* to vampires—if they had information she needed, she would force it from them. Sarah hoped Christopher was still alive.

Evidently, Nikolas had the same thought, because Sarah saw instant hatred on his face. He stepped forward a pace and Adianna drew her knife.

"Come any nearer, and you won't be pleased with the results," Adianna warned.

"Tell you what," Nikolas said slowly, glancing from Adianna to Sarah and then back. The other vampires had disappeared, leaving Nikolas alone with the two hunters and a scattered handful of groggy humans; Sarah could tell he was stalling for time. "Only Sarah is in my plan for tonight. I'll let you leave safely, if you will do so now."

Adianna did not wait for him to continue but attacked instantly. No hesitation, no thought, just pure Vida skill.

Nikolas dodged, but Adianna turned quickly, cutting into his side. Sarah had just drawn her knife to join the fray when something struck her from behind, sending her stumbling. More astonished than frightened, she twisted and detached the human who had attacked her, knocking the girl out with a small burst of power.

A quick scan revealed two more humans on their feet and ready to fight if necessary, but Nikolas did not need the help. Sarah heard something in Adianna's arm snap as the vampire slammed her back into the wall.

"Nikolas, let her go!" Sarah shouted.

"Why?" he asked, his hand over Adianna's windpipe, ready to crush it.

"Adianna isn't involved in this—she only came because she heard I was here. Let her go."

"Christopher wouldn't have told her where I was unless she hurt him," Nikolas growled.

Sarah advanced, careful to keep the humans from her back, and Nikolas's grip on Adianna's throat tightened. "The hour has fallen, Sarah—I could kill her before you could get near enough to hurt me, and you know it."

"Then how about I leave now, while you are busy with her?" Sarah bluffed. "It would ruin your plans for tonight, wouldn't it?"

Nikolas hesitated. "I suppose it would dent them a bit."

"Let her go, Nikolas." Adianna was turning blue from Nikolas's grip, and it took all of Sarah's will not to attack.

"You are in no place to make demands, Sarah, but I'll make a deal with you anyway. Marguerite?"

One of the humans answered. "Yes?"

Sarah spared a glance and recognized the girl from SingleEarth. Nikolas's marks on her dark skin looked like pearl inlays.

It was not these designs, though, that sent dread down Sarah's spine. There were two more on her left arm, which must have been tucked under the girl when she had been brought to SingleEarth: one was a teardrop, and the other was a second signature.

Kristopher.

"Sarah," Nikolas said, "Give your knives—all of them—to Marguerite so she can bring them upstairs, and I will let your sister go safely."

She believed him. However warped, somewhere within Nikolas's twisted mind was a sense of honor.

Of course, if she relinquished all her weapons, Nikolas would probably kill *her*. And it was *completely* against Vida rules to surrender arms to any leech.

"Fine," she answered, drawing the first knife from her back.

Nikolas loosened his grip on Adianna's throat enough that she could breathe, and Adianna immediately said through her teeth, "Sarah, what are you *doing*?"

She did not answer.

Adianna had never broken the rules. She hadn't befriended the vampires or made deals with them. She hadn't revealed her powers to a human boy. Stronger and colder, Adianna was the one more likely to survive after this night, and so Sarah had to do what she could to help her. The Vida line had to go on, and Adianna was a better Vida than Sarah could ever be.

It seemed to take a long time before Sarah had finished stripping herself of weapons, but it was all too soon that Nikolas asked Marguerite to bring them upstairs, and Sarah was left standing before the vampire unarmed. Nikolas pulled Adianna away from the wall and disappeared with her.

He reappeared alone in an instant. With luck, he had simply put some distance between Adianna and this house. With less luck, she was somewhere in Europe, trying to find a phone to call Dominique to arrange a plane home.

# CHAPTER 20

"Now what?" Sarah asked.

"No fight, Sarah? No bold words?" he asked, stepping toward her. "Are your knives all that give you courage?"

"My knives are necessary for me to kill your kind," she answered. "But they aren't my courage. I'm not begging for my life, either."

"You never will, will you?" he asked, as he took hold of her right arm. He bent his head down to the rose and licked away the thin line of blood that had gathered on the stem. Then his lips moved to her throat.

Once again she started to pull away, but this time she had no knives to threaten with, and Nikolas's grip was tightening. His fangs brushed across her throat and she braced herself for pain.

He raised his head to look her in the eye.

"It doesn't hurt, Sarah," he said, as if reading her mind. "And I'm not going to kill you. What are you afraid of?"

*The unknown,* Sarah thought. What exactly did this creature have planned? But she didn't ask, because she didn't really want to know. "Just get on with it."

With his free hand he leaned her head back, his fingers running through her hair, strangely gentle.

"Nikolas, let her go."

Nikolas raised his head, allowing Sarah just enough room to look to the speaker.

"Christopher." Nikolas's eyes lit up as he whispered his brother's name. "Care to join me?"

"Let her go, or I will take her from you," Christopher ordered, his voice unwavering.

"You can't," Nikolas answered. "You *could*, physically—you know I wouldn't fight you—but you can't by law." Nikolas gestured to the thin line of blood on his side where Adianna's knife had pierced the skin. "Her sister drew blood. I have claim on Adianna and her relations."

Blood claim was one of the few laws vampires regularly followed. In return for the blood Adianna had drawn from Nikolas, no other vampire was allowed to interfere if he wanted to harm her or anyone in her family.

Christopher closed his eyes for a moment, taking a deep breath. "Don't hurt her."

"Whoever said I was going to hurt her?" He sounded so innocent, it made Sarah nervous.

"I *know* you, Nikolas," Christopher argued.

"Once you did," Nikolas said quietly, sadly. "We— not I, but *we*—were the most feared of our kind. Rome, Paris, New York—every city in the world was ours. What happened to Kristopher and Nikolas, who would hunt side by side, sharing the blood, dancing in the streets?"

Nikolas gestured to the wounds on Sarah's arms. "These marks were *ours*, not mine, and everyone knew it. Now, even the hunters have forgotten you. When was the last time I saw you place your mark on your prey?"

"Marguerite," Christopher answered, lost in memory. He stepped forward until he was standing in front of his brother. "She was the last."

"Why?" Nikolas asked, voice barely audible.

"Let it go, Nikolas," Christopher ordered, his voice shaking slightly. "That was fifty years ago."

"I can see it in your eyes, Christopher," Nikolas whispered to his brother. "You remember. Why did you leave me?"

"I stopped killing, Nikolas—"

"You stopped living!" Nikolas shouted, his emotion breaking any control he had. "I look at you, and all I see is pain. For you I tried to survive on anything but the blood of humans, but I couldn't stand the pain. I couldn't walk in the sunlight. I couldn't stand to be near humans. One day I ran into a human girl on the street, and before I knew it she was dead in my arms. An *innocent human girl*, Christopher, who didn't deserve to die."

Sarah's confusion escalated. Since when did Nikolas care if his victims were innocent or not?

"You were always stronger," Nikolas finished. "I don't have your control."

Christopher looked anything but strong. Sarah could see the bloodlust close to the surface. She was still trapped in Nikolas's arms, and her wounds had opened enough for blood to bead around the edges. The scent of her witch blood was in the air, laced with power and a hint of danger.

"Why did you leave me, Christopher?" Nikolas asked as he reached around Sarah to take his brother's hands. She was trapped between the two vampires, and not sure how to react. Christopher's control was obviously slipping—if she fought now, she would destroy it altogether. She did not want Christopher's life to be the price of her escape.

"You remember Marguerite," Nikolas said. "She picked *us*. She knew what we were and what she wanted—"

"She said she wanted to die," Christopher whispered. The memory was so strong in his voice that Sarah could almost imagine the scene, and the vision caused her to pull at Nikolas's grip for a moment before she forced herself to stop.

Christopher's control was so thin. If he could contain the bloodlust long enough to get his brother to let her go, she would be grateful. If he lost it, she would fight.

It no longer mattered who was speaking as they continued the tale, both lost in memory. "Two of us, like a mirror. We both fed on her, you on the left, and me on the right. You marked her first, putting your signature forever on her skin, and then I followed."

"And when she woke she was afraid, but there was passion there too. She was given the finest wines and the softest silks to wear, rich foods, chocolates—"

"We approached her again, both of us taking her blood, but this time we only took a taste—".

"And then we both cut ourselves, here, just below our throats, and she leaned forward to drink."

Disgust flashed in Sarah's mind, as she weighed the brothers' every word for a hint of what their next action would be. So the girl had wanted to die. Instead they had blood bonded her, given her all but immortality.

Nikolas drew his brother forward, and then placed Christopher's hand over the uncut skin on Sarah's left wrist.

"Why is there nothing here, Christopher?"

Both of the brothers seemed entranced by their pasts. Finally, Sarah spoke.

"You said you haven't hunted since Marguerite, Christopher," she said, loudly, in an attempt to break the spell. "Why?"

Christopher blinked and looked at Sarah as if he were seeing her for the first time.

"Nissa took him away from me," Nikolas answered sullenly.

"Nissa needed me," Christopher answered tiredly. "You saw how she was, Nikolas. She hadn't fed in a week. If I hadn't—"

Nikolas's voice was quiet as he interrupted. "Don't you know how lonely it is hunting without you?"

"No," Christopher answered, still looking at his brother. "I don't. I've never hunted alone."

Nikolas once again drew his brother forward, this time placing Christopher's hand just above the pulse on Sarah's throat. She checked her reaction to jerk back, knowing that an attempt to flee would only bring out the predatory instincts that Christopher was fighting.

"Can't you feel the life there, Christopher?" Nikolas pressed. "Don't you want it?"

Christopher closed his eyes, turning his head away.

"Christopher—"

"Sarah, don't talk," Christopher said quickly, sounding pained. He jerked his hand out of Nikolas's grasp and stepped back.

"Christopher, don't leave me again," Nikolas pleaded, childlike in his fear of loneliness. "I don't want to be alone anymore. Nissa needed you then, but I need you *now*."

"Let Sarah go." Christopher's voice wavered.

"She *hurt* you," Nikolas argued. "I *saw* you after she turned you away. You wouldn't even talk to me. I can't stand to see you in pain, Christopher. In the old days we would have hunted her down together."

"I don't want to kill her," Christopher said. He finally gathered the strength to meet his brother's gaze again. "And I won't let you."

"I won't kill her if you don't want me to—if I was willing to do that she would have been dead the instant she entered my home. But you know I can't just turn her loose. She hunted me down once. Do you really think she would stay away if I let her go? Do you really think her family wouldn't track down you and Nissa if they couldn't find me?" Nikolas's voice was cold, but filled with pain.

"Nikolas—"

Nikolas removed his knife from his pocket and opened it.

"Nikolas, what are you doing?" Christopher demanded, but his brother did not answer as he caught Sarah's right wrist in a grip she could not break, and

skimmed the blade across the back of her hand, drawing a thin line of new blood.

"Damn it, Nikolas!" Christopher shouted, spinning
sharply away so the blood was not in his sight. "Don't
do this to me!"

"Just once, Brother, be the Kristopher I know."

Christopher was trembling as he fought the bloodlust.

"Please, Brother. For me, kill the pain." Holding
Sarah by the throat with one hand, Nikolas reached out
and turned his brother around with the other.
Christopher's eyes immediately fell on the blood that
was dripping from Sarah's hand.

"Christopher, no—"

"*Shut up*, Sarah!" Christopher shouted when she
tried to argue, his voice strained. He turned to his
brother. "We're both damned. You know that, don't
you?"

And then Christopher took Sarah's hand, lifted the
wound to his lips, and licked the blood away.

"Christopher, I'm your friend—"

"No, Nikolas." Roughly, Christopher shoved himself
away from her, sending Sarah stumbling back into
Nikolas. She could see him shaking from the effort it
took him to break away.

"Kristopher, have you forgotten everything?"
Nikolas pleaded, the hurt clear in his voice.

"Please, Nikolas, let her go."

"Why?" Nikolas's voice was childlike, hurt. "You
were the first one," he reminded his brother, "to pick up
a knife."

Sarah felt Nikolas's hold on her wrists lessen as he focused on his brother; if he continued to be distracted, she stood a chance of getting out. She had lost hope that Christopher would help her—he wasn't strong enough to ignore his bloodlust.

"Please, Kristopher," Nikolas implored.

"Not Sarah."

That last, painful argument almost caused her to hesitate, but even as she yanked her arms out of Nikolas's grip she had made her decision. Survival. She threw herself forward, and before either vampire could react, she had pinned Christopher to the floor, a hand over his throat.

"Sarah—"

He didn't have another chance to speak before she violently dragged at Christopher's power with her own. He gasped, unable to fight back, and she winced at the pain she knew her magic caused him.

There were nine energy centers in the body, called chakras, that witches could use to manipulate the energies of another, usually in order to heal. Her line had learned another way to use them, one no witch would ever use on another mortal creature: to inflict pain, and to kill.

It was a desperate move. Any vampire strong enough to control his own power could reach along the line she had opened and attack her, and she would have no defenses.

But Christopher had not fed on humans for too long. He was powerless against the deadliest of her attacks.

Nikolas froze when he heard his brother scream.

Sarah saw him hesitate as he tried to figure out what she had done.

"Let me go, Nikolas," Sarah demanded. "Call that girl back down and tell her to get my knives *now*, or I will drain every drop of power from your brother's body."

"You wouldn't," Nikolas answered softly, a small amount of fear in his voice.

"He just licked blood off my hand," she growled. "That gives me the motivation to cause some exceptional *pain* if you do not give me back what is mine and let me out of here." She didn't want to kill Christopher. She didn't even want to hurt him. But the choice was between letting him go and having Nikolas kill her, and hurting him and living through this night.

Nikolas stepped forward and she once again reached into Christopher's power and *twisted* what she found there.

He shouted out in pain and Nikolas winced, stopping.

"I can kill him in less than a second if you make another move toward me," she warned, and it was true. As entrenched in Christopher's power as she was, she could tear, tangle, or destroy with a thought.

"Marguerite, get the knives," Nikolas whispered, and the human who had been watching from the doorway ran upstairs. Sarah had seen the fear on the girl's face— fear for Christopher's life, for the vampire who had fed on her years ago when she wanted to die, and then given her this life in exchange for the one she had abandoned.

Nikolas took a step back, but Sarah could see pure hatred smoldering in his eyes as he did so.

Marguerite returned and held Sarah's knives out to her. Keeping her right hand over Christopher's throat, she returned all the knives to their rightful places with her left. Still holding Christopher by the throat, she stood.

"I am going to let him go, and you are going to leave me alone. Do we have a deal, Nikolas?"

"I'm going to kill you the first chance I get," he growled back, and Christopher once again shouted out in pain.

*"Do we have a deal, Nikolas?"*

"For tonight, I will let you leave safely," he answered.

"Agreed," she said, as she relaxed her hold on Christopher, who collapsed to the floor. "He's going to die if he doesn't feed soon, Nikolas," she warned before he had a chance to make a move.

Without hesitation Nikolas drew Christopher to his own throat.

# CHAPTER 21

"WHAT IN THE WORLD did you think you were doing?" Adianna demanded the instant Sarah entered the house.

Sarah pushed past her sister without answering. She was too tired to deal with questions tonight.

Adianna followed in silence, waiting to speak until they were almost in Sarah's room. "You aren't invincible, Sarah, and you well know it. Yet you're always throwing yourself into these situations, going alone where no hunter in her right mind would—"

"I couldn't bring you," Sarah interrupted tiredly. "I can't explain, but it wasn't just because I like doing things alone."

"You don't have to protect me," Adianna stated.

"This time I did. This is something between Nikolas and me."

"No, it's *not*," Adianna argued. "You are a Daughter of Vida, Sarah. A witch. A hunter. He marked you, and for that you are seeking vengeance. But that is *not* what you are here for. You are here to protect the humans who cannot protect themselves. Not to get yourself killed for a personal insult."

"I've heard the lecture before," Sarah snapped, her frayed nerves ruining the last of her patience. "Now, please, leave me alone."

"You're acting suicidal, Sarah."

"Good night, Adianna." Sarah slipped into her room and closed the door on her sister. Adianna knocked a couple of times, but finally gave up and let Sarah alone.

Nissa was the one she was worried about. The girl didn't take human blood meals, but if the other hunters learned Nikolas was her relation, she would never be able to rest safely. The last thing Sarah wanted was for hunters to push Nissa into killing to defend herself.

Christopher . . . what was she going to do about Christopher? She might have just helped Nikolas convince his brother to start killing again, but it was what she had needed to do to survive.

*It wasn't her fault.* She had never asked for any of this. She had never asked for anything more complex than the simple definitions of good and evil she had been raised on.

All she could think was that she was marked, that Nikolas had signed his name on her skin as if she were some kind of object, and now he was hunting her. All to defend his brother. Wouldn't she have done the same— worse, actually—to someone who had hurt Adianna?

She shook her head violently, trying to let go of these dangerous thoughts, and threw herself down on the bed, hoping for a sleep that eluded her.

She would kill him.

If she could.

If she could turn her heart into stone and make her knife her only morals, if she could stand to kill Christopher and Nissa when they came to avenge Nikolas's death, if she could stand living after killing her friends, then she would kill Nikolas.

# CHAPTER 22

SARAH INTERCEPTED ROBERT by his car at the end of the next school day.

"What's up?"

She was aware that she looked very different than when they had last spoken. Her black jeans and white shirt were plain, not exactly her style, but she wore them because she planned on visiting someone who wasn't fond of colors. Her leather jacket covered her arms. She had not bothered to replace the bandages after last night. Her blond hair was down, slightly wild, stirred up by her running to the parking lot. Her eyes smoldered with intensity and purpose.

"I need to talk to your sister."

"Not likely. I told you already, Kristin doesn't talk to anyone. She barely even *sees* anyone anymore."

Sarah leaned back against his car door, and repeated herself. "I need to talk to Kristin, and I'm pretty sure she'll talk to me."

He snorted. "I'm not bringing you to her. If she notices you at all, she'll just freak out."

"Robert—"

"Leave me alone, okay?" he snapped. "I get it. I'm not as . . . important . . . as you are. I'm human, yeah, fine. I talked to your mother, and she made that quite clear. Now leave me alone."

"No," she answered calmly. She felt a little guilty about sending this human to her mother, but he had received no colder welcome than any other hunter had. "I need to talk to Kristin, and I thought it would be more polite to ask than to break into your house."

This time he tried to muscle past her, pushing her to the side. He was bigger than she was, but he hadn't counted on her strength; his shove didn't even knock her off balance.

"Robert . . . , " she said, trailing off. There was only one way to get his attention.

Show-and-tell. She shrugged off the leather jacket and watched Robert's eyes widen at the sight of her fresh wounds. "I know a lot more about him than you do. I've fought him twice, and I know he plans to try to kill me soon. I need to know what Kristin knows, and if she knows some way to hurt him."

Robert hesitated, then stepped back reluctantly. "Fine." He got in his side of the car and reached over to unlock the passenger-side door. "I can't guarantee she'll talk to you, but if you think she can help you get that monster . . ." He trailed off. "Get in the car."

# CHAPTER 23

THOUGH THERE WAS COLOR in it, Robert's house seemed bleached of life.

"Kristin's room is upstairs," Robert said quietly, and led Sarah up the blue-gray carpeted stairs. Just outside his sister's door, he spoke again. "If you can help her, or get her to help you, fine. But Kristin . . . isn't all there. She probably won't even notice you. Don't bully her— she doesn't need any more abuse."

Kristin was dressed in a long white nightgown with a high collar. Her hair had been dyed black, though the natural brown showed for about an inch at the roots.

The room was devoid of even gray—black paint covered every spot that might have been colored, and flaked off the handle of the hairbrush Kristin was using.

Nikolas's house had been just as colorless, but that had been neat, artistic somehow—this was just sick.

"Kristin, I need to talk to you." The girl didn't look up, but continued brushing her hair. "Kristin?" Still there was no reaction from the girl. "I need to talk to you about Nikolas."

The brush paused.

"Kristin . . ." The girl returned to brushing her hair, and Sarah sighed.

Sarah knelt, moving the marks on her arms into Kristin's line of sight, and finally the girl looked at her.

"*He* sent you?" she asked, and the hope in her eyes was strong.

There was pain in Sarah's voice as she answered, "No. But I need to talk to you about him."

"I . . . I don't know much. It was only one party—"

"Just tell me what happened there."

"I don't—" She looked at her brother and shivered as her eyes fell on his washed-out blue shirt; he took it off, throwing it from the room.

"Better, Kristin?"

She nodded slowly and Robert left to get a different shirt.

"This girl Heather invited me to the party. She said the people were cool, and the music was awesome, and the guy she was going with was completely hot . . . which was strange, 'cause Heather is so cold, not really caring about anything . . ."

Sarah choked back her revulsion. The Heather whom Kristin was talking about was probably the one Sarah had seen at Nikolas's bash, asking Kaleo to bite her. What kind of human invited other, defenseless humans into that kind of place?

Kristin had trailed off. "Tell me about the party," Sarah prompted, and Kristin nodded.

"The house . . . there was so much color in it, like walking into a kaleidoscope . . . one room was all red . . . it scared me . . ."

"Was Nikolas there?"

"The people . . . it was strange, the groups. Some of them were like me. They didn't seem to know what was going on, really, and the house unnerved them a bit. Others were like Heather. They had connections. And others, so detached, so . . ." She shook her head, unable to find the description she was looking for.

"And then there was *him*, Nikolas . . .

"He was so beautiful, completely in contrast with everything else . . . his skin was so pale, and he was wearing all black . . . beautiful. He asked me my name and I told him it was Christine . . . he didn't like that. He didn't say anything, but I could tell."

Christine . . . did she remind Nikolas of the Christine who had hurt his brother? Had some slight nuance of expression been so important that the girl now refused to respond to her real name?

"But he asked me to dance, and I thought I might just *die*, because he was *so* handsome and . . . unearthly. I'd say like an angel but he wasn't at all, he was like . . . I don't know . . . seductive, just by *existing*."

Kristin sighed, then continued. "After the dance he held me in his arms a minute longer, and I remember . . . I remember his lips on my throat and I just *relaxed*, because it felt so good . . ." She gestured to the marks on her arms. "I don't remember when he made these . . . they didn't hurt . . ." She paused.

"And then?" Sarah said, and the girl blinked.

"No, I don't want to talk anymore."

"You started telling us, Kristin—you have to finish," Sarah said, meeting her eyes. She wasn't as good as the vampires at influencing human minds, but Kristin's defenses were weak.

Kristin nodded. "He . . . he didn't really take much blood. I remember not wanting him to stop when he pulled away, because it felt so good . . ."

Robert made a sickened sound, but Kristin didn't notice as she went on. "And he said . . . he said, 'I want to make you mine.' And I said yes and yes was all I could say for a moment, but then I said no." She shook her head, trying to clear it. "And he . . . he looked so *surprised*, and he just asked why . . . and I . . . I said, 'Because I need to go home,' and he asked why again, and I said, 'Because my brother will be sad if I don't go home, and he'll be lonely.' "

She put her head into her hands and started to cry. "And he . . . he pushed me away and said, 'Get out,' and that's all he would say to me. I didn't understand and I tried to talk to him, but he pulled some other person over and said, 'Get her out of here.' "

"And then?"

"Then . . . the other guy asked, 'And do what with her?' and Nikolas said, he said, 'I don't care, just get her home to her brother.' And . . . no."

"Go on, Kristin," Sarah urged, but the girl just shook her head.

"No, no . . ."

Despite Sarah's encouragement, Kristin would say no more. The block was partially vampiric mind control, but mostly simple, human denial.

# CHAPTER 24

ALL THREE OF THEM jumped at the knock on the door.

"Who is it?" Robert called.

"Is Sarah in there? It's Nissa—I need to talk to her—"

Robert had opened the door before Sarah could tell him otherwise. Sarah fell back into a fighting stance, unsure what Nissa wanted.

"Sarah, I'm glad I tracked you down. Nikolas is calling for your blood. What the hell did you do to Christopher?"

"I did what I needed to do to survive," Sarah answered, but Nissa's attention had left her and moved onto Kristin, who was huddled in a corner, sobbing.

"God . . ." Nissa looked at the marks on Kristin's arms, and then said, "Nikolas didn't do this to her. These are his marks, but he would never . . . leave someone like this."

Robert frowned. "If he didn't, who did?"

"What are you doing here?" Nissa asked, as if just realizing that the human boy was in the room.

"I live here," he answered. "And since you're in my house, maybe you should answer my questions."

Nissa just shook her head. "What happened to her?"

"Why do you care?"

"Why do I care?" Nissa said between her teeth. "I care because she is a living human being, and she's . . ." She shook her head violently, and then put a hand on Kristin's shoulder. The girl looked up at Nissa, who caught her eye.

Kristin screamed again, bolting from Nissa's hold.

"What the hell did you do to her?" Robert demanded.

"I just tried to find the memories of what caused . . . *that*," Nissa spat, looking at Kristin. "I should have known this is the kind of mess Kaleo would leave behind."

"*Kaleo?*" Robert repeated. "Who the hell is Kaleo?"

Nissa laughed, a pained sound, but she did not answer. Instead, she turned back to Kristin, who was sitting silently in the corner, terrified. "I don't think I can help her. Kaleo has her blood bonded to himself, and I'm not strong enough to reach her mind through that."

"You mean someone stronger could help her?" Robert asked, catching the unspoken statement.

"I don't know exactly what *caused* this, but if someone could reach her mind through all the mess he's put in there, they could help."

Robert stalked over to where Nissa was standing. "I don't want to know what you are or what relation to Nikolas you have. If you can help my sister, or get someone who can, I don't care if you're the devil herself."

Nissa shook her head. "I don't think—"

"Please. If you know how to help her, you have to. She wasn't like this before. She was . . . colorful. Alive. Intelligent. Kind. She had dreams. But the monster who did this took all that away."

"I know someone who would be strong enough to help her," Nissa said slowly, but she looked over Robert's shoulder and met Sarah's gaze. "But he—"

"Then get him to do it!" Robert ordered, but Sarah was very slowly shaking her head.

"Sarah?" Nissa left the rest of the question unspoken.

"Would he help?" Sarah asked quietly. "Or would he do more damage than Kaleo did?"

"I think he would help," Nissa answered, and Sarah nodded.

"Fine, then." She was leaving sanity in the hands of the insane. Since when were the monsters called in to heal the innocent?

Nissa disappeared, and Robert shouted, "That . . . that . . ."

"Was one of the simplest vampire tricks you will ever see. She could be in China now with no more effort than you would use to blink."

Robert sat down, his legs folding under him.

"Is she gone?" Kristin whispered as she lifted her head.

"For the moment," Robert answered, still dazed.

While Nissa was gone, Sarah drew the knife from the sheath on her back, unsure what was going to happen once she reappeared.

"What's that for?" Robert asked, nervous.

"Just in case I need it," she answered. She moved so her back was to a wall, and crossed her arms. She could defend herself if necessary, but she didn't want to start a fight if Nikolas was going to help Kristin.

"You just carry that thing around?"

"This and two others," Sarah answered. "Sometimes more. It depends whether the knife sheaths match my outfit."

Robert looked at her as if she might be crazy, but then seemed to realize she was making a joke. He *didn't* realize that she was also telling the complete truth—she tried to wear as many knives as her outfit would safely hide.

Then Nissa reappeared with Nikolas and everything happened at once.

Robert's eyes narrowed as he realized who Nikolas must be—*black and white*.

Sarah and Nikolas locked glares, and he took a step toward her.

Nissa stepped between Nikolas and Sarah.

Kristin vaulted across the room and fell at Nikolas's feet.

Nikolas's attention snapped away from Sarah as he pulled Kristin up, looking at her quizzically. Sarah could see recognition in his eyes.

"Christine," he recalled aloud.

The girl did not argue the name, but instead nodded, leaning against him. Nikolas tensed for a moment, and then put a comforting arm around her, looking over her to where Robert was standing.

"You're the brother?" Robert nodded. "I sent Christine home. What happened to her?"

Robert opened his mouth, closed it, opened it again. "I thought . . ."

"She told us what happened up until you sent her off," Sarah said. "Then she broke down, hysterical. Nissa said Kaleo did this." *Since when did Nikolas turn into a cuddly sweetheart?* Sarah wondered cynically, seeing the tenderness with which Nikolas held Kristin.

Nikolas's eyes narrowed. "It would be like him." He looked around the room, taking in the lack of color, perhaps seeing even more in it than Sarah had. "This isn't his, though . . . Kaleo likes color, especially red."

Kristin shivered, and put her head down on Nikolas's chest, crying.

"She can't stand color anymore," Robert explained, watching his sister in Nikolas's gentle embrace. "She screams at anything red."

Nikolas nodded, and then returned his attention to Kristin, lifting her face.

"What happened after I sent you away, Christine?"

She shook her head violently. "No, no—"

"Christine, look at me!" Nikolas ordered. He put his hands on her shoulders and forced her to meet his gaze. Sarah heard the echo of his voice in her own mind, and she could tell that Nikolas was forcing his words into Kristin's mind as he spoke aloud. *"You're . . . safe, Christine. No one is going to hurt you. Calm down."*

Kristin relaxed a bit as his mind reached into hers, speaking his words directly to her thoughts.

*"Now tell me what happened."*

"No, I—" She broke off, finally looking away from his black eyes. "You sent me away, and he took me outside . . . he said you didn't care what happened to me . . ."

"Go on."

"And he . . . he bit me, but it wasn't like when you bit me, it *hurt* . . ." She moaned. "I tried to push him away but it just hurt more . . ."

She collapsed back into sobs and he put his arms around her, comforting. He ran his fingers through her hair, and Sarah saw him hesitate when he noticed the dye.

"Go on, Christine. He isn't here; it doesn't hurt anymore."

"I think I blacked out, and when I woke up I was in a hospital, and people were asking me questions, about *you*. That's all they cared about. The police thought you had hurt me, and I told them no, you tried to send me home, but no one would believe me. And they had an IV in me, and the blood was so red . . ."

She was babbling now, but Nikolas simply held her, looking over her shoulder as if he couldn't stand to see the mess she had become.

"Christine," he said, looking her in the eye. "It's over now—"

"*No!*" She screamed it. "They keep telling me it's *over* . . . that there's nothing to be afraid of, that . . . but it *isn't* . . . it *isn't* . . ."

Now she did collapse, and Nikolas caught her easily. He whispered into her ear and she moaned in unconsciousness. Suddenly his eyes narrowed as he found something in her mind he didn't like.

"I'll kill him, Christine," he said softly, speaking to

the unconscious girl. "I wasn't strong enough to protect Father, but for this, Kaleo is dead." Looking up, he spoke to Robert. "I'm taking her with me."

*"Like hell you are!"* Robert started to lunge at Nikolas, but Nikolas pulled his knife from his pocket and snapped it open, tilting it toward Robert.

"You don't understand, boy. Kaleo has been feeding on her—not just once, but ever since he found her," Nikolas snapped. "And he has blood bonded her to himself, which means he has complete control over her mind. I'm taking her someplace safe until I can stop him. Then, if she wants to return, I'll bring her back."

"Like I would believe you."

"I never lie," Nikolas answered, and Robert glared at him. "Normally, the humans invited to our circuit are loners—they don't have anyone to miss them, or anyone to miss. Christine should never have been invited in the first place. Once I am satisfied she is safe, I will let her come home. I would not take her away from her brother."

Robert was unconvinced. "Let go of my sister."

"I was asked to help her—do you really want me to leave her here until Kaleo drives her completely insane?" Robert took a step back, but his glare didn't soften. Nikolas sighed. "Did she ever once say I hurt her?"

"You knifed her!" Robert shouted.

"I *marked* her. That should have protected her from Kaleo. But I told him I didn't care what happened to her, so long as she got home. Did she ever say I *hurt* her?"

"What are you trying to prove?" Robert demanded.

"I do not torture my prey the way Kaleo does." Sarah smirked, and Nikolas commented, "As I recall, Sarah, you were trying to kill me. You're a Daughter of Vida, and you broke into my home. I would hardly consider you prey."

"You don't torture your prey," Sarah challenged. "You just kill them."

Nikolas shrugged, acknowledging the truth. "Yes, I kill. I have no reason to deny that fact." Turning to Robert, he said, "But I will not kill Christine." He whispered something else, and Sarah thought she might have heard him say *"Again."*

"Just for the record, what happens once you're satisfied she's safe?" Sarah asked.

Nikolas looked up and then tossed something in her direction. She caught it instinctively, and Nikolas disappeared, taking Kristin with him.

# CHAPTER 25

SARAH CAUGHT NISSA'S ARM before the other girl could disappear, and herded her into another room.

"What is he up to?" she demanded instantly.

Nissa looked startled. "What?"

"Nikolas is a self-admitted killer. Suddenly he's all heart."

Nissa shook her head slowly. "Nikolas is . . . Nikolas," she answered vaguely. "His marks make him more blatant among vampire hunters, but he isn't even as bad as most of my kind." She sighed. "You see him only as a killer, the same way he sees you only as a threat to himself and Christopher. Nikolas has rules of his own, and he would never torment an innocent girl like Christine.

"Nikolas sees you as his enemy because you threatened someone he cares about." Nissa sighed, grasping for the words. "But Christine is someone he has chosen to defend. Nikolas is a harsh enemy, but much of that is because he is a fierce protector."

Sarah shook her head, not understanding. "So he chooses to protect Christine . . . but at the next bash, or probably even tonight when he hunts, he will kill some other girl who might as well be her."

Nissa looked heavenward as if for assistance, which was not forthcoming. "You know my brothers used to hunt together. They had—and Nikolas still has—scores of admirers, all of whom were completely safe. They were more than willing to donate blood, and beyond them, people would come to my brothers who wanted to die. I will never understand how my brothers' minds work, but they aren't . . . evil. They could never be that."

Robert entered the room and Sarah jumped at the sudden intrusion.

He turned to Nissa. "Is my sister going to be safe with this guy?" he demanded.

Nissa nodded. "With Nikolas is probably the safest place she could ever be."

Robert nodded sharply. Then he groaned, and leaned back against the wall. "What the hell am I going to tell my parents?" He turned back to Nissa. "Never mind. I don't care about my parents. Thank you. Tell Nikolas that too. I just want my sister to get better."

Nissa smiled faintly. "I'll tell him, the next time I see him."

She disappeared, and Sarah finally relaxed. Remembering the note she was still holding, she quickly skimmed over the words.

*Cold as winter, strong as stone;*
*She faced the darkness all alone.*
*A silver goddess; a reflection.*

*A mirage; a recollection.*
*No return; no turning back.*
*The past is gone, the future, black.*
*Serpents gather in their nest,*
*And she stands above the rest.*
*Shadows hunt; she hunts the shadow.*
*The moon is risen; she stands below.*
*She views her world through the eyes of others.*
*Black and white; there are no colors,*
*As she looks down upon a shattered youth.*
*A shattered mirror shows a shattered truth.*


The poem reminded her of the notes Christopher sent to her.

On the back of the paper was a drawing of Nikolas, standing back to back with Christopher . . . or a reflection of himself. At the bottom of the paper were three words, written in black ink: *Midnight; my house.*

"I don't think so," she whispered.

Robert looked over at her shoulder and read the message. "You going?"

"I already gave him a free shot at me. I'm not really suicidal," she answered absently.

"Huh?"

"He said he would help your sister," Sarah snapped. "That doesn't mean he's suddenly a good guy. He isn't particularly fond of me, and if I go there, he will try to kill me."

"He didn't act like he wanted to kill you," Robert pointed out. "And what's this poetry about—"

"Robert, give it up!"

"I think you're misunderstanding something—"

"Robert, I'm a vampire hunter. Nikolas is a vampire. He has a million and one reasons to kill me and not one to let me live. Don't let poetry and a moment of kindness on his part fool you. Nikolas has only one way of dealing with things, and that's by killing. You heard it when he was talking about Kaleo."

"The guy who did that to my sister deserves to die," Robert growled. "I'd kill him too."

"I'll deal with Kaleo later. The only one on my hit list right now is Nikolas."

"No," Robert said.

*"What?"*

"No," he repeated. "If you kill Nikolas, what's going to happen to Christine?" he demanded. "Kaleo will keep hurting her, and—"

"Doesn't anyone remember that Nikolas is a killer?" she hissed.

Sarah cut off his answer and left abruptly. Robert didn't understand, and she didn't know how to explain to him. Instead she went home and collapsed onto her bed, still holding Nikolas's invitation.

# CHAPTER 26

SARAH RETURNED to wakefulness gasping, struggling to fill lungs with air thick as charcoal ashes, and struggling to clear vision fogged with . . . she didn't know. She could see, but the sight seemed imperfect and she could not tell why.

"Sarah Tigress Vida, stand up."

Her mother's voice, formal and cold, instantly cleared Sarah's mind despite the disorientation she could not seem to shake. She felt off-balance as she found her feet, trying to keep herself from shaking. She sought uselessly to smooth her wrinkled jeans.

Adianna stood behind Dominique, her face pained as she sought Sarah's gaze. Sarah opened her mouth to speak, but Dominique cut her off before she could say a word.

"I want no excuses," Dominique stated flatly. "I am not a fool, and I have known what has been going on since the start of these events." At these words,

Adianna's gaze fell. "You were warned, and you had more than one chance to halt this . . . disgusting infatuation. Now this." Dominique threw to the ground Nikolas's poem-invitation.

"Mother—"

Dominique held up a hand to halt her daughter's words. "I might have turned a blind eye upon your association with the vampires at your school, since you would have in time come to your senses, but *this* . . . lying about this killer, *protecting* him," Dominique spat, "this I can not forgive."

Succinctly and in order, Sarah's crimes were listed. Befriending her prey. Lying to her kin. Endangering her kind by revealing them to the vampires when she told Christopher the truth. Bargaining with Nikolas, and giving up her Vida knife. Telling the human Robert who she was without Dominique's permission. The list went on and on, including transgressions so minor they would have been overlooked any other time, and through it all Sarah had no choice but to try to stand without swaying.

Sarah reached for her power to steady her nerves, but found herself grasping at air. She could feel the magic still humming deep in her blood, but Dominique had bound it—that explained the disorientation she had felt when she had first awakened, and that was why every sense seemed dulled. Without her magic available, she was little more than human.

"You have until tomorrow night to prepare yourself," Dominique announced at last.

To prepare herself for the trial, Sarah knew. By then

Dominique would have gathered the leaders of the other lines, and Sarah doubted she would be acquitted. Every word Dominique had spoken had been true.

When Dominique turned and left the room, Sarah sank back onto the bed, dazed. Again she tried to reach for her power; she could sense it so clearly, but could not use it. What would it feel like to have it stripped away completely?

It was only eight o'clock at night. So early, but it might as well have been the end of the world.

"Sarah . . ." Adrianna's voice was soft as she closed the door and sat beside her sister. "I'm sorry. I thought you had the sense to break it off with them, and I thought you would be better off if Dominique knew right away rather than finding out sometime later . . ." Adrianna shook her head. "I never should have let it get this far."

Sarah's eyes widened as Adrianna quietly ordered, "Get out of here. As it is, your magic will come back in a few days, and you still have your knife. But if you're here tomorrow night, Dominique will disown you and take it all away."

"I'm not going to hide from her."

Adrianna shook her head violently. "This isn't about your pride anymore, Sarah. This is about your *life*—"

"And when Dominique asks where I've gone? Will you lie for me?" Sarah demanded. "I won't have you killed for me."

"I won't be," Adrianna answered calmly. "Besides Dominique herself, no one will fault me for defending my sister." When she saw Sarah's hesitation, she added, "It's your only choice, Sarah."

"To hide for the rest of my life from every one of my kind doesn't seem like a very good choice."

Adianna swallowed thickly. "Better than being dead." Her gaze still locked on Sarah's, she stood up and turned away. "I'm going to bed, Sarah. I'm going to lock my door and turn on loud music, and if I don't hear a car leaving, that's not my fault." She shrugged. "Good night."

After Adianna closed the door, Sarah sat for a moment more.

To hide forever was not a very good option. Neither was being disowned—and she had no hope that she would be found innocent of the crimes Dominique had listed.

Her gaze fell on the invitation Dominique had thrown to the ground, and her decision was made. There was only one way out.

She spent about an hour orientating herself, getting used to using her body without the sixth sense her magic usually provided, and she was confident she could do what she needed to.

She needed to kill Nikolas.

Sarah wrote a note to Adianna and Dominique, stating her intent. Dominique had accused her of endangering her kin and protecting Nikolas—which, in her attempt to protect Nissa and Christopher, she had done. The only possible way out of this mess was to confront Nikolas.

In truth, Nikolas wasn't the worst of his kind—he didn't torture his prey, and he didn't kill nearly so wantonly as his strength would allow. He hunted, as all vampires hunted, to kill the bloodlust. His marks were the only element that made his kills more obvious than kills by others of his kind. Had Christopher not separated from his brother before Dominique had started organizing the chaotic mess her predecessors had allowed the Vida records to become, his marks and name would have been just as infamous as his brother's.

This was not the time to ponder Christopher's guilt or Nikolas's innocence. This was the reason hunters knew better than to mix with their prey. It created shades of gray, where there had once been just black and white.

She didn't know what she would do when Nissa and Christopher hunted her down. She refused to kill them. But she also refused to run; hiding until she died, old and lonely, seemed worse by far than dying the quick death every hunter knew marked the end.

She didn't bother to hide her knives when she left, but instead put on a black tank top and black shorts; over everything she threw her leather jacket, so the weapons wouldn't be quite so obvious while she was still in the human world.

After taking the keys to her Jaguar from the dresser, she went outside and started the car.

The clock read 11:59 as she pulled into the driveway at Nikolas's house.

# CHAPTER 27

NIKOLAS TOOK HER COAT as she entered. The house was empty except for the two of them.

*Three of us,* she realized, as Nikolas led her into the living room, where Christopher was pacing.

"Are you losing your resolve, Sarah?" Nikolas asked, and Christopher halted in his pacing. "You've been near enough to kill me for a whole two minutes, and you haven't even drawn a knife."

"Is Christine okay?" Sarah asked, not acknowledging Nikolas's question.

Nikolas sighed. "Christine is fine. Even Kaleo is still alive. In fact, I haven't had a chance to kill anyone noteworthy in the ten hours since I last spoke with you. Does that settle your curiosity?"

Sarah ignored the taunt. "Christopher, what are you doing here?"

Christopher shrugged. "My brother asked me to come."

He looked much the same physically as he had the

last time she had seen him, but there was an energy about him that was different.

Christopher had fed. Though she could read his aura easily enough to know he had not killed, he had obviously taken human blood, probably just after their fight, when his bloodlust had been so overwhelming.

Sarah examined his face for a sign of whether he was going to help her or hurt her, but though his expression showed no anger, it showed no compassion either.

"Can I get you something to drink?" Nikolas offered, and Sarah laughed.

*Sure,* she thought sarcastically, wondering what vampires served to drink. *A Bloody Mary — shaken, not sliced.*

"What are you up to, Nikolas?" she asked instead.

"I invited you to my home. I can at least be a gracious host before you try to kill me."

He was going to wait for her to move? That could make this a very long evening indeed, because she had been planning to wait for his attack. If she killed Nikolas now, unprovoked, she had no illusions that she would not need to kill Christopher, too.

"I'll have something."

Sarah turned to see a girl no older than sixteen. She was wearing a white cotton dress with silver embroidery, and her skin was fair, but not ghostly. Her hair was dark brown.

"Christine?" Sarah whispered, hardly able to believe it. Could this girl be the same wraith Sarah had seen earlier that day, huddled in a corner? She had obviously been cleaned up, dressed, fed . . . the change was so amazing, it seemed impossible.

"Yes," the girl said lightly. "I never caught your name, though."

"Sarah," she answered. She shook Christine's hand as if this were a normal situation, though it was absurd to be introducing herself to this girl now, in the midst of a den of monsters.

*She views her world through the eyes of others./Black and white; there are no colors,/As she looks down upon a shattered youth./A shattered mirror shows a shattered truth.*

Sarah had never doubted herself before, but this nymph in white caused her hatred of Nikolas to fade a bit. Christine stood on tiptoe to open a tin that was sitting on the mantel above the fireplace.

"Chocolate?" she offered, but Sarah shook her head.

"No, thank you."

Christine glided out of the room again and Sarah watched her go, entranced.

"Nikolas, what do you want?" Christopher finally asked once Christine was out of sight. He sounded drained, tired. "Why am I here?"

"I wanted to give you a chance, Brother," Nikolas said. He reached into his pocket, pulled something out, and tossed it to Christopher.

For a moment Sarah thought the knife was Nikolas's, but as Christopher snapped it open she realized the handle was black with white inlay, the reverse of Nikolas's—Kristopher's, Sarah assumed, left over from the time when the two brothers still hunted together.

Christopher closed the knife. "A chance to do what?"

"To share this one with me," Nikolas answered, and Sarah realized it might be time to start fighting.

But she didn't move.

"You're going to blood bond her to yourself," Christopher said, knowing how his brother's mind worked. "That's why you didn't kill her when you marked her."

"For you, Brother. You wanted her, but she turned you down, Christopher," Nikolas answered. "Now's your chance to make her yours. To make her ours."

"Like Marguerite," Christopher whispered, understanding. "Nikolas, no. Marguerite wanted it. Sarah doesn't."

"She *hurt* you, Christopher," Nikolas said, pleading. "I *heard* you scream. You told me not to kill her—fine, I won't kill her, but there are very few choices left. I can let her go, in which case her own family is going to kill her, or I can blood bond her to myself."

"I'm not going to help you with this, Nikolas—"

"Fine," he answered, his voice childlike and resigned at the same time.

Sarah stepped back out of Nikolas's line of sight, and saw him turn to keep her in his view.

She went for her knife, and an instant later Nikolas was behind her, with his hand around her throat. She drew the knife from her thigh and flipped it in her hand, driving it into his side.

Nikolas cursed, throwing her away from him, and Sarah landed awkwardly on her knife, slicing open her right palm. A moment later a knife blade was at her throat.

Christopher's.

Christopher had Sarah pinned on the floor, with the blade of his knife against her skin.

"Slice me open, Christopher," she hissed. "If you're really willing, then do it."

Though Christopher didn't let the knife cut her, he pressed the blade harder against her skin. If she moved, she would slit her own throat.

Nikolas recovered and knelt by his brother's side, then reached toward the knife on Sarah's back so he could disarm her. His brother caught his wrist, stopping him, and Nikolas nodded.

Christopher moved his knife away and pulled her to her feet, and then he let her go.

Nikolas followed Sarah with his gaze. "Christopher—"

"I'm not going to kill her for defending herself," Christopher interrupted.

"The Kristopher I used to know—my *brother*—would have killed her as soon as he found out she was a Vida. You've tasted her blood. How can you not want it?"

"I want it," Christopher said softly. "I want it as much as humans want to breathe, but I have control."

Sarah backed away, and noticed that, though Nikolas kept a hawk's gaze on her, Christopher was only watching his brother. When she realized how easy it would be to kill him, bile rose in her throat.

"Come back to me, Kristopher. Hunt with me," Nikolas pleaded. He stepped toward his brother, moving closer to Sarah at the same time—he obviously did not trust her at his brother's back. "Why do you let the bloodlust burn you every night and every day? We need to feed to survive. Would a starving man on the verge of death turn down a dinner because it was chicken and he was a vegetarian? Or would he eat it anyway, because it was all he had that could stop the pain?"

Sarah did not wait for Christopher's answer. Instead, she drew the knife from her wrist. The blade had barely cleared its sheath when Nikolas pounced, sending her to the ground; the breath rushed from her lungs, but she kept her grip on her weapon.

Christopher reacted instantly and grabbed his brother's arm, dragging Nikolas to the side, ignoring Sarah as if she posed no threat. Slaughtering her sense of fair play, Sarah rolled, knocking the momentarily defenseless vampire away. Nikolas cried as her blade touched his skin, and the sound caused Sarah's gut to clench. He looked so much like Christopher—so vulnerable.

She realized that she had hesitated only when Christopher's hand clamped over her wrist, stopping the knife from completing the killing blow. He tightened his grip until she dropped the weapon, and Nikolas tossed her knife away while Christopher dragged her away from his brother.

Most vampires were solitary hunters. Sarah had been trained to take down enemies one by one, but Nikolas and Christopher fought like one entity. When one was in danger, the other reacted.

Self-preservation replaced all loyalty to her friend as Sarah slammed an elbow into Christopher's gut, forcing him to release her, in the same moment that Nikolas knocked her legs from beneath her.

She rolled away from both vampires, drawing her last knife. Breathing heavily, she paused, waiting for one of the vampires to move.

Nikolas edged toward her slowly, and she found her

feet, her eyes never straying from him. Her right hand was still bleeding, and she saw his gaze fall to it, and the knife she was holding.

She was watching Nikolas, but it was Christopher who caught her wrist, Christopher who was suddenly restraining her. She had fallen for the same mistake he had, only moments before—she had assumed he would not hurt her unless she attacked him, and so had not been paying attention when he had disappeared from in front of her.

Christopher had lost his reasons for refusing, and all three of them knew it. Sarah's blood was in the air, along with the tension from the fight. Christopher's control was already weak, and now the predator had taken control.

Nikolas reached around Sarah and held her wrists, as Kristopher wrapped an arm around her waist to hold her still.

Sarah gasped as twin sets of fangs pierced her skin, Kristopher on the right and Nikolas on the left. Without her magic she had no further defense, and she collapsed beneath the combined pressure of their minds. With Nikolas and Kristopher still at her throat, she sank to her knees.

Both brothers pulled away after a few moments, and their gazes met for barely a second.

Nikolas turned away first, bent to retrieve Kristopher's knife from where it had fallen, and handed it to his brother.

Kristopher took the knife as if he were in a trance and made a cut just below his own throat.

Sarah turned her head away, but Kristopher forced her to look at him—and at the line of blood that beaded on his skin. They had barely taken any of her blood, but even so she could feel the thirst that always fell on a vampire's prey, and she could not look away.

"No." Her voice was soft, almost frightened.

Kristopher touched his fingers to his own blood and painted her lips with it, forcing her mouth open. She tasted the blood of the damned, and she could not resist.

Leaning her head forward to the cut on his chest, she drank. The blood was sweet and thick and magical, and she wanted it so much—

He pushed her away after a moment, and Nikolas turned her to himself, drawing his blade across his own skin, a mirror wound to Kristopher's.

Once again she drank.

Then Nikolas pushed her away too, and she felt her mind spin downward as the blood entered her system. Blackness finally swallowed her, and she fell into the oblivion of unconsciousness.

# CHAPTER 28

ADIANNA HAD HER KNIFE in her hand as she shouldered open the front door, but she already knew there were no vampires within a mile of her. Her senses were stretched so far she could feel the heartbeats of the human inside and those of most of the humans on this block. Worse, she could feel Sarah, her aura muted from Dominique's binding of her powers, and her heart beating frantically.

All this she knew before she even stepped into the front hall of the house. Her eyes took in, but her mind ignored, the artwork, the roses on the table, and the open box of chocolates on the mantel.

More vividly she saw the droplets of deep red blood, not yet dried, but scattered as if from a minor wound on a fighting person.

She should have guessed what Sarah would do. Adianna herself would have done the same, if somehow she had ended up in the same situation. Better to die than to face the humiliation of being disowned. Better to die with your pride intact than to live without it. They had both been raised that way, but Adianna had hoped so fiercely that Sarah would choose life. It had been almost two hours later that she had sneaked back to Sarah's room, only to find her already gone.

Sarah's spilled blood, blond hair, and flushed skin were the only color in the room. She lay on a plush black couch, where it seemed someone had gently set her down. Adianna could see the faint mark that attested to an almost-healed wound on Sarah's right hand, though she knew there had been no mark there earlier in the night.

The fact that the new injury, no doubt the source of the blood on the floor, was nearly closed scared Adianna more than anything had since their father had died. No witch healed that fast.

Her power flared as she knelt by her sister's side. She was dangerously close to losing control, but she knew of nothing on earth that would make her pause to regain it.

Sarah's skin was hot to the touch, and Adianna clamped her jaws tight as she saw the faint blush of blood on Sarah's mouth. Reaching out with a tendril of magic, she found the poison in Sarah's system.

They had given her their blood. Whether they had intended to blood bond her or to end her life did not matter. Sarah was a Daughter of Vida; her witch blood would destroy the invading vampiric blood, and probably destroy the body it was inside in the process.

A healer might have been able to do something, but any healer would have consulted Dominique before treating Sarah, and Dominique would have told them to let her die. Adianna would have to try on her own.

She knew what the consequences could be. This had not been attempted since Jade Arun had tried to heal her young daughter thousands of years ago. Since then every witch in the Arun line had been born with vampire blood. But if that was the price, Adianna would pay it.

She placed her hand over Sarah's feverish brow, closed her eyes, and tried to sever the bonds the vampiric blood had already made on Sarah's flesh.

She knew from the start it was a lost cause. The infection was too deep, and it had leached onto Sarah's blood too firmly.

"Damn it, Sarah!" Adianna's own shriek startled her back to the real world. "Don't you *dare* die on me. Do you hear me? Don't you *dare*." The last words were whispered, as she threw her mind and magic headlong into the swift tide that was Sarah's power.

The effect was similar to jumping into freezing river rapids headfirst, bogged down by pockets full of stones, with salt in her eyes, and every inch of skin raw to the bone. First she severed the ties Dominique's magic had fastened over Sarah's, and then steeled herself for her next move.

Sarah's magic was killing her as it killed the vampire blood. If Adianna could not pull out the vampiric toxin, then the only thing she could do was cut away the magic that was fighting it.

She was in Sarah's mind as well as in her magic, and even though she did not want to hear, she knew the truth. She could save Sarah's life by destroying her magic, but she knew quite clearly that her sister would rather die.

She held Sarah's life and magic between two fingertips. She could snap each with a thought.

Instead, trembling, she withdrew, breath dragging through her lungs with difficulty. The sun had completely risen while she had been drowning in Sarah's power, and she knew that the faint, cool sensation of someone's aura brushing over her was not new. He must have been there for hours, kneeling silently, slightly behind her and to her left.

She turned slowly, drawing the knife from her wrist as she did so, and he did not move to stop her.

"How is she?" Christopher asked, his voice soft.

Her voice cut as sharply as could her blade. "How did you think she would be after you gave her your blood? She is going to die."

Christopher's carefully neutral expression crumbled. The vampire leaned back against the wall and his eyes closed for a moment.

"I didn't think," Christopher answered quietly, raising his black gaze to meet the hunter's. "I lost control."

Adianna was Dominique Vida's older daughter. She had always been the strong sister, the one who honored the line, the one who made Dominique proud. She, more than anyone, knew exactly how much could be destroyed by losing control even for a few moments. She could also see how painful the confession was to the vampire.

Perhaps seeing Adianna's reluctant understanding, Christopher added, "I love her, and I never meant to hurt her. And I *will not* let her die because I screwed up." Though he spoke softly, Christopher's voice was rich with self-directed anger.

He stepped toward Sarah, and without thinking, Adianna moved between the vampire and her sister. "Get away from her."

"You're Sarah's sister," Christopher said, his voice tight. "Do you really want her to die?"

Adianna flinched at the accusation; her nails bit crescents into her left palm as she clenched her hand into a fist. "How do you intend to help her?" she asked, but she knew the answer.

"I took her blood, and possibly her life," Christopher said. "It's only right if I give her mine." The meaning was clear. He meant to change her, to make her into one of the creatures that Sarah had spent her whole life hunting. Christopher must have seen some sign of revulsion in Adianna's face because he added, "She would be alive."

"She would be a . . ."

"Yes, she would be a vampire," Christopher snapped. "But she would be *alive*. Isn't that all that matters? I would prefer to change her and risk having her hate me even more for it than to let her die without giving her a choice."

Adianna could not agree. To allow her own sister to be turned into one of their kind would be worse than letting her die.

Before Adianna could raise the protest, Christopher calmed his voice and added, "If she wakes up and doesn't want it, Sarah is strong enough to fall on the knife. At least this way she *will* wake up."

Adianna choked on her own argument, and turned away from Christopher and Sarah. "Do what you have to do." Her voice broke on the words.

She stepped aside, but could not force her gaze away. Her resolve almost broke as the leech bared Sarah's throat; she leaned back against the wall and sank to the floor.

*Get out of here, hunter. You don't want to watch this.* The vampire's voice in her mind was loud, strengthened by the witch blood he had in him. Adianna felt the bile rise in her throat.

She stood, and turned her back on the pair. One step, two. She was almost at the door when, like Orpheus, she had to take one last glance—just in time to see Christopher draw his knife across his own skin, and to see Sarah latch on to the new wound like a suckling child.

Adianna lost control, and sprinted the rest of the way to her car. Twenty minutes later she convinced herself to slow down when she found herself pushing ninety-five on the highway; no matter how far or how fast she traveled, Adianna knew she would never outrun that last image.

From this night on, whether she chose to live as a vampire or kill herself, Sarah was as good as dead. Adianna prayed she would never see her sister again.

# CHAPTER 29

AT SUNSET, Kristopher still sat by Sarah's side, waiting anxiously for her to stir.

Had he been too late? He cursed himself for wasting time arguing with the hunter, but he doubted that Sarah would have forgiven him if he had hurt Adianna. His system still hummed with the power of Sarah's witch blood, and if he had fought the hunter he probably would have killed her out of reflex.

His brother was pacing in the back of the room, his power crackling around him like a net of sparks, and as always Kristopher could feel the connection between them. Nikolas had a right to be there; they were in his house. It had been the only location that Kristopher had trusted to be safe enough.

A less intrusive presence, Nissa waited calmly in one of the other chairs. He wasn't sure why his sister was there—maybe to diffuse the situation if Sarah woke up hating him.

He brushed a long black hair from his face, the only

movement he had made in almost twenty minutes, and glanced briefly at the abstract black-and-white clock on the wall. The sun should have set by now. She should have awakened.

Finally, Sarah moaned lightly, and Christopher's guilt came around to hit him again as he heard the pain in her tone. He knew that a newborn vampire, before she had ever hunted, was wracked by bloodlust so strong it could drive reason completely from the mind. Without killing, it was almost impossible to sate that hunger.

Sarah moaned again and sat up slowly, blinking to clear her vision. They all knew her mind was foggy. Her memory might not even return until after she fed. Kristopher and Nikolas both reached to help her up.

Sarah could barely stand on her own, and she leaned on Kristopher as he held her. "I need to bring her someplace she can feed safely," he told his sister. Once Sarah had fed she would probably hate him. Worse, she might put her own knife through her heart.

Nissa stepped forward and put a hand on his shoulder. "Don't let her kill anyone, Kristopher."

Nikolas laughed, and Nissa flinched at the cutting tone. "That's impossible, Nissa. She's a new fledgling, and her change wasn't nearly as easy as yours was—if she doesn't take a life, she won't be able to sate the bloodlust, and you well know it."

"She's a Daughter of Vida. She won't take a human life," Nissa argued.

Nikolas looked at Sarah doubtfully as Kristopher gently smoothed a hand down her silky hair, trying to comfort her as much as he could while his siblings argued.

"I'll take her," Nissa said, her voice strong. "There are people I know at SingleEarth who will be willing."

Kristopher mirrored his brother's expression, doubtful. "Not willing to die." Like his sister, Kristopher had gone through the change easily; only Nikolas had woken to the mind-numbing pain that Sarah was going through.

Nikolas and Nissa continued to argue, but Kristopher had already made a decision. Human blood was too weak to sate the bloodlust without a kill. Witch blood would have been best, since it was strong enough to quench the thirst without killing the donor, but every instinct rebelled against bringing Sarah to her kin. The witches answered to Dominique, and Dominique was the last person who could know what had become of her daughter.

There was only one choice left—had always been only one choice. Tilting his head back, he drew Sarah to his own throat.

# CHAPTER 30

GODDESS, IT HURT. Fire and glass were being forced through her veins and she could do nothing about it.

*Drink,* she heard in her mind, and suddenly she was aware of the sweet scent that filled her senses.

Sarah's instincts took over as Kristopher pulled her to his own throat. Graceful as any predator, she wrapped a hand around the back of his neck and sealed her lips over the pulse point. She felt the weight of her own fangs in her mouth, the moment of resistance as they pierced the skin, and then only the rich, warm blood that flowed over her tongue.

Then there was only the sweet, rich taste, and a million images that accompanied it. She was not prepared for the flood of memories and emotions, but she understood that Kristopher could not have blocked her from his mind if he had tried. Not while she was this close, not while his blood flowed past her lips.

Some of the memories were pleasant, some harsh, and as she flickered among them she lost track of her own self.

*"Nicholas, or Christopher?" the girl asked with a toss of her golden curls. Dressed in pale cream, with an ivy wreath and a white rose in her lap, Christine Brunswick was every inch the May Queen. He flinched at the question, but it was common enough. Only from Christine did it have the power to cut.*

*Power like lightening struck him, knocking him away from their willing prey. Pain worse than even the searing torture of the bloodlust, as Elisabeth Vida's knife sank into his chest, only missing his heart because his brother had hit the witch's arm. He thought he was going to die, like this, but somehow they got the knife out. The witch's blood was sweeter than the richest honey, and the pain dimmed as he took it, with his brother beside him.*

*He remembered when the human world had found her body. The names Nikolas and Kristopher had been on the lips of the world that they had lost. Christopher Ravena—the name he had been given when he was born—was not a hunter, and so he had changed the name when he signed it on his prey. Such a small change, but a symbol of his difference, the last break he had made from the world he had been born in.*

*Nissa, at one of their bashes, the first time the brothers had seen her since they had been changed a hundred years before. She was nervous of Kaleo and the others, but eventually she relaxed in the heady atmosphere of predatory contentment. No one here hid his nature.*

*One human got out of hand and made the mistake of insulting Nissa while her brothers looked on. He never would have lived through the night, and Nissa had known that. The Devil's Hour fell, and no one thought to stop Nissa as she bared the man's throat and fed.*

*Nissa, dying as she refused to feed again. Dying as her own guilt tore her apart. He wasn't sure he could survive without Nikolas, but he knew Nissa couldn't live without him. Later, when she was strong again, he could go back to his brother, but right now . . . she needed him.*

*Even before he spoke to her, he adored her. Her beauty, her grace, and the thoughtful expression she wore that told him she was not listening to a thing the teacher was saying . . . all of that enthralled him. After he spoke to her, after he had laughed with her and learned about her, he could not have helped being fascinated by her. She was too polished, too impossible, and he kept wondering what lay beneath.*

*Sarah Tigress Vida, youngest Daughter of Vida. Finally he understood the strength he had seen in her. And only then, when she told him to leave her alone, did he realize that he loved her.*

*Fighting the desire to argue, he had fallen back into the neutral mask Kristopher wore when he was not in friendly territory. He wanted to kiss her, but instead he had been cold, because otherwise he would not have been able to keep himself from asking her to defy all the rules. He would never ask her to give up so much, not for him.*

When the spell finally broke and Sarah stepped back, the hunger and the pain were gone, but a duality remained. Though Sarah tried to ignore the sensation, it was like turning her back to a conversation. The direct thoughts and memories disappeared, but there remained a lingering sense of Kristopher's mind.

Kristopher stepped back, and Sarah knew that he would have blocked the connection, if it had been his decision. The wound that Christine had left was still healing. He had adored Christine; she had been the most beautiful woman he had ever seen. The last thing he wanted was for Sarah to see what Christine had been to him.

"Kristopher?" The question came from Nikolas, who had been standing quietly at the other side of the room.

Kristopher shook his head as if to clear his mind. "I'm . . . fine," he answered finally. Forcibly turning his mind from the memories, he raised his gaze to Sarah's and said simply, "What you do now is your choice."

He was not going to mention it aloud, but she could easily feel his fear, and she understood it. He was worried that she was going to kill herself.

But if she didn't, what could she do? Her life and everything she had known were gone. Her own mother would kill her if she tried to go back.

A true Vida would have fallen on the knife the moment she had become a vampire, but Sarah did not want to die. She had made friends with Nissa, and with Christopher, and they had taught her that the vampire blood did not turn a person into a monster.

# CHAPTER 31

WHEN SHE GAVE NO RESPONSE, Kristopher took a breath. After a hesitation that told her he was bracing himself for her answer, he said, "Sarah, I don't give a damn about your past—I love you. If you want to, you're welcome to stay with us."

She saw Nikolas's surprise when he heard the "us," but the vampire didn't argue. The idea gave Sarah pause, however.

If the "us" had meant Christopher and Nissa, she would have said yes immediately. But she knew how Nikolas lived, how he hunted. He killed, and whether his prey was willing or not didn't matter to Sarah. She couldn't live that way.

Before she could voice her refusal, Nikolas spoke.

"Sarah . . ." He paused and looked to Kristopher for a moment before he continued, as if for approval. "I'm not expecting your instant forgiveness. I'm not even asking for it." He started to take a step in her direction, but then seemed to think better of it and stopped. "But if nothing else, trust me when I say I won't ever hurt my brother, or let him be hurt if I can stop it." Again he glanced at his brother, but this time only for a moment, as if he already knew how Kristopher would react. "We don't own you. Whatever you choose today . . . I'm no threat to you. But don't blame Kristopher for what I've done, and don't leave just because I'm here."

Sarah opened her mouth to disagree, but then closed it as Nikolas's words sank in. Her instinct was to argue with anything he said, but right now what he said made sense.

She couldn't stay, but it wasn't because of Nikolas. Quite abruptly she realized that her hatred for him seemed to have faded. Her brush with Kristopher's mind had caused some of that; it was nearly impossible to completely hate Nikolas once she had felt the intense love and loyalty Kristopher held for his brother.

Yes, he had hurt her physically, but pain was only fleeting. Honestly, the most brutal thing Nikolas had done to her had been to open her eyes and force her to see reality—the shades of gray that existed in the world, beyond the world of stark black and white, of evil and good, that Dominique had taught her long ago.

She took a breath, but her mind was made up. "I can't stay," she said finally, and she saw—and felt— Kristopher flinch. "You know I can't survive—and hunt—the same way you do. Even if I could, I don't like to be dependent. Give me some time to find my own way to live." She lifted her gaze and met Kristopher's. His fear, which was still ringing clear in her mind, prompted her to add, "I don't hate you, Kristopher. I don't hate you or your brother." On a burst of impulsiveness that would have made Dominique cringe, she stepped forward and hugged him. "I'll miss you, Kristopher, but I can't stay here. For now at least."

"We have forever. I'll see you again," he answered with certainty. "But before you go—"

Kristopher tilted her face up and kissed her.

It occurred to Sarah then that she had never been kissed, really kissed, before.

However, as first kisses went . . .

Like all of Kristopher's art, his kisses were expertly done.

Kristopher was the one who broke the kiss, though he kept his arms around her and did not pull back far. "I'm sorry. I've wanted to do that for"—he shrugged— "too long."

"That is a moment you never need to apologize for."

He smiled, and in the expression Sarah saw the true Christopher, whom she had come to know and trust.

"There are a million other moments, both past and future, that I should apologize to you for," he said lightly. "I might as well start earning credit."

A million moments, both past and future. Thousands of years of hatred, between both their kinds, could hardly be undone quickly. Even in the eternity that she potentially had ahead of her, she didn't think she was up to a job as a peacemaker. But if she had been . . .

SingleEarth would take her in if she asked. Nissa could teach her how to survive without killing. There were pockets of peace in the world, and if she could just find one of them, she could make a life there. As Kristopher had pointed out, she had forever.

# MIDNIGHT PREDATOR

Midnight Predator *is dedicated to my father, William Michael Rhodes, for inspiring me in this project. When I stopped two hundred pages into the first version of this book, you suggested that the whole thing could be summed up in one brief sentence. Lo and behold, it worked. I love you, Dad.*

*For technical knowledge, I must thank Karl Horlitz, a wonderful friend, Eagle Scout, excellent researcher, and fountain of arcane knowledge. If I need anything, from caring support to a new skill, I can turn to him. Thank you for the Boy Scout handbook, thank you for all you taught me, and thank you for one a.m.*

*My most profound thanks and eternity of worship must go to Valerie and Irene Schmidt, who, in addition to being two of my best friends and Jaguar's two greatest fans, are also two of the most amazing editors I know. Their suggestions helped shape this from the bulky, rambling stack of papers it was at first to the novel you are reading now.*

*I send sincere gratitude and love to everyone else who contributed to this work, including raVyn, Kelly Henry, Haley Ulyrus, Jesse Sullivan, and Kyle Bladow. I never could have done this without your support. Thank you all.*

She made a little shadow-hidden grave,
    The day Faith died;
Therein she laid it, heard the clod's sick fall,
    And smiled aside—
"If less I ask," tear-blind, she mocked, "I may
    Be less denied."

She set a rose to blossom in her hair,
    The day Faith died—
"Now glad," she said, "and free at last, I go,
    And life is wide."
But through long nights she stared into the dark,
    And knew she lied.

*The Dead Faith*
Fannie Heaslip Lea

# CHAPTER 1

*SOME PEOPLE USE THINGS; they destroy. You're a creator, a builder.* The words came unbidden to her mind, completely inappropriate at the moment.

Distracted by the memory, Turquoise missed a block. She hissed in pain as the knife cut deep into the meaty underside of her arm. She caught her attacker's wrist and twisted, sending the young woman attached sprawling to the ground, as her father's words faded from her mind. Once, they might have been right, but now, they could not have been further from the truth.

The woman Turquoise was fighting wasn't clumsy for long. In a near-blur of burgundy hair and black leather, Ravyn Aniketos sprang to her feet.

Turquoise rolled her shoulders, trying to work out the kinks in them, and blinked quickly to clear her tired eyes. This match had been going on for too long. She was bleeding from where Ravyn's knife had sliced through her arm, and she could feel the warm, sticky drip of blood down her back from a second wound on her left shoulder. Ravyn's black leather pants had been slit open in the thigh, and she had a shallow wound low on her jaw, which would probably heal without scarring.

Earlier, there had been other combatants; most slunk out the back door, defeated, within the first few minutes.

The fight was a competition of stealth and hunting ability. In near darkness, the competitors found and marked one another—a quick knife slice, just enough to draw blood. If a hunter was marked three times, he or she was out of the running. Turquoise was pleased to have lasted so long, but only victory would satisfy her pride. Ravyn likely felt the same. The next one of them to land a blow would win, becoming the leader of Crimson, the most elite unit of the Bruja guilds.

Somewhere in the building, a clock struck, once, twice . . .

Turquoise lost track of the clock's tones as she struck again. Ravyn cursed as the blade narrowly missed her stomach, and Turquoise barely managed to evade an answering strike to her cheek.

They were both getting tired, and tired quickly became clumsy. Only the fact that they had both been fighting for hours kept them evenly matched.

The clock finished its song, and left the room in eerie silence, broken only by the ragged, heavy breathing as the two fought.

"Ravyn. Turquoise."

Turquoise slid a fraction of her attention to the voice but did not allow her gaze to leave Ravyn.

"Sheathe your weapons," Bruja's leader, Sarta,

instructed. Someone flipped the switch and both fighters blinked against the sudden light. "I have a feeling that this competition could go on for days if I let it," she announced, "but Bruja law does call for a limit."

Ravyn licked the blade of her knife clean, her cranberry-colored gaze resting on Turquoise all the while, as if daring her to react. Ravyn had no fetish for blood, and she professed to hate vampires, but she did love to give a show.

"Well, Sarta, if you're going to call a halt to our fun, do you also plan to name a winner?" Ravyn was still panting slightly, but not enough to affect the smooth drawl in her voice.

Turquoise wiped her own blade on the leg of her ruined jeans. She didn't speak yet, preferring to catch her breath. If it was ten now, then she and Ravyn had been sparring for almost five hours. This fight had begun at sunrise.

Five hours, and they were left in a draw. Turquoise's muscles ached with fatigue, but she would rather have finished this than stopped now. She wanted the title.

Crimson. It was the most elite of the three Bruja guilds. Cold-blooded as snakes and vicious as hyenas, members of Bruja were the best predators in existence. To be recognized as the guild's leader would fulfill the promise Turquoise had once made. She had sworn that no one would ever mistake her for prey again. If that meant abandoning a few of the social mores of the daylight world, as Bruja members so frequently did, so be it.

The leader of Crimson was second only to Sarta, the leader of all three Bruja guilds. Turquoise had trained and fought and competed for the position. She knew she was the best Crimson had. She could out-stalk and out-fight any vampire and had, many times. She would win this title, whatever it took.

"Rematch," Sarta said simply. "Onyx and Frost still need to compete today. You two are obviously matched evenly with daggers, but a Bruja member needs to be able to use any weapon at his or her command." She paused for dramatic effect. "A tie is decided in a private duel, one month after Challenge, witnessed only by the other leaders. The weapon is decided by the member who has been in the guild the longest—in this case, Ravyn—and the bout goes to third blood."

Ravyn sighed, looking at Turquoise past burgundy lashes. "In one month, and I choose the weapon. In that case . . ." She walked around the room, examining the walls, which were decorated with weapons of all sizes, all shapes, and all designs.

She paused to run a finger down the blade of a broadsword, but then shook her head and moved on. She glanced at the crossbows, but they were the traditional weapon of Crimson's sister guild, Onyx—not appropriate for a Crimson duel. She passed foils, epées, and sabers, and did not even pause to glance at the thick wooden staves.

Finally, she pulled down two leather whips, and cracked one expertly. "I choose these."

Ravyn tossed one of them to Turquoise with a sly grin, and Turquoise almost let it fall to the ground before reflex made her catch the handle. Of the entire selection of weapons in the Bruja hall, the whip was the only one she hated. Ravyn could not have made a better choice.

"Turquoise, do you accept the challenge?" Sarta asked.

"I accept." She was grateful that her voice stayed even. She hated whips. She could use one if she needed to, but not with any precision.

"Then get out of here," Sarta ordered. "Come back the day of the next full moon. The match will begin at sunrise."

Turquoise nodded, then turned her back to Sarta and Ravyn, and stalked as gracefully as she could from the fighting floor.

She paused next to the cork assignment board, collecting herself before she left the halls.

Ravyn had come up behind her to look at the board. Turquoise's instincts told her to leave. Ravyn, like all Bruja members, was not someone Turquoise trusted at her back. So of course she forced herself to stay and read the notices.

Turquoise ignored most of the posts. She was a mercenary, but she had standards, and she preferred vampires as her prey. There were numbers up on a couple of shape-shifters, but none sounded interesting. Besides, Turquoise was still a little wary of putting a knife in something that breathed and bled like a human, even if it did grow fur, scales, or feathers occasionally.

The rest of the posts she tried to avoid reading. She liked to think no amount of money was worth stalking human targets, but she knew most Bruja members disagreed. Some argued that cowardice kept her from hunting her own kind. When Turquoise had first joined Bruja, the older members had taken bets on how long it would take her to make her first human kill.

They were still waiting.

Turquoise finally slipped away from the hall, stretching as she shouldered open the door to the bright outside.

A stranger, a young woman no more than twenty-five years old, was waiting for her. She held up her hands to show she was unarmed. "Turquoise Draka?" she inquired. Her voice was polished, the accent vaguely English.

Turquoise nodded cautiously. Her eyes had adjusted to the sunlight now, and she sized up this woman. She looked fairly harmless, with brown hair pulled back in an elegant twist, and wearing a cream business suit over a chocolate-colored blouse. A leather folio leaned against the wall beside her.

However, the woman's heels made no sound on the stone walk as she approached, and even in the mid-June heat, her face showed no hint of sweat. Turquoise trusted her ability to recognize a vampire on sight, but just because this woman was not a bloodsucker did not mean she was human.

"Ah, and here is Ravyn Aniketos," the woman called, as Ravyn slipped tiredly through the door. Though she must still have been sunblind, Ravyn drew a dagger instantly upon hearing her name.

Ravyn and Turquoise exchanged a look, and a mental shrug passed between them. Although they were enemies at times, rivals for power always, they were both intelligent enough to put their differences aside if confronted by a threat. Vampire, witch, shape-shifter, or human, this woman didn't stand a chance if her intentions were less than friendly.

"Something I can help you with?" Turquoise inquired warily.

"Yes. My name is Jillian Red." The name had the sound of a pseudonym. Jillian extended her hand, but did not seem surprised when no one reached out to shake it. "I have been following your careers for about a year now. You both hold quite impressive ranks, and have shown a certain rancor toward a breed I am not too fond of myself."

Bored already, Turquoise assumed the woman's lengthy speech was just winding toward another job.

Ravyn had actually started to walk away. Turquoise debated doing the same, but was stopped by the woman's next words.

"You both show a certain promise in your history, namely, some unpleasant experiences with the trade."

Turquoise did not need to ask which trade. From the sudden tension that pulsed through Ravyn's body as she turned back, she had understood the words just as well.

"And what do you know of our history?" Ravyn asked, voice silky as a black widow's thread.

Jillian Red sighed. "You, Ravyn, first came to vampiric attention when you were fifteen, and were brought into the trade by a low-power mercenary named Jared. You were lucky enough to avoid the professional slave traders, but unlucky enough—"

Ravyn shook her head, sending silky cranberry hair shuddering about her shoulders. "This is unnecessary."

"Unlucky enough," Jillian continued, "to be in the midst of vampires who respected Jared's claim of ownership and because of it would not come to your aid no matter how much they disapproved of his treatment of you."

Ravyn was by this point visibly simmering, her frame so rigid Turquoise suspected bone and sinew would shatter if the hunter tried to move.

"Shortly after he acquired you, Jared was found dead," Jillian finished, "and about a week after that, you entered Crimson."

"What is the job?" Ravyn snapped.

"Shall we find someplace to sit and discuss the particulars?" Jillian suggested. "Even if you choose not to accept my offer, which I doubt, you will be well paid for your time."

"Lead the way," Turquoise said, when Ravyn did not immediately speak. If this woman knew as much about Turquoise's history as she did about Ravyn's, that knowledge could make her inconvenient, if not dangerous. It would not hurt to learn what she wanted.

# CHAPTER 2

FIFTEEN MINUTES LATER, they were gathered around a small table in Jillian Red's hotel room, looking at pictures the woman drew out of her briefcase.

"This is a copy of a painting made back in 1690," their host explained as she placed the first print on the table. "I don't suppose either of you recognizes it?"

The painting focused on an intimidating building, the outside walls of which were painted black with an abstract design in red. The grounds maintained the pattern with burgundy-leafed ground cover that had been carefully planted around black stone. A path of white slate wound sinuously up to the door, which was flanked by lushly growing roses. The blooms, which had been carefully depicted by the artist, were pure black.

The painting looked familiar, but Turquoise could not place it.

Jillian Red launched into a history lesson. "In the early sixteen hundreds two sisters, vampires both,

founded an empire they called M
was the heart, the symbol so to speak,
They were less than five hundred years old, y
pared to most of their kind, but they both were
less, and more organized than their elders; their
determination allowed them to take control swiftly."

Jillian glanced at the white stucco ceiling, and continued, "Jeshickah, the younger of the two sisters, was the absolute ruler of Midnight. For a few hundred years, she controlled nearly all the vampires, the shapeshifters, and the witches. As for the humans . . . they were little more than cattle. If a human was sold into Midnight, that was the end."

"You keep saying Midnight *was,*" Turquoise thought aloud, anxious to get to the present and learn what the job was. She was not a fan of history, and she already knew more about the vampiric slave trade than she cared to. "What is it now?"

"I'll get there," Jillian chastised. "In the early eighteen hundreds, Midnight was destroyed by a group of older, stronger vampires. The building was leveled, and every living creature caught inside was killed. Of course the vampires survived, but with the property and slaves lost, the empire lost its heart, and the rival power was able to take control.

"The new leaders banned the slave trade—they did not approve of caged meat—but as you two have witnessed, the laws have slackened over time. The original vampires of Midnight were able to pick up the trade again." Jillian sighed. "That might have been bad enough, but . . ." She reached into her briefcase again, and this time pulled out a glossy eight-by-ten photograph.

"This was sent to me a few days ago."

The photo did not need to be explained. Someone had rebuilt Midnight.

"The trade has been pulled together by a new master, one of the trainers from the original Midnight. My employer, who wishes to remain anonymous, was unconcerned about Midnight's revival until recently, when the original founder returned. With the groundwork already in place, Jeshickah is expressing an interest in taking charge again. My employer would like that threat eliminated.

"The offer for Jeshickah's death is a half million to each of you, with that much again to split as you wish if the job is done within the next week. I am only the agent, and have only been contacted via writing, so I can offer little more information than I have given you. Are you interested?"

"Why hire two Bruja to go after one leech? It's a waste of money," Ravyn asked, the question both practical and suspicious. An anonymous employer could mean many things. It could be he had no intention of paying, or more likely it meant that he feared his target.

"My employer has a wish to have this job over quickly," Jillian answered. "Hiring two of you is insurance. If one of you does not succeed, the other might."

In other words, they were expendable, and Jillian's anonymous employer wanted to have a backup in case one of them got killed. Someone either didn't have much faith in Bruja abilities, or had more information than Turquoise and Ravyn were receiving.

"Sounds fun," Ravyn acknowledged, scraping away a speck of blood she had just noticed on one of her burgundy nails. "With luck, we won't have to worry about the rematch, either," she added to Turquoise.

Turquoise shrugged. This job was worth too much to turn her back on. Besides, she had never met a vampire she couldn't beat. "You say get inside," she inquired, tacitly accepting Jillian's terms. "How?"

"That's one of the reasons the job isn't cheap," Jillian said, a slight smile on her face. "You're on your own to get into Midnight. You'll have to use any means necessary, Turquoise."

Turquoise knew what Jillian was hinting at. "I need to make a call."

An hour later, Turquoise found herself in yet another hotel room, this time with a fairly attractive, dark-skinned gentleman three or four hundred years old. It was hard to tell exactly, since in appearance he was twenty-five at the most. As broaching the topic of any vampire's past could be dangerous at best, Turquoise had never asked.

"Milady Turquoise," he greeted.

"Nathaniel, always nice to see you," she responded sincerely. Nathaniel was a vampire, true, and that was not his only flaw; he was also a mercenary and an assassin, as necessity dictated. However, since Turquoise also fit most of those descriptions, she did not hold Nathaniel's profession against him.

Luckily, Nathaniel's line thirsted more for money than for blood. If anyone thought it strange that a vampire and a human had a close business relationship, no one had spoken of it. Nathaniel had taught Turquoise most of what she knew. He had taught her what a mercenary was, the value of her talents—among them hunting—and most importantly, where to find buyers for the skills she was willing to sell. He had also once saved her life, not to mention her sanity.

"I don't suppose this is a social call," Nathaniel stated. "You on a job?"

She nodded, debating how much she needed to tell him. Though he would offer her a chance to buy his silence, Nathaniel would be willing and able to sell any information she gave him.

"I need to get myself and another woman into Midnight." The slight widening of Nathaniel's eyes was the only sign that she had surprised him. "And I need to do it without getting tied up or beaten bloody."

Nathaniel sighed and leaned back against the wall. "You don't ask for much, do you, Turquoise?" he said with heavy sarcasm. "Are you trying to get yourself killed?"

She frowned at the tone of his voice. It was unlike Nathaniel to object to anything someone else was doing, especially if he was likely to get paid for it.

"Will you get us in?"

"I could sell you in," Nathaniel responded bluntly. His gaze flickered down and up her body, a critical sizing up. "You would fetch a high number, I'm sure. Attractive, healthy, strong, intelligent . . . or I thought you were. Are you really so anxious to sell yourself back into slavery, Turquoise?"

No. She had been in once; she had no desire to return. However, to return with a knife, as an experienced hunter, was a great deal different than returning unarmed, as the innocent she had once been.

"Is there any other way?"

Nathaniel shook his head, and inventoried her price in a cool tone that sent shivers down her spine. "The scars on your arms will lessen your value by a couple hundred. Unless you would like me to offer you to Daryl? He would pay dearly."

She recoiled as Nathaniel said her once-master's name.

Gathering her pride, she stated, "If he's involved in Midnight, I'm definitely going in. He's deserved a knife for a long time."

"You weren't always so tough, Turquoise," Nathaniel said softly. He had been the one who had given her the name Turquoise Draka, a new identity to replace the one Lord Daryl had destroyed. He had provided her with contacts to Bruja, and had taught her about fighting back instead of cowering. He had never told her why, and she had never asked. "I've seen you pull stunts that left me wondering if you had a death wish. You push yourself hard enough to kill a weaker human, and accept jobs that should be suicide missions just to prove you can handle them."

She shrugged, and found that her shoulders were painfully tight. "I've never lost," she pointed out. "And I've never known you to argue with me before."

Nathaniel just sighed. "It's your life," he finally relented. "You know the slave trade better than most freeblood humans will ever imagine it."

He paused, and then named his price. "Forty thousand, in advance. And I'll take whatever I can get for selling the two of you. I haven't dealt in flesh since the old Midnight was destroyed, but I've had enough pressure to return to it that my selling a couple of humans for a profit won't surprise anyone. Deal, milady?" Nathaniel had returned to his usual cool composure, and the familiar tone helped soothe her jangled nerves.

She nodded. "Deal."

"Shall we find your companion?"

Again she nodded. They walked down the hall to the room where Ravyn and Jillian were waiting.

A few paces from the doorway to Jillian Red's hotel room, she asked, "Why does Midnight scare you so much?" It was not a polite question. Asking any vampire about his fear was like asking a parent why his child was diseased.

She half-expected him to clam up, but instead he leveled a dark gaze in her direction.

Then he looked away, flashing a handsome smile at some memory as he stepped toward the doorway. "Because I was part of it once," he answered. "I know Midnight and the woman who once ran it better than you could ever imagine; I understand what went on inside. And while I'm not nearly so mad as the people I surround myself with, I seem to have a rather unprofessional desire not to see you kill yourself."

Turquoise was still trying to decide whether that last bit was an insult or a compliment when Nathaniel knocked on Jillian Red's door.

# CHAPTER 3

RAVYN HAD SEEMED to be thoroughly amused when she learned of the masquerade she would have to play in order to earn her money, but as they went over the finer points of slavery at a Chinese restaurant along the way, she became decidedly less delighted.

Nathaniel spoke between sips of tea and polite bites of sesame chicken. Turquoise wondered whether he liked the taste, or was just willing to eat so they would look normal, as the vampire certainly did not need the human food.

He explained calmly, "If you don't want to be bound and thrown into a cell, you're going to need to pass for a tamed slave. No trainer will believe you are broken, but if you're careful, he might be satisfied that you're smart enough to be obedient. I've heard that Midnight isn't as brutal to its slaves as it once was, so a bit of servility should buy you enough time for your job." For Ravyn's benefit, he elaborated. "Your master is more than your owner—he is your life, the only thing that matters. Nothing comes before his wishes. What he says, you do, without hesitation. Until you're sold, that master is me. When we get to Midnight, keep your eyes on me. If someone tells you to do something, look to me. If someone asks you a question, look to me. Once you're sold, the same applies to whoever your new owner is. A slave isn't supposed to think; she just obeys.

"Never address the vampires by name unless given permission to do so. I know of very few who would hesitate to give a slave a beating if she forgot a title. In general, address any of my kind as 'milady' or 'milord' until told otherwise."

He paused. "The present Master of Midnight is named Jaguar. He was a trainer in the original Midnight—one of the best. Avoid him as well as you can, because he'll see through your act quickly."

"Tell us about this Midnight," Turquoise pressed, when Nathaniel paused again.

"I have avoided this new Midnight so far, but I knew the old one too well," Nathaniel answered. "I've seen humans bred like cattle, beaten bloody for meaningless trifles. Worse, I've seen freeborn humans as strong willed as you two reduced to the servility of well-trained pets." He raised his gaze to meet first Ravyn's then Turquoise's, scanning each of their expressions. "I've been told that Jaguar is changing some of the rules. People have been objecting that he's too gentle with humans now, but no one with the power to overthrow him has bothered to do so. Don't let his seeming kindness fool you. After Jeshickah, Jaguar was the most vicious trainer in Midnight. Even if he has somehow gained a set of morals, old habits die hard.

"Once I sell you in, you're on your own. None of Midnight's followers will go against a claim of ownership, so even if you want to pay a mercenary for help escaping, he won't be able to take you out."

Nathaniel was giving them one more warning. He had been the one to remove Turquoise from her first master's possession, but only after Lord Daryl had thrown her away in a rage and ordered the mercenary to take her.

"It won't be a problem," Ravyn replied, though Turquoise could hear strain in her voice. According to Jillian's recital, Ravyn had found herself once before in the uncomfortable situation Nathaniel was describing. The hunter was putting forward a brave front. "Tell us more about this Jeshickah you mentioned."

"Jeshickah . . ." Nathaniel shook his head. "She gathered her trainers and taught them their trade. She picked the slaves who would be bred and the slaves who would be culled. After her Midnight was destroyed, she withdrew from vampire society." He continued, "So far, she doesn't seem to be involved with Jaguar's project. Jaguar was Jeshickah's favorite—brutal, and perfectly obedient to her. It isn't surprising that he would attempt to re-create the environment in which he had power." He turned to describing the trainer instead, leaving Turquoise unable to press about Jeshickah without revealing that she was their target. "Don't trust Jaguar, and don't irritate him unless you are willing to take a beating for it. It takes a lot to get his temper riled, but once it is, you're in trouble. In general, don't give him any reason to touch you, especially in anger, but don't fight him if he does. *Never* raise a hand against a trainer, not unless you know you can kill him."

"Is he usually armed?" Turquoise asked the question out of habit. Both hunters were leaving their weapons behind; there would be no way to explain if someone noticed they were carrying when they entered Midnight. However, there were always ways to find weaponry, especially if one's prey was wearing it.

"Jaguar rarely uses a knife," Nathaniel answered. "He favors a nine-foot leather whip, which he is an expert with. I've seen him slice open the arm of another vampire, then pull a bird unharmed from the air with the back snap."

Ravyn shook her head, sipping her water in contemplation. Turquoise found that burgundy gaze risen to meet her own. "Something wrong, Turquoise?" she drawled. "You look a bit pale."

"Just annoyed," she answered briskly, forcing her composure to return. Knives, crossbows, swords, staves . . . why did it have to be a whip?

*It's practical.* The voice in her memory was Lord Daryl's, answering that question, asked three years earlier. *A knife is more likely to scar, or do greater harm than intended. It is easier to establish discipline with a more versatile weapon.*

Lord Daryl had been able to snap a whip softly enough to sting the flesh, or hard enough to draw blood, depending on his mood.

Nathaniel's gaze met hers across the table; he no doubt knew what she was thinking. Then he looked away, his eyes rising to flirt with the waitress who had just returned to refill their water glasses.

As soon as she was gone, Nathaniel continued. "Turquoise, you might want to go back to using your birth name; it will make it easier to convince anyone you see that you have been bounced around inside the trade the last few years. Either way, don't use Turquoise Draka—it's too easy to trace. Ravyn, how likely are you to be recognized?"

Ravyn shook her head. "All the vampires I've ever known are dead." Nathaniel gave her a look that said he heard both the implied threat and the lie, but Ravyn volunteered nothing more.

Nathaniel took another sip of tea. He held the liquid in his mouth a few moments, as if thinking of something else. "I normally don't make a point of arguing the plans of someone who is paying me, but you both know this is insanity, don't you?"

"Insanity makes the rivers flow," Ravyn replied nonsensically.

"Any more advice you're willing to share?" Turquoise asked, ignoring Ravyn as well as she could. She bit back a yawn, and then frowned at her watch. It was only noon. Grudgingly, she admitted to herself that even she had limits. She had been up since three in the morning, and had spent much of the time fighting Ravyn. Still, there was enough adrenaline left in her system that she had expected to be wired until next Tuesday.

Nathaniel paused. "None that's going to mean much to you. With luck, you won't have any trouble dealing with Jaguar. He's probably stronger than the vampires you've faced before, but he's weak compared to

Jeshickah. If Jeshickah or Gabriel are there, pray you don't run into either of them."

Ravyn's gaze snapped up from what had been a sleepy-looking contemplation of her chopsticks when she heard the second name.

"Something wrong?" Nathaniel inquired.

She shook her head. A frown crossed her brow briefly, and Turquoise saw her stifle a yawn. As always, the yawn was contagious.

The waitress had returned with their check. By the time Nathaniel had taken the appropriate number of bills from his wallet, Turquoise was taking deep breaths in an attempt to keep awake.

*One foot in front of the other,* Turquoise ordered herself as she followed Nathaniel to the car. He opened the two passenger-side doors before walking around to the driver's side. The passenger's bucket seat sank beneath Turquoise invitingly.

Turquoise was nearly unconscious before she turned her doubling vision on Nathaniel.

*You drugged us?* It took two tries to form the thought coherently, and then her lips seemed too dry to say it aloud.

*Sleep, Turquoise,* Nathaniel returned, speaking with his mind as he started the car. *It's a long drive to Midnight, and there's no reason for you to know the way.*

*But . . .*

*Sleep.*

# CHAPTER 4

THERE WERE THREE cartoon characters to choose from, though of course the best ones were on the square bandages and the tiny ones, the ones no one ever had a use for.

"There, all patched up," Cathy announced. "You take care of Bert for me," she commanded. The eight-year-old boy grinned, any pain from the scrape on his shin forgotten in the swath of Sesame Street bandages, and kissed his sister on the cheek before hopping down.

Tommy scampered off about the time that her dad descended the stairs. "That boy gets into more trouble in one afternoon . . ." He shook his head, still smiling. "He's lucky to have you. Most fifteen-year-old girls have better things to do than take care of their brothers."

Cathy shrugged. It sounded like Mr. Minate was about to launch into another of his inspirational talks.

"Honestly." Right on cue. "Some people only care about themselves. They use things; they destroy. You're . . . you're a creator, a builder. A healer, not a user."

Cathy shook off the words using the traditional "nod and

*smile" approach. Her father seemed to realize he had descended into the depths of hokey advice again, and gave her an impulsive hug. "Don't let anyone change you, Cathy."*

The dream crumbled, and Turquoise wrenched herself away from sleep, trying to gather her bearings. *You are not that innocent girl anymore. You are Turquoise Draka, a high-ranking member of Crimson, and a vampire hunter—one of the best.* She pushed the memories away.

She was on a job. Memories had no place here.

She was sprawled across the passenger seat of Nathaniel's car, with a kink in her back where someone seemed to have tied the muscles into a square knot. She rotated her shoulders, cautiously peering out the car's window as she pushed the remnants of her dream away.

They were parked at a gas station. Through the window, she could see Nathaniel speaking to the cashier, an attractive young woman.

*Flirt,* Turquoise thought without bitterness, as she saw the cashier leaning forward, giving her customer an excellent view. Her hand lingered, fingers brushing over Nathaniel's as she handed him his change.

Turquoise heard Ravyn starting to come to, as she waited for Nathaniel to get back in the car so she could grill him. It was dusk already; she wanted to know when they would arrive in Midnight.

She had just reached for her door handle, ready to confront the vampire, when she saw how the cashier's flirting had paid off.

Nathaniel was holding the girl gently, almost in an embrace, one arm around her waist and his other hand on the back of her arched neck.

Turquoise stretched, turning away from the scene, and then fumbled with the radio dial for a few seconds, finding only static. Nathaniel was too discreet to kill the girl, and he had to feed sometime.

Ravyn grumbled a curse. "What the hell?" she snarled. "That—"

"We didn't pay him to tell us where Midnight was," Turquoise interrupted the other hunter. She had worked with Nathaniel numerous times; she knew how he thought. "And most likely, someone is paying him not to give Midnight's location away."

Ravyn grumbled an insult that Turquoise pretended not to hear. "What's all the drama about this job? I've killed older bloodsuckers than this Jeshickah. She might have a bad rap, but that will all change once she's got a knife in her."

Turquoise did not respond except to shake her head. Nathaniel obviously did not know that Jeshickah was back. Jillian had said her return was very recent, and since Nathaniel had been avoiding Midnight, it was not surprising that his information was out of date. However, it was always worrisome when a prime source of information was wrong.

She sat back, forcing herself to relax. She could plan once she knew the score; until then, worrying about details was pointless.

Ravyn continued to grumble as Nathaniel bid the cashier adieu. She sank groggily to the floor, and the vampire returned to the car with a new bounce in his step.

Opening the door, he tossed a box of donuts and a soda at Turquoise, who took the drink gratefully; her mouth was dry as cotton. When Nathaniel offered one to Ravyn, the other hunter refused to do more than glare at the bottle.

"It's sealed," he assured her.

"No thank you."

"Suit yourself." He dropped the soda into the cup holder. "We're about ten minutes away from Midnight. If you want anything to eat—"

"No," Ravyn said again.

Nathaniel chuckled lightly, shaking his head. "Turquoise?"

She dug into the donuts. The drug had made her hungry, and who knew how often Midnight fed its humans?

Lost in her own thoughts, Turquoise still could not have missed the shift into Midnight's territories. The hair rose on the back of her neck, and the skin of her arms tingled; she saw Ravyn shudder as they passed through the almost solid wall of magic.

"Midnight has always had witches on its payroll," Nathaniel informed them. "They keep unwanted pests from stumbling in."

They had driven on a single-lane road from a suburban town, through whatever veil Midnight's witches had put up, past a thick wall of oak and pine trees, and into a different world. It was dark by now, and even the full moon above was all but obliterated by the thick leaves of this unnatural forest.

"We're here."

Turquoise found herself looking at a menacing building that could only be Midnight. A path of white marble led from the gates of an imposing iron fence guarded by iron ravens to the opulent, carved doorway, around which black roses grew. Though the red ground cover was slightly less overgrown, the building had obviously been designed in imitation of the antique painting Turquoise had seen.

Nathaniel swore under his breath, driving off the road to avoid an oncoming car. Sleek claret, the car all but screamed money.

Ravyn whistled, leaning forward in her seat. "Who's got the Lamborghini?"

"Shut up." Nathaniel's voice was crisp. He pushed open his door, every movement tense—not quite fearful, but wary and displeased. "Stay here."

Turquoise caught his eye, but Nathaniel avoided her gaze. Instead, he approached the woman who had just stepped out of the Lamborghini. Suede encased her long legs—tall, black boots that laced from ankle to mid-thigh over a pair of black pants. The archaic-style boots contrasted with the modern styling of her shirt, which was the burgundy color of an especially bad bruise.

"Nathaniel," she greeted. Her tone was not friendly, but neither was it openly threatening.

"I heard you had decided not to involve yourself with Jaguar's project here," Nathaniel returned, nodding in the general direction of Midnight's main building.

"That was my plan," she responded dryly, "but Jaguar's games here have recently ceased to amuse me."

"How so?"

"This place is a mockery." She shook her head in disgust, and then her gaze fell on Turquoise and Ravyn, who were waiting in the car. "That one looks familiar. . . ." Turquoise's heart stopped. She had not known her name, but she remembered this woman on sight. Mistress Jeshickah had been a frequent visitor to Turquoise's tormentor's home. She had been the only creature in the world Lord Daryl would admit to fearing. Belatedly, Turquoise realized where she had seen the painting of Midnight—also in Lord Daryl's manor, hanging on the wall of his office. However, Jeshickah's gaze had settled on Ravyn. "Jared's pet, wasn't she?"

"Perhaps." Nathaniel glanced at Ravyn absently. "But I don't recall anyone quite like her."

Throughout the exchange, Ravyn's gaze had remained on the car door. Her expression, however, she could not control.

"She's not broken," Jeshickah observed.

"Not quite," Nathaniel agreed. "I thought Jaguar might enjoy that. I was going to present the girls to him directly."

"There was a time when you would have enjoyed them yourself," Jeshickah responded. Turquoise saw Nathaniel's expression cool to a blank, unreadable mask. The words had struck a nerve.

"Jaguar is much more qualified than I ever was," he answered.

Jeshickah growled a rather unflattering expletive under her breath. Aloud, she added, "The little cat had talent, but I'm afraid time has liquefied his brain. I think I'll come with you and see what he makes of this fine pair. Jaguar will certainly deal with their pride." She sighed, and with an air of regretful practicality, added, "Or he won't, and I'll tear out the bleeding heart he's developed and make him eat it." She said the last words brightly and with a smile as she led the way toward Midnight, not even bothering to glance back to see if Nathaniel had heeded her commands.

"You two, follow," Nathaniel ordered Turquoise and Ravyn. The tone was surprisingly similar to the one with which Jeshickah had spoken to him, and as the mercenary had obeyed, so did the hunters.

# CHAPTER 5

JESHICKAH'S BOOT HEELS made a sharp *click*
each time they struck the marble walk. Turquoise had
to resist a wince at every strike; it was the kind of
sound that would give a tic to anyone who had to listen
to it for too long.

The imposing, carved door opened to reveal a young
boy, probably no older than fourteen. He started to
walk outside, and then froze when he saw Jeshickah.
His aborted step turned into a stumble, at the end of
which Turquoise flinched to hear the impact of the
boy's knees on marble. He moved as if to stand, and
then rethought the action.

Jeshickah regarded the boy as if he were a sickly
dog.

"Can I help you, milady?" His voice was soft, and he
kept his eyes carefully on the ground.

"Stand up and get out of the way," she suggested.
Carefully, the boy rose to his feet and slid aside, still
never raising his eyes. He waited for Jeshickah,

Nathaniel, Ravyn, and Turquoise to pass before slinking after them.

"Mangy cur," Jeshickah growled under her breath. She ignored the boy, who was following them, and spoke only to Nathaniel. "His name is Eric. Jaguar treats him like a son, gives him free rein of the building and grounds, even lets him into town when he wants to go. The creature is obedient, but spoiled."

Jeshickah led the way to Midnight's interior, which was slightly less intimidating, but no less elegant. An oaken panel ran halfway up the wall, where it broke into a rich jade green. A carpet of oriental design covered the floor, soft and plush enough that Turquoise could feel it through her sneakers.

Near the end of the hall, Jeshickah pushed open a door and let the party into a dimly lit room.

Long ago, Turquoise had learned that the most evil creatures in the world were frequently the most beautiful. The Master of Midnight was no exception.

Jaguar—and it could only be him—was sprawled on his back across a black leather couch, one hand beneath his head, with his eyes closed. His skin was the color of a deep, golden tan, and his hair was black, perfectly straight and long. When he stood, it would probably hang to his lower back. He was wearing soft, black pants that hugged a body that Turquoise tried valiantly not to stare at.

That was it—no shirt, no shoes, no jewelry. The whip Nathaniel had mentioned was curled on Jaguar's chest like a black viper. His hand resting on the handle reminded Turquoise of a child with a beloved stuffed animal.

As she paused in the doorway, the vampire's eyes

fluttered open—black eyes, like obsidian, they seemed to reflect the light cast from the lamp in the corner. They lit on Jeshickah instantly, and the expression on his face snapped from sleepy contentment to wary aggression as he stood.

Turquoise expected the two to come to blows in the moment of silence that passed, but instead Jeshickah spoke. "Have a good nap, pet?" she purred.

It took obvious effort for Jaguar to ignore her as he spoke to Nathaniel. "These the girls you called me about?"

The tension that Turquoise had seen in Nathaniel the instant he had sighted Jeshickah's car was either gone or flawlessly hidden. He nodded, explaining, "They aren't perfectly broken, but they're smart enough not to give you any trouble. Besides that, they're both healthy and fairly attractive. There's some scarring on that one," Nathaniel continued, gesturing toward Turquoise, "mostly on her arms, but nothing unusual."

"Let me see." The command came from Jeshickah.

Nathaniel had prepared Turquoise for the inspection, and so she was wearing her only tank top, over which she had thrown a cotton shirt despite the August heat. She hesitantly removed her outer layer.

The scars had been hers for nearly three years; she had hidden them for nearly that long. With only the tank top, she felt half naked.

"Whip?" Jaguar asked, frowning at the semicircle of scarring around Turquoise's left wrist, a smooth pearl bracelet cut into her skin.

Turquoise felt the muscles between her shoulder blades tense, but she kept her eyes down. She had already concocted the story she could tell if asked about her past. Only Lord Daryl would be able to contradict her, and she counted on his pride to keep him from doing so if the opportunity arose.

"Her first trainer wasn't as careful as most," Nathaniel answered vaguely.

Jaguar seemed to accept the answer. "How much for the pair of them?"

Nathaniel was in his element now. He was a green-blooded mercenary. Any fondness he had for Turquoise or distaste he held for Jeshickah or Jaguar faded as soon as the question of money was raised.

Jeshickah forestalled any bartering. "Allow me, kitten. You need a few more toys around here." Jaguar's glare met the nickname, but Jeshickah had already turned away from him. "Nathaniel, shall we haggle in private while Jaguar gets to know his new acquisitions?"

Jeshickah wrapped an arm around Nathaniel's waist. They walked out together, but the contact did not appear friendly.

In the silence of their departure, tension began to drain from the room. Jaguar let out a slow breath. Vampires by nature did not need to breathe, but human habits died hard.

Without speaking, he walked around the two humans, a silent inspection. It occurred to Turquoise that they were lucky to have this job so shortly after Challenge. They both had plenty of bruises and new cuts, the absence of which would have been suspicious. Turquoise watched her new master as long as he was in her line of sight. Jaguar moved like his namesake, all grace and muscle. His black hair was a black pelt smooth against his skin.

"Names?" he asked finally.

"Audra." Turquoise understood Nathaniel's suggestion not to use the name Turquoise Draka—her name was well known as a vampire hunter's—but there was no power on Earth that could make her start using Catherine again. Catherine had been innocent, a child—defenseless prey. The memories of that girl's life, her family and friends, were bittersweet at best.

"Ravyn," the other hunter answered defiantly, stupidly ignoring all advice.

Jaguar gave no sign of recognizing the girl. Instead, he offered, "If you have questions, ask them now."

"Are there any rules we should know, sir?" Turquoise could not have managed to say "milord" or "master" without choking.

She knew the one general rule of slavery: Do whatever you are told to do. However, there were always household rules; there had been many of those in Lord Daryl's manor, most of which Turquoise had learned painfully.

"Eric will find you something to do. So long as you get your work done, you may go almost anywhere in the building. I suggest you avoid the west wing unless you plan on a little bloodletting. Beyond that, if a door is locked, you aren't welcome." Jaguar paused, considering. "I don't mind intelligent conversation, so feel free to speak as you wish to me. If you bother me, I will tell you to shut up; I don't feel the need to hit people for talking. Around others of my kind, hold your tongue. Most aren't as lenient as I am." These last words were accompanied by a glance through the door which Jeshickah had passed. "Understand?"

"Yes, sir," Turquoise answered. Ravyn echoed her assent, though her "sir" sounded like it was spit out through clenched teeth.

Jaguar gave the girls a sharp look. "You'll want to practice that for Jeshickah, but I'm not fond of titles. Jaguar will do just fine."

Ravyn nodded, her lips just barely curled into the edge of a smile.

"You'll find I give few orders, especially once you get an idea as to how this place is run. If you choose to do everything I say, fine."

"If?" Turquoise prompted. He was all but telling her that she could disobey him. "Since when has a slave had a choice?"

Jaguar laughed, a rich laugh that startled Turquoise with its warmth. "If you choose not to obey, I suppose we will discuss that then, won't we?"

Completely shocked by the lack of threat in his words, Turquoise could not speak for a moment, during which Jaguar decided the conversation was over. "Eric, come here," he called. The boy who had avoided Jeshickah like a beaten dog entered the room confidently. He did not seem afraid of Jaguar.

"Eric, get these two situated, and find something to keep them busy. I have other work I need to get done." With the words, Jaguar effortlessly changed from what for a moment had seemed like companionable bantering, back to the arrogant Master of Midnight. "Dismissed, all of you."

# CHAPTER 6

ERIC CHATTERED ALL THE WAY down the hall. "This whole building is pretty much a square surrounding a central courtyard. We're in the northern wing now. There are a couple of shape-shifters housed here, but mostly it's sitting rooms. There's a seamstress, and her office is at the end of the hall, right there." He pointed, and then led them through a dark oak door. "This is where most people sleep." Turquoise noted his avoidance of the word "slaves," though that was obviously who he was talking about.

The décor in this wing was just as elegant as Jaguar's sitting room, if not quite as dark. The oaken panel and chair rail continued from the north wing, but the floors here were polished wood, and the walls textured, pale honey-beige. Sponge painted? Turquoise wondered, amused by the thought of a vampire sponge painting a wall. Though of course, human slaves would have done all the work. Lamps set in the ceiling provided a soft glow.

"Who did the painting?" Ravyn asked, apparently as curious as Turquoise.

"I did," Eric replied proudly. "It was white before. There aren't any windows in Midnight, so I thought something warmer would be better for the sanity of us humans. That's my room," he added, pointing to the first room in the hall. "And here is where you two will be staying."

The room was simple—two stacked beds, currently unmade, sliding doors Turquoise assumed led to a closet, and an empty table. A second door was set in the side of the room.

"There are sheets folded in the top of the closet," Eric said. "Bathroom is through that door; you share it with Lexi and Katie, who are your neighbors. Katie is the woman to talk to about clothing, toiletries, and stuff like that. Lexi . . . she doesn't say much, but she works with Katie. They both usually sleep until about midnight, but after that you'll find them either in their room or in their workspace in the northern wing. Anything else you need?"

Turquoise did have one gnawing question. "How old are you?" Jaguar seemed to trust this boy, and Eric certainly seemed to be in charge of the humans when Jaguar was not.

Eric seemed startled by the question. "Fourteen. I think. Yeah, fourteen." After a moment, he seemed to understand what she was really asking. "I've been here since I was eleven."

Turquoise felt her stomach churn.

"It's not that bad," he said softly. "And honestly, I've got nowhere else to go."

She didn't want to hear this. This boy was her brother's age—the age her brother would have been, her mind forced her to remember. He was what Tommy might have become, if he had lived.

Eric must have translated Turquoise's distressed expression as skepticism, for he continued, "Jaguar found me with the vamps that had killed my parents. He bought me; saved my life." He shrugged. "He trusts me. And I can run this place cold." With a half-smile that seemed forced, he added, "I'm actually one of the lucky ones. Some of the people here with different owners, they don't even know their own names anymore."

Turquoise understood, and did not want to know more. She had seen the human dogs Lord Daryl surrounded himself with. Only through pure luck and dumb stubbornness had she avoided becoming one of them.

Ravyn flopped down to sit on the lower bed, asking, "How many humans are in here?"

"Eighteen in the building," Eric answered promptly. "That's including you two and myself. Two cooks. We could use one more; can either of you cook?" he interrupted himself.

Ravyn nodded. "I can cook."

Eric smiled, and continued, "Great. Besides them, of course there's Katie and Lexi. Two more people work in the infirmary in the south wing. I'll show you there later. That's it."

"That's nine," Turquoise stated.

Eric gave her a look, and then his eyes fell. "The vampires need to eat, you know." The message was clear. "A few vamps live here permanently, and other

vampires come and go. Most of them aren't too threatening, but you should be careful. They've been starting
to grumble that Jaguar won't let them treat us like they
want. Jeshickah showed up about a week ago, bringing
her own pair of . . . pets," Eric finished, voice apologetic
at the last word. "She's staying in the first room in the
west wing, and she doesn't care what Jaguar says she
can or can't do. Be careful around her. If she hits you,
don't get up. She's less likely to hit you again if you stay
down." With that less than cheerful advice imparted,
Eric glanced around the room, double-checking to
make sure he had not left anything out. "That should be
it," he finally decided. "Get some rest; I've got some
stuff to do, but I'll be back about midnight to show you
the south wing. Oh," he added, "meals are served at
sunrise, sunset, and midnight. There aren't enough people awake at noon to make it worthwhile to cook.
Nothing fancy is made, but if you want something special, you can feel free to ask. Generally, sunset is breakfast food and the other two are dinner."

"Thanks."

Eric disappeared out the door.

"Should we ditch and explore?" Ravyn suggested
languidly.

"We need to talk first," Turquoise responded.

"I suppose." Ravyn yawned. "This looks like an easy
job. Get a knife. Put it in the bloodsucker. You can take
Jeshickah and I'll get Jaguar, or the other way around,
if you'd prefer."

"The assignment was to get rid of Jeshickah,"
Turquoise reminded her, "not Jaguar."

"Jaguar's the one running things right now," Ravyn

pointed out. "We take down Jeshickah, you don't think he's going to object?"

Turquoise shook her head. "Let's avoid picking random targets until we know what's up, okay?"

Ravyn shrugged dismissively, not agreeing. "Once the job's done, suppose I can steal her car?" the hunter asked. "Lamborghini Diablo . . . that thing's worth three hundred thousand easy, half mil maybe."

"Could we stick to the problem at hand?" Turquoise interrupted.

Ravyn gave her a look as if Turquoise were mad. "It's a nice car. Besides, it'd be fun to figure out. I hear they're almost impossible to steal. I prefer the black, but all things considered—"

"Ravyn." Turquoise's patience was at an end.

Ravyn glared back. "You are no fun."

Turquoise debated strangling her detested partner, but elected to find sheets and make the top bed— Ravyn was still sitting on the bottom one—instead.

Ravyn finally acceded, standing and following Turquoise's example. The sleepy expression she usually wore was gone. "Let's see if Jeshickah is really planning to run Jaguar through. If she isn't . . . Even unpaid, I wouldn't mind putting a knife in the creature that runs the slave trade." For the first time, Ravyn's voice didn't sound tailored.

"How'd you end up involved with the trade?"

Ravyn shrugged. "Wrong time, wrong place, wrong life. Stumbled across a vamp with a taste for exotics." She said the words emotionlessly, as if she were quoting.

Exotics. It sounded like a sign that should be in a pet

store, advertising parrots or rare snakes. Hearing Ravyn apply it to herself was sickening. Knowing that Ravyn's burgundy hair and eyes made the description appropriate was worse.

Still, condolences were out of place. There was no friendship between her and Ravyn, and likely never would be. "How'd you get out?"

Ravyn's smirk returned. "Friends in low places," she explained crisply. "I made a couple deals with vampires who hated Jared to begin with. They might not have stopped Jared from taking a two-by-four to me, but at least they didn't stop me from slamming said beam into his skull before I put a knife in him."

After that, Ravyn lost interest in talking except to ask for the top bed, which Turquoise gave up without much of a fight. She wouldn't sleep well in either place.

# CHAPTER 7

"I CAN'T BELIEVE I...I'm so stupid." She took another large gulp of milk, trying to stop the tears.

"No you're not," her father argued. His face still held a look of dazed shock, as it had ever since the police had woken him in his hotel room nearly eight hours ago. "Listen to me, Cathy."

She lifted puffy, crying eyes to her father.

"You're Catherine Miriam Minate," he said, as if that explained everything. "You're proud, and you have every right to be. And no one—no one—can take that away from you unless you let them. You're safe now," he assured her. "You can't let this creep have the satisfaction of hurting you. No one can make you a victim but yourself."

She shook her head, remembering how dumb she had been. A strange city, a strange hotel, a strange guy . . . why had she trusted him? Even at home, she wouldn't have let a stranger get so close, no matter how nice or cute he seemed.

Mr. Minate stood and hugged his daughter close. She could feel his fatigue and his fear. He knew the danger was over, but was still near to panic.

✿    ✿    ✿

Turquoise had forgotten to consider one fact when planning their trip to Midnight: she was claustrophobic. Not terribly; she wouldn't end up huddled, screaming, in a corner, but she hated to be stuck in one small room.

She alternated between napping and pacing. When she slept, she dreamed, and the dreams were rarely pleasant.

Asleep or awake, vivid memories of Lord Daryl's manor assaulted her.

There had been four floors to the house. The top level had held the kitchens, laundry rooms, and quarters for Lord Daryl's numerous common slaves. Turquoise had not been allowed there, but she had explored it once while Lord Daryl had been away. He had beaten her unconscious when he had returned.

The third floor had held mostly bedrooms—hers, Lord Daryl's, and guest rooms. Lord Daryl's studio had been on that floor, a large room in the northern side of the house. It had been the only room in the house with a window, an almost solid wall of glass, and once or twice a month, when she had been desperate for sunlight, Catherine had crept in there despite Lord Daryl's rules. The glimpse of life beyond her slavery was always worth risking a beating.

The second floor had held an office, a desk with drawers that were always locked, the dining room, and the library. Catherine had spent hours reading history, which was a subject on which Lord Daryl had numerous books. She ate alone. Lord Daryl's slaves, even when serving her meals, were silent. Unless Lord Daryl spoke to her, Catherine heard no voice, no sound at all.

The first floor had been one large, elegant ballroom, complete with grand piano, polished dance floor, and a chandelier Catherine never saw lit. Lord Daryl was possessive and paranoid, and kept her away from the rest of his kind. When he hosted parties, he invariably locked his pet away in the next room, where she would barely hear music and distant voices.

That room, the little sitting room next to the ballroom, had been Catherine's sanctuary. The carpet had been soft and black, and the walls had been burgundy so dark that only direct light would make the red visible. The room held a couch and matching love seat covered with black suede. A small bookshelf in the corner held photos of people Catherine did not know, and books in languages she could not read.

Turquoise wrenched her mind away from her past. She glanced at Ravyn, who was lying on her bed and pondering the stucco ceiling, and rejected as impossible the idea of intelligent conversation. Instead, she dropped to the floor and started doing push-ups. Generally, she ran for four miles and then used weights, but this little boxy room wouldn't allow for that.

She did fifty on her right arm, and was up to thirty-seven on her left when someone knocked on the door.

"It's Eric. May I come in?"

"Go ahead," Ravyn called. She jumped down from her bed, commenting to Turquoise, "I'm tired just from watching you."

"I promised you a tour of the south wing," Eric

reminded them. "I thought you might want to eat first," he told Ravyn. "Sound fine?"

"Peachy," Ravyn answered.

Eric seemed unnerved by the bright response, but he did not comment.

He showed them to the kitchens, where the midnight meal was being served. They ate, and Eric introduced Ravyn to the others she would be working with.

Afterward, he briefly showed them the infirmary and the weight room. "Keeps people busy in their down time, and gives them something to do to keep healthy," Eric explained about this last.

"What's through there?" Turquoise asked, pointing to a heavy oaken door in the interior wall that seemed out of place.

"Courtyard. It's off-limits. The door's locked anyway," Eric explained briskly.

*If a door is locked, you're not welcome,* Jaguar had said. Instantly, this courtyard interested Turquoise. "What's in there?"

Eric shrugged. "You'll have to ask Jaguar about that. Speaking of," he continued, changing the subject, "if you can find Jaguar sometime before you turn in, ask him if I'm allowed to bring you outside. Probably not, but that's where I really need the most help. Otherwise, you'll either be cleaning or bloodletting, whichever you prefer." The boy's tone made it clear he'd have no respect for her if she took the second choice.

They split up. Ravyn returned to the kitchens to learn the ropes, Eric disappeared into his room, and Turquoise sought out Katie. She gave the woman her measurements, and was rewarded with the necessities of life: three full outfits, as well as a toothbrush, hairbrush, soap, washcloth, and two towels.

Next, Turquoise went looking for Jaguar. If all went well, she'd find him quickly and ask about going outside. That should grant her enough free time to explore. She wanted to see the western wing, and she wanted to get into the courtyard.

There were two locked doors in the northern wing; the shape-shifter rooms, Eric had said. The inside wall was empty—no courtyard door here. Jaguar was not in any of the sitting rooms, though she did have to skirt one room where Jeshickah was arguing with a vampire Turquoise did not recognize. The glimpse she caught as she walked by was of an attractive man of maybe twenty years, with a strong build and elegant features.

His words caught her attention, enough that she paused just past the room. "Are you going to kill him?"

Jeshickah paused to consider the other vampire's question. "Jaguar is trying my patience, but he's too valuable to put down so quickly." She sighed. "I'll give him a few days; maybe he just needs a reminder of his place. If he still hasn't come to heel, I can take Midnight back from him."

"He might fight you on it," the other vampire pointed out. "However it happened, Jaguar has picked up a fair amount of independence since Midnight burned."

"And then who will you back?" The vampiress sounded unconcerned.

"The only person I would rather put a knife in than Jaguar is you." The comment was made as if the knowledge was well known and unimportant. "But if it comes down to a fair fight, you'll win. Who's the human?"

The change in topic startled Turquoise, and she felt a chill as she realized the question was about her.

"Jaguar's new toy. Girl, come in here."

Turquoise obeyed, knowing delay would be painful; she forced herself to recall all of Nathaniel's suggestions, as her excuses came quickly to her tongue.

"Yes, milady?" Eric had used that title without being hit; hopefully she could do the same.

*Ow.* Her right knee struck the floor hard as Jeshickah's companion kicked it out from under her, inelegantly but effectively forcing her to kneel.

"She suit your fancy, Gabriel?" Jeshickah asked.

So both of the vampires Nathaniel warned Turquoise about were in the same room, while she was alone and unarmed. Fate had a twisted sense of humor.

But Gabriel just replied, "She's more Jaguar's taste than mine." This was not a fun conversation; Turquoise's fingers ached to be wrapped around a knife. Her leg was starting to go to sleep below the knee. "What are you up to?"

The question was addressed to Turquoise. "I'm sorry for interrupting, sir. I was told to speak to Jaguar, but I don't know where he is." The building wasn't that large; she would have found him eventually. But so long as she was playing the part of a dumb slave, she might as well take advantage of its excuses.

Gabriel looked to Jeshickah. "How long has he had her?"

"A few hours."

Without warning, Gabriel dragged Turquoise to her

feet; she had to check her desire to slam an elbow into his gut and wrench her arm out of his bruising grip. "The guard on the western wing will direct you to your master. In the future, I suggest you remember to refer to him as such."

He released her. Turquoise resisted both the urge to rub the new bruise on her arm, and the desire to turn about and slug him in the jaw. She left their presence quickly, trying to rid herself of the creeping feeling that she was lucky to still be walking.

A raven shape-shifter blocked the door to the western wing. She shifted into human form as Turquoise approached.

"You have business here?" the girl asked.

She recalled Gabriel's "suggestion" bitterly as she spoke. "I'm looking for Master Jaguar. I'm supposed to—"

Her explanation was cut off as the girl pushed open the door. "Jaguar's study is the third door on the right. If he's not there, you can wait."

Excellent. Apparently, Jaguar's lax rules extended to his guards, who were allowed to send people into his rooms. Turquoise looked forward to the possibility of snooping.

She knocked lightly, and was disappointed to hear Jaguar's smooth voice call out, "Come in."

As she entered the room, Jaguar pushed away from the desk where he had been working and stretched. "Audra, nice to see you. You want something?"

"I didn't mean to interrupt," she apologized, speaking softly and dropping her gaze. The unfamiliar name did not sound strange to her. Outside Bruja, she changed her name with each assignment. She had no fondness for any particular combination of syllables; Audra was as good as Turquoise or any other.

Jaguar shook his head, looking vaguely amused. "Submissiveness does not become you. Don't worry. I would much rather talk with you than do paperwork." He frowned suddenly. "What happened to your wrist?"

A glance revealed red marks where Gabriel's grip had held her. She flexed the wrist, but it was only bruised, nothing more. "One of your guests corrected my misuse of your name," she answered. "It was my mistake."

"I take it your old master wasn't overly fond of titles?"

Honestly, she answered, "Only his." Lord Daryl had not expected her to speak of others of his kind at all. Referring to another vampire as "master" or "milord" in front of Lord Daryl would get her beaten, as if she was acknowledging ownership by another as opposed to him.

Jaguar shook his head. "Please, sit down." He motioned to one of the free chairs as he collapsed back into his own. Turquoise took a seat, though she could not begin to relax as easily as Jaguar did. "Did you come to keep me company, or do you have a question?"

"I spoke to Eric about getting an assignment," she explained, grateful to change the subject. "He wanted me to ask you if I could work outside, since he needs the most help there."

Jaguar paused, and his gaze flickered down her form. "Jeshickah knows you aren't broken. She'll feel the need to correct that error much more quickly if you're working outside. You don't want to encourage her to do that," he recommended. "What other jobs does Eric have?"

"He said cleaning or bleeding."

"Neither of which sounds very fun for you," Jaguar offered.

Turquoise did not argue with him, even though he was more than half wrong. There were humans who chased after vampires all their lives, addicted to the sweet, intoxicating rush of having their blood drawn. It could be very pleasant, if the vampire wanted it to be.

Perhaps that was why it frightened some hunters so much. It took effort to live, to fight for one's life and one's pride. It was too tempting to simply relax and let the blood flow. Too tempting to let yourself slip up in a fight.

Turquoise shook the thoughts from her mind. She had no desire to die, and she certainly had no desire to become some vampire's pet bleeder. She only had to look at the scars on her arms to remind her why.

Like all hunters, she hated putting herself in the prey's position, but unlike most, she did not mind letting a little blood if doing so was an occupational necessity. A bleeder in Midnight would be closer to the vampires than any other human.

"I was a bleeder before Nathaniel bought me," Turquoise explained, modifying the truth as necessary. Lord Daryl had taken her blood occasionally, but he had owned a score of other slaves for such practical matters. She had been more like a lapdog in his manor, ornamental but essentially ineffective.

Jaguar looked surprised. "I wouldn't have expected that."

Turquoise reminded herself that he was a professional, and decided to keep the lies to a minimum. "My first master wasn't much in the way of a trainer, but he did teach me not to fight his orders. After that . . ." She shrugged. "It isn't unpleasant, and it's a lot better than some of the alternatives." Turquoise had seen slaves whose sole purpose was as beating posts to their masters' rage. She knew many who would argue, but she would rather feel teeth at her throat than a fist in her gut any day.

"If you want into that group, go ahead," Jaguar answered, either taking Turquoise's story for the truth or not caring about the lie. "Most of them take the sunrise meal for supper, sleep most of the day, and do as they want at night. Your only other chore is to stay healthy." He continued, "Several of my kind already reside in Midnight, and Jeshickah and Gabriel have both been threatening to move in. Theron doesn't like titles—he generally doesn't want to be addressed by humans at all, so that shouldn't be a problem—but any of the others will hit you if you forget one. If you run across Daryl, tread lightly; his temper is unpredictable." Turquoise was very proud of herself—she kept breathing, kept standing, and kept her expression the same, even hearing that name. "Avoid Gabriel unless you're fond of pain. You aren't, correct?" he asked worriedly.

She rubbed absently at her wrist as she shook her head. "I never have been."

"There are a few others who come and go, so don't be surprised if one of them pulls you aside. I'll tell the guards on the west wing not to challenge you." Jaguar paused, and she could see indecision on his face before he said, "You can go if you want to."

It was not a command, and she wondered why he was offering the permission. He had already made it clear that she could speak freely, and she assumed asking to leave was within the realm of what she could say.

Absently, she brushed back some of the hair from her face, and she saw as Jaguar's eyes followed how the long strands slid across her throat. Though his dark skin did not show pallor as clearly as Lord Daryl's had, Turquoise could tell Jaguar had not fed yet, and she recognized the hungry look in his black eyes.

Testing, she stood, the movement appearing reluctant. "I'll leave you to your work if you'd like."

He answered the way she had expected him to. Not raising his gaze from her throat, he said, "Come here." Though the words were an order, the tone left room for argument.

For a moment, Turquoise almost felt guilty. She was intentionally manipulating him. A feeding vampire is an easy target; most of them completely lost sense of their surroundings as they drew blood. Jaguar did not even try to catch her mind as his lips fell to her throat. If she had been armed, it would have been revoltingly easy to kill him.

# CHAPTER 8

JAGUAR RELEASED TURQUOISE reluctantly, holding her wrists until he was sure she could stand on her own. She took a deep breath and leaned back against a wall. He had taken a little more than she would have lost in a hospital blood donation, but it was enough to make her light-headed.

The sound of a throat being cleared in the doorway brought her back to her senses. When she saw who stood there, an instant of frozen panic shoved the fuzziness aside.

Lord Daryl. He wore his customary steel-toed boots; just seeing them made Turquoise's ribs ache in memory. She knew his charcoal gray pants would be dry clean only, as would the blue silk shirt. His hair reflected any color around him like a raven's feathers, and just now it appeared black with blue highlights.

His features looked sculpted from ivory, with just a faint flush—he had fed tonight, but not recently.

And he was beautiful. Why were vampires always beautiful?

In her years as a hunter, she had looked for answers to this. She knew many of them had been changed because their beauty attracted attention. She knew that the vampiric blood erased all the little human flaws, smoothed the skin, firmed the muscle, and in general perfected their form. But knowing intellectually was not the same as seeing.

Beautiful like the Devil, and twice as frightening. Turquoise's heart was suddenly pounding so hard she could feel it against her temples; she knew Jaguar and Lord Daryl both would be able to hear it, but she could not focus enough to slow it. Two years of Bruja training might as well never have occurred.

"What do you want, Daryl?" Jaguar snapped. Clearly, he did not like his guest. He held Turquoise against himself, either protectively or possessively. Turquoise liked to think it was the first. But Jaguar's protection had its dangers, too. Lord Daryl had always been jealous.

"New acquisition?" Lord Daryl bit out, his gaze falling on Turquoise with instant recognition before it rose to meet Jaguar's in blatant hatred.

"A gift from Jeshickah. What do you want?" Jaguar repeated, his feelings for Daryl mirroring Daryl's for him.

"Has Jeshickah decided whether she is going to stay?" Lord Daryl responded, apparently in no hurry to get to the point.

Jaguar shook his head. "She hasn't told me her

plans. If you've got nothing better to do than chat, Daryl, I must ask you to leave. I have work." Daryl started to argue, but did not manage to get a word out before Jaguar added, "Dismissed, Daryl," in a voice so cold it made gooseflesh rise on Turquoise's arms.

Lord Daryl stalked out, fury written in every movement.

"You can just order him around like that?" Turquoise asked, before she could bite her tongue to stop herself.

"Supposedly, everyone in this building is under my command."

"Why supposedly?"

"There are always exceptions," Jaguar answered dryly.

Jeshickah, Turquoise guessed. And maybe Gabriel.

"Go find something to entertain yourself with, Audra," Jaguar sighed. "I should speak to Jeshickah before Daryl goes whining to her."

Jaguar preceded her into the hallway, which Turquoise entered only with great trepidation. Lord Daryl had barely acknowledged her in Jaguar's presence, but he had recognized her. If he caught her alone she imagined no leniency.

Turquoise halted in the hallway and watched Jaguar leave, leaning back against the wall as if a bit faint, until she could focus and plan her next move.

Lord Daryl was an unexpected danger she would have to cope with. She had her own agenda, to accomplish with or without him in the way.

Right now, she wanted to see the courtyard. She could check the door to the south wing, but she imagined it would be inaccessible at this time, as too many people would be within sight. She would never be able to pick the lock and get inside without being seen.

As she stepped into the hallway on her way to the south wing, Turquoise bit back a curse. Ravyn. Whatever she was doing here, it wasn't in line with their plan to lay low until they understood what was going on.

Ravyn didn't seem to be in trouble yet, but she looked pretty near. Gabriel was leaning back against the wall, arms crossed over his chest, and regarding Ravyn with skepticism as she spoke.

Huffily, Ravyn turned away and started toward the south wing; her vampiric companion grabbed her arm, pulling her back. Turquoise started to approach, but Ravyn caught her eye and shook her head minutely. She did not look distressed, so Turquoise would let her handle this on her own.

Turquoise returned to her room and paced, waiting for Ravyn. Her energy was ferocious behind the docile front she had to display; she wanted to fight something. She was anxious to complete their mission and leave; she was doubly anxious to know what trouble Ravyn had gotten them into.

Jeshickah couldn't be that difficult a target. Jaguar detested her so Turquoise doubted he would protect her. All Turquoise needed was a knife and a moment of opportunity.

Of course, if she misjudged and Jaguar did get in the way, he would probably have to go, too.

Finally the door opened, and Ravyn sauntered in. The girl looked a bit pale, tired, but pleased as punch.

"What was that?" Turquoise immediately snapped.

Ravyn just stretched, yawned, and without bothering with pajamas climbed up to her bed. "It's almost sunrise, Turquoise. Get some sleep."

Sleep? Strangling Ravyn seemed once again like a very good idea.

"Ravyn—"

"I am tired," Ravyn responded. "And incidentally, I have a plan. Let me sleep, and I'll tell it to you. Later." She pulled the pillow over her head.

Damn that girl.

Sunrise. Most of the vamps would be bedding down to sleep. They weren't comatose under the sun, but a sleeping vampire was still an easier target than a fully conscious one. Sunrise would have been a perfect time to execute whatever Ravyn's plan was.

Turquoise stalked out of the room. The kitchen was full of people eating dinner. She joined them, and lingered until the kitchen closed, at which point most people retreated to their rooms to sleep.

She spent an hour in the exercise room, and then took a quick shower and changed, by which time it was late morning and the wing was almost empty. She remembered Eric mentioning that not enough people were awake to make a noontime meal worthwhile, so midday seemed to be the best time to make an attempt at the courtyard.

Turquoise had snatched a large safety pin and a pen from Katie's office earlier. Unbending the pin and pulling the shirt clip from the pen provided a low-tech but workable pick set, which she quickly employed on the courtyard door.

The lock wasn't particularly complicated, about as sophisticated as most house locks. Turquoise's tools were less than wonderful, but she had practiced this art a great deal, and within three minutes she felt the tell-tale click of success.

# CHAPTER 9

THE COURTYARD WAS STUNNING.

The area was surrounded by the walls of Midnight, their natural stone texture enhanced with crawling ivy, and the ground beneath her feet was soft with thick green moss, dotted with smooth gray stones that rose in tempting seats. Low-growing trees decorated the ground, young willows and Japanese maples that bowed gracefully to their visitor. Slender irises grew from the edge of a small pool, their blooms past but their green leaves rising regally from their mossy bank.

*I can see why someone would want to protect a place such as this.* However, she could not see why Jaguar—a trainer, a slave trader, and a vampire—would care for the beauty of irises and ivy, no matter how kind a master he seemed.

She entered the courtyard with careful but quick steps, keeping her eyes open for anyone else that might be here. Jaguar was probably asleep at this hour, but she did not know if any humans or shape-shifters had permission to be inside these walls.

She was nearly at the center of the courtyard when a rustling of leaves caused her to turn, her excuses already on her lips.

"I was just . . ." The words died, useless.

The animal stalked silently from the grove of willows, its dark-amber eyes regarding her carefully.

Turquoise was no expert on felines; she simply knew this one was big. The creature was probably longer than she was tall. It stretched lazily and she saw extended claws press into the moss; one swipe could probably take off her hand. She didn't know enough to identify the breed by its spots, but considering the master of this place, she could make a reasonable guess as to which this one was.

*These two,* her mind amended, as a second jaguar emerged from the undergrowth. This one was smaller and lighter, and a ragged line of scar tissue marred her muzzle, running to her ear and leaving a trail of pearl where one beautiful golden eye had been destroyed.

Turquoise knew not to panic. These creatures were bigger than most dogs, but they were still animals; she knew better than to run from them.

Instead, she made her voice smooth and calm as she spoke to the female, whose lead the larger jaguar seemed waiting to follow.

"Milady, I didn't mean to invade your courtyard." *One should always address a large, potentially dangerous animal with respect.* She smiled, recalling her father's words on the subject. Of course, he had been speaking about a stray dog at the time—dangerous, but not a jaguar. Her father's mishmash of wisdom and advice formed most of the only good memories she still had.

As she spoke, she edged toward the doorway, careful neither to run nor to turn her back on the jaguar. "I didn't realize this area belonged to anyone but Jaguar, and if you wish, I will certainly leave."

She found her way blocked by the larger jaguar, and had to circle around to avoid him. He stretched in the shade directly in front of the doorway and closed his eyes to return to the nap she had probably interrupted.

"How like a cat," she murmured. "Well, milady, I don't suppose you're going to ask him to move, are you?" The words got no response, but her attempt to edge past the male jaguar did: he drew back his lips, just near enough to a snarl to make her back off.

She could try the other door, but she hesitated to walk into the west wing without knowing what was going on. She would give it another hour or so. With luck, the jaguar would move from the south wing doorway. If not, she would have to try her luck in the vampire's corridor.

To pass time, Turquoise ended up sitting in a patch of sunlight near the pool, working on her story to Jaguar for when he found her here, trying to do nothing that would aggravate the two felines.

The smaller jaguar was the more inquisitive. She joined Turquoise in the sunlight, and shortly proceeded to give her new human companion a cat-bath. Turquoise endured the sandpaper tongue on her back and shoulders, hoping it was a good sign.

Despite her size and capacity for ferocity, the jaguar

acted much like any cat: independent, assertive, but at the moment playful. She nuzzled Turquoise in the side until the human stroked a hand down the jaguar's beautiful fur, and then sprawled ungracefully on the ground to chew on a blade of iris.

The larger jaguar had not moved. Turquoise gave up on hoping, and reluctantly approached the west door. She hesitated as she saw the male lift his head. She was near the doorway when it yawned, showing a threatening expanse of teeth, and stood.

The female shouldered her in the backs of the knees and she nearly ended up on the ground again, but she just barely managed to keep her balance.

"Milady, I'm sorry if I'm being rude, but—"

The male jaguar pounced.

With no time to prepare, Turquoise hit the ground on her back; though uninjured by the fall, she braced herself for the feel of the jaguar's teeth snapping her neck.

She peeled open her eyes after a moment to find a very large cat standing over her, its front paws perched on her shoulders.

She might have blinked; she wasn't sure. Either way, it was suddenly Jaguar who was pushing himself to his feet, and offering her a hand to pull her up.

Mutely, she stared at the hand for long seconds.

Within the sunlit boundaries of the courtyard, Jaguar looked as much at home as he had in the exotic confines of Midnight's interior. The sunlight caused his dark hair to come alive with highlights of warm chestnut; his dark skin took on a rich bronze tone.

Recovering quickly, Turquoise stood without his help. "Jaguar—"

All he said was, "Audra, I don't believe I invited you here." His tone was light, almost playful, and she distrusted it instantly.

"You—"

Before she could form the sentence, Jaguar collapsed to his knees next to the other cat, which nuzzled at his shoulder companionably. "Allow me to introduce Shayla, the most beautiful creature living in this building." He paused, tracing the rosettes on Shayla's fur. "Though I doubt Shayla would ever protest being called 'milady.' "

Turquoise's head was still spinning, and the only answer she could form was, "It's what my father used to call our tabby cat when he needed her to do something."

"Shayla is naturally distrustful of most people," Jaguar explained. "And since every enemy I have, she has as well, there is ample reason for her to be wary. You're lucky she took to you so quickly."

"If she hadn't?"

Jaguar's black eyes were unreadable as he turned from Shayla to meet Turquoise's gaze. "You wouldn't be standing here now." He looked away, and when he continued his voice was once again light. "Shayla is an excellent judge of character. Since she deems you worthy, I'll allow you to be here."

"Thank you, milady," Turquoise said with mock formality, addressing Shayla, who did not look up from meticulously cleaning her right forepaw.

Shayla seemed to sense that the atmosphere had mellowed; she chose that moment to pounce, which engaged Jaguar in a round of kittenish play.

Turquoise could not keep herself from laughing. She was watching a vampire *romp*.

Shayla was the one who disengaged first, when Jaguar managed to roll her nearly into the irises. She walked off with her ears perked, her posture saying, "I meant to do that," as she retreated to the trees.

Jaguar remained lounging on the ground. He propped himself up on his elbows to look at Turquoise. "I've been told that I spend too much time in jaguar form, and it affects my behavior. Do you think it might be true?"

"Definitely." He had given her leave to speak as she wished with him, and she sought to explore how far the limits on that freedom stretched. "How long have you known Shayla?"

Jaguar sighed. "I've known her family since her great-grandfather was a kitten. Shayla was injured by a hunter a few years ago; she lost one eye and nearly lost the other, and she still walks with a slight limp where the bone was set too late. She never would have survived in the jungle, so I brought her here." Jaguar glanced toward Shayla, and Turquoise followed his gaze; in response to the attention, Shayla yawned widely.

"A lot of the older cultures in Central and South America thought jaguars were gods, or messengers of the gods," Jaguar noted absently.

The comment prompted Turquoise to ask, "Your homeland?"

His expression cooled slightly, but he answered, "My mother's." His voice was carefully neutral as he added, "My father was Spanish."

He turned away abruptly, and Turquoise berated herself for asking the question. She would never have asked any other vampire, as they tended to respond violently when questioned about their origins. For a moment, she had almost forgotten what Jaguar was.

Now would be a good time to back off and let him simmer alone. Vampiric tempers could be volatile, and when set off they could be deadly.

"Jaguar—"

He had assembled his walls again. "It's almost noon, Audra. I'll speak to you later."

She nodded, and watched in mute fascination as he returned to jaguar form and loped back into the grove of trees.

*You can stay here as long as you like,* he offered belatedly. His voice slid through her mind, unwelcome and threateningly open, almost an apology about his abrupt brush-off.

Turquoise had to fight her instant impulse to throw up walls and keep him out of her mind. While most hunter groups taught how to guard one's mind at least partially against vampires, that was not a skill most humans had, and doing so while Jaguar was already in her mind could only make him suspicious.

As it was, she sensed him pulling back mentally. When he spoke again, his mental voice was fainter, and carried none of the flavor of Jaguar's mind. *Relax, Audra. Enjoy the sunlight.*

She could not tell whether he was sincere or sarcastic.

Shayla tilted her head, curious, as Turquoise sighed

heavily and sat on one of the stones. Turquoise regarded the puzzled jaguar tiredly.

"Do you understand him any better than I do?" she found herself asking. Shayla reacted to the words by nuzzling at Turquoise's side.

Why bother to understand Jaguar? The most obvious answer was so she could predict him. An unpredictable opponent is far more dangerous than one whose moves can be guessed ahead of time, and Jaguar would figure prominently in any move Turquoise and Ravyn made against Jeshickah. But nagging at her was the thought that she wanted to understand Jaguar simply because he confused her, and she was not used to being confused.

She was human. She was mortal. She recognized the fact that she was not all knowing. However, in the two years she had spent hunting vampires, she had never met a creature she so completely failed to grasp.

Nathaniel had painted Jaguar as a dangerous, cold foe; she had wanted to plant a knife in the creature upon hearing the mercenary's words. Yet Nathaniel's arrogant Master of Midnight had turned out to seem sincere and open, and she found herself wondering about the contrasts in his character. One moment he was coldly dismissing Lord Daryl, and the next he was affectionately wrestling Shayla. Turquoise did not understand him, and for that reason above any other she did not trust him.

Trust. That was a word she had long ago learned to avoid. The only thing anyone could trust was that everyone else would look out for himself first.

Shayla was trying for Turquoise's attention again; the jaguar was as bad as a kitten wanting a playmate—a very large, deadly kitten, but just as spoiled and restless.

Barely noon, and Turquoise had little she could do for hours. Ravyn had looked exhausted; she would sleep for a while yet. The courtyard, while beautiful, had proved far less interesting than when it had been forbidden. And fortunately, the vampires would mostly be asleep at this time.

She stretched out next to Shayla. The sun felt wonderful on her bare arms. She was pale, having spent most of the past two years following the nocturnal schedule of the creatures she hunted; she could not remember the last time she had simply lazed an afternoon away in the sunlight.

That was exactly what she decided to do. She had not slept much, and combined with the loss of blood, she was tired. She dozed, and then wrestled with Shayla for a bit, then dozed again.

# CHAPTER 10

"*FIRST LESSON: TITLE,*" he said calmly as Catherine struggled for breath past the pale hand wrapped around her throat. "*You will address me as Lord Daryl.*"

"Get your hands off me," she hissed in return, her voice made hoarse by the difficulty of drawing breath. Lord Daryl backhanded her nonchalantly, and sparks danced in her vision.

"Say it," he ordered, one hand still wrapped around her throat and holding her against the wall.

Instead, she tried to kick him; with reflexes faster than a striking snake he caught her ankle and pulled her off her feet. Her back slammed against the ground hard enough to knock the already scant breath from her lungs, and she choked around a gasp of pain as her head snapped against the polished wooden floor. The world swam; she could not have stood if she had tried.

"Well, Catherine?" he prompted.

"My lord," she growled in response, "you can go to hell."

She started to push herself back to her feet and he kicked her down again, the tip of one steel-toed boot glancing off the side of her ribs hard enough that breathing became instant agony and *she wondered if anything was broken. Another couple of those love-taps would probably kill her. But why should he care? He had already killed her family.*

*The thought gave her the energy to try to stand again despite the ache in her ribs and head, but the attempt was rewarded by another blow.*

*"Lord Daryl," she whispered, still on the floor, unable to get the breath to speak louder. "You happy now?"*

*He nodded, those fair, sculpted features betraying nothing past a cool mask of derision. "Almost."*

She woke struggling for breath, aching from phantom injuries long healed. That first beating, the first night she had woken in Lord Daryl's manor, had been minor compared to what she had later endured, but it had been the first and that made it the most terrifying in her memory.

A modern American teenager in a white-collar, preppy town, Catherine Minate had never been hit in her life until Lord Daryl had entered the picture. The remembered terror and pain of that first encounter left her with the taste of fear on her tongue, bitter, metallic, and hot.

Shayla had curled up beside her, and the mixture of the midafternoon sun, the jaguar's own heat, and the nightmares had left Turquoise uncomfortably sweltering. Carefully, she moved back into the shaded grove where Jaguar had retreated.

His animal form remained still, curled up on the soft moss, as his voice flitted in her mind. *You okay, Audra?*

She nodded, realized he could not see her, and then formed the thought clearly in her mind: *Fine. Just bad memories.* She doubted Jaguar would be surprised to learn that a slave had a few bad memories, especially a slave who came with such a brutal history written on her skin in scars.

Jaguar startled her by standing and loping toward her. She smiled as he brushed along her side, a soothing but amusingly feline expression of comfort. Again she had a brief touch of his mind, wordless this time, but offering sympathy nonetheless.

He stretched out again next to her, and Shayla lay down at her other side, as if Turquoise was a frightened kitten to be guarded.

Maybe she was. Either way, sleeping with a protecting jaguar on each side successfully chased the memories away from her dreams. She could see why the old culture's had worshipped these creatures: beautiful and proud, they also radiated savage, protective strength.

# CHAPTER 11

SHE FELL ASLEEP resting against the beautiful, soft fur of a jaguar; she woke in a very different situation. Sometime while they had both slept, Jaguar had returned to human form. Now he lay on his back, so that Turquoise woke to find herself snuggled against his side, one of his arms casually draped around her waist.

For a moment she paused to admire the beautiful form stretched out beside her: the black silky hair tousled on the ground, the smooth golden-tanned skin that was warm as any human's.

The illusion did not last. Her cheek rested on his chest, and beneath it there was no heartbeat.

Jaguar woke at the sound of her sigh. She felt his chest rise and fall in a silent breath, and his arm around her waist tightened for a moment in a companionable hug. "Evening."

Evening? Had she slept so long?

Yes. The sun had set, and in the darkness his voice was soft and a little too warm for her liking.

"I'm sorry," she apologized by reflex, as she started to push herself to her feet.

"No need to be," he responded. He did not release her instantly, and she found herself hesitating, trying not to stare into black eyes that at the moment were frighteningly intense. "It's not an unpleasant way to wake up."

*Maybe not to him,* her mind argued bitterly. He was the owner, not the slave. The choices were his.

He let her go and she stood hastily; Jaguar followed more slowly, but as she stepped out of the grove and into the open starlight he caught her arm.

Her mind kept flashing snippets of memory as she tried to deal with the present. Lord Daryl had mostly treated her as a disobedient pet. More than once she had fallen asleep—usually still bruised and aching from the last beating—with her head resting on his knee as he worked on some carving, and woken curled in his arms like a child's favorite toy.

"Audra, there's no need to be frightened."

Only when he said it did she realize she *was* frightened, enough that she could feel her heartbeat in her temples and wrists, fast with nervousness. Jaguar and Lord Daryl were nothing alike; she repeated the words in her mind over and over.

The fact that he was a vampire did not scare her; she had hunted enough vampires over two years that they no longer forced terror into her mind.

The fact that she had let her guard down, forgotten even so briefly what Jaguar was, that frightened her. The fact that she actually found him likeable, with a sense of humor and compassion, *that* terrified her.

She might need to kill him; she did not want to start thinking about how human he seemed.

"What are you afraid of?" Jaguar asked, as she yanked her arm out of his grip. "You had no fear in you until this instant."

She ignored him, picking her way carefully around stones in the darkness and trying to remember which wall the door was on.

"You've bared your throat to me, Audra. You aren't afraid of what I am," he stated. "What else is there?"

She turned back to face him, wishing she could simply sink into the wall she leaned against. "I can't explain."

"Why not?" he asked, and though his voice was gentle she could tell he was not going to let her worm her way out of this easily. "Who is stopping you? I'm your only master here, and I'm not going to hurt you for anything you say."

He stepped toward her, and Turquoise flinched as he planted one hand on the wall to each side of her shoulders. "What are you afraid of?" he asked softly. "Are you afraid I'll recognize that you're pretending to be a slave when you have as much free will as I do? Or are you afraid I'll recognize these . . . ?" With fingertips that barely grazed her skin, he traced the scars on her right arm, finally settling on the ring around her wrist. "And that I'll know whose weapon made this mark?"

Her throat was choked around the knot that must have been her heart, which jumped from her chest at the mere suggestion of Lord Daryl.

"Afraid I'll remember stories I've heard, the ranting complaints of one of my associates? Pretty, but very disobedient, he said. And strong—but of course he would call her strong, since he couldn't seem to tame her. She had a natural resistance; he couldn't get into her thoughts, and didn't know any other way to break her. He called her Catherine."

The silence after he finished speaking seemed to last forever.

She jumped when he reached for her again, but all he did was brush a lock of hair out of her face. Jaguar's proximity was awakening more than her hunter's instincts.

"I'm not going to hurt you," Jaguar repeated. He lowered his lips to her throat, and she relaxed in the familiar position. "What is it that terrifies you not of this . . ." She felt the sharpness of fangs against her throat, not pressing quite hard enough to pierce the skin. ". . . but of this?"

He kissed her.

He kissed slowly, unhurried, as if he could stay all day and not miss a beat. At the same time he was demanding, deepening the kiss before she knew what was going on. Gentle he was not, but the aggressive edge of his kisses was like the sweet rush of adrenaline so dear to a fighter.

Of course, he had a few hundred years of practice, and Turquoise had very little to compare him to—human boyfriends, mostly, and all of those a long time ago. And Lord Daryl.

The last thought made her jump. Jaguar's kiss had none of the violence of Lord Daryl's, but the undertone of possessive dominance was the same, and that made Turquoise recoil the instant she recognized it. She pulled back, slamming her back against the stone wall as she pushed Jaguar away.

"Audra—"

"Jaguar, let go of me."

He hesitated. "Audra—" he began again, and again she interrupted, "Let go of me."

He released her so suddenly she had to bite back a gasp. "I'm sorry."

Turquoise saw the newcomer enter the courtyard before Jaguar did. The vampiress glanced at Turquoise for a brief moment before turning her gaze to Jaguar. She caught him by the shoulders and whispered, "How touching, kitten. It seems you've made a new friend."

Jaguar spun around in a movement too fast for Turquoise's human eyes to follow, recoiling from the vampiress behind him. "Jeshickah." The name fell off his lips as a mixture of greeting and fear.

"Are you enjoying your new pet, little cat?" Jeshickah purred, inclining her head toward Turquoise. Turquoise's hand itched to reach for a knife—if only she had one—the instant those black eyes fell on her.

At the same time, Turquoise heard Jaguar's silent voice. *Kneel.* She cringed at the invasive feel of his command in her head. Jaguar's expression did not change, but his voice was desperate as he added quickly, *Don't fight me now, Audra. Not unless you want her to hurt you.*

The sensation was like sandpaper scraping down her throat as she swallowed her pride and went down to one knee, lowering her gaze so "Mistress" Jeshickah would not see the blatant hatred there. She had been prepared for moments of subservience, but that didn't make her enjoy them.

To Jeshickah's question, Jaguar answered aloud, "Audra has been keeping me entertained."

"She's not very well trained," Jeshickah observed.

Jaguar shrugged. "She's adequate, and I don't have time to work with her."

"Adequate?" Jeshickah's voice sounded amused.

"Do you need something?" Turquoise marveled at how perfectly cool his voice was, after he had been so obviously frightened by her sudden arrival. "You aren't supposed to be here."

"Do I need your permission to enter?" Jeshickah's voice had picked up a dangerous tone, but it was light again when she added, "Besides, I would have hated to miss such a touching little scene with the girl."

Turquoise wondered how much Jeshickah had seen. She also wanted to know when she could stand up; her neck was getting a crick in it.

"As for what I *need*," Jeshickah continued, "we were supposed to have a meeting several hours ago that you neglected to attend."

"I told you I had other obligations," Jaguar answered. Of course, the fact that he was blatantly lying showed his disregard. He had done nothing all day, unless Turquoise had slept through it.

Jeshickah's voice carried a threat. "And I told you to cancel them." Turquoise could only see Jeshickah's feet as she strode forward, until she and Jaguar were nearly touching. "I've been amused so far by your toy replication of my Midnight, and because of that I have allowed you to rule, but I am not amused by what I see now. I am most disappointed with what *you* seem to have become."

"Then go away," Jaguar suggested tiredly. "I've no desire to turn this place into what you made of the last one."

He stumbled back as she shoved on his shoulders. "Don't forget, cat, everything you own is mine. Even the blood that runs in your veins is what I have given you. If I say I want your slaves washing the floors with their tongues, you will make it so. And if I say I want her broken," Jeshickah finished softly, "you will do it."

"I will not," Jaguar responded, his voice just as soft, just as poisoned by anger. "The humans in Midnight are exactly as I wish them to be. Audra is exactly what I wish her to be. Understand?"

The air grew taut with Jeshickah's rage, and this time she slammed Jaguar up against the stone wall hard enough that Turquoise flinched, glad she had not refused to kneel.

"I understand that you think you aren't a trainer any more," Jeshickah spat. "I understand that you think yourself to be in charge here. And I understand that you are a pathetic beast who thinks no one remembers who he used to be."

"Get out of my courtyard."

Again Jeshickah bristled; pale fingers wrapped around Jaguar's throat, holding him against the wall. "You can impress the others, but not me. You were a slave to me, Jaguar. I've seen you bleed. I've seen you cower. I've seen you beg." She pulled him away from the wall just long enough to throw him against it again. "All the power you have now, all the power you use to rule this Midnight — I gave it to you. Displease me, and

I will take everything you have and break you over my knee. Do you understand?"

Jaguar stayed against the wall, his eyes lowered, for a moment of painful silence before he finally raised his gaze and, with a voice dangerous as black ice, answered, "Yes. Now get out of my courtyard."

"For the moment." Jeshickah disappeared, and Jaguar slumped back against the wall suddenly enough that Turquoise worried that he really was hurt. She started to move toward him, but the lingering reminders of the moments before Jeshickah had appeared—her still racing heart and the light ache in her head—made her hesitate.

The indecision was solved when Jaguar pushed himself back to his feet. He glanced at Turquoise, and then turned away. "Go get something to eat, Audra."

"Jaguar—"

"Out, Audra." His voice was hard with the order. Turquoise hesitated one heartbeat, worrying about the emotional exhaustion she could see in Jaguar's gaze, before hastening to obey.

# CHAPTER 12

"DAMN YOU, TURQUOISE," Ravyn growled when Turquoise slipped into the kitchen looking for her. "You disappeared all day, and then you weren't at the sunset meal—"

"Calm down, Ravyn," Turquoise interrupted. "You don't need to worry about me. I can take care of myself. And keep your voice down, unless you want someone to run tell Jaguar two of his slaves are arguing in his kitchen."

Ravyn looked appropriately chastised for perhaps a quarter of a second. Then Turquoise noticed the bruise blossoming on the left side of the burgundy hunter's face, mostly hidden by her long hair. "What happened to you?"

Ravyn's hand flew to the bruise on her cheek. "Our favorite queen leech thought I was a bit cheeky. If she hadn't had another two vamps within arm's length, she would be dead now."

"You armed?" Ravyn didn't look like she was wearing

a knife, but Turquoise knew there were many ways to conceal a weapon.

Ravyn's gaze flit briefly to the doorway to double check that they were alone, and then she responded, "The vampire you saw me with was Gabriel Donovan. He is one of the only people here who isn't terrified of Jeshickah. He deduced our reasons for being here, and donated a pair of knives to our cause."

"Out of the kindness of his undead heart, I'm sure." From the pieces of conversation she had heard, Turquoise wasn't surprised that Gabriel was willing to help kill Jeshickah. She was only wary of why he would help a pair of slaves do it. "What's between you and this vamp?" Turquoise pressed, remembering Ravyn's reaction every time Gabriel's name had been mentioned.

"I've worked with him in the past," Ravyn answered vaguely. "He knows I'm a hunter, but my profession has been beneficial to him before, so he won't be a threat. He's been helpful enough that I'll forgive him for never informing me of his connection to this trade." Returning to the subject at hand, she continued, "You'll find your blade beneath the pillow in your room. Once you get it, I say we make this a race: whoever brings down the target first gets Ms. Red's bonus. You game?"

Turquoise found herself answering Ravyn's bluster in kind. Meeting Ravyn's eye with a level gaze, she challenged, "How about the loser forfeits the title?" Turquoise wouldn't be able to beat Ravyn with a whip, though Ravyn probably didn't know that. She also knew where Jeshickah slept, and as a bleeder she could easily put herself in the vampiress's path.

Ravyn hesitated; she did not want to admit uncertainty in her skills by declining the bet, but she did not want to risk her title by accepting.

The burgundy hunter's intense expression suddenly disappeared, changing to one of modest boredom, as her gaze shifted past Turquoise. "Eric, hey," she greeted. "The meal's over, but if you're hungry I can dig something out of the fridge."

"I was looking for Audra, but thanks," the boy responded, oblivious to the conversation he had just interrupted. "You have a chance to talk to Jaguar?" he asked Turquoise.

Her last conversation with Eric seemed a very long time ago now, but she dredged it up in her memory and answered, "I'm not allowed outside."

Eric frowned in annoyance. "That's a pain." He turned, sensing the vampire behind him before anyone else did.

Turquoise looked up and recognized the vampire; her mind spun and stalled instantly.

Ravyn glanced at Turquoise and seemed to see the other hunter faltering. With a superb imitation of humility, she asked, "Can I help you, milord?"

Lord Daryl barely paused to look at Ravyn before answering, "You're dismissed." Ravyn exited swiftly, her eyes never leaving the vampire. She paused in the doorway and glanced at Turquoise, who nodded minutely, before disappearing into the hall.

"Eric, you have work to do," Lord Daryl added.

Eric looked at Turquoise for a moment, silent apology clear in his features, but he did not argue with the vampire. With him gone, the room was cleared but for Turquoise and Lord Daryl.

Black, unreadable eyes watched Turquoise as she took in the smallest details of his appearance, remembering vividly how those slender artist's hands could deliver a beating so severe she had begged forgiveness for whatever imagined or real transgression had set it off. Remembering the sharpness of fang in her throat, the seductive pull of his mind as he drew her blood. And of course, remembering the instant pain of his whip turned on her once in a fit of fury.

"Lord Daryl." Her voice was so soft even she could hardly hear it.

"Catherine, how nice to find you here," he greeted, and his tone was polite with an undercurrent of anger, a tone she would have stepped back from had she had anywhere to go. "Imagine my surprise when I saw you with Jaguar earlier." Without warning, he backhanded her hard enough to send her reeling. "Where have you been?"

Turquoise grasped for her lies, searching for a story she could tell to this creature, but all of her clever tales slipped from her reach. Catherine was not a vampire hunter. She was just a girl, a girl Lord Daryl had abducted and terrorized, a girl with no guile and no defense.

"Never mind," he snapped when she took too long to respond. "Come here."

"No," she replied instantly, backing away toward the kitchen. His black gaze fixed on her in anger, and he grabbed her arm; Turquoise wrenched out of his grip and took another step back. "Don't touch me." She could not feign sycophancy, not with Lord Daryl. If he had been any other bloodsucker, she could have played the part of subservient slave, but she did not have the strength to kneel to this beast from her past.

She couldn't fight back, either. Rationally, she knew that fighting would make it obvious that she was a hunter. Irrationally, every fighting move she had ever learned had disappeared from her head the instant he had touched her.

"Don't argue with me, Catherine," he warned.

She stopped backing up. "Don't call me that."

"Catherine?" He laughed as he said it. "It's your name, in case you've forgotten."

Laughter was a good sign—it meant that he was not in the mood to injure. Keeping him in that mood, however, was nearly impossible unless she wanted to beg forgiveness for the last two years of her life.

"Audra," she answered instead. "I'm going by Audra now. I haven't been Catherine in years."

"I really don't care," he answered, and this time he grasped her wrist in a grip she could not easily break. "Come here."

"No," she snapped, putting all her weight into an open-handed blow to his face. The heel of her palm hit just below the eye hard enough that it would have broken something if it had contacted with human flesh and bone. Four bands of crimson appeared where her nails raked across his skin.

Lord Daryl hit back harder, a reminder that if she wanted to trade punches, he would win. Black spots danced in front of Turquoise's eyes, and her back hit against the sharp edge of the counter as she tried to avoid falling.

"I'm leaving, Catherine, and you're coming with me."

"Don't you think you should discuss that with me, Daryl?"

The new voice came from the doorway. It was calm, almost a purr, but laced with threat all the same.

Lord Daryl grimaced, glanced back at Turquoise, and offered reluctantly, "I'll pay you whatever she cost."

"She isn't for sale to you."

"Really?" Lord Daryl asked, voice dangerously level. "Just to me?"

"To anyone," Jaguar admitted, "but you especially. I happen to be fond of her, and it doesn't appear that she wants to go with you."

Turquoise took a step away from Lord Daryl.

"Fond of her, are you?" he whispered, voice low. Jaguar seemed to sense that he had made a mistake; he said nothing, but looked to Turquoise.

"Lord Daryl—"

She didn't get any further before he struck her across the face hard enough that she stumbled. Before she could even think of defending herself, he had grabbed her by the throat and thrown her against the wall. A gasp of pain came from her throat, along with another attempt at, "Milord, please—"

"And how have you earned his favor, Catherine?" he demanded. "Does the jaguar think you're *his*?" He hit her again, this time sending her to the floor. "You're *mine*. Don't you understand that?"

"Milord, I didn't—"

A sharp kick caught her in the side, once again forcing the air from her lungs.

*Damn him to hell and back, why am I groveling?*

Yet she was, because she had always done so. "Milord, he didn't mean —"

The crack of a whip caused her to jump, expecting to feel the leather slice her flesh again; instead, Jaguar's whip wrapped around Lord Daryl's throat, drawing blood. Lord Daryl stumbled, and while he was off balance Jaguar untangled the whip. Then he grabbed Lord Daryl's throat and threw the other vampire against the wall as easily as Lord Daryl had thrown Turquoise.

"You have no right," Lord Daryl protested, shoving Jaguar away. Jaguar gave ground, but stood between the vampire and Turquoise.

"Right of ownership. Even your twisted little mind can understand that one. Jeshickah paid for her, and then gave her to me. She is my property." Each word was clipped, spoken coldly, as if he was talking about a pet. Lord Daryl's eyes narrowed.

"She is not *yours*, Jaguar," he growled. "She was mine to begin with, before you ever bought her."

"And it seems you lost her, didn't you?"

"I didn't . . ." Lord Daryl paused, then smiled cruelly, his hand going to the cheek Turquoise had hit and the four quickly healing lines of blood there. "She wounded me. She drew blood, Jaguar. Even if you have ownership, I have claim."

Turquoise painfully turned her head away, knowing what the outcome of this argument would be. Blood claim was one of the vampires' highest laws. The blood she had drawn from Lord Daryl entitled him to do with her as he pleased; no other vampire was allowed to interfere if her once-master wished to beat, maim, or kill her.

She thought Jaguar might sigh, or even curse in frustration, but she expected him to give in. After all, there were some laws that none of their kind argued with, and blood claim was one of them.

She expected him to do anything, except what he did.

Jaguar laughed.

Lord Daryl looked shocked for a moment, before Jaguar began to speak.

"You're foolish enough to call blood claim here?" Turquoise did not understand what he was saying, and from the expression on Lord Daryl's face, he did not either. Jaguar went on, "Don't bother complaining that you were weak enough for a human to injure you, because I don't care. If you want to cower behind those laws, go to New Mayhem and serve the rulers there. Of course, they do have those nasty restrictions against the slave trade, but if you grovel prettily they might not kill you for disobeying." Lord Daryl nodded slowly, though none of the hatred left his eyes.

"Fine," Lord Daryl whispered. "Do whatever you want with her. Just watch that she doesn't put a knife in you before I can do it." He stalked out of the room.

Jaguar knelt beside Turquoise. He reached toward her and she flinched.

"Are you okay?" he asked, not touching her, afraid of causing further injury.

Cautiously, she tried to stand. Her left eye was swollen from Lord Daryl's first blow, and there was no doubt a lump growing on the back of her head from when she had been tossed against the wall. The left side of her rib cage was bruised, but she did not think anything was broken.

He had given her beatings worse than this one.

"I'll be fine," she whispered, leaning against the wall as she tried to get her bearings.

"Normally, one warning is enough for Daryl, but Jeshickah's been favoring him lately, and he thinks that gives him power. If I'd realized how smug he's gotten, I would have intercepted him before he could get to you," Jaguar apologized.

Turquoise shook her head, and then flinched at the pain the movement caused. "Lord Daryl will try to kill you, if you don't let him have me."

Jaguar sighed in annoyance. "I don't like murdering my own kind, but for Daryl, I would gladly make an exception. He knows it, too."

He tried to offer a hand when she pushed herself away from the wall, but Turquoise avoided it. She was sore, and would feel worse tomorrow after all the bruises and bumps stiffened up, but Lord Daryl had never intentionally given her any permanent injuries. Even the majority of the scars on her arms had been accidental, not part of a beating.

Right now, though, she could not accept help from his kind. She would not let this small injury be a weakness. It was bad enough that she had frozen when fighting him, bad enough that she had lost every defense she had learned in two years the instant he had spoken her old name. She would not let Daryl turn her into weak prey again.

# CHAPTER 13

JAGUAR ESCORTED TURQUOISE back to the courtyard, and brought ice from the infirmary for the bruise spreading on her face, as well as some water and some aspirin, all of which she accepted gratefully.

Turquoise forced herself to stretch to avoid the stiffening of her aching muscles. Doing so hurt, but it was better than running into Lord Daryl again when she was too stiff to lift an arm in self-defense.

She was antsy to get the weapon Ravyn had promised her, but Jaguar, while not exactly hovering, refused to leave. He tumbled with Shayla a bit, and then took a break to leaf through some papers.

"Does Midnight own the town it borders?" she asked, trying to kill time as well as to understand.

Jaguar nodded. "Not quite the entire town. Two apartment complexes, most of the stores, and a couple neighborhoods. The local paper is independent, as are the schools and most of the housing."

"Impressive." She meant it. Running Midnight was

one thing; slaves were relatively easy to handle. Running a town filled with free-willed people must have been more difficult.

She didn't want to kill him. Turquoise realized that fact quite suddenly. She did not think Jaguar would try to protect Jeshickah, but any vampire might try to destroy two hunters he found in his territory, and if he did, Turquoise would have to kill him.

*Deal with that later,* she told herself.

When and if the problem arose she could think these thoughts. For the moment, Turquoise needed this time to return her body and mind to fighting condition. She couldn't afford to face Lord Daryl or Jeshickah as unfocused as she was, and she desperately needed to regain control after the last humiliating confrontation.

As Jaguar continued to work, Turquoise ran through a stunted exercise routine, just enough to warm her up. She didn't have the energy to do her normal full set.

She collapsed onto the moss-covered ground, pausing to catch her breath, and then worked on honing her other senses. Humans relied strongly on sight, but a hunter had to be focused in all ways if she was to survive. Hearing and smell could impart much knowledge about the terrain as well as about the enemy. More important still was the animal instinct for predators.

Humans had no natural predators, and so, like smell, they mostly ignored their latent sixth sense. Strong vampires put off an aura that made even dull-witted humans edgy; a more sensitive human would avoid the leech instinctively.

A trained hunter, like Turquoise, could consciously

feel a vampire's presence. The ability made it harder to be startled, and it sped up reaction time in a fight.

She could feel Jaguar's presence, faintly, a tingling on the surface of her skin. From the same direction, she could hear the faint rustling of papers, and the soft sound of his breathing.

Breathing? She opened her eyes. Jaguar was paying no attention to her, and so she had an opportunity to observe him. She was startled to realize that he was breathing, regularly, as a human did. While Turquoise had heard them sigh or yawn or express other emotions, she had never known one who had retained this constant human habit. It was a rather endearing detail.

Jaguar seemed to sense Turquoise watching him; he rolled onto his side, for all the world like a cat himself, to look at her. "How are you feeling?"

"A little sore, but I'll be fine," she answered. "Get anything productive done?"

Jaguar shook his head. "I never get anything done. If I work in my room, someone usually shows up to threaten my life or sell something to me. If I work out here, this girl gets restless." He rubbed his hands down Shayla's muzzle affectionately.

Jaguar's voice was reflective as he mused aloud, "In the original Midnight, Jeshickah had an albino leopard that lived in the courtyard. Nekita, she was called."

"I wouldn't think Jeshickah much of a cat person," Turquoise responded. She tried to picture Jeshickah tumbling with her leopard as Jaguar did with Shayla, and failed.

"When Jeshickah got angry, she'd tie people to the

trees in the courtyard so Nekita could sharpen her claws. Usually the victims were humans, or occasionally shape-shifters. Sometimes they were other vampires."

Turquoise grimaced. She did not ask—did not want to ask—whether Jaguar had ever been Nekita's target. "I take it that's part of the original Midnight you decided to change?"

He nodded. "Shayla is very gentle. She'll hunt the prey I bring into this place—rabbits mostly, or birds if they land here—and she'll attack if she's frightened, but if given the chance she would rather retreat than give pain. Only humans have it in their nature to torture."

"And vampires?"

"You think vampire blood gives one the desire to hurt another?" Jaguar responded. He shook his head. "A feeding vampire is as natural and simple as a wolf or a lion. It's only when the human mind is in control that any creature has the desire to give pain."

He gazed at Shayla fondly, and Turquoise recognized longing there—longing to be so innocent. She wondered how Jaguar had survived so long. Sentimentality was a deadly flaw in a predator. Even Turquoise could recognize Jaguar's weakness the way a wolf recognizes the stragglers in a herd.

"The more you describe the original Midnight to me, the less I can picture you as one of its fearsome trainers." Before he could speak, she added, "You don't seem like someone who would enjoy living there."

Jaguar looked surprised for a moment. "You mean the type of person who would enjoy power, wealth, luxury, instant obedience, and virtually anything else I ask for?"

"I mean the type of person who would enjoy manipulating another living creature."

"Why not?" Jaguar responded unnervingly. "We all do what we're good at, and manipulation is a skill I learned very early."

Turquoise shook her head. "You're trying to scare me again."

"Maybe," he answered. "Maybe I don't need to try. Maybe I just need to be honest. I refuse to work as a trainer anymore," he stated, "but that doesn't mean I never did, and that is not work any creature can ever forget. The instinct to analyze, manipulate, destroy, and dominate never goes away. Reason and . . . morals can overlap and control instincts, but they can never destroy them."

He shook his head, his gaze distant. His voice was soft as he added, "I don't want to have to break you."

She didn't like the way he phrased that.

"If Jeshickah takes over Midnight, she won't let you stay here as freeblood. Either she'll kill you, or she'll have someone tame you."

"Lord Daryl didn't manage it," Turquoise stated, bravado in her voice.

"Daryl is too soft," Jaguar stated coldly, and this time Turquoise did recoil. Soft? The creature of her nightmares, soft?

Then Jaguar's voice was in her mind. *Daryl decided to act as a trainer because it was profitable, and he liked power. He can't read people very well, and he certainly has no idea how to control them.*

Turquoise would not look away, though she wanted to get as far from the vampire in her brain as possible.

*A trainer who knew what he was doing* . . . For a split second images came to her, vivid and painful; her knees gave out and she fell to the ground, the phantom taste of blood in her mouth. *You're strong, Audra. But you don't know what you're up against.*

He paused.

*Would you like me to let you go?*

Yes! Her mind was still reeling from the brief taste Jaguar had given her—a taste of what it was like to be in a trainer's cell, one that would keep her awake at nights longing for the more gentle memories of a beating from Lord Daryl.

*Think I have somewhere else to go?* she answered, as soon as she could gather her thoughts. She would love to go, to get as far away from Midnight as possible, but she had a job here and would not leave until it was finished. Besides, if she ran now she would need to run forever. One was either predator or prey; a person could not be a hunter if she hid from that which she hunted.

"As you wish." She could feel Jaguar leave her mind, like a subtle pressure draining away. "I'm sorry I hurt you. I wanted to make sure you knew what there was for you to fear."

"Thanks," she answered hoarsely, not yet trusting her legs to hold her if she stood. She forced herself to focus on the job. Information was safe, safer than memories, anyway. "Why is Jeshickah so upset about how you're running things here?"

Jaguar sat beside her. "She wants me to rule Midnight like she used to."

"Don't you?"

Jaguar's expression was shocked. "You don't know

much about the first Midnight, if you ask that question."

"Then tell me."

Jaguar's expression was distant as he spoke. "The
east wing was a row of cells, each of which usually
housed a litter." He hesitated with distaste, and then explained. "The humans were bred for beauty and obedience. Eight or nine children were usually born each
year, but it was rare for more than four or five to live
past the first culling."

Turquoise choked back bile as Jaguar continued.

"The first-generation slaves, the ones brought into
Midnight from the outside, were kept in the combined
lower cells, or on occasion in individual trainer cells if
they had caught someone's attention." He paused, and
then gave an example. "Jeshickah's idea of a well-
trained slave would make most of Daryl's dogs seem
rowdy, and her methods make Daryl himself seem like
a humanist."

Audra nodded, remembering the silent slaves Lord
Daryl had surrounded himself with. To her eyes, they
had been perfectly obedient, eerily so.

"You don't want to know more," Jaguar stated
bluntly, and of course he was right. She had not wanted
to know as much as he had already told her. "I worked
in the original Midnight for almost two hundred years,
until it was destroyed."

"Why did you rebuild it?" Turquoise asked quietly.

Jaguar looked surprised. "Someone was going to."

"Why?"

"Why not?" he responded. "Wealth. Power. The
vampire who was threatening to rebuild at the time was

generally disliked, and an old enemy of mine." His gaze searched her face for a moment as if wondering whether to say something. He continued, "Daryl, to be exact. You know him well enough to understand that it would have been disaster if he had taken control. Jeshickah had disappeared after her Midnight burned, and Gabriel didn't want to lead, so I was the only one with the power to challenge Daryl." He shrugged, but there was pain in the movement.

"Is he really so strong?" Turquoise asked. Though there were crevices in her soul that held a particular horror of him, a panic that appeared when he was near, in her rational mind she knew he was not powerful.

"Physically, no, but he has political power. He was called a trainer in the original Midnight, and even though his methods were often ineffective, that title gave him a following." Jaguar shook his head. "Still, no one would back him against one of Jeshickah's blood. I'm not quite the strongest in my line, but I'm close enough that the people who originally followed her will follow me."

"How . . ." She broke off, unsure that she wanted to know the answer to the question she had been about to ask.

Jaguar looked at her questioningly. "What?"

"How were your methods different from Lord Daryl's?"

He looked away from her, but still answered. "Daryl's line is known for its ability to manipulate the minds of humans, and he depends on that talent. He uses a simple mixture of brute force, physical and mental, to twist his slave's minds into what he wants them to be." There was contempt in his tone as he continued, "It works about half the time. Frequently, he ends up with products too damaged to be of use. Scarring, for instance," he added, his tone apologetic, "is common on Daryl's projects. I knew you were once his the instant I saw your arms."

Turquoise swallowed the lump in her throat, and forced herself to say, "And how did you work?"

"Pain . . . is easy to give." His voice was remote, and his gaze rested on some distant point. "Daryl doesn't have the patience necessary to bide his time and observe. Every person has her own weaknesses, physical, emotional, spiritual. After a while, finding those weaknesses and pressing against them becomes a habit, almost a game."

Turquoise remembered uneasily how Jaguar had done just that when she had woken that evening and pulled away from him. He had reacted to her fear almost angrily, like a shark that had caught a blood scent but did not want to acknowledge his attraction to it.

When he spoke to her, was he sizing her up, testing her as a possible opponent? He said he did not want to break her. Did that mean he saw her, a human being, and was content with her actions and reactions? Or was she just a slave he happened to be fond of, and which he would wait to tame until she ceased to please him?

Her thoughts were cut off as Jaguar looked up abruptly. He muttered a curse under his breath and then jumped to his feet.

*Stay here.*

Turquoise ignored the words and followed Jaguar.

She swore at a rock that nearly tripped her, and arrived in the southern wing just in time to hear the crack of Jaguar's whip and a loud string of colorful expletives from Ravyn. Ducking, she narrowly avoided the knife that Jaguar's whip had caught and tossed across the room.

*I thought I told you to stay put.*

She did not respond to Jaguar, and he did not insist on an answer. They both had more pressing issues to deal with.

Ravyn had her back pressed to the wall; her hair was in disarray, and she stood stiffly, favoring her right leg. Her gaze flickered to Turquoise briefly, and then returned to the two vampires in the room with her.

Jeshickah was leaning against a table; despite a slit in the side of her shirt, which had probably been made by Ravyn's knife, she looked unfazed. Her gaze was fixed on Jaguar.

Jaguar snapped the whip to disentangle it from Ravyn's wrist; Ravyn hissed in pain, and from the doorway Turquoise could see blood on the burgundy hunter's skin.

"Are you in the practice of letting dangerous pets run about like feral dogs?" Jeshickah asked acidly, causing Jaguar to stiffen. "Or are you completely out of control of your own property?"

*Audra, out.* The command was forceful, inviting no disobedience.

However, one does not leave one's allies to get slaughtered, even if those allies are the likes of Ravyn Aniketos.

*Audra.* The second voice rolled through her mind like

honeyed blades, a combination of sweetness and threat. *Aren't you going to obey your master?*

The words loosed a vivid memory, intentionally Turquoise knew.

Catherine, *aren't you going to obey your master? The vampiress's voice slipped into Cathy's mind at the same time that Jeshickah said aloud, "Your pet is rather poorly behaved, Daryl."*

*Lord Daryl wrapped an arm around the human's waist, and attempted to pull her back against himself, saying, "She's a work in progress."*

*Cathy slammed a heel down onto the bridge of Lord Daryl's foot and wrenched herself out of his grip, asserting, "I am not your pet."*

*Lord Daryl was trying to impress this Jeshickah, whoever she was. Cathy refused to be a good little slave so he could flaunt his power.*

*She saw amusement in Jeshickah's expression, and then fierce rage in Lord Daryl's, and belatedly realized that making him look like a fool in front of this particular member of his kind had been a really bad idea.*

*The first blow brought the taste of blood to her mouth. The second was a slug to her gut, and it sent her to the ground, gagging. The third was a kick to her rib cage. Normally, he would stop hurting her once she was down, but normally he wasn't nearly this furious.*

The memory was enough to kick the hunter into action.

Turquoise dove, trusting the vampires to be unprepared; she rolled, grabbing the knife Ravyn had lost, and was almost to her feet by the time Jeshickah reacted.

Jaguar shouted, but Turquoise did not turn her attention to him; instead, she tried to keep Jeshickah's backhand from striking her across the side of the face. The blow would have been crippling, had it connected.

Every fighter has an instinctual tendency to defend first, then attack; that tendency has ended many a hunter's life. Only one ineffective defense means death, but only one effective attack means victory. If that attack is fast and hard enough, there is no chance of losing because an opponent has no chance to fight back.

Her left shoulder contacted with the vampiress's gut, knocking her off balance. In the instant before Jeshickah could recover, Turquoise raised the knife in her right hand.

The crack of a whip echoed dimly in the back of her mind.

Then blackness.

# CHAPTER 14

*LORD DARYL SHOVED HER AWAY, toward Nathaniel. She couldn't get up again. Everything was bleeding, bruised, throbbing. She barely heard her master's voice, shaking with pain and fury, order Nathaniel, "Get her out of here."*

*"And where should I take her?" Nathaniel responded, barely glancing at the human who had collapsed at his feet.*

*Lord Daryl spat another curse, and then disappeared, leaving Turquoise alone with the other vampire. Nathaniel hooked an arm around her waist to help her stand, and wrapped a cloth around her bleeding wrist as he told her, "You have no idea how many people have wanted to do what you just tried. For that alone I'm willing to help you. Can you walk?"*

*He set her on her feet, and his answer came immediately; her legs buckled, and the world slid into gray oblivion.*

Turquoise forced her eyes open, dragging herself out of an unwanted sleep. Despite the agony of the memory, there was a faint smile on her lips as she remembered the feel of the knife slicing open her master's skin. If only that first, painful attempt had worked.

The smile disappeared as she sat up and became aware of the chain connecting her left wrist to the wall. The back of her head pounded where Jaguar's whip had hit her. She was chained on one side of a large cell; Ravyn was similarly bound a few feet away.

Arguing voices made her headache worse.

"Hunters," Jeshickah spat, pacing angrily, and Turquoise winced at the sharp sound the vampire's boots made as their heels contacted with the cold stone floor. "How could you be so stupid?"

Jaguar did not rise to the bait. "If memory serves, you used to collect hunters. And incidentally, you were the one who bought them."

Jeshickah tossed her mane of black hair in a dismissive gesture. "There is a difference between keeping a well-caged rattlesnake on the shelf to display and letting it slither between your bedcovers," she pointed out acidly.

"I doubt the hunter ever posed any great threat to you."

"Of course not," Jeshickah answered haughtily, "but it's the principle of the thing. You can't allow your pets to go around attacking the guests."

"They were well behaved with me. What exactly did you do to her?" Jaguar leaned back against the wall. He glanced in Turquoise's direction once, but did not acknowledge if he had noticed she was awake.

"Nothing unexpected." With a frosty look at Ravyn's slumped form, Jeshickah added, "Though I suppose your lapdogs don't expect their masters to hit them, do they? Not when you shower them with praises and treats all day long."

Ravyn moaned as she woke, her hands flying to massage her temples, the chain from the wall to her wrist scratching loudly over the stone floor. She raised a brazen, garnet glare toward the two vampires, who returned it with twin expressions of distaste.

"Either deal with that," Jeshickah drawled lazily, "or give it to me and I will."

"I'll deal with her. I don't prefer your methods," Jaguar answered.

Jeshickah replied glibly, "Oh? And what do you think would be appropriate? A hug and a lollipop?"

Jaguar started to respond, but Jeshickah interrupted him.

"Deal with it, Jaguar," she ordered. "If you don't, I will. I know a few people who would pay dearly for them, after I break them."

"I'll take Catherine back." That voice belonged to Lord Daryl. He had been standing in the corner, so silent that Turquoise hadn't noticed him.

"They're mine," Jaguar argued, barely sparing a glance for Lord Daryl. "I'll deal with the two however I like, and that is not going to involve turning them over to either of you."

Jeshickah's black gaze smoldered. "They are yours, little cat, but *you* are mine. Blood and body, mind and soul, you belong to me and always will." Jaguar took a step back from her. "You've had long enough with them." Jaguar started to argue, but Jeshickah interrupted him. "You aren't the girl's nursemaid. Daryl's incompetent, but at least he isn't a softhearted baby-sitter."

Lord Daryl's insulted protest was ignored.

Turquoise could see Jaguar thinking quickly, trying to come up with a way to keep her from Jeshickah and Daryl. "Give me three weeks with them," he bargained.

"I don't think you could handle the both of them," Jeshickah argued.

"Let him keep the red-haired one," Lord Daryl suggested. "I want Catherine."

"Did I tell you to speak?" Jeshickah snapped, before turning back to Jaguar. "A few hundred years ago, a couple days would have been more than enough for you."

"She's spent too much time with Daryl; she's built defenses," Jaguar swiftly countered. "Give Ravyn to Gabriel; she's his type."

"One week with Daryl's pet," Jeshickah allowed.

"Two."

"Unnecessary," Jeshickah argued.

"Jeshickah—" Lord Daryl again tried to interject his opinion, only to be cut off as Jeshickah tossed him casually against the far wall. Lord Daryl stayed sulking in the corner.

"One week," Jeshickah repeated. "No special privileges or protection, no silken pillows or puppy treats. I want her licking your boots, or I'll take her from you, train her myself, and have her slit your throat. Understand, kitten?"

Jaguar lowered his gaze for a moment, and then returned it to her face. The moment of submission was brief, but visible all the same. "I understand," he answered, voice tight with barely controlled anger.

"Good." She disappeared, at which point Jaguar swung around and slammed the heel of his palm into the wall. Turquoise winced at the sound of flesh meeting stone, not sure whether the sharp *crack* came from the stones breaking, or Jaguar's hand.

Turquoise had not stood. Instead, she had discreetly worked the safety pin and pen cap out of where she had taped them to the inside of her pants cuff. Her body shielded from view her right wrist as she worked on the lock.

Trying to ignore Lord Daryl, who was glaring at Jaguar but had not yet spoken, Turquoise raised her gaze to Jaguar's.

"What now?" Her voice was calm, and betrayed none of her thoughts. The lock was a tricky one, and doing it one-handed behind her back did not make the job any easier. Once it was open, she had no idea what she would do, but she didn't have many other options.

"Get out, Daryl," Jaguar ordered.

"I think I would like to hear the answer to Catherine's question first," Lord Daryl replied.

Jaguar glared at the other vampire, whose expression instantly shifted to surprise. Turquoise could tell there was some silent communication going on between the two, and she would have given good money to know what it was—especially when Lord Daryl smiled.

"That settled?" Jaguar asked coolly.

Lord Daryl nodded slightly. "Fine."

Focused on their exchange, Turquoise's concentration broke. The safety pin slipped, and she heard the lock click back into place.

"Would you like me to unlock that?" Jaguar asked, hearing the sound.

"That would make things easier," Ravyn drawled. "While you're at it, would you mind opening the doors and then going out to lunch?"

Lord Daryl's lips twitched again in amusement; Turquoise was beginning to get nervous.

Jaguar smiled wryly. "You," he told Ravyn, "are not my problem anymore." He tossed the keys to Ravyn, who had her lock undone in an instant. She stood, eyeing Jaguar and Lord Daryl warily.

"You're not going to let her out," Lord Daryl argued.

Jaguar ignored him, and continued to speak to Ravyn. "You'll be in the west wing as soon as you go through that door. Gabriel is staying in the second room. I hear you two have a . . . business relationship?"

Ravyn nodded, handing the keys back to Jaguar. "We're very close," she purred. She started to leave, the grace of her exit marred only by a slight stiffness in her walk.

Lord Daryl grabbed Ravyn's arm, and the hunter froze, her gaze flashing to Jaguar. She was obviously sizing up the situation, debating whether to fight Lord Daryl off.

"She isn't yours." Jaguar's voice was cool, the very absence of expression in it a warning.

"She isn't yours, either," Lord Daryl countered.

Jaguar stepped forward, and put a hand on Lord Daryl's wrist above where the vampire was clutching Ravyn's arm. Lord Daryl's grip on Ravyn tightened, and Jaguar's grip on Lord Daryl did the same.

Turquoise saw Ravyn's eyes flicking from the faces of the two vampires to the doorway.

"Gabriel will not be pleased if you mark her." Lord Daryl winced as if Jaguar's grip was getting painful.

"She can't just wander around." There was a moment of pause, and then Lord Daryl added, "Let me go."

Turquoise leaned back against the wall, content to watch the vampires engage in their game of male dominance.

She flinched at the sound of bones crunching.

Lord Daryl shouted a curse, flinging Ravyn away, and swung a punch at Jaguar. Ravyn instantly took advantage of her freedom to disappear out the door.

Jaguar grabbed Lord Daryl's wrist before the blow hit and twisted it behind the fair-skinned vampire's back; Turquoise heard the wet snap as tendons in the elbow joint tore. Lord Daryl whimpered, and Jaguar wrapped a hand around his throat.

"Midnight is my property," Jaguar stated, "and so long as you are here, you will obey me. Understand?"

Lord Daryl started to struggle, and Jaguar's grip tightened until Turquoise looked away from the sickening sound of her former master's windpipe collapsing.

"Understand, Daryl?" Jaguar repeated.

Jaguar dropped his captive, and Lord Daryl fell to the ground, his hands at his throat. Turquoise watched, her emotions a mix of distaste and surprise. Here was the creature who had tormented her, terrified her, emitting soft sounds of pain from his crushed throat as it quickly healed. For the first time since the day she had first learned his title, this black-haired creature ceased to be Lord Daryl. He was still stronger than she was, physically, but he was no one's master.

Daryl slid away from Jaguar. He pushed himself up, and coughed a couple times before answering, "Fine." He leaned back against the wall, and rubbed his throat.

"Out, Daryl," Jaguar ordered again. This time Daryl obeyed without hesitation.

# CHAPTER 15

"AS FOR YOU . . ." He tossed the keys to Turquoise and then sat cross-legged in front of her. "I could not let you kill Jeshickah. The woman has very powerful friends who would have killed you shortly after. I didn't expect that to be a problem when I hired Jillian Red to find me some hunters, but unfortunately I seem to have become quite fond of you, and it would distress me to see you tortured to death." He spoke with a calmness that belied the violence of his fight with Daryl.

Turquoise unlocked her cuff. "You hired her?"

Jaguar nodded. "She's a witch, very powerful and very well informed. I believe she worked with Nathaniel to destroy the original Midnight, so I didn't think she would have any hesitation to help this time."

"I'm confused," she protested. "You worked in the old Midnight, but aren't upset it was destroyed. You founded this Midnight, and are actually trying to ruin it."

"I'm very happy with Midnight as it was two weeks

ago. Jeshickah wasn't. Her authority always has been and always will be higher than mine. Either I can let her turn my haven into her own empire again—and she has the power to do it—or I can get rid of her."

Turquoise nodded, contemplating. "How long have you known who Ravyn and I were?"

"I was suspicious the moment I saw you," Jaguar answered. "Nathaniel rarely trades in flesh, and his selling me two strong women, both unbroken, just a few days after I hired Ms. Red . . ." He shrugged. "I wasn't sure until I saw you go for the knife, though. Jillian picked you well. I knew you used to belong to Daryl, and Ravyn's description rang a few bells when I asked around. The more I learned, the more likely it seemed that you two were both exactly what you were pretending to be—two humans who got tangled up in the trade, and were lucky enough not to be broken yet."

"It's the truth," Turquoise answered, with a bit of a smile. "You just neglected to account for the two years after I got out."

"It also didn't occur to me that anyone who had escaped the trade would ever be mad enough to put herself back in," Jaguar pointed out.

Turquoise shrugged. "You're the second person who's called me mad in relation to this job," she commented. "How will you get rid of Jeshickah now? And what do you plan to do with me for the next week?" Unless Jaguar could get rid of Jeshickah before those seven days were up, either Jaguar was dead or Turquoise would once again be a slave ready for breaking. Turquoise would trust no one to put his life above her freedom.

"I have a few ideas for Jeshickah, but none of them are quick," he answered. "As for you . . . I don't know."

Turquoise didn't intend to give Jaguar time to make a decision. She would get out of Midnight today, if he left her alone for more than five seconds. This job had gone bad. If Jaguar had been honest in his warning that killing Jeshickah would bring about deadly retaliation, then Turquoise needed to backtrack and plan again. Confronting Jillian Red and Nathaniel about whether she and Ravyn had been sent on a suicide mission sounded like a good idea.

Getting out shouldn't be too difficult. It would be the easiest thing in the world to scale the courtyard wall and go over the back of the building. The iron fence was high, but she could manage it. Turquoise wasn't worried about Ravyn; the hunter could look out for herself. Whatever Ravyn's relationship was with the vampire to whom she had been sold, Turquoise was more than happy to turn her back on the pair.

She was silent for too long, debating. Jaguar asked casually, "What's Catherine's story? How did she end up in Daryl's care?"

"Doesn't he acquire most people the same way?" Turquoise retorted defensively as she tried to avoid answering.

Jaguar nodded. "He buys most of his slaves from other trainers." He added, "And he doesn't buy anyone who isn't broken. That means he picked you up somewhere else."

"Guess so." She did not feel like sharing her life history today.

"How many people did he kill to get you?"

The words were blunt, and Turquoise knew her shock showed on her face. Most of the scars on Turquoise's arms were from when Daryl had thrown her father through the second-story bay window, and she had almost followed through the broken glass. Before she meant to, she answered, "My mother. My father. My brother." *Tommy.* The thought of her little brother made something in her gut wrench. He would have been fourteen now. "How the hell did you know?"

"I don't know your exact history with Daryl, but I know his methods. He wouldn't have taken a freeblood human without making sure she didn't have a home to return to."

She shrugged. "I wouldn't have had anything, even if they had been alive. How would they ever have understood?"

Jaguar didn't argue with her. "You miss them?"

Turquoise shrugged. "I miss Catherine's old life, sometimes. Her friends, her family. Mostly, the sense of safety she lived with. But I can't go back, no matter how much I would like to." Recklessly, she asked a question that she knew would end the conversation. "What about you? When Jeshickah changed you, did you miss your past?"

Jaguar recoiled as if she had struck him, but he matched her honesty as he told his own brief story. "My mother was a shape-shifter. Midnight's laws didn't allow for shape-shifters to be traded, unless they were first sold into it by their own kind. My father was happy to oblige." He gathered himself quickly, but his voice was still sharp when he answered, "He sold me to

Jeshickah for less than the cost of a bottle of whiskey. I could have fought him on it—I was twenty years old, and held almost as much power in the estate as he did—but I was glad to leave." He stood, turning away from Turquoise, each movement slick and angry like a restless, caged beast.

"Why did Jeshickah want you?" Though anxious to leave this fouled job behind, she was genuinely curious about his background.

Jaguar rounded on her, asking, "Why did Daryl want you?"

"Answer for an answer?" she translated. At Jaguar's nod, she explained as succinctly as possible, "My father took me to New York for my eighteenth birthday, to see a musical. We got in late, and my father went to bed, but I stayed in the hotel lobby to people-watch. I was a naïve idiot; when Daryl came up to me, I didn't think past the fact that he was handsome and seemed to be flirting. We were in an open area, surrounded by people. No danger. I never recognized what he was—never even knew vampires existed—until he bit me."

"Daryl's line is weak physically," Jaguar commented, "but if you let one of them in your mind you won't ever think to fight them. Against an unprotected human mind, he wouldn't need to be strong."

Turquoise raised one brow. "Apparently he did need to be." She finished the story quickly. "Or maybe he was just careless. Either way, he didn't manage to catch my mind. I started to fight him, smashed my soda glass against his temple, kicked . . ." She remembered fondly that memory, less fondly the one after. "I caused enough of a scene that he couldn't keep people from noticing, and had to let me go . . . for the moment, anyway."

Jaguar nodded, knowing the gist of the rest, if not the details. Daryl did not kill most of his prey, but he did not like losing one. If Catherine had not fought him, her interaction with the world of vampires might have ended on that night. But thwarted once, Daryl had been twice as determined to claim her.

"Daryl hates you too much to have let you go willingly," Jaguar observed, "and even with his temper, he wouldn't have scarred you unless he planned to kill you. Yet you somehow managed to get out and become a hunter. How?"

"I fought him. I got out. I joined Bruja," Turquoise answered vaguely, her tone adding the words *end of subject.* One of Nathaniel's conditions for his help had been her silence about his part in her escape. "What about my question?"

"Jeshickah picks her trainers for physical beauty, mental acuity, moral void, and what she calls a trainer instinct—the instinct to watch a person, determine her weaknesses, and destroy her." He paused, and then added, "I had shown a knack for such. It also didn't hurt that Jeshickah had a fondness for shape-shifter blood." He said the words dispassionately, the same way Ravyn had referred to her master's taste for "exotics." Turquoise wondered if she would ever be able to look at her own experience as a slave so unemotionally.

Turquoise had seen how deeply Jeshickah's claws of ownership went. Unless she counted the years before his father had sold him—a very small portion of his long life—Jaguar had never been free.

Physical beauty and mental acuity—Turquoise could still see those descriptions applying to Jaguar. Moral void, she could not. "What changed?" she asked.

"A hundred years without Jeshickah," Jaguar answered. He spoke slowly, choosing his words with care. "There was a slave of mine who survived when Midnight burned. I had owned her since she was four, when I had bought her in one of my many attempts to annoy Jeshickah—she had been born blind, and Jeshickah had been planning to kill her." He smiled a bit at the memory. "She was faultlessly obedient. That was unsurprising; she had been raised a slave in Midnight. Only after Midnight burned did I realize that I had never once struck her. I had never needed to."

He sighed, his expression distant. "Over the years I realized I didn't want to own her; I wanted to know her. I enjoyed her company, especially once she grew brave enough to speak freely with me. She trusted me implicitly, and I was wary of betraying that trust.

"I'd had people fear me, hate me, envy me. . . ." He shook his head. "Trust was new, and it was precious. It took me a long time to figure out how I had managed to earn it."

"And when you did?" Turquoise asked, caught up in the story.

"I realized I didn't think of her as a slave, and that I hadn't treated her like one since Midnight's walls fell. You can't earn a slave's trust, or loyalty—only her

obedience. But blind obedience doesn't make for interesting conversation or companionship; I prefer spending time with a defiant equal more than an obsequious
slave." Jaguar shrugged. "I'd be lying if I said I always
enjoy the challenge. The relationship between master
and slave is clear-cut, easy, and sometimes it's tempting
to slip into the familiar role and demand submission
from someone who is refusing to give me what I want."

"Such as?" Turquoise pried, thinking of how easily
he had ordered Daryl away, and wondering whether
that was an example of his giving into temptation, or
simply a good decision.

Jaguar laughed a little, shaking off the question.
"You don't want to know the answer to that one."

She frowned, wondering if he was laughing at her or
at himself.

"We should go outside," Jaguar said. "I need to find
Jeshickah before she starts hurting my people, and the
courtyard is the only area in this building that's free
from Daryl."

He escorted her to the courtyard, his mood contem-
plative. Heavy clouds hid stars and moon from sight,
and Turquoise welcomed the darkness that matched
her mood.

She jumped as Jaguar caught her shoulders, pulling
her forward in an impulsive embrace. He kissed the top
of her head.

"I know," he said, holding her loosely enough that
she knew she could pull away if she tried, "that you are
going to disappear as soon as I turn my back."

Turquoise did not argue; there was no point to it.

"That being so, I have one favor to ask." He nodded

toward the alcove where he usually napped during the day, and Turquoise's eyes reluctantly made out Eric's form there. The boy was watching them warily, as if thinking he should leave but not wanting to. "Take him with you?"

"What?"

Eric would be a liability. If Turquoise had to protect him, that would make facing anyone she encountered on the way out more difficult. Eric would slow her down. Unless Jaguar was willing to help . . . no. Jaguar would give her the opportunity to leave, but he couldn't afford to help her.

Jaguar all but echoed her thoughts. "In a couple weeks, Jeshickah will be . . . out of the way. Until then, she's going to cause trouble. I doubt she'll kill me." *Isn't that reassuring?* Turquoise thought, as Jaguar continued, "But she won't hesitate to hurt me, or to go through my possessions to do so. She knows I'm fond of you, but you can handle yourself against Jeshickah. Eric . . ." He shook his head. "He's tough, but he's a kid. I can protect him against almost anyone else, but Jeshickah could destroy him, and she will, because she knows I would keep him safe."

What on Earth would Turquoise do with a kid once she got out? Eric had no place in Bruja—he was a victim, not a fighter—but Bruja was all Turquoise knew. Bringing this boy along would play hell with her plans.

But leaving him behind would be leaving him to die.

She nodded sharply.

"After you get out, I recommend laying low until Jeshickah's gone. She'll be raising merry hell."

Turquoise smiled wryly.

He hesitated, and Turquoise could read fear, desire, longing, and an oversized portion of regret on his face. "I doubt you'll want to come back to my world, even after Jeshickah is gone. Would you mind if I came to visit yours?"

Turquoise swallowed, trying to shove down the lump of nervousness in her throat. Jaguar had disrupted her life enough as it was. Eric was going to mess it up even more. Continuing her association with the vampire any longer than necessary was a bad idea.

"I'm planning to disappear for a while," she answered. "If I don't want you to find me, you won't." That was honest, and it would give her a chance to think.

He accepted the answer. "Best of luck, Audra."

And then the world shifted, and he was gone.

# CHAPTER 16

THE AIR BARELY CLOSED on the space Jaguar
had occupied when Turquoise turned to examine the
wall. The natural stones would be perfect for climbing,
with plenty of handholds; scaling it would be easy.

Reluctantly, she turned toward Eric. He was fourteen, still a kid no matter what he had seen. He needed
a family; instead, he had Midnight. He needed a father;
instead, he had Jaguar, who was so tangled in webs of
dominance he could hardly help himself.

She was getting sentimental, and that was dangerous. Time to get out of Midnight while she still could.

"Do you want to come with me?" she offered, while
the sane part of her mind berated her with every possible insult it could consider.

Eric nodded.

"It's going to be rough," she warned. "I'm no good at
taking care of other people." A vision of Tommy assaulted her suddenly, a vision of Daryl striking him

down. She tried to shake it off, but it wouldn't disappear.

"I'm okay at taking care of myself," Eric assured her.

*Please, don't let me let him get hurt,* Turquoise pleaded of whatever powers existed.

"We're going over the back wall. Stay low at the top. Can you climb?" she asked belatedly.

Eric nodded.

Turquoise boosted the boy up, making sure he could find handholds in the rough stone before she followed. They stayed low on the roof to avoid making themselves into silhouettes, and crossed quickly to the back.

The wall here was smooth, and offered no purchase for climbing down. The guard was nowhere to be seen as Turquoise turned and gripped the edge, lowering herself as far as possible before letting go and falling. The impact was jarring, but she knew how to take a fall. She reached up to catch Eric, who mimicked her strategy.

Turquoise's peripheral vision caught movement the instant Eric dropped, a faint blur of color—a cougar. She saw its muscles bunch to pounce.

She twisted awkwardly, pushing Eric behind herself and out of the cougar's way. Off balance, she took the brunt of the creature's initial rush; stars spattered her vision as her back struck the gravel, and she felt claws bite into her skin.

The guard's hesitation was her salvation. Turquoise belonged to Midnight, and the cougar was reluctant to permanently damage her. Turquoise took the moment to get a knee between herself and the cat and shoved full force, sending the guard stumbling a couple feet.

Turquoise was now at a disadvantage. She wasn't sure what the best way to fight a large feline was, but run and hide sounded like her best option. She thought she could make it over the gate before the cougar could follow, if she could delay it long enough for Eric to get out of the way first.

"Eric, over the fence," she ordered.

The cougar moved to intercept the boy, and Turquoise pounced, throwing her entire weight against the cat's side. It snarled, turning on her.

Luckily, the shape-shifter was just trying to contain Turquoise as it waited for its master to appear. Turquoise was grateful for the guard's unwillingness to harm its employer's property, and tumbled at the large cat recklessly, keeping it occupied as Eric scaled the fence.

The hair on the back of Turquoise's neck rose as a familiar aura brushed her senses.

Daryl. She turned and struck in one movement. It's just Daryl. Not Lord, not Master. Just Daryl.

This creature was only another leech, no matter what else he had been to her in the past. He was vulnerable, and she had spent the last two years of her life learning how to make use of that fact. Unfortunately, without a weapon, she still stood about as much chance as a Hawaiian snowman. Still, she would fight rather than submit to this beast.

Her first blow caught Daryl in the solar plexus; it was not as incapacitating a blow on a vampire as it would have been to a human, but it did hurt, and interrupted any attack he had been making. At the same time she knocked out his knee with a side kick, striking just below the joint in a move banned from martial arts competitions because it was crippling to a human.

Crippling for a vampire meant he stumbled. The joint dislocated, and Daryl tumbled with a curse. A dislocated knee, which on a human might never completely heal, would take a vampire two or three minutes to recover from.

Daryl had a low pain tolerance for one of his kind; as she fought, she saw that weakness come into play. He had been startled by her initial attack, and now pain was making him take too long to defend himself.

A fight between a vampire and a human almost always goes one of two ways: either it ends instantly, or the human dies. A vampire is stronger, faster, and can heal more than any human. If a fight lingers, the human will always tire first. Once prepared for a fight, all a vampire needs to do is wait, providing minimal exertion to defend himself.

She had a chance for one more attack while Daryl was bent over, a side kick to his temple. It was a risky move; he could catch her foot and tear it off if he recovered enough to react. However, a broken neck would get him out of her hair long enough for her to get away.

Daryl did not manage to turn her attempt against her, but he did get out of the way to turn her paralyzing attack into a minimal nuisance.

Nursing his injured knee, the vampire did not bother to stand. He swiped Turquoise's back leg out from under her before she had recovered her balance from the miss, and the only thing she could do was control the fall.

She let herself fall away from Daryl, so that when she landed she was the perfect distance for another kick to his already broken knee.

She turned quickly, but Daryl was quicker. Still fighting from the ground, he dragged her to him and hit her squarely across the jaw. He did not need to bother striking sensitive areas or waiting for opportunity; his strength made any blow strong enough to daze.

Turquoise turned her face away from the blow, moving with it to absorb the brunt of the force and retaliating at the same time. Sparks crossed her vision even as her attack snapped the weak floating rib off Daryl's rib cage, driving it back and causing him to release her.

He rolled away, and shoved himself up. She did the same, both of them momentarily too hurt to press an advantage.

She got to her feet first; Daryl was still struggling with his knee. He wasn't in too much of a hurry. Most vampires instinctively discounted humans as a threat, no matter how many kills a hunter had on her record or how the fight was going. Vampires were called "immortal," after all. No human could kill them.

Daryl was pushing up from his knees when Turquoise repeated her earlier attempted attack, striking his head hard and fast. She felt the impact all the way up her leg as the kick made contact, the resistance of bone that gave way with a *crunch*.

His neck snapped, and the vampire tumbled back to the ground. A broken neck is paralyzing to any creature, even one that can survive and heal the injury.

Turquoise hated running, but short of tearing Daryl's

head off, she knew no way to kill a vampire without a weapon. Like most humans, she wasn't strong enough for bare-handed decapitation.

But retreat chafed on her nerves. One thing Crimson always taught: eliminate your enemies. Leaving prey alive gave it a chance to recover and win the advantage next time. A second fight rarely went as well as the first.

The cougar had fled somewhere during her fight with Daryl, probably distressed to see the vampire losing. Eric was waiting for her on the other side of the iron fence.

She barely remembered scaling the fence. She remembered Eric asking if she was okay, and nodding sharply before leading the way into the forest behind Midnight. She had no idea how far away the town was, but she would not stop until they were out of Jaguar's land.

Later, she could examine the painful swelling of her jaw. Later, she could wash and bandage the wounds from the cougar's claws. Later, she could pause to wonder what on earth she was going to do with a fourteen-year-old boy. Now, she just wanted to go to ground and disappear.

They reached town at a slow limp at about noon. Eric obviously wasn't used to so much walking, but he never complained. Turquoise's adrenaline carried her through the many miles, leaving her with the focused energy and feeling of immortality that always followed a fight. More than anything, she wanted to go back and pound the cougar, which must have called to Daryl when Jaguar did not respond to its summons.

Instead, she found a pay phone in some hole-in-the-wall town a couple miles down from the end of Jaguar's territory. The street signs declared this to be Main Street, in some town called Logging.

"Yes?" Nathaniel's faint voice over the static-filled telephone wires was the sweetest sound she had ever heard.

"It's Turquoise," she said quickly. "I need a place to stay for a couple days where I can't be tracked."

"Until the waters cool?" Nathaniel responded. "I've got a place you can borrow. I'll lend you some cash so you don't get traced pulling out your funds. Tell me where you are and I'll pick you up."

She told him, wondering how much this was going to cost her. It didn't really matter though. She had made enough in Crimson—vampire hunting could be a lucrative business—that she could comfortably retire for the next seventy years if she wanted. Whatever price Nathaniel charged, it would be worth it.

"Wait fifteen minutes so I can make a reservation for you, and then check into the inn down the street. I'm a few hours away, so you'll have a chance to patch up and get some sleep."

Blissful advice.

"I'll see you soon," he bid her. She responded in kind, and then found the phone dead in her hand.

No barter, no price. Nathaniel was as proper a mercenary as there came, and when he made a deal, he kept it. He never forgot to include a price, but he had agreed to give his help without stating one, and couldn't change the terms later.

She would puzzle it out later. For now, she turned back to Eric. "Just a block more, and we can get some sleep."

The kid smiled. *Smiled,* after all he had been through, and despite the exhaustion that was clearly written on his features. Miracles do still happen after all.

# CHAPTER 17

"CATHERINE, PUT THE BOY DOWN," Daryl commanded, "and I won't have to hurt him."

She reluctantly set Tommy down, though his small, trembling hand gripped hers tightly enough that her fingers were going numb. "Tommy, run," she commanded, pushing him away.

The boy hesitated, long enough that the creature reached forward and twined pale fingers in Tommy's soft brown hair. "You love your sister, Thomas?" the creature asked softly, kneeling so he was looking the young child in the eye.

"Let him go!" she shrieked, launching herself at the pair, trying to separate them. The creature simply glanced in her direction and backhanded her casually, a light tap compared to what he would do later.

He released the boy and caught Catherine's arm as she tried to hit him, brushing his fingers across her cheek. She jerked back from his touch. "Catherine—" he began, but before he could continue she lashed out, striking him in the throat with all the force of terror, hatred, and fury.

The creature cursed, releasing her, and she was off in a

*sprint. She had barely reached the driveway when it caught up, and a shove sent her sprawling. Her palms and knees tore open as she struck the pavement, less than a foot away from her father's body. Where was Tommy? Had he gotten away, or . . .*

*"Catherine." He dragged her to her feet, his grip on her wrist bruising. "Never hit me." He hit back. She tasted blood in her mouth for a moment before she fell into the encroaching darkness.*

Turquoise woke to find herself coated in a sheen of cold sweat. She was lying on a bed in a room she did not know. The dream left a sour taste in her mouth, and agitation in her mind.

She sat up quickly, and was rewarded by a series of shooting pains.

Sunlight was streaming in through the nearby windows. She closed the curtains, which caused the throbbing in her head to subside a bit, and pushed her bitter history from her thoughts.

Slowly, more recent memories returned to her. Nathaniel had picked her and Eric up, and brought them here. Driving through it, the town had seemed as familiar and as alien as all small towns were to her, though she hadn't seen much before she had slept.

Turquoise stood and forced herself to stretch. She walked to Eric's room, wincing at each step she took; a glance through his partly open door revealed that he was still sleeping soundly. Then, having reassured herself that he was safe, she took a hot shower and put on clean clothes.

"Is this yours?" she had asked, when Nathaniel had handed her the key to the house.

He had nodded slightly. "I haven't stayed here in a while, though. At the moment, it belongs to this girl here," he had added, tossing her a leather wallet. Examining the contents, she had found a license with her picture on it, a platinum Visa, a bankcard, a library card, and three twenty-dollar bills. "Since you can't tap into your accounts from here without being traced, I thought you could use a new identity with access to a little cash," Nathaniel had explained. "I also took the liberty of swiping some of your clothing from your Bruja house; it's in an overnight bag in the master bedroom's closet."

She hadn't ached so much then. During her sleep, all the muscles she had abused the evening before had stiffened.

The house was a small one-story, with two bedrooms, a bathroom, a kitchen, and a wraparound porch. Though clean, it had a feeling of emptiness that their presence had not yet eased.

The kitchen had a pale blue-marble linoleum floor, dark blue counters, and pine cupboards. The refrigerator was completely empty, and warm; Turquoise had to find the plug and turn the thing on. The burners on the stove looked unused, and the cupboards were equally bare. There were no pots or pans, no silverware, no paper towels or plastic bags, no toaster, and no can opener—a vampire's house. Nathaniel didn't need to eat here.

There was, however, a phone and a phonebook. Pizza sounded like a grand breakfast. But first she had to call Nathaniel and find out what the hell was going on. She dialed his number from memory, and waited three rings before remembering that it was midmorning and Nathaniel was probably asleep.

An answering machine clicked on, and a mechanical voice informed her, *"There is no answer. Please leave a message after the tone."*

"Nathaniel, I need to talk to you. Give me a call whenever you can." She hesitated, and then awkwardly added, "Thanks," before hanging up.

Nathaniel didn't approve of thanks. He always assured his clients that he did everything for his own gain, not theirs, and that gratitude was therefore out of place. Turquoise had believed him, until today. Twice, once when he had taken her from Daryl and now with all this, Nathaniel had helped her without asking for payment.

Turquoise shook her head. He would call or he wouldn't; until then, she might as well get settled and fed.

She didn't have long to wait before Eric emerged from his room. His stomach was rumbling as loudly as hers, and he had no objection to takeout.

"I'll go shopping sometime today," she assured him, as they munched on their cheese pizzas. "If I can find a grocery store." She frowned. "And someplace to buy silverware." Shopping was probably her least favorite thing to do. A waste of time, by her book, it was an excellent practice in tedium.

Eric nodded. "I saw a little houseware shop in town. We drove right past it. I can walk there."

Startled, Turquoise had to remind herself that Eric had been the human liaison to Jaguar's town from

Midnight. He was young, and depended on others for security, but he had taken on adult responsibilities in Midnight and hadn't lost that experience now that he had left—temporarily anyway. Once Jeshickah was no longer a threat, Eric would probably want to return to Jaguar's Midnight. His life was there.

"I'll drive you," Turquoise offered. "I don't want to split up." Eric's gaze fell, and she recognized that he was hurt. He didn't want her to treat him like a kid. "Anyway, we need too much for you to carry it all back," she assured him. He didn't look like he bought the explanation, but she couldn't soothe his ego. He didn't think like a kid, or act like a kid, but that didn't mean she felt any less protective.

Eric's houseware store proved a success; they found all they needed to stock the kitchen easily and hit the grocery store next. Turquoise wasn't a picky cook—she usually ate cereal in the mornings and something canned in the evenings—so Eric insisted he would cook. She trailed along behind, unable to stop herself from scanning the aisles as if looking for threats.

Her eye paused at a boy about her age, who looked vaguely familiar, though she couldn't place him. He was browsing the Asian specialty food section, but happened to glance at her as she passed.

The boy did a double take, and then turned. Turquoise started to fall instinctively into a fighting stance before she reminded herself that this boy was human and she was in a public area.

"Cathy?" His voice held surprise, and wonder. "I

haven't seen you since . . . I guess since I went away to college. How are you?"

She looked at Eric as if for help, but he was without answer. "I'm okay," she answered vaguely. *Who was this guy?* Clearly, someone who had known her before Daryl. So many memories from that time had faded, unnaturally so. "How are you?"

"I'm okay," he answered, apparently unaware of her discomfort. "Graduated last spring. I'm a history major." He laughed. "For all the good it will do me."

History . . . yes, she vaguely recalled a friend interested in history. Oh, she did remember this guy now. She had dated him, when she had been a junior and he had been a senior. But she could not for her life remember his name.

He had been away at college on her eighteenth birthday, when all hell had entered her life.

"Where are you now?" he asked.

"What?" *Great, intelligent conversation, Turquoise.*

"You were looking at Smith when I fell off the edge of the earth," he reminded her cheerfully. "Did you end up going there?" She was spared the need to respond when the boy noticed Eric. "Is that Tommy?"

Turquoise shook her head, and her voice was just a little too sharp as she answered, "No." Seeing the boy's confusion, she lied, "He's the neighbor's kid. I'm baby-sitting for him."

"Oh. That's cool," he answered.

She had to get out of here. The last thing she ever wanted to do was chat with Greg.

Greg. That was his name. Randomly, she remembered helping him with a senior prank. They had stolen one of the dissection rats from the bio lab, put bread around it, covered it with plastic wrap, and planted it in the middle of the sandwich bar in the cafeteria. What kind of bad luck had put him into her path now?

"What are you doing here?" she asked.

The words came out a little sharp. Greg looked startled, but responded with the same light humor. "I've got an apartment in town. I know, I said I'd never live in a small town, but I guess I was wrong." He checked his watch, and winced. "I've got to go, but I'll give you a call sometime. We should get back in touch. Do you live nearby?"

Didn't he know Catherine Minate was *dead*? Her body had never been found, of course, but she was as dead as any corpse in the ground. Turquoise still had some of her memories, though all of them had faded to a frightening extent, but she was not the innocent, mischievous girl who had planned pranks and gone to parties with Greg.

"I'm in town, but I just moved in. . . . I don't know the number." That at least was honest. *Please, leave me alone,* she added mentally. If she hadn't been worried about running into him again, as she was likely to do if they were living in the same small town, she would have lied.

She did not know why she felt the incredibly strong desire to run, but at the moment, she wanted to flee from this specter of her past.

"Oh, well, my apartment should be in the phone book," Greg said, undaunted. More quietly, he added, "I've missed you, Cathy."

*So have I,* Turquoise thought. She missed Cathy Minate more than anyone else could.

"I'll see you around," she said as Greg hoisted his basket of groceries.

"Yeah, I'll see you."

She fled the aisle as soon as he had turned away. Quickly Eric finished shopping, and just as quickly they paid and hurried to Turquoise's car.

"So who was that?" Eric asked.

"An old friend," Turquoise answered vaguely. She looked at the store, but could not see Greg from where they were parked.

Eric turned toward her with worry drawn on his face. "He talked like you two were close."

"He and Cathy were close," Turquoise amended.

Eric frowned. "Aren't you Cathy?"

"No," Turquoise argued. "Cathy was . . . stupid. She couldn't defend herself. Blissfully ignorant," she added dryly.

"Innocent. Not stupid."

"What makes you so wise?" Turquoise grumbled, mostly to herself. She started the car, attempting to drop the conversation.

Eric wouldn't let it drop; he answered her question. "It's the same thing the vampires do," he answered, "and I've spent a lot of time around them. You don't want to think of Cathy as you because she had weaknesses. You're a hunter, so you're not allowed to have weaknesses. A predator doesn't like to admit it's ever possible it can be prey." Quietly, he added, "And maybe you don't want to think that the girl Greg dated was capable of killing."

Turquoise realized her knuckles were white from

gripping the steering wheel too hard. She bit back a sharp criticism, remembering at the last moment that she had agreed to bring him, and had not been forced into it. "Cathy couldn't make herself crush a spider walking on her bedside table," she argued, her voice tight. "She *was* weak, and Daryl destroyed her."

"Cathy is *you*," Eric asserted again. "Daryl couldn't destroy her. He just made her a little harder, a little more scared—yes, scared," he continued, ignoring Turquoise's protest. "Cathy didn't need to hunt because she wasn't afraid of life."

"Okay, then I'm scared," Turquoise growled. "But I can't go back. I know what's out there, and if I turn my back on it, that won't make it disappear."

"You'd rather admit Daryl won than admit you were ever prey," Eric said softly.

"Daryl *did* win—that battle." She was nearly shouting now. "He murdered my father and my ten-year-old brother in front of me, and I couldn't save them. I couldn't fight him. I couldn't do anything. I spent one year in his house, little better than a pet, and I couldn't do anything about it. Cathy died in there—her innocence, her illusions, her dreams—"

"Your dreams," Eric interrupted. "What are you now? A hunter; I know that. Anything else?"

The question stymied her. Anything else?

Turquoise Draka was a high-ranking member of Crimson, and one of two competitors for the position of leader. She had a web of contacts and associates, but friends? Those were scarce, if they existed at all. She had a love of the hunt, an addiction to the sweet rush of adrenaline. Anything else?

Probably another ten or fifteen years of life. Though the lifespan of a member of Bruja was slightly longer, most hunters didn't live past their mid-thirties. Age could catch up, making the hunter slow. But mostly death came in the form of the inevitable slipup. Carelessness. Human imperfection.

"Let it drop, Eric," she ordered, or tried to. Her voice wasn't hard enough to be commanding.

"What did Cathy want to do?" Eric pressed, his voice more gentle now.

"I said, let it drop."

Cathy had wanted to help people. She had wanted to go into medicine, or teaching. She had wanted to work with children; Turquoise remembered that. She had cared about everything.

And everything had been able to hurt her.

*Some people use things—people, objects. They destroy. You're a creator, a builder, a healer, not a user.* That line came to her mind time and again, no matter how wrong it now was.

Now she was a killer, a mercenary. And that was all.

# CHAPTER 18

NATHANIEL WAS WAITING in her living room when she got home. Lounging on the couch in jeans, a T-shirt, and a denim jacket, he looked casual and chic at the same time. Moreover, he looked comfortable, as if brightly lit suburban homes were a natural part of his life.

He rose to his feet like a cat, in one smooth movement, to greet them. "Eric, it's good to see you safe. Milady Turquoise, you look like he's been tugging your chain."

"A bit." Turquoise worked to wipe the frown from her brow.

Eric looked between the two of them, and then announced, "I'm going to put stuff away."

"I can help—"

He shook off her offer. "No problem."

"That boy is about a hundred years old," Turquoise sighed.

"Too much time around vampires," Nathaniel agreed.

"He's not worse off than you are, though." In response to her wary expression, he added, "I've no plan to chastise you. Your life is your own."

Not wanting to dwell, Turquoise broke right into her questions. "Did I get set up for a suicide mission?"

Nathaniel sat back down. "If you were after Jeshickah, yes. There are vampires thousands of years older than she is that would love to destroy her, but know better than to put the knife in place themselves."

"Why? She isn't so strong," Turquoise asserted. "A knife in her heart would kill her. Who's protecting her that can make other vampires wary?"

"Jeshickah's sister is one of Siete's fledglings." Seeing Turquoise's confusion, he elaborated, "Siete is the creature that created our kind. He's ancient; people say he's truly immortal. If you killed Jeshickah, her sister would demand your death, and Siete isn't a creature you could fight." He shook his head. "When you asked to get into Midnight, I'd thought you were after Jaguar. If I had known who your target was, I would have stopped you."

"Why?" she pressed. "I've never known you to watch out for anyone else, not unless you were paid for it. Why now?"

"This might surprise you," Nathaniel retorted, and Turquoise realized suddenly that she had insulted him, "but I was human for twenty years before I was changed, and unlike some of Jeshickah's fledglings, I actually had a soul. I consider you a friend, Turquoise. Is it so shocking that I wouldn't want you to die?"

No words came to Turquoise's lips. Completely taken aback by his revelation, she could only shake her head.

"I was one of her early experiments," Nathaniel explained. "Her third fledgling. She intended for me to be a trainer; I was the first person to refuse her and survive." His gaze flickered to the kitchen, where Eric was busy ignoring them, and then returned to Turquoise. "After me, she started looking for those who already showed the tendencies she wanted. Gabriel was her favorite, but she was too fond of him; she never managed to own him, not the way she did the others.

"The others, of course, included Jaguar."

A moment of silence passed before Turquoise ventured, "But why, however many years later, did you save me from Daryl? You're not evil, but you say it yourself—you're no white knight."

"I don't know." He shook his head. "Daryl wanted to get rid of you anyway, so it was no skin off my back. And maybe because you reminded me of myself."

"Of you?" The words came out a startled yelp.

"When I was a human," he clarified, "in Jeshickah's Midnight."

Turquoise stood, too frustrated to stay still. "You were another one of her . . . pets?"

"Never," he quickly replied. "She tried. She lost her temper before she broke me, and she hurt me too badly for me to survive as a human. She preferred to change me rather than admit defeat, and by the time she realized she couldn't control me, I was too influential in her empire for her to destroy me." He continued before Turquoise could respond. "It sounds like Jaguar has experienced the same sense of familiarity with you," Nathaniel added.

"You, I could believe," Turquoise retorted. "But I've

heard enough about Jaguar's life to know we have nothing in common. Cathy had a perfect life before Daryl took her." She could hear the bitterness in her voice. She had spent eighteen years as a blissful innocent before being thrown abruptly into pain. She had barely survived the break.

Would she rather have had Jaguar's life? She had lost everything to Daryl, but at least she had good memories, faded as they were.

Nathaniel shook his head. "Jaguar's trying to break away from Jeshickah. He won't be able to do that until she's dead, and even then I doubt he'll ever fully manage it. You're trying to break away from Daryl—"

"I *have,*" Turquoise corrected.

Nathaniel just nodded, and tactfully changed the subject. "What's your plan now?"

"I don't have one," she answered honestly.

"Are you going back to Bruja?"

"Of course. I've got Challenge to fight," she responded immediately, though the moment she said the words she wondered about them. Eric's questions about Cathy's dreams fluttered around in her brain, brushing uncomfortably against her thoughts.

Nathaniel had introduced her to Bruja. She had entered the guild as a chance to get strong, and to learn to defend herself. She had not intended for it to be her whole life, but hunting had consumed her. What else was she supposed to do? Sitting in classrooms didn't strike her as something she could survive. Chatting with Greg had given her a good idea of how distant her life was now from the one she had once planned.

Nathaniel sensed her uneasiness, and turned the

conversation from personal to general. "They say one of the original founders of Bruja was a vampire."

"It wouldn't surprise me," Turquoise answered. "The guilds aren't known for their humanity. Is the vampire still . . . alive?" It seemed strange, asking if a vampire was alive, but English didn't have a better word.

"She's alive," Nathaniel answered. His voice was light, almost humorous. "But she refuses to answer whether the rumor is true. She alternates between living as a reclusive artist, and cutting an unmerciful, bloody swath through human society. Everyone needs balance, I suppose."

Turquoise chuckled, imagining the contrast.

Nathaniel's expression clouded; he reached into his jacket pocket for something. "Jaguar suspected you would be in contact with me. He wanted me to give you this." Reluctantly, he handed over a sealed letter.

"Have you read it?" Just because the letter was sealed didn't mean Nathaniel hadn't opened it.

"Jaguar paid me well," Nathaniel replied. "He's worked with enough mercenaries to mention I wasn't allowed to read it." If Jaguar hadn't specifically included that clause, Nathaniel would have broken the seal without hesitation. A major part of his business was information.

On the flip side, if Nathaniel took money for his client's confidentiality, he would never violate it.

As Turquoise slit the envelope, Nathaniel added, "He's trying to respect your wish for privacy, but if you really don't want him to know where you are, you have to get rid of the boy." Turquoise's gaze lifted in an involuntary glare, in response to which Nathaniel flashed a harmless smile. She had agreed to take care of Eric; she wouldn't ditch him. "I had a feeling you wouldn't go for it. But the kid belongs to Jaguar. Any trainer can track his slaves, no matter where they go."

She absorbed the information as she read the short note Jaguar had written, which invited her to meet him at a place of her choosing, at a time of her choosing. She could send an answer via Nathaniel.

What did she have to lose? She wanted to know what was happening with Jeshickah, and when Eric could safely return to the place he considered his home.

Honestly, she admitted to herself that she also missed Jaguar. He had been a rare curiosity, a splash of warmth and sincerity after two years in the cold darkness of a hunter's life. Even embroiled in all the power struggles and chaos of his world, Jaguar had a kind of wistful innocence that Turquoise could not help but envy.

Besides, a little companionship would be nice. Greg was sweet, and she was sure he would be willing to fill the empty hours she had on her hands, but it was hard to imagine a close friendship with him. He didn't know, couldn't know, what her life was like. How close could she get to someone who didn't even know the monsters existed, after she had fought them tooth and nail for her very sanity?

She invited Jaguar to meet her in a café in the town center.

"I've told you before, you're mad," Nathaniel informed her, as he took the message. "But it's never seemed to change your mind."

# CHAPTER 19

JAGUAR SHOWED UP exactly on time. Turquoise blinked at her first glimpse of him in the doorway, trying to assure herself it was really the vampire she knew.

Jaguar would attract eyes everywhere he went; he would never be able to blend into a small town. But he was trying.

His hair had been brushed back from his face and tied, so from the front it appeared short. He was wearing jeans; that alone was weird. They were black, faded a bit at the knees, but seeing Jaguar in denim was a shock. He was also wearing a very simple dark green T-shirt. Turquoise had grown so used to seeing bare caramel skin that he looked odd fully dressed.

He could pass for human. When he tried, he could look almost normal. If they had been in any city, no one would have looked twice at him.

"You're looking . . . bland." The words were out of her mouth before she could consider them.

Jaguar laughed, sliding into the seat opposite her. "I

could veil the mind of every human in here so they wouldn't notice me, but it requires more concentration than I feel like expending."

"You're getting stares, anyway," Turquoise pointed out, nodding toward a teenage girl a few tables away.

Jaguar glanced at the girl, who suddenly turned back to her food as if she had forgotten Jaguar was present. The brief display of power was unnerving.

"Man of many talents," Turquoise murmured.

"And I'll admit to at least half of them," he quipped.

Since she knew Nathaniel's words would eat at her thoughts until she had the answer, she ventured, "Nathaniel said something about your being able to track Eric if you wanted to. That another of your talents?" At Jaguar's nod, she asked, "How?"

"Eric's mine," he answered, as if that explained it. Turquoise's confusion must have showed, because he elaborated, "The connection's not as strong as a blood bond, but I recognize his mind, and I can find it if I look. I don't work as a trainer anymore, so I don't usually take advantage of the bond, but it's still a habit to make the connection with any mind not strong enough to lock me out."

Turquoise remembered with distinct disquiet the times when Jaguar's mind had brushed hers. "Does that include me?"

"You put up walls that keep everyone out," Jaguar answered. The lack of a yes or a no made Turquoise uneasy. "You've dropped them around me before. I try not to take advantage of people who trust me—they're rare enough as it is."

Trust was an almost obscene word inside the mercenary world; it meant you were always susceptible to betrayal. Turquoise was struck with the desire to argue with Jaguar as soon as he spoke the word, but he was right. She *did* trust him, to the point where she had not even flinched for a knife when she had seen him. She had taken him at his word that he meant her no harm in this visit.

Jaguar changed the subject. "You might like to know Jeshickah will be out of the way very soon. There's a Triste by the name of Jesse who seems to think he has enough allies of his own to risk offending hers, and is willing to deal with her for a highly exorbitant price." Tristes had the strengths of vampires and witches combined, as well as blood that was deadly to any vampire that tried to feed on them. It made them the perfect vampire hunters.

"How long will this take?" Turquoise asked. Vampires often judged time differently than humans did.

"A few weeks, maybe a month," Jaguar answered.

"I assume then Eric will be able to go back safely?"

"He may be a kid, but he did a lot of work there; it's chaos without him," Jaguar admitted. "You'll be welcome back once she's gone, too," he ventured. "Not as a slave. Just a guest. Or, if you ever get bored with Bruja, the town of Pyrige has plenty of spaces for people willing to work."

"I'll consider it." She shrugged. "What's happening with Ravyn?"

"She's living it up, enjoying abusing Gabriel's power. It's more likely she'll enslave him than the other way around." He smiled wryly. "Gabriel has a fondness for women who are willing to kill him; it's a dangerous habit of his."

"And yours," Turquoise observed.

Jaguar paused for a reflective moment. "I like to think you would at least hesitate before trying to kill me. If I'm wrong, kindly don't correct me. I enjoy my illusions," he added, attempting to lighten the mood. "Ravyn said something about hoping you still plan to show up for Challenge?" His tone made the words a question.

"Ravyn and I are rivals. Challenge will determine who gets to lead Crimson. If I don't show, Ravyn gets the title." She was about to add, *"If I do show, she'll beat me, then get the title,"* when she remembered who she was talking to. "Would you like to help me practice?"

"What's the weapon?"

"Whip."

He looked intrigued. "You know how to use one?"

"Just barely."

Jaguar shrugged. "There's not much time, but I'll teach what I can. Maybe you'll turn out to have a knack for it."

"Or maybe I'll take out my own eye," Turquoise retorted. In a way, she hoped she would lose miserably, and have an excuse to quit Bruja. Recent events had given her too much doubt.

As always, Jaguar was painfully astute. "Do you want to win?"

"Yes." After a moment, she changed her answer to, "I don't want to lose to Ravyn. I'm just not sure I want the title."

Jaguar nodded. "There's something that might help you make your choice," he informed her. "Ravyn's worried you'll chicken out of Challenge, so she made a deal with Gabriel. He bought you from Jeshickah; if you win at Challenge, he'll make you legally free-blood."

Turquoise frowned. "I'm free now. I don't care about the legalities."

"Maybe not," Jaguar acknowledged, "but if you want to work in our world you will." He continued, "Shape-shifters and witches are born free. Only their own kind can sell them to Midnight. Humans don't have that protection; any vampire can pick them up and claim them, just like Daryl did with you."

"And if I take this title Gabriel is offering?"

"Freeblood means you'll be treated like one of us. It doesn't mean no one's allowed to kill you, but it does mean none of us can claim you. It means the next time you work with our mercenaries, you don't have to worry about having someone like Daryl pay them to turn you over instead of helping you. And it means that you can walk into Midnight and even Jeshickah wouldn't be able to break you."

"And if I kill Daryl?"

"I'm not going to stop you," Jaguar answered. "Neither will Gabriel. Jeshickah might cause some trouble, but she isn't fond of him either, and she'll be out of the picture soon anyway."

"And then . . . what if I said that I wanted to give up Bruja?"

Jaguar appeared skeptical. "You can't go back to what you were before Daryl. You're still human by blood, but in your mind and in your soul you're no more human than most of the vampires I know."

Turquoise responded flippantly, "Maybe I can't go back. But what's the other choice? Ask you to open a vein so we fix that little problem of blood?"

She had not considered the words, but once spoken they did not surprise her. If she wouldn't stay in the twilight, and she couldn't go back to Cathy's daylight world, then of course, vampire blood would be the only choice.

Voice cool and level, Jaguar answered, "It's a viable choice, but not from me. Find someone who's freeblood if that's what you want—your mercenary friend Nathaniel, for example. He didn't hesitate to burn Midnight the first time, or to sell two hunters into it. I'm sure he wouldn't have any scruples about giving one of Bruja's best immortality. And get rid of Daryl first. He might have no legal claim over you, but you don't want him arguing ownership for the next millennium."

Turquoise had hunted vampires for two years. The idea of becoming one of them should have been sickening.

*Should have been.* She found herself contemplating it for a moment.

"I don't know," she said. She seemed to be saying that a lot lately.

"Go to Challenge," Jaguar recommended. "Win. Then decide. If you decide to become one of us, you'll be strong. If you don't, you'll still be able to survive."

Turquoise nodded, taking the advice. Face Challenge now; save the future for tomorrow.

Jaguar frowned, looking past her, then spoke quietly. "I think this one is looking for you."

Turquoise turned, following Jaguar's gaze, and ended up looking at Greg.

The human's gaze was resting on Jaguar with what wasn't exactly anger, but wasn't warm fuzzy friendship, either. He looked away from the vampire to greet Turquoise, but his proverbial hackles were up.

"Cathy, hey." He glanced at Jaguar again, and seemed to decide to be polite. "I noticed you and figured I'd swing inside for a moment. Am I interrupting?"

Flustered, Turquoise looked between the two, caught briefly in a hazy shadow. Greg and Jaguar didn't belong in the same world.

Jaguar covered for her, standing and offering his hand. "I'm Kyle Lostry, one of Cathy's friends." Having Jaguar use her childhood nickname struck her in a most unpleasant way.

Greg banked his hostility, and accepted Jaguar's gesture of civilized greeting like someone who had never been lied to or manipulated, someone who expected sincerity. "Greg Martin. I knew Cathy in school," he offered, looking to Turquoise, "but we've been out of touch for a while." He backed off, aware enough to sense awkwardness. "I've got to get going; I'm on my way to a job interview." He looked at Turquoise, and the expression on his face was honest, unschooled. "Give me a call?"

"I will."

Watching his back as he left, she knew she would. To forestall Jaguar's questions, she asked, "Who's Kyle Lostry?"

Jaguar looked startled, as if he had not thought about the name when he had used it. "Someone I knew once—and wish I'd had a chance to know better."

She sensed that there was a story behind the words. "Is he . . ." She broke off, not wanting to ask whether this phantom was alive or dead.

Jaguar volunteered no more. "Is your Greg why you're thinking of leaving Bruja?" he asked. Turquoise couldn't tell from his tone or expression what he thought of Greg, or the idea.

She shook her head. "I ran into him yesterday. He somehow managed to remind me of all the things I left behind, after Daryl. . . ." She trailed off. "I don't know whether I could still follow any of those dreams, or whether I would still want to, but it hurts to know I threw them away."

Jaguar was still watching Greg, who had paused on the sidewalk to talk to someone else. "He's too innocent for you. His life is too innocent for you."

"I know."

Jaguar shook his head. "I've never known anyone who joined our world and then managed to go back to the human one." Turquoise could see in him the same longing she had once seen as he watched Shayla, and could tell he had tried. "You could thrive in my world; darkness suits you. But if you want it, Greg's world— the world his Cathy came from—might still be worth fighting for."

# CHAPTER 20

DURING THE NEXT MONTH, Turquoise's days and evenings became an interesting study in contrasts.

Her mornings were usually domestic. She or Eric would make breakfast and eat together. A couple of times Greg joined them. Turquoise tried valiantly to bridge the gap to the human's world. He thought she was a freelancer for a small newspaper, a lie that seemed to work well enough. He also thought she was dating Jaguar, a.k.a. Kyle Lostry. The lies were imperfect, but at least it kept him from getting the wrong impression. She could handle having Cathy's old boyfriend as a friend, but she quickly realized that they would never be as close as they once were. There was too much of her life she could never share with him. The mischief they had planned together and the dates they had gone on were still bright spots of humor and happiness in his mind, whereas Turquoise remembered them as if they were faded black and white photos. Someone else's memories, from someone else's life.

In the afternoons, Jaguar came over, and they practiced until midnight every night. During their breaks, Jaguar would fill her in on what was going on in Midnight, and in his town. The owner of the town's only inn had decided to elope with a young woman he had met on vacation, and the building, one of the few remaining properties Jaguar had not owned, had gone up for sale; now he was just looking for someone to manage it. He was less than subtle in suggesting that Turquoise could have the position, if she wanted it. She dodged him and they went back to practice.

The owner of the local community recreation center wanted to start a course in self-defense for teenagers, and was looking for an assistant. The job sounded more up Turquoise's alley, but she still shook her head. Challenge first. Then she planned to kill Daryl. Then she would see to the future.

Over the weeks of practice, Turquoise's own whip had given her almost as many bruises as Daryl ever had, before she had gotten the knack of it and learned not to hit herself. She was lucky Jaguar had amazing reflexes, or she probably would have taken out her own eye more than once.

She and Jaguar dueled occasionally. She used every move, piece of furniture, and dirty trick she could think of, and he kept most of his talent in check to avoid giving her more welts than she cared to receive.

At first she was hesitant to really fight, but Jaguar had offered no mercy until he was sure she was using her full force. He would heal from any wound she managed to give him, but if she got used to trying not to hurt her opponent, the habit would cripple her in a confrontation.

That was not to say Jaguar ever allowed her to hit him. Mostly he managed to evade her blows, recognizing from her form which direction the weapon would move and where it would land. Occasionally he used his own whip to catch hers, snagging the weapon out of her hand until she learned not to relinquish her hold on it.

Two quick snaps from Jaguar, and Turquoise found an X cut neatly into the stomach of her shirt.

"Careless," Jaguar chastised. She had tried an overhand snap, which left her mid and lower body unprotected, while Jaguar was in a position to attack the vulnerable area. "Do you need a break? It's late."

Turquoise took the opportunity, and faked a setup for a low crack. Jaguar moved to avoid the blow, and she brought the movement around a full circle to strike high. It had taken her days to get over her desire to wince at doing so, but she checked none of her ability; the blow landed home, and cut open Jaguar's skin.

He ignored the injury, which healed too quickly to even bleed, and soon they were again engaged in a no-mercy duel.

It was well past midnight when they finally took a break, and collapsed onto the dew-dampened grass.

Turquoise's gaze alit on the nearly full moon. Another few days, and she would have her chance to beat Ravyn in the Challenge rematch for leader of Crimson—and she *could* beat the other hunter. She had been practicing with an expert, and had no doubts as to her skills.

She just didn't know if she wanted to.

She was getting used to companionship. Eric's company was always entertaining. She enjoyed having him there for her noontime breakfast, and chatting with him during the day. He liked cooking, and she well-appreciated having dinner made for her; cleaning up afterward was a small price to pay. While domestic chores such as shopping and laundry were dreadfully dull, she was getting into the habit of seeing people.

And as annoying as it could sometimes get to discuss college, work, the news, and whatever else was on the all-too-human young man's mind, she was even getting used to Greg. His conversations were about normal, innocent life; it was so exotic to her that she could listen to what would otherwise have been dull chatter for hours.

But she couldn't juggle the two lives forever. As fond as she was becoming of her suburban life, she could not ignore what she knew. A human life would never completely suit her, because most humans would deem her mad if she tried to confide even the smallest hint of her past. And, "Yes, I work nights as a vampire hunter," usually wasn't a good line to make new friends with.

Maybe Cathy wasn't dead, but she had grown. Turquoise couldn't fit into that old life. Besides, as fond as she was of having companions, sitting around in suburbs was making her gray matter go stagnant. She needed challenge; a break was nice now and then, but boredom was not a state she would tolerate for long.

*Save tomorrow for tomorrow. Deal with now first.*

# CHAPTER 21

THE BRUJA HALL was not imposing from the outside. Anyone looking at its exterior would see nothing more important than a redbrick house with black trim and white shutters that were always latched.

A phrase was written in Latin beside the door. Translated, it meant, "Enter the den of the hunters."

The door was unlocked, and Turquoise opened it, stepping forward into the main room of the Bruja hall with Ravyn and, strangely enough, Gabriel at her back. He confirmed Jaguar's message about the deal Ravyn had made: legal freeblood status to the hunter who won today.

The floor was black marble, with Bruja's motto carved into it. The light was too dim for Turquoise to read it, but she knew the words by heart: *In this world, there are predators and there are prey; only the former survive.*

Turquoise entered the hall knowing she didn't want to lead these hunters.

However, she knew from experience that when a

vampire involved in the trade made a deal, his word was as good as law. When Turquoise won against Ravyn today, the burgundy hunter's blood would buy her opponent's freedom. Then Turquoise could kill Daryl without worrying about whether Jaguar had gotten rid of Jeshickah yet. Then she could get on with her life.

As soon as they entered, Sarta approached. "Ravyn, Turquoise? Are you ready?"

Ravyn walked toward Turquoise, a graceful predator's walk. She snapped her whip, and it cracked little more than an inch from Turquoise's skin, then wrapped around the hunter's throat harmlessly. "I'm ready when she is."

Turquoise shook Ravyn's whip from her neck and lashed out, catching the handle of the other hunter's weapon. One quick tug before Ravyn could react, and Turquoise caught Ravyn's whip as it jerked from the woman's grip.

Sounding amused, Sarta simply said, "The fight is to third blood. Ravyn Aniketos and Turquoise Draka, you may begin."

Turquoise tossed the whip back to Ravyn, who accepted it with a glare, and the duel began.

Ravyn lazily snapped her whip in Turquoise's direction, though Turquoise had already put herself out of reach. She was testing her opponent's reflexes.

The opponents circled each other on the cold Bruja floor, watching each other for weaknesses.

"You're not going to win," Ravyn said.

Meanwhile, Turquoise watched Ravyn's arm carefully, waiting for telltale signs that the hunter was about to move. The muscles tensed.

Turquoise saw the movement before Ravyn actually attacked with the whip, and raised her own. The two leather braids twined around each other. Ravyn pulled hers away with a practiced flourish, and then attacked low.

The material of Turquoise's pant slit, but the blow wasn't hard enough to draw blood.

"Are you playing with me, Ravyn?" she asked. Turquoise flicked her own whip, which cut open the stomach of Ravyn's shirt, and Ravyn jumped back a pace. The wound did not bleed, but she could have made it do so if she had wanted. Turquoise saw the unease that slid behind Ravyn's eyes as she realized her opponent had more skill than she had suspected.

Ravyn masked the emotion. "And here I thought you had no taste for fun," she teased. This time when her whip cracked, it fell where Turquoise's left cheek should have been. Turquoise ducked out of the way, cracking her own whip as she moved.

"You little brat!" Ravyn's free hand went to the new cut on her weapon arm.

"First blood, Ravyn," Turquoise said calmly, hyperfocused.

Ravyn's whip came down hard, too fast for Turquoise to get out of the way, and landed on Turquoise's left shoulder at the hardest part of the snap. The skin split.

"First blood, Turquoise," Ravyn said sweetly. "I saw Daryl a day ago," she commented. "He gave me some pointers."

Turquoise let the barb bounce off her ears. Ravyn's whip cracked again. Turquoise moved slightly, and her opponent's whip wrapped tightly around the handle of her own. Yanking, Turquoise pulled the other hunter off balance. Before even bothering to untangle the two weapons, she flicked her own, and it cut open the back of Ravyn's left shoulder. Second blood.

Ravyn rotated the shoulder that had just been hit, and pulled her weapon away as she again moved back to gain distance.

"A little more practice, Turquoise, and you could be quite good at this," she encouraged. Ravyn liked the sound of her own voice, apparently. Turquoise personally preferred a silent fight, but many hunters liked to talk; it helped them focus, and their opponents were more likely to be distracted by engaging in dialogue.

Turquoise refused to banter, and attacked again.

Her strike fell short, but she managed to evade Ravyn's next one. There was blood running down her back from the wound on her shoulder. It wouldn't be fatal, but Turquoise was annoyed to realize that she would have yet another scar.

Ravyn sidestepped Turquoise's next attack. Her whip hit Turquoise's right wrist and snapped around it, a mirror to the blow that Lord Daryl had given her years ago.

She hissed in pain, but forced herself to keep hold of the whip. Her wrist was bleeding heavily. This fight would be over soon.

They were both at second blood. Whoever hit next would be the winner.

Ravyn attacked again, and Turquoise collapsed to the ground to dodge. Then, before the other hunter could react, Turquoise snapped her whip around Ravyn's ankle and yanked as hard as she could.

Ravyn lost her balance and fell to the floor hard on her back. Before she could recover, Turquoise struck with the whip one more time, drawing a fine band of blood from Ravyn's left cheek.

"Third blood," Turquoise announced, rising to her feet. The movement was more painful than she would have expected.

Ravyn silently raised a hand to the mark on her cheek. "If this scars, I am going to be *really* angry," she snapped as she pulled herself off the floor. "Cheap trick, Turquoise."

"It worked."

Sarta had come to Turquoise's side, and started to wrap a bandage around her wrist wound to stop its bleeding.

"Congratulations, Turquoise," she began, but Turquoise shook her off, and wrapped the bandage by herself.

"I hope Daryl snaps your neck," Ravyn growled.

With a chuckle, Gabriel wrapped an arm around his burgundy-haired friend's waist, pulling her away before she could attack her bleeding adversary. The vampire turned Ravyn toward himself, and licked the blood from her cheek.

Ravyn shoved him away.

Gabriel laughed again. He caught the hunter's wrist, and again drew her toward himself. He licked the blood from her arm, and Turquoise saw Sarta shake her head in disgust. To Turquoise, Gabriel said simply, "You're freeblood, Turquoise. Go put a knife in Daryl for me."

Ravyn leveled her garnet eyes in Turquoise's direction.

Turquoise tossed the whip down at the burgundy hunter's feet. "Take the title, Ravyn. I don't want it." She saw the shock on Ravyn's face, but did not bother to stay and explain her decision.

She didn't want to be leader of Crimson.

She ducked Ravyn's punch, and ignored the ungrateful threat, then walked out of the Bruja hall for perhaps the last time.

# CHAPTER 22

THE BUS RIDE HOME—to Nathaniel's house, Turquoise hastily amended—was painfully long, and stifling. She wished she had driven, but had not wanted to risk needing to drive home injured. With a light jacket on over the black tank top she had worn to Challenge, Turquoise could feel sweat dripping down her spine. The wound on her shoulder ached as the salt found its way beneath the bandages.

She gave in, and took her jacket off, trying fiercely to ignore the looks people gave her. Maybe it was the wildly tousled hair, or the adrenaline-induced flush to her cheeks that made them stare. Or maybe it was the fact that the bandage on her wrist was highly visible.

She decided she didn't care. None of these people knew her, or wanted to know her. They weren't concerned enough to question a stranger.

*Now what?* she wondered. She was through with Bruja. She would need to kill Daryl eventually. His pride wouldn't allow him to ignore her forever, and even if she had been willing to hide from him—which she wasn't—he worked with mercenaries even more than she did, and would be able to track her down eventually.

*What else?* Eric's words echoed in her mind.

She needed action, movement, adrenaline. A tame white-picket-fence life would never suit her; it would bore her to death. She also didn't want to ditch Jaguar and Eric now. With Jeshickah out of the way, Midnight might even prove interesting for a while.

For a while. But forever? For as long as a vampire could live? She didn't know.

The bus stop was about a mile from Nathaniel's house, in the center of town. Turquoise would have to walk home, but the day was beautiful and she had plenty of energy.

Hearing her stomach rumble, she took a detour into a gas station convenience store. She slipped her hand into her pants pocket, double-checking to make sure she had enough cash on her for some donuts and a soda. The thought amused her. She had eaten the same fare on her way to Midnight.

"Are you okay?" The old man at the register asked, a worried frown on his face as Turquoise approached to buy her snack.

Turquoise could not conceal her surprise. She had forgotten to put her jacket back on and her battered body was visible. As long as she had been in Bruja, she had stuck to anonymous cities. No one asked questions. But this town was so small and she had chatted with this man on a couple of occasions in the last month. He would know that something was wrong, and feel comfortable enough to ask.

"Yeah . . . had a fall." As a lie, it was awful.

An awkward moment ensued. The old man's eyes were questioning.

"I'm a little accident prone," she lied, trying to make the words sound realistic when they made almost no sense. She added, "I fell off a table when I was little, into a window." She tried to add a smile and a bit of a "no big deal" laugh as she said it, but the memory was too raw. Vividly she remembered catching her father's arm as Daryl shoved him back through the window. Daryl had grabbed her and tossed her onto a table, where broken glass had sliced open her arms and the backs of her shoulders.

The old man looked unconvinced. He patted her hand sympathetically as she handed him the money for her purchases. He handed her change, with a "Have a good day" goodbye.

She left quickly. Where was her jacket? She swore as she realized she must have left it on the bus.

She swore again when she recognized Greg a block down the street, walking toward her. She considered ducking back into the convenience store, but didn't want to face the old man's silent questions.

Too late anyway. Greg saw her, and waved hello, then sped up his pace to meet her.

"Cathy, hi. I . . ." He broke off, his light jog turning to a sprint as he hurried to her side. "What happened to you? Are you okay?" Then he seemed to notice that most of the scars were years old, and his eyes widened more. "What the hell? I mean, I'm sorry, but . . . what the hell?"

Turquoise's nerve ran out. She had known living here wasn't going to work from the start. She didn't have the patience to deal with him now.

"Greg, I'm a mercenary," she said coolly. "Mostly, I hunt vampires for a living. I've been debating quitting my job and teaching middle school, but I hear it's a little rough there." The words dripped with bitter sarcasm.

She knew what his reaction would be—disbelief, fear—and didn't want to see it. She pushed past him, walking quickly in the direction of her house.

Greg hurried after her, and caught her shoulder. She winced, pulling away as his touch hit the new injury.

Unsurprisingly, he was looking at her as if she had sprouted a second—no, third—head, but he *was* trying to keep up with her.

"You mean vampires like . . . um, some criminal person, right?" he said hesitantly, trying to figure out her speech. "You're a cop or something?"

He was so damn innocent. How could she ever hope to convince him?

She didn't need to. He deserved his innocence.

She backtracked, slowing her pace a bit so he could keep up. "I'm sorry. It's been a rough day," she said, stalling as she tried to add to what he already tentatively believed. If she tried, she could convince him of the reality of vampires. She could tell him what had really happened to Cathy and the rest of her family. But Greg didn't need to know. He was happy. "You know I was interested in psych, right? I got into criminal psychology in college, and I do some work with some people." She made the lies intentionally vague, as if she wasn't supposed to tell. Actually, she had no idea who she would possibly be working for; she knew nothing about the government or law enforcement. But Greg probably knew less than she did.

Greg said something noncommittal along the lines of "Uh-huh." He kept walking with her, not talking for a bit, as if digesting what he had heard.

Humans had an instinctive desire to remain at the top of the food chain. Unless forced to see reality, most of them would believe almost anything before believing that vampires and other such creatures existed.

"So. You're with the government or something?"

Crimson was about the antithesis of the United States government, but Turquoise answered, "Yeah." She added, "I'm not really supposed to talk about it." That was vague enough. It would tickle his imagination, without straining against what he believed.

Greg walked her home. They didn't talk much, though occasionally Greg made some attempt to start a new conversation. Turquoise wasn't much in the mood to chat.

"Smells like someone's having a bonfire," he commented, blinking at the faint smell of smoke. "Speaking of, some friends of mine are having a picnic next weekend. Would you like to go maybe?"

He sounded so hopeful, she had to smile. She started to say no, but then changed her mind. "Sure. Why not?"

His expression lit up.

Before he could speak, the fire truck rumbled by. They both looked after it anxiously.

"I hope everything's okay," Greg said worriedly.

Turquoise picked up her pace. The smell of smoke was thicker now. A coil of fear was making its way from her stomach to her throat to choke her.

A few houses down, she began to see the flames. She sprinted, until a fireman caught her arm, pulling her back.

"Ma'am, this area isn't safe for bystanders—"

"I live here," she spat, shoving away from him. "What . . ." She broke off. *Eric? Where was Eric?* She frantically scanned the area for the boy. "My brother was here when I left. He's fourteen. Have you seen him?"

The man hesitated. "Please wait here, ma'am."

If he was hurt . . . if one hair on his head had been singed . . .

Greg caught up to her, panting and coughing around the smoke. "What caused it?" he asked instantly. "Do they know?"

"I don't even own a toaster," Turquoise growled back. Faulty wiring was impossible. Nathaniel wouldn't have had a house that had been poorly made. The stove and oven were new, and Eric was too experienced a cook to ever mistakenly leave one on unattended. If this wasn't arson, she'd eat the cinders.

A police officer returned from the jumble of people, leading an ash-streaked Eric. The boy broke from his escort and hurried toward Turquoise.

She couldn't help herself. She pulled the boy against herself, so grateful for his safety that she didn't care about the house. Nathaniel could deal with losing a house. Turquoise could pay for a house. There was nothing in there she could not replace.

"Are you the owner?" the officer asked.

Turquoise nodded, not really paying much attention. Instead, she spoke quietly to Eric. "What caused it?"

Eric grimaced. "Your favorite vampire," he answered, under his breath so no one other than Turquoise could hear him. Greg must have picked up a word or so. The boy took a few steps back, looking awkward.

"Ms. Emerette?" Turquoise looked at the officer dumbly before remembering that the name on her license was something Emerette. Margot, maybe? She couldn't remember. She was glad Greg was still dealing with his new belief that she worked for the government, or else he might have tried to correct it.

"Yes?"

"Would you mind coming down to the station to answer a few questions?" he asked.

"Right now?" Right now, she would rather go kill something than talk politely with these friendly officers. Specifically, she wanted to deal Daryl a long, painful death for destroying Cathy's life, for making it impossible for her to pick up where she had left off with Greg, and most of all for frightening her.

Greg came to her rescue. "She doesn't need to talk now." He spoke like he knew what he was doing. "We'll come down after she and the kid are cleaned up, okay?"

The officer seemed to hesitate. Turquoise offered a watery smile. "Please," she added to Greg's words.

The man nodded finally. "I suppose there's no hurry.

I know this is going to be a difficult time. Do you have a place to stay?"

"Yes, she does," Greg answered for her.

They walked back to Greg's car, which he had left near where he had met up with Turquoise.

"My sister's visiting, and she probably has some clothes that will fit you," Greg offered to Turquoise. "You two can come over and clean up, then figure out whether you want to talk to the police or what."

Turquoise shook her head. "I can't."

Greg didn't seem to know how to handle that one, so Turquoise didn't make him respond.

"There's something I need to deal with first," she explained. Taking Greg up on his offer would put him in danger, at least until Daryl was dead.

"How are you going to get there?" Eric asked practically, knowing that she would go to Midnight.

That was the most difficult part of her plan.

Greg was a lifesaver. He chewed his lip for a moment, and then asked, "Do you need to borrow my car?"

*There is a God.* She gave him a hug. "I'll be back in less than a day." She was still armed from Challenge, and she could pick up a few more weapons from her Bruja house before getting to Midnight. It was almost on the way.

"Sure," Greg answered nonchalantly. "Just be careful with her, okay?"

It was hilariously easy for Turquoise to get inside Midnight. The raven guards at the gate did not challenge her; they were too shocked that a human was willing to fight to get *into* Midnight. Her fury was visible in every movement she made, and no one approached her until she was almost to Daryl's door.

"You no longer annoy me." The voice behind her caused Turquoise to turn, a knife instantly in her hand. She hesitated upon seeing Jeshickah, willing to wait for the vampiress to either push a fight or back off.

"Always nice to gain a new friend," the hunter retorted.

"I wouldn't go that far." Jeshickah's voice was dry.

Belatedly, Turquoise informed the vampire, "Gabriel made me freeblood."

Jeshickah nodded. "I'm aware of that. His foolishness is why I am speaking to you, instead of chaining you down so I can break every one of your bones before removing your skin and making it into a nice pair of pants." Jeshickah's expression of polite amusement never left her face as she spoke.

"Pleasant image," Turquoise answered. Impatience was gnawing at her, but she was smart enough to avoid antagonizing Jeshickah by ignoring her.

"I have determined my reasons for detesting you," Jeshickah stated. "You are too like my own pets. The traits are attractive in a man I own. They are less so in a human girl."

Turquoise thought with unease back to Jaguar's words. *Jeshickah picks her trainers for physical beauty, mental acuity, moral void, and what she calls a trainer instinct — the instinct to watch a person, determine her weaknesses, and destroy her.* Surely she didn't fit that description.

"I'm not one of your pets," she argued.

"You're willing to sell yourself, your principles, for

power, strength. You'll lie, manipulate, or kill for money. And may I say you are very good at it; you have my Jaguar eating out of your hand." There was bitterness in the statement. Or jealousy? Was Jeshickah jealous?

"Do you have a point?" Turquoise spoke to keep from laughing. She didn't think Jeshickah would appreciate amusement.

"Go ahead and kill Daryl if you wish," Jeshickah purred. "He's too stupid to live anyway. But then go home. Get a job, breed, do any of the tedious things humans do. Get old and gray, and stay that way. If you take vampire blood from any of my brood—either Nathaniel or Jaguar would give it to you, at your request—know that I will control you."

That sounded unpleasant.

The conversation skidded to a halt as Jaguar stepped into the hall. His step faltered as he noticed Turquoise and Jeshickah, and when he approached, he did so cautiously.

He addressed the vampiress first. "Your Triste is requesting a meeting with you."

"That creature is no end of trouble," Jeshickah grumbled.

Jaguar shrugged. "You hired him."

"There seems to be a shortage of gray matter this century." To Turquoise, she offered, "Enjoy your sortie, girl. Don't make too much of a mess."

"How long until she dies?" Turquoise growled, as soon as the vampiress was out of the hall.

Jaguar smiled; the expression looked too wary to be hopeful. "Not long, if Jesse does his job. Jeshickah hired him for his kind's talents at restraining vampires. It's something he is very good at." The smile was gone as he asked, "You're after Daryl?"

She absently checked one of her knives. "I've waited too long already."

"You know that if you get yourself killed, I'm going to hate myself for not stopping you," he informed her.

"I'm not planning to die."

"No one ever is." He hesitated, but then turned away. Jaguar, like most of the vampires in the building, would turn his back and not hinder her, but he wouldn't help her.

She didn't want the help. This was her fight to win or lose alone.

Turquoise kept one knife in her hand as she turned the knob and entered Daryl's room. If he wasn't in, she could wait.

# CHAPTER 23

NATHANIEL HAD SAID he was there to conduct business; he didn't say what type. He had seemed surprised when she, a slave, had spoken to him, but he was willing to talk.

Despite knowing what Nathaniel was and despite knowing that Lord Daryl would be furious to find someone in his home when he returned, Cathy was grateful for the vampire's companionship.

"Would you help me kill him?" she asked, in a moment of frustration.

Nathaniel looked at Cathy as if she had finally done something interesting. "Is that really a road you want to travel?" he asked.

"Is there another choice, besides dying here?"

"You could have asked for help escaping," the mercenary pointed out.

"He killed my parents and my brother," Catherine argued. "I want to see him dead."

✳ ✳ ✳

Daryl's room in Midnight brought back unpleasant memories, even once Turquoise had assured herself that he was not in it. From the delicate glass etching on the chair, to the whip lying ominously on the cluttered desk, every object reminded the hunter of the creature she had come to kill.

Turquoise paced restlessly, waiting. She killed some time working at the tight braid of his whip with her knife, and unraveled enough to make it harmless if Daryl got his hands on it. She started to go through the desk, and found more cash than she had ever seen, then amused herself imagining a Midnight Savings Bank.

One of her Crimson knives, a slender weapon with a blade of expensive firestone, was in her hand before Daryl finished opening the door; she saw Daryl hesitate when he caught sight of her. "Catherine," he greeted her. "I thought you would find your way back here. A slave without her master is lost, after all."

*"You don't seem to understand your situation," the vampire said coldly. He reached past her to shut the door she had been trying to escape through, and she recoiled from his proximity. "I own you, Catherine, as surely as I own the shirt I'm wearing, and you don't want to make me mad."*

That had been her introduction to the concept that a human being could be property. The concept had been beaten into her time and again; the more she fought, the more she had been forced to realize how powerless she was.

She actually smiled at the memory. She wasn't

powerless anymore. She certainly wasn't this creature's slave. "You're not my master."

"You're human, Catherine," Daryl argued. He closed the door and leaned against it, and Turquoise realized that, while she would never prove the point to him, she no longer felt the need to argue. He continued, "Ours is simply a higher race. You are a slave by blood, and that is all you can ever be."

Without words, Turquoise attacked.

Daryl was prepared for a fight this time, and he dodged her first attack easily, and then drew his own knife.

It would have been so much easier—for Turquoise, at least—if he had just tried to bleed her. Trying to kill a feeding vampire is as easy as trying to kill a blind deaf-mute.

*"Revenge," Nathaniel paraphrased. "It sounds sweet, but it doesn't make for a good life."*

*"Maybe not, but in this case, I think I wouldn't mind it." Bravado. Did she really think he would help her? And could she really kill, even Lord Daryl?*

*Nathaniel drew a knife from his boot and handed it to her, handle first. "If you're willing to kill, wait to strike until he's feeding. Go for the heart—it's the only place that will be fatal."*

*She hesitated. Cathy wasn't a killer; violence made her stomach turn. But as her hand closed over the knife's handle her decision was made.*

Daryl caught Turquoise's wrist and knocked the first knife away. Fortunately, she had others, and Turquoise's left hand was almost as good as her right.

Daryl hissed in pain as the next knife raked across the skin of his chest, but a hasty block knocked the blade from its aim and kept it from piercing the rib cage.

*Lord Daryl stormed back into his home, his temper already hot and looking for an outlet. He found one as soon as he saw Nathaniel waiting in his parlor.*

*"What is he doing here?" Lord Daryl demanded of Cathy, as if the human should have been able to make Nathaniel leave.*

*"I have business with you," the mercenary replied. Lord Daryl ignored him; Nathaniel leaned back against the wall to wait.*

*Lord Daryl pulled Cathy against himself, wrapping her hair around his fingers to yank her head to the side and bare her throat. She shivered with the pain as his fangs pierced the skin.*

*The knife was in her left hand. The vampire obviously didn't see it as a threat, if he noticed it at all. Across the room, she saw Nathaniel make an X over his heart, a reminder.*

*But she missed the heart. The blade hit a rib and skittered across his chest, and her master threw her away with a curse.*

Turquoise pulled away abruptly before he could retaliate, but his grip on her wrist didn't falter. Instead, he used the hunter's momentum to throw her.

The breath hissed out of her lungs as her back slammed into the wall, and Turquoise stumbled to her knees before she could recover it.

*She hit the wall hard, and fell. The next moments were unclear; she only remembered fear, pain, and anger. Because in that moment she heard a sound that had never been directed toward her before—the crack of Lord Daryl's whip.*

*The weapon wrapped around her wrist, tearing open the skin; he yanked her forward, and her shoulder screamed in pain, probably dislocated.*

Breathing tightly past pain that seemed to pulse from her fingers to her shoulder, down her back and through her gut, she tried to move the arm, then nearly blacked out. *No, we won't be trying that again.* In all her years as a vampire hunter, she had yet to break a bone, but there was a first time for everything.

*Again came the crack. This time the whip cut open a line above her left collarbone.*

*Desperately, she dove with the knife. Lord Daryl didn't react quickly enough to avoid the blade, but she could not reach his heart. Instead, the weapon cut into his stomach.*

*Lord Daryl growled a curse, and shoved her away, toward Nathaniel. She couldn't get up again. Everything was bleeding, bruised, in pain. She barely remembered hearing him order Nathaniel, "Get her out of here."*

She had been lucky then to have Nathaniel to save her. This time, she had only training and her wits to help her.

Her knife was still in her hand, held by a death grip, but only because instincts died hard. Turquoise was lucky it had not sliced her open when she fell.

Daryl was already standing above her, expression unconcerned. "You can't fight me, Catherine," he said calmly, and the words ignited her rage. "I am your master, and I will be for as long as you live. Did you honestly think you were better than I am?"

✻   ✻   ✻

*"You're Catherine Miriam Minate," her father had said, after she first met Daryl, as if that explained everything. "You're proud, and you have every right to be. And no one—no one—can take that away from you unless you let them."*

Turquoise answered with a single word: "Yes."

She started fighting again, this time a series of lightning thrusts and dodges that left him off guard. The knife sliced along his arm as he fumbled a block. She barely managed to dodge his blade, by stepping in closer. Her knife cut along the back of his hand, and he dropped his weapon with a hiss of pain.

*"Some people only care about themselves. They use things; they destroy," Mr. Minate told his daughter. "You're . . . you're a creator, a builder. A healer, not a user."*

*Cathy shook her dad's words of wisdom off as hokey.*

*Some people use things*—people, objects. They destroy. Some creatures needed to abuse others in order to thrive. This one had picked the wrong life to try to steal.

"I might never have come back here," Turquoise stated, as she fought. She moved closer, and then dodged back as Daryl tried to retaliate. "But you did something very dumb." Another series of attacks, and another quick retreat. "You threatened—" She blocked a blow; the effort sent a series of black waves through her vision. "—Eric. And you tried—" He caught her around the waist, and pulled her forward. "—to ruin the life I had just barely created again." She slammed a knee up, and Daryl shoved her away with a sound of pain.

He was expecting her to fall, or at least be delayed. Instead, she instantly swung her weapon arm up, at the same time throwing her weight forward to add power to the blow.

Finally the knife found its mark, and the creature collapsed, as a marionette will when the puppeteer cuts the strings.

Turquoise nearly fell with him, but somehow managed to lean back against the wall and grit her teeth against another wave of dizziness.

*"You'll do something amazing with your future," her father stated with surety. "You've got so much passion, so much talent . . . you'll be something incredible, I'm sure."*

He hadn't been talking about hunting vampires.

Funny, that wasn't what she was thinking about, either. She had two worlds to pick her future from: human and vampiric. Or both.

First, she was going to need to see a doctor. She had no illusions about what she was at the moment—human—or about how much damage she could do to herself if she didn't get to a hospital soon to get the arm set. After that . . .

*You're a creator, a builder.* Who knew? Maybe she could try to find that part of herself again.

Maybe she would take Jaguar's job for long enough to decide she was bored with it, and then ask Nathaniel to change her; maybe she would salvage what Daryl had tried to destroy, and realize she was content in human life.

She had choices, and if she didn't have all of eternity, she had some time. She also had freedom.

Wryly, she mused, *In the end, my father was right.*

Carolynne Bailey

**Amelia Atwater-Rhodes** grew up in Concord, Massachusetts. Born in 1984, she wrote her first novel, *In the Forests of the Night,* praised as "remarkable" (*Voice of Youth Advocates*) and "mature and polished" (*Booklist*), when she was thirteen. The books in the Den of Shadows quartet are all ALA-YALSA Quick Picks. She has also published the five-volume series The Kiesha'ra: *Hawksong,* a *School Library Journal* Best Book of the Year and a *Voice of Youth Advocates* Best Science Fiction, Fantasy, and Horror Selection; *Snakecharm; Falcondance; Wolfcry,* an IRA-CBC Young Adults' Choice; and *Wyvernhail.* She is also the author of *Persistence of Memory* and *Token of Darkness,* which will be available from Delacorte Press in the spring of 2010.